TURNS *of* FATE

BOOKS BY ANNE BISHOP

The Isle of Wyrd Series

Turns of Fate

The Others Series

Written in Red

Murder of Crows

Vision in Silver

Marked in Flesh

Etched in Bone

The World of the Others

Lake Silence

Wild Country

Crowbones

The Lady in Glass and Other Stories

The Black Jewels Series

Daughter of the Blood

Heir to the Shadows

Queen of the Darkness

The Invisible Ring

Dreams Made Flesh

Tangled Webs

The Shadow Queen

Shalador's Lady

Twilight's Dawn

The Queen's Bargain

The Queen's Weapons

The Queen's Price

The Ephemera Series

Sebastian

Belladonna

Bridge of Dreams

The Tir Alainn Trilogy

The Pillars of the World

Shadows and Light

The House of Gaian

TURNS *of* FATE

AN ISLE OF WYRD NOVEL

Anne Bishop

ACE
New York

ACE
Published by Berkley
An imprint of Penguin Random House LLC
1745 Broadway, New York, NY 10019
penguinrandomhouse.com

Book design by Ashley Tucker
"Between Stone and Sky" copyright © 2024 by Jennifer Crow. Used with permission.

Library of Congress Cataloging-in-Publication Data

Names: Bishop, Anne, author.
Title: Turns of fate / Anne Bishop.
Description: New York : Ace, 2025. | Series: An Isle of Wyrd novel
Identifiers: LCCN 2025001606 (print) | LCCN 2025001607 (ebook) |
ISBN 9780593954089 (hardcover) | ISBN 9780593954096 (ebook)
Subjects: LCGFT: Detective and mystery fiction. | Paranormal fiction. | Novels.
Classification: LCC PS3552.I7594 T78 2025 (print) | LCC PS3552.I7594 (ebook) |
DDC 813/.54--dc23/eng/20250326
LC record available at https://lccn.loc.gov/2025001606
LC ebook record available at https://lccn.loc.gov/2025001607

Printed in the United States of America
1st Printing

The authorized representative in the EU for product safety and compliance is Penguin Random House Ireland, Morrison Chambers, 32 Nassau Street, Dublin D02 YH68, Ireland, https://eu-contact.penguin.ie.

For Deb, Pam, and Jen

and

for all the people who loved *The Twilight Zone*

CAST OF CHARACTERS

PENWYCH

(town in Eastwood County)

Police, 13th precinct special investigations team

Benjamin Reynolds—*officer*

Beth Fahey—*junior detective*

Charles Forrester—*captain/detective*

Ian Kuhn—*detective*

Jim Monkton—*officer*

Tom Castelletti—*senior detective*

Police, 12th precinct

Amanda Gibson—*detective*

Residents

Acid—*student; one of Dare's Doggs*

Aisha Forrester—*Charles Forrester's wife*

Albert Palmer—*Darren's father*

Butch—*student; one of Dare's Doggs*

Colin Forrester—*Charles Forrester's son*

Darren (Dare) Palmer—*bully; leader of Dare's Doggs*

Davie/Davinia Madison—*Jazz's friend*

Devl—*student; one of Dare's Doggs*

Edwena Bang—*mayor*

Gerry Palowski—*bought the use of a ghost gun*

Jazmin (Jazz) Forrester—*Charles Forrester's daughter*

Melissa Stevens—*student*

Mrs. Myers—*neighbor of Beth Fahey*

Stick—*student; one of Dare's Doggs*

Ted "Tedious" Ocampo—*friend of Colin Forrester*

KING'S HILL

(town in Westwood County)

Police

Grace Russell—*captain/detective*

James Lamb—*officer*

Laci Tower—*officer*

Markus Seibert—*senior detective*

Residents

Alistair Hampton—*brother of Reginald Hampton III*

Casey—*young girl*

Jeremy Swayne—*works for Alistair Hampton*

Martin Chandler—*Alistair Hampton's head of security*

Mr. Danvers—*bank manager*

Rachel Nightingale—*writer; Alistair Hampton's fiancée*

Reginald Hampton III—*controls the Hampton family's wealth*

JACKSON

(town in Westwood County)

Police

Sheina Kali—*detective*

Residents

Yaron Kali—*professor at Jackson University; Sheina's husband*

BARKER

(town in Northwood County)

Residents

Alan Naylor Jr.—*son of Alan Naylor*

Emma Naylor—*wife of Alan Naylor*

CARTER

(town in Northwood County)

Residents

Chloe Peterson—*young girl*

LOVECRAFT

(town in Eastwood County)

Police

Jeni Slown—*welfare officer*

Leanne Curran—*officer*

Stan Wozniak—*captain/detective*

Other people mentioned

Alan Naylor—*disappeared many years ago*

Arianna Greenwood—*Arcana*

Bonnie Wilson—*Beth Fahey lived with her for several years*

Chad Forrester—*Charles Forrester's brother; deceased*

Maxine (Maxie) Greenwood—*half Arcana*

Molly—*Ted Ocampo's cousin; died from complications of eating disorders*

Patrick Russell—*Grace Russell's father*

Richard (no last name)—*private investigator hired by Bonnie Wilson*

ISLE OF WYRD

The Arcana (mentioned by name)

Ashley Laxton—*works for Lucas Frost*

Deerman—*patrols the park*

Ethan Sharpe—*runs the armory*

Ferryman—*runs the ferry that brings visitors to Destiny Park*

Jack Frost—*Lucas's brother; an assassin*

Justine Frost—*one of the Ladies Three; Lucas's wife*

Kia Dance—*medic*

Lucas Frost—*Wyrd's Sorcerer King*

Lysandra—*one of the Ladies Three; Justine's older sister*

Mia Skov—*works in the park*

Zerah—*one of the Ladies Three; Justine's younger sister*

Other residents of Wyrd

Betsy Richens—*runs the library in the Teeth*

Chase—*works at Destiny Park's hotel*

Faulkner—*a crow*

Katherine Rose—*works in the pavilion; reads cards*

Rya Hedden—*runs the mobile library; half Arcana*

Tia Downing—*runs the trading post in Llamalidia*

GHOST SHIPS

***Bonnie Lass*—three-masted schooner; pirate ship**

Sheridan Gray—*captain / pirate queen; Arcana*

Wing Kei Lee—*first mate*

***Last Breath*—fishing trawler**

Carver—*first mate*

Fletcher—*crew member*

Flint—*captain; Arcana*

Skinner—*crew member*

BETWEEN STONE AND SKY

Take a step into the unknown
And learn who you are:
Past experience all that you own
In this place, and afar.
So this passage between
Stone and sky begins
A journey to truth, now,
Or a vengeance if your sins
Have gone unanswered. How
Can you grow without
Shedding old selves, serpent-mind,
As you choose hope not doubt
And focus on the kind
Of new beginning you wish
To have beyond this arch,
The place you belong, your need a dish
Served in this moment's march
Into moon's embrace.
Your heart will make the measure of this place.

—Jennifer Crow, translated from the Arcana language

TURNS *of* FATE

PART ONE

COINS FOR THE FERRYMAN

SEPTEMBER

1

Detective Beth Fahey opened the next "solved" case file and wondered if reading through these reports was really necessary or if this was busywork her colleagues had found for the new, and only, female detective on the Penwych police force's special investigations team. She'd been told these files were examples of what the team investigated when called in by any of the police in the six towns located on the outer bank of the Fate River.

This case from the police in the town of Barker, for example.

A man who went out hunting with some friends had shot and killed a migratory goose (no mention in the file about whether shooting geese was legal at that time of year). Instead of taking the goose home, he gave it to his friends, because his wife was severely allergic to feathers.

The next day, the wife heard strange sounds coming from their backyard and discovered their in-ground pool was packed with geese. In fact, their entire yard was packed with geese. When several geese rushed toward her in a threatening manner, the wife went inside, screamed for her husband, and managed to call emergency services before she began wheezing and struggling to breathe, either from the number of feathered assailants in her yard or from a panic attack.

Coming out of the family room to see what his wife was fussing about, the man heard her wheezing, saw the geese, and fetched his rifle instead of having the sense to stay inside and let the authorities handle rounding up the geese.

He stepped outside, raised his rifle, and was immediately attacked by several geese. The unanticipated attack threw off his aim, and instead of shooting any of the geese, he managed to shoot the fuel tank on his neighbor's fancy new grill. The grill exploded, and the resulting fire not only damaged the neighbor's house but cooked a couple of unlucky geese.

The special team was called in because the wife claimed she'd had her tarot cards read the week before by the acquaintance of a friend, and it had been predicted that a disaster would occur if her husband tried to shoot creatures that were unable to defend themselves. (There was some debate about whether geese qualified as "unable to defend themselves.")

An inquiry was made. After talking to the individuals who ran Destiny Park, it was concluded that, while the series of events was strange, the Isle of Wyrd was not involved, and neither the man nor his wife had made a bargain with the Arcana.

Beth shook her head. She didn't discount tarot readings or any other means of tapping into a person's intuition, but why did the towns around the Fate River need a special team to investigate things like geese in someone's yard?

Then again, this had been one of the few "amusing" cases she'd reviewed. The others . . .

How was anyone supposed to deal with what she'd seen in some of those crime scene photos?

Maybe that was the point of this review—to find out if she *could* deal with the gruesome cases the team was required to investigate. Last fall, there had been four detectives on the team, along with two officers and Captain Forrester. Something had happened. No one would—or could—say exactly what that was, but one of those detectives transferred out of the 13th precinct to avoid any contact with the team, and another detective was on extended medical leave and wasn't likely to return.

She had been hired to fill one of those positions. She'd been given a week to find a place to live in Penwych and get herself settled before reporting to work. She'd spent last week reading old reports and looking at crime scene photos. And yet when she studied some of those photos, she could almost see dark and seductive shapes in the background, could almost hear words whispered in a language that might be understood in dreams.

Looking beyond the deaths, she could almost see the terrible married to the sublime and hear the warning: *they chose this.*

Not thoughts she would acknowledge to the psychologist who had the task of assessing police officers' mental health. She was sure there was already a notation in her file about her interest in macabre imagery and dark fantasy artwork, courtesy of Bonnie Wilson, the woman she had lived with while growing up—a woman who preferred religious pictures that included self-flagellation and went beyond what Beth considered gruesome and gory.

Tom Castelletti, the team's senior detective, walked into the area of the 13th precinct that was reserved for the special team, glanced at Captain Forrester's closed office door, and placed a file on Beth's desk.

"This one is hot," he said. "Read it. I'll be back with Kuhn in a few minutes, and we'll do the coin toss to see who has to cross the river."

He left, glancing again at the captain's closed door.

The coin toss had been mentioned once before. Beth thought it was an odd way to decide which detective on the team had to interview . . . What, exactly? A confidential informant? A local politician? Another cop?

According to Castelletti, all the detectives on the team participated. The two most senior officers began the coin toss. It was elimination in reverse, where winning the toss meant you were excused.

Shaking her head, Beth opened the file and focused her attention on this current case. She read the information, then read it again. It had to be a joke, because what the autopsy said wasn't possible. *Couldn't* be possible, and yet . . .

The frisson that ran through her told her that what she was reading was true.

Tom Castelletti and Detective Ian Kuhn returned.

Castelletti gave her a long look, then gestured to indicate she should join them around the big evidence table. "You've read the file?"

"I don't understand it, but I've read it," Beth replied.

"One of us is going to have to cross the river and make inquiries." Castelletti studied her. "You remember what we said about the coin toss?"

She nodded.

Castelletti lost the coin toss to Kuhn, and Beth lost to Castelletti, who looked relieved and uneasy.

He's spooked, she thought as a door opened.

Captain Charles Forrester stepped out of his office and looked at his officers, his eyes almost, but not quite, skipping over her. "Who lost the coin toss?"

"Detective Fahey, Captain," Castelletti said. "She'll need to get her skates on if she's going to catch the next ferry and not get stuck doing an overnight."

Forrester stared at the men so hard that they looked away. Looked ashamed. "Neither of you was given this kind of assignment when you first joined the team."

"She wanted to participate," Kuhn protested.

She hadn't been told she had a choice. In many ways, Castelletti and Kuhn acted like she was a placeholder, like they didn't expect her to be around in a couple of months. "I can handle this, Captain."

Forrester turned his stare on her. "Can you? With me, Detective." He stepped over to her desk, scooped up the folder she had been studying, and went into his office. When she walked in after him, he said, "Close the door. Then tell me what this says."

When he held out the folder, she took it. "Gerry Palowski. Twenty-five-year-old male, unemployed. Is—was—living with a current girlfriend but had a five-year-old daughter with a former girlfriend. According to statements made by both girlfriends when they were stable enough to be interviewed, Palowski wanted to go to a party with his ex and 'have some fun'—and he wanted the current girlfriend to babysit his daughter. She refused to stay home and babysit, and then his ex refused to go to the party, and that deprived Palowski of his fun. The next day, Palowski purchased a gun—"

"Transacted for the use of a gun," Forrester corrected.

"—and went over to his ex's apartment, where he shot his ex and their daughter before going back to his apartment to shoot his current girlfriend for spoiling party night. No fatalities. All three people are in the hospital in serious condition but are expected to pull through."

A miracle by anyone's definition. At close range, Palowski should not have missed a kill shot once, let alone three times, but the bullets did something impossibly crazy in terms of entry and angles that left three people wounded instead of dead.

"And Palowski?" Forrester asked.

Beth hesitated. In the crime scene photo that was taken where he was found, Palowski still looked like a hard-living twenty-five-year-old man sitting in the park, sleeping off a bender or some drugs. But the autopsy indicated that all of Palowski's internal organs belonged to a man in his nineties and that he died of natural causes—if aging seventy years in a matter of hours could be considered natural.

"You'll note that the report speculates that the same ghost gun used for the shootings has been used in other unsolved cases over the past eighty years or more."

"Ghost gun? An illegal firearm?"

"More than that. The gun comes from the Isle of Wyrd. It can't be traced or found beyond that point—and it always returns to the island after being used."

"So you know where it came from."

Forrester nodded. "I even know who, most likely, sold the use of it to Palowski. Having lost the coin toss, you are going to Wyrd to find out the terms of use and confirm that the gun returned to the island."

"I'm going undercover to try to purchase one of these ghost guns?"

"No." Forrester's voice turned sharp. "There is no such thing as undercover in Wyrd. Pretending to be someone you're not would be a death sentence for people like us."

"Like us, sir?"

"Normal people." Forrester hesitated. "People who aren't part of the threads that make up the supernatural on that island. There are other places like it around the world, but in this part of our country, the uncanny is concentrated on Wyrd and then ripples through all the towns on this side of the river." He stopped and seemed to focus on his breathing before he continued. "Have you visited the Isle of Wyrd, Detective Fahey?"

"No, sir." There hadn't been time for sightseeing between her hurried move to Penwych and reporting to work.

"Then let me explain what you're about to face."

Forrester took out his wallet, removed two fifty-dollar bills, and held them out to Beth. "Take it," he said when she didn't move. "I'll put in a chit for it."

"I can . . ."

"The ferry makes a trip across the Fate River every hour on the hour between sunup and sundown. When you get to the pier where the ferry takes on passengers, you'll see a booth where you'll exchange the money for the coins that are used on the island. Ask for six gold coins and eight silver coins. The gold coins are worth ten dollars; the silver are five dollars. The ferry usually costs a silver coin, but if the Ferryman asks for gold, don't argue."

A coin for the Ferryman? Was Forrester kidding? "They have flexible fees?"

"For everything."

"Why couldn't the patrol boat take me across the river?"

"Even a patrol boat doesn't dock anywhere on that island without an invitation," Forrester replied quietly. Then he continued in a normal voice, "You'll probably be met by Lucas Frost. He rules Destiny Park and sometimes acts as a liaison. Tell him we have a shooting with a strange outcome and think a ghost gun was involved." Forrester gave her a hard look. "Whatever he tells you, accept without question."

"Why?"

She had the impression that her captain was trying to decide how much to say.

"The Arcana control Destiny Park and the pavilion. Their influence extends over the whole island, but the pavilion is where they make transactions with people like us."

"Meaning non-supernaturals."

"Yes." Forrester let out a careful breath. "By our standards, they are amoral, but they are honest and honorable in their own way. Any bargain they make with you, they will keep. It just might not be in the way that you expect. And you had better keep any bargain you make with them, because if you fail, they can be unforgiving and brutal when extracting compensation." He paused. "The Arcana are very dangerous. Never forget that, Detective. When I say your fate lies in their hands, I am not exaggerating."

"Yes, sir."

He held out a hand. "It's forbidden to bring a weapon to Wyrd. The Arcana will overlook a pocketknife because they consider that a practical tool, but they won't overlook a gun, not even for a cop. I'll keep yours secured until you return."

Beth gave him her holster and weapon.

After locking them in a drawer in his desk, Forrester said, "Ask the questions you're allowed to ask about Palowski and the gun. If there is time, see a bit of the park while you're there to get a feel for the place. Then get yourself back here."

"If I miss the ferry, is there a place—"

"I don't care if you have answers or not, you will make damn sure that you don't miss the last ferry."

His anger was a heat that filled the space between them.

"Why is it so important?" she finally asked.

"Because things . . . change . . . on Wyrd after dark, and you don't want to be there when that happens."

Charles Forrester escorted Beth Fahey to the patrol car that would take her to the ferry's pier. Then he returned to his office and closed the door before making the phone call.

"Frost." A voice that resonated with a power that made people hesitate to enter shadowy places.

"It's Charles Forrester." No response. There wouldn't be. The Arcana didn't waste time on small talk. "My new detective is on her way to the island to ask for your assistance in confirming some details on a case. She's green as grass and unfamiliar with Wyrd."

"You know how things are done here."

"I do. I'm asking for your understanding if she makes mistakes when dealing with you or your kin."

"When is she due to arrive?"

"She'll be on the next ferry."

"Soon, then."

"Yes."

"Anything else?"

Charles considered the question carefully. You never accused the Arcana of wrongdoing. They didn't care about such things when it concerned the mundane world. The Arcana in Destiny Park simply facilitated people who either tried to change their fate or wanted to fulfill their destiny. "A man from King's Hill has hired a private investigator to find his missing spouse. I have an appointment with the PI and should have more details later this afternoon. Apparently, the wife is mentally fragile, which is why the husband is particularly concerned about her disappearance—and why the PI is checking in with police stations all along the river."

"Anything else?"

He hesitated, then said, "Nothing from my precinct."

"Then I'll look for your detective at the dock, and we'll see what answers we will give."

Charles understood the distinction between *can give* and *will give*. Someone like Frost could give a cop a lot of answers—but not everyone was suited to dealing with what lived on Wyrd. It was Charles's luck, or misfortune, that he could work with the Arcana.

By the time the sun went down, he'd know if Beth Fahey could work with them too.

2

Access to the ferry was made up of a pier and floating dock. The pier was connected to the shore and secured with pylons sunk into the riverbed. The floating dock, which contained the currency exchange booth and access to the ferry, was connected to the pier in a way that made it easy to separate the two.

At first Beth thought the arrangement was to accommodate the rise and fall of the river, and that might be part of it. Then she realized that any attempt at theft could be thwarted simply by detaching the dock and setting it adrift. That would leave the person in the booth vulnerable to a thief who would, most likely, be armed with some kind of weapon, but perhaps it was assumed that person would jump into the river and brave the currents until being rescued.

She reassessed her thinking when the woman in front of her stepped aside and she got a good look at the individual in the booth.

A woman. Maybe. Long hair that was a steel gray mixed with white. Stringy muscles in the arms, but those muscles gave the impression of strength rather than weakness. The face didn't register as male or female, and the voice had a pitch that could go either way.

"First timer?"

"Yes." Beth handed over the money Forrester had given her and asked for the coins per his instructions.

"Police?"

"Yes."

"On business?"

"Yes."

"Seeing Lucas Frost?"

"Yes."

"Pay the Ferryman a silver coin."

Beth tucked the other coins into her pockets and kept a silver one in her hand as she carefully stepped onto the ferry. There was some seating outside, and it looked like there was some seating on the upper deck, but most of the ferry was a cabin with seats and large glass windows. Next to the entrance was a small black cauldron with a padlocked lid that had a slit for the coins and a sign that read PAY THE FERRYMAN.

The honor system of payment—or a test?

Did the crew keep watch somehow? She hadn't seen anyone who looked like they worked on the ferry, but someone had to secure the lines that held the ferry to the dock, and someone had to cast off when the ferry was ready to leave. And someone had to be at the wheel when the ferry crossed the river.

Unless the ferry was sentient and crossed the river by itself.

Stop it. You're just spooking yourself.

But the possibility gave her a tiny thrill.

Beth dropped the silver coin into the cauldron and chose an indoor seat next to a window.

Two young men came in—late teens or early twenties. One of them gave her a look and hesitated, as if considering making a move on her. Then he glanced at the person who had taken the seat behind her and joined his friend in seats across the aisle.

"I wonder what happens if you don't toss a coin in the pot," the boy said loudly, as if volume equaled bravado.

"Nothing good comes from cheating the Ferryman," a voice replied quietly.

The voice came from whoever was sitting behind her. Something about that voice made Beth think of someone trying to claw their way out of a grave.

That voice took the sass out of the young men. They remained hunched and wary for the entire ride to the dock at Wyrd.

Before leaving the precinct, Beth had studied the map of Wyrd that was stapled to the wall in the special team's area. The island looked like a human skull in profile, and the only things identified in pencil on the map were Destiny Park, which was located where the eye socket would be, and Destiny Bay. The whole interior of the island was blank. Unknown. Forbidden?

Beth pushed that thought away. She didn't have time for mist and bones and graveyard stones, despite how much shadowy and creepy things fascinated her. What would her colleagues say if they saw her box of drawings and prints, images that gave her a shivery thrill every time she looked at them? She'd almost been thrown out of the police academy because Bonnie Wilson kept writing letters to the administration, telling everyone that Beth was an "unnatural child with a dark, bent nature."

Fortunately, the psychologist at the academy hadn't believed that having a taste for fantasy art was unusual or a cause for concern, pointing out the number of people who attended fantasy conventions every year. But Beth had wondered if Bonnie's letters had influenced someone higher up the chain of command, and that had limited the jobs available to her after graduation—and that was the reason she had ended up at Penwych's 13th precinct under Captain Forrester's command.

She thought she caught a glimpse of someone securing the lines when the ferry docked on the island side of the river, but other passengers were gathering up belongings and moving about, so she wasn't sure she'd seen anything.

Then she stepped off the ferry and, feeling a pang of disappointment, wondered if Wyrd was just a strange tourist attraction.

A long stretch of golden sand. To the right of the dock, she noticed buoys evenly spaced in the water. Markers to indicate a safe place to swim? She'd heard the Fate River had strong currents, and there had been bodies that had been swept out to sea, only to be returned elsewhere along the island's shore.

As she followed the boardwalk that kept her off the sand, she noted the row of cabins above the beach on her left. Rentals? Or the homes of whoever worked at the hotel that was on her right? The hotel gave her the impression of luxury and expense, but that could be just the difference between cabins that looked like they'd emerged from the ground and something so obviously, and shiningly, human.

Of course it was human. And so was the rest of this place.

Then she saw the man standing at the end of the boardwalk,

watching the arrivals. Suddenly, she wasn't sure there was *anything* human on this island. Which was . . . foolish, bordering on hysterical. She was a cop, for pity's sake. She didn't do hysterical.

She also usually didn't have a fanciful turn of mind, despite being drawn to the shadowy strange, so maybe instinct was trying to tell her something she couldn't put into words.

A tall man with a perfect amount of muscle for his size, with black hair, blue eyes, and lightly tanned skin. He wore jeans, work boots, a leather jacket, and a blue chambray shirt.

He looked right past her and lasered his focus on the two young men who were jostling each other and starting to get rowdy—no doubt as a way of blowing off steam after the uneasy ride out here.

They saw him—and Beth could feel their bravado wither, making her glad she wasn't the focus of that man's attention.

Then that focus settled on her when she reached the end of the boardwalk.

"Forrester sent you?"

Cool air after summer heat. Heavy silk laid over grass. Lightning and summer storms. A voice designed to make a person want the wild—want to absorb a taste of something feral.

It was also the voice of a ruler powerful enough to demand absolute obedience—and receive it.

"I'm Detective Fahey," Beth replied. "You're Mr. Frost?"

"Lucas Frost, yes."

Must be more than one Mr. Frost, then.

Where the sand changed to grass, dirt paths branched out from the boardwalk. One headed toward the cabins; one headed toward the hotel. The last one headed straight toward something unseen.

"This way," Lucas said, taking the straight path.

"I'm here to get some information about a ghost gun that was used in a multiple shooting." Beth lengthened her stride to keep up with him.

"I know."

"Are you psychic?" The words sounded snarkier than she'd intended, but given the way she'd been picked for this assignment, she still expected some kind of prank.

"Not on this occasion," he replied. "Your captain called and asked me to meet you at the dock since this is your first visit to Wyrd."

"Oh." She sighed. "Sorry. I'm the new guy at the precinct and still settling in."

"You're not a guy; you're a woman." He stopped walking and studied her. "This is Wyrd, Detective Fahey. Don't be careless with your thoughts or words. Not here."

Threat? Warning? She wasn't sure, but his words chilled her.

The path was on a mild incline—just enough to block the view of what lay ahead. When they reached the top, Lucas stopped again. There were a handful of food stands near small open-sided pavilions that held tables and chairs. There were also a few picnic benches. And there were benches in the open for people who wanted to sit and enjoy the view. Some benches faced the river; others faced the park that spread out below her.

"That's Destiny Park. This area"—Lucas waved a hand to indicate the ground where they were standing—"and the area that includes this beach, the hotel, and the cabins is considered neutral ground—at least during the day."

"And the dock?"

He shook his head. "That is the Ferryman's domain." He headed toward a large moon gate, the biggest one she'd ever seen. "Visitors can go through the moon gate to reach the pavilion, or they can go around. Their choice determines what doors in the pavilion will be open to them."

"I don't see a sign explaining the choices."

"There isn't one. Prey instinct provides a better understanding than words." A beat of silence. "People who come purely for fun tend to avoid the moon gates in the park—especially this one. However, your quest requires you to go through this gate." Another beat of silence. "Or you can choose to walk away."

Beth had seen photos of moon gates in gardens. Except for being larger, this one didn't look any different.

Gray stones, she thought. *The color that endures.*

Was that a quote from something distantly remembered? Why did she think of it now?

She didn't see any marks or symbols on any of the stones, including the keystone. Nothing to tell her what was supposed to happen when she walked through the opening.

Drawing in a deep breath, Beth stepped through the moon gate—and felt an odd tingle. Not unpleasant, just . . . odd.

Frost wasn't looking at her as she went through the gate. He watched something on the stones. When Beth turned to look, she saw symbols on some of the stones, fading too fast for her to identify any of them.

But they seemed to mean something to Frost.

"You don't have to go through the moon gate?" she asked when Lucas headed for the pavilion.

"No."

She noticed people walking down terraced slopes to reach the park without going through the pavilion. Unless there were ramps discreetly tucked away behind some landscaping, the only way down to the pavilion itself was a double set of wide stairs. And with every step she took, she felt that odd tingle.

The pavilion had the feel of an old place lovingly tended. The long, wide central aisle had some conventional lighting, but it was also lit by sunlight coming through the stained-glass skylights. The open doors at the other end revealed a statue that must be the centerpiece of an ornamental lake. On both sides of the aisle were archways that opened on to rooms. Since one discreet sign said TAROT, Beth assumed these were where the practitioners of the supernatural did their business.

Frost stepped inside. Beth followed.

To the right of the entrance was a table made from a slab of polished, free-shaped wood balanced on . . . Beth wasn't sure what the creatures carved from other slabs of wood were supposed to be. Something about them made her queasy, and she couldn't force herself to look at them long enough to focus on details.

The box on the table was also made of wood and elaborately carved, but it was beautiful, and she released her breath in a sigh of pleasure.

A sign next to the box read: ONE FOR SILVER, THREE FOR GOLD.

Lucas gestured to a wooden wheel that was also on the table. "After you put a coin in the box, you turn the handle on the wheel, and a small disc with a number comes out of the slot. The number indicates the door and the individual who will read your fortune. If you put a gold coin in the box, you can turn the wheel three times for three numbers. Many do when they come here for fun. If you seek an answer from the Ladies Three, you put a gold coin in the box and take one of those bone discs." He pointed at a bowl beside the wheel.

"I'm here on business, Mr. Frost."

"If you want answers, Detective Fahey, you will put a gold coin in the box and take a bone disc. That is the only way to see the Ladies Three."

Beth dropped a gold coin in the box and took a disc. "What kind of bone is it?"

"The Ladies determine how many questions you may ask. Do you want to waste one by asking about a disc?"

"No." Beth tried to smile. "None of this was covered at the police academy or the extra training to become a detective."

"It wouldn't be." Frost headed for the other end of the pavilion. "This way."

The archways on the left-hand side of the pavilion had signs and numbers to indicate the practitioner's specialty: tarot, numerology, astrology, colors, palmistry, and gems and crystals. The last archway simply said CARDS, which sounded like it wasn't the same as tarot.

There were archways on the right, but those were darkened spaces—an unnatural dark, since there should have been enough light coming in to reveal *something* about whatever was beyond the arches.

Halfway down the length of the building, they reached another archway. Frost stepped aside and indicated that she should go through.

"Start on the left," he said. "Put the bone disc in the bowl on that table and follow the instructions."

Beth entered the room and tried not to stare at the three women sitting behind three tables. They looked similar enough to be sisters, or at least closely related, and they looked gorgeous one moment and ugly the next, as if Beth's eyes couldn't settle on what they were seeing. Interesting women. Arresting.

Terrifying.

Maybe they weren't any of those things, but like her experience of looking at the legs of the wooden table, trying to focus on the women made her queasy, and that reminded her of how vulnerable she was in this place.

But not alone, Beth reminded herself. Captain Forrester knew where she was and would expect her to report to him when she returned. He would know if she didn't return. Inquiries would be made.

Yes, inquiries would be made if she went missing, but that didn't mean she would be found.

Swallowing fear, she approached the woman sitting at the first table and put the bone disc in the bowl.

From a decorated porcelain tray, the first woman picked up a long piece of polished wood that had a rounded top covered with what looked like fine black leather and handed it to Beth. Next, she chose one of the decks of cards and spread them in an arc.

"Choose three cards. Touch them with the wand." The woman stared at Beth. "What happens here is not a game. Choose with intention."

The words shivered through Beth, and the air in the room had a tang that usually signaled an oncoming storm.

Beth slowly moved the wand as she followed the arc of the cards, careful not to touch any of them as she thought about the reason she was here in this place, on this island. Reaching the last card, she moved the wand in the opposite direction and felt . . . something. A tingle. A pull. Something that made her hand dip until the wand touched a card. Touched another. Touched the third.

The woman pulled those cards from the deck but didn't turn them over to reveal whatever images were on the other side. Instead, she gathered up the rest of the deck and set it aside before selecting another deck and spreading out those cards. "Choose two more."

Beth did as she was told. When those two cards were selected, the woman turned over the first three, then the other two.

The first woman looked at the woman sitting at the middle table and nodded.

"Go to her now." The woman with the cards held out a hand for the wand.

Beth gave her the wand. "Aren't you going to tell me what the cards mean?"

"No." The first woman pointed to the middle table. "She will tell you the cost for you to acquire what you seek."

Scales of justice, Beth thought uneasily as she approached the middle table. The old-fashioned brass scale sat in the exact center of the table, its two bowls perfectly balanced. One side of the table held weights made of various metals and carved stones of various sizes and shapes.

"Put something you value on one side of the scale," the second woman said.

Would she get it back? She wore an antique ring on her right hand—a ring set with a small moonstone and carved with odd symbols that were so worn down they were barely visible. She didn't remember where the ring came from, but she'd had it for as long as she could remember. She did value it, but it was personal, and she wasn't here for personal reasons.

Beth took her detective's shield out of her pocket and set it in one of the bowls. The bowl sank until it almost touched the table.

"What is it you seek?" the woman asked.

"Answers about an incident that happened in Penwych," Beth replied.

The woman stared at the detective's shield as she reached for one of the weights—a weight that looked heavy enough to balance the shield.

The moment the woman set the weight in the other bowl, that bowl sank as if the shield weighed nothing.

The woman looked surprised, but her eyes remained focused on the detective's shield while she tried a smaller weight. Then another.

Frowning slightly, the woman removed the weight, and the side of the scale with the shield once more settled close to the table. Then she set a bone disc in the bowl.

Too light to do anything, Beth thought. And yet . . . That side of the scale moved.

The woman put a second bone disc in the bowl and watched the scale. When she put a third disc in the bowl, the two sides of the scale were balanced.

Shouldn't be. Beth had held one of those discs. No way three of them equaled the weight of her detective's shield.

"The cost of receiving the answers you seek is your assistance to us on three occasions," the woman said. "Three favors, if that is wording you prefer."

Beth pushed words past a suddenly dry throat. "I can't break any laws I swore to uphold."

"We will not ask you to break any of your laws, but we do require that you respect the laws that apply here." A pause. "These are the terms. Do you want the answers to your questions?"

She was here for answers. "Yes."

"Then ask—but remember that words have power here."

Heeding the warning, Beth thought for a moment before she spoke. "A man named Gerry Palowski recently purchased the use of a ghost gun. He shot three people, one of them a child. They were seriously wounded, but they will live. Palowski was found on a park bench, dead of natural causes, with internal organs that indicated he was in his nineties. The police—Captain Forrester—would like to know how this is possible."

"Pick up your shield and go to our sister for your answer." The woman made a graceful gesture to indicate the woman sitting at the third table.

This woman's eyes were heavily filmed and she stared at nothing. Yet she seemed to be filling a page on a sketch pad with multiple drawings. When Beth approached her table, she closed the sketch pad. Then she closed her eyes. When she opened them, her eyes were clear and her gaze sharp.

She rose and opened a pair of pocket doors that formed a wall behind her. There were shelves filled with paper on both sides of a room that seemed to go on forever.

Maybe it did.

The woman ran a finger along the edge of the papers on a shelf closest to the pocket doors. Removing a single sheet, she returned to the table and held up the paper for Beth to see.

Two . . . timelines, for want of a better word, both beginning with Palowski as he had been—a twenty-five-year-old man who lived hard and cared for no one but himself.

In the first timeline, Palowski was sketched with his daughter and two other children, the hardness in his face slightly softened as he looked at the children. That sketch blended with another where he wore a hard hat, seemed to be working a construction job. That sketch blended with a middle-aged Palowski, still wearing a hard hat but looking more like a foreman or management. That sketch blended with an elderly Palowski smiling at his daughter while he held what might have been a grandchild. That sketch blended with an old man who had found death in his sleep.

In the second timeline, Palowski, looking dark faced and furious, held a gun aimed at a woman and child. That sketch blended with three gravestones that were partly drawn. That sketch blended with Palowski sitting on a park bench—exactly as he'd been found.

Beth studied the sketches that filled the page, then looked at the woman.

"He wanted a gun that couldn't be traced by the police," the woman said. "He wanted a weapon from Wyrd. The price for the use of the gun was ten years of his life. The price for each bullet used was twenty years. You will have to ask Ethan Sharpe, but it appears the man used three bullets."

Beth swayed, dizzied by what she'd heard. "Gerry Palowski aged *seventy years* in a matter of hours as payment for this ghost gun?"

"For the use of the gun." Lucas Frost had stayed near the archway while she made her transaction with the Ladies Three. Now he stepped up beside her. "He aged ten years the moment he walked out of the pavilion with the gun. Even if he'd changed his mind before reaching the ferry and brought the gun back here, he had already forfeited a decade from his potential ninety-five years. But he left, and he chose to use the three bullets he'd been given and spend the sixty years he could have had to live a different life."

That was an explanation, of sorts, for Palowski. But . . . "Even if he'd never fired a gun before, Palowski was too close to his victims to miss, and yet the bullets . . ." *Did crazy things that shouldn't have been possible based on any law of physics.*

The woman pointed to the gravestones in her sketch. "It wasn't their time. But for one of them, their time will be shorter because of this."

Beth studied the gravestones. One stone was little more than the base and a lightly penciled arch that indicated the final size. One was completed halfway, so finely wrought she could see the texture of stone on the paper. The third stone's form was between the other two.

"Do you know whose time will be shorter?" she asked.

"No," the woman replied. "They didn't stand before us. He did."

She thought for a moment. Even if Palowski doubted that payment really would be deducted from his potential lifespan, he would look for a way around paying. "What if he got the gun here but purchased the ammunition from a sporting goods store in Penwych?"

"The guns that come from here only work with bullets that come from here," Frost said. "When you deal with us, you must pay what is owed."

"Why couldn't he buy ammunition that was the same caliber and get around your price that way?" Captain Forrester had told her not to argue or question, but she was trying to understand. And Frost? Did "cartridge" and "bullet" mean the same thing to him, or was he using the word he meant to use?

Frost gave her a predator's smile. "If someone tried that, the gun would turn on him—or her—before returning home."

One of the cases she'd been given to review. A man with a grudge against someone, standing in a parking lot waving a gun while he shouted obscenities. Witnesses agreed on that much. They also agreed that the man took aim at someone—but as he pulled the trigger, the gun twisted in his hand, and the bullet he'd intended for someone else hit him instead, killing him instantly.

The police found one spent cartridge next to the body along with five other cartridges that matched a box of ammo found in the man's car.

Despite everyone swearing that no one had gone near the man, the police never found the gun.

Beth wondered if there was anything else she should ask these women. "Could I see the gun?"

A silence before Frost said, "This way." He led her to a darkened arch and stepped through.

Beth hesitated and turned back to look at the women. "Thank you for assisting in our inquiries."

They didn't reply, so she walked through the archway. She expected to find a dark place. Instead, she stopped and blinked at the sunlight filling the room.

The front part of the room was empty, much like the room overseen by the Ladies Three. Glass cases filled with a variety of weapons divided the room in half.

Beth approached the cases, alarmed by how much destruction could be wrought by the array of weapons that could be grabbed by a quick thief.

Except . . . The more she looked at the weapons, the more she realized they were a ghostly image that could be seen but not touched.

"Detective Fahey, this is Ethan Sharpe," Frost said. "He runs the armory and is the caretaker of the weapons and ammunition that come from Wyrd."

Beth glanced at the man. Like the women, she couldn't quite bring his features into focus, so she focused on the weapons. "This is like a history lesson in violence. Some of these weapons look like they were made centuries ago."

"Some of them were," Sharpe replied.

"The detective would like to see the gun that returned recently," Frost said.

Sharpe slid open a wooden door on the back of one of the cases and reached for a six-shooter—a gun that seemed more appropriate for an Old West shoot-out than a modern-day killing.

Beth expected his hand to go through the ghostly image, but as Sharpe's hand closed around the weapon, it took on substance, took on weight. Became real. Removing the gun, he placed it on a mat and looked at Beth.

She reached for it, wanting confirmation of the reality of what she'd just seen. Then she remembered what it cost Palowski and jerked her hand away.

"She is a detective and works with Captain Forrester," Frost said. "This is an inquiry into a death."

Something about the way the words were spoken made Beth think that much more was being said.

"Ah," Sharpe replied. "Police. In that case, you may examine the weapon in this room without cost."

"Thank you." Beth picked up the revolver and opened the cylinder, checking to make sure the chambers were empty. Then she examined the weapon. Nothing wrong with the sights, no reason Palowski's victims weren't killed when he fired.

Except it wasn't their time, according to the women in the other room. The outcome of a bargain made here wasn't determined, then; only the cost to the person using the weapon was set.

Beth placed the gun on the mat. "Thank you for allowing me to examine the weapon."

Sharpe put the gun back in the case. As he closed the sliding door, Beth watched a tangible weapon become a ghostly image again.

Frost led her to a darkened archway at the front of the room and stepped through. This time Beth hesitated only a moment before following him.

They were back in the pavilion's wide central area. She looked at the dark archway.

"One way, like many things in Wyrd," Frost said. "A person can't reach the armory without seeing the Ladies Three first."

Beth nodded, not sure what else she should ask—or wanted to know.

"This way." Frost headed toward the end of the pavilion, where the archway leading outdoors revealed a statue rising from a large ornamental lake.

"I should—"

"Come this way." A command.

Beth followed Frost, not sure what to expect.

"You have some time to look around Destiny Park before the ferry makes the next crossing to your side of the river," Frost said. "If you heed the warnings, you should come to no harm."

What warnings? With her eyes on the statue, Beth took a step forward. Suddenly her focus readjusted, forcing her to look at two signs that blended into the area between the pavilion and the lake so well she hadn't seen them.

Or had they appeared because she had crossed some invisible line?

DESTINY PARK

Be Careful of Your Thoughts,

Your Words, and Your Intentions.

MOON GATES ONLY GO ONE WAY.

DO NOT GO THROUGH A GATE

WITHOUT SUPERVISION.

"What does that mean?" Beth asked.

"Exactly what it says," Frost replied. "Since Captain Forrester expects you to return to the police station, don't walk through a moon gate, even if it's open. You might not find your way back—or, depending on the gate, you might not recognize yourself if you do manage to return."

"I walked through the gate when I first arrived."

"With supervision." Frost paused. "I'll meet you here in an hour and escort you to the ferry."

Finding her way back to the dock and the ferry should be easy enough. Then again . . . "Thank you."

Frost turned and walked into the pavilion.

Beth followed a path around the ornamental lake. As she came abreast of the statue, she glanced at it and had a dizzying moment when her eyes wouldn't focus. When she thought she saw something else—something darker and dangerous.

The moment was gone, and the lovely woman with feathered wings once more stood on a pedestal in an ornamental lake.

The place smelled earthy and rich. There were mulch or gravel lines of demarcation between different areas of plants, but it still felt less like a conscious design, more like something formed by nature.

After checking her watch to make sure she had time, Beth chose a path that led away from the lake. Cultivated flower beds and small meadows still full of wildflowers. The coolness of autumn as she passed beneath trees shading the path. And sculptures. Not statues placed to be a point of interest, although those were there too. She passed a bearded man resting on one knee, looking down at her from his perch on the stone that he had sprung from. Not a benign face; not hostile either. Watchful. Considering.

Hearing shouts and laughter and that particular kind of taunting that sometimes occurred between male friends, she hurried down the path and spotted the two young men who had been on the ferry with her.

Friendly pushy-shovey? Or something more?

As she stepped out of the shadows under the trees, they spotted her. She didn't think they were predators in the truest sense, but there were two of them and they might have liked their odds for harassing a female on her own.

Then they spotted something else in the shadow of the trees and hurried away.

Beth stepped forward but saw nothing that would have alarmed two boys that age. But she *felt* something watching them. Watching her.

A glance at her watch had her moving quickly, retracing her steps back to the lake and the pavilion. Should she let Lucas Frost know there were a couple of rowdy young men in the park who might be tempted to cause some trouble as a way to restore their bravado? Or was the park's security already aware of them?

Did the park have security?

And what could she tell Frost? That a couple of boys were being rowdy? There was no law against *that*. And yet . . . She didn't have her service weapon, but she knew how to defend herself. Another woman, walking alone and thinking she was safe, might not have that experience.

When she spotted Frost, she lengthened her stride until she reached him. "It might be nothing, but I wondered if there was any security in the park?"

He studied her. "Why is that a concern?"

"It isn't always safe for women to walk alone, so I—"

"Were you threatened?"

Something in his voice made her shiver. "No. Nothing happened. I just wondered." She didn't want to cause trouble for anyone.

"Would you have reported this *nothing* to Captain Forrester?"

She hesitated, then nodded. "No laws were broken. The two young men didn't even approach me, but I feel concerned that other women walking alone in the park might be harassed—and I would have suggested to Captain Forrester that park security be made aware of potential problems."

"It is not your place to interfere with someone else's fate unless their fate is connected with yours," Frost said.

I'm a cop. It's my duty to interfere. Except she had a feeling they weren't talking about quite the same kind of fate.

"Come. The ferry will start taking passengers in a few minutes."

She waited until they were approaching the beach before asking, "That hotel is for visitors who want to stay overnight?"

"Yes," Frost replied.

Maybe when she had a couple days off, she would make an overnight visit and spend some time in Destiny Park. She'd barely had a chance to see anything. She hadn't seen any of the other moon gates, and she was curious about why they required supervision.

Just before she boarded the ferry, she turned to Frost. "Thank you for your assistance." She reached into her pocket, then hesitated. "If I'm asked for a gold coin, would two silver coins be acceptable?"

Frost almost smiled. "Yes. They would have the same value. But your fee for the ferry is one silver coin." A pause. "Hold on to the remaining coins. You'll find them useful the next time you visit."

Beth boarded the ferry, paid her silver coin, and found a seat inside.

Did Frost assume there would be more police inquiries in the future? Or did he sense that she was curious about the Isle of Wyrd and would come again for her own reasons?

Some commotion and a belligerent male voice had her half rising out of her seat. Then everything was quiet, and whatever had happened . . .

The ferry pulled away from the dock. The ride across the river was uneventful. When she reached the other side and left the area around the pier, intending to hail a cab, Beth spotted the patrol car parked in a pickup and drop-off zone. Jim Monkton and Benjamin Reynolds, the officers assigned to the special team, stood near the car.

Monkton raised a hand, so she headed toward them.

The two men studied her with an odd intensity before Reynolds said, "You okay?"

Puzzled, because it sounded like he'd expected her not to be okay, she replied, "I'm fine. I think I was given most of the information Captain Forrester needs."

Reynolds opened the back door of the patrol car and waited for her to get inside and settled before he and Monkton got in the car and they drove to the station.

No chitchat, no small talk, no comments. She didn't know these men well, so maybe that wasn't unusual. Maybe they would have been the same way picking up anyone who had just come from Wyrd.

She didn't know. But she did wonder what these officers had seen in the eyes of other detectives who had crossed the river that made them relieved to have the metal grill between them and her.

3

Charles Forrester listened to Beth Fahey's report, surprised—and a little uneasy—that she'd been told so much, shown so much. He'd expected her to meet the Ladies Three, since that was the only way she would have received any answers. He wasn't surprised that she'd met Ethan Sharpe, but to be allowed into the armory, allowed to *see* all the weapons that could come into someone's hand if that person was willing to pay the price? His other detectives had been shown a weapon brought to the Ladies' room, but they hadn't been allowed to handle it. *Couldn't* have handled it once it left Sharpe's hand. And yet this young woman had done exactly that. The Lady who sketched out the potential life paths that were used to decide on the price for the Arcana's assistance had *shown* her the drawing. Palowski's three victims. Not their fate to die that day.

He hoped his expression didn't reveal his surprise or uneasiness. She'd been shown too much on her first visit, and he didn't know what that meant. But he did know what question to ask when she finished her report.

"What was the price?" He smiled tightly when she looked startled—and a little guilty. "The Arcana don't give away that much information without getting something in return. What did you have to pay?"

Beth hesitated. "I owe them three favors."

Charles sucked in a breath.

"Nothing that would compromise my oath as a police officer or break any of our laws," she added hurriedly.

None of his men had been asked for anything more than a couple of gold coins. "Anything else?"

Another hesitation. Then she told him about the two young men and how they might have harassed her if something hadn't spooked them. Something that was in the shadows watching them—or watching her.

More likely watching her. Why so much interest in Beth Fahey? Because she was the first female he'd sent to Wyrd? Or was it something more?

"I'll add this information to the report," Forrester said. He unlocked his desk drawer and returned her service weapon. "Good work, Detective. Go home. Get some rest. I'll see you in the morning."

Beth pushed up from the chair but didn't move away from his desk. "I asked Frost why someone couldn't purchase the use of a gun from Wyrd but use regular ammunition to get around the per-bullet payment. He said if someone tried that, the gun would turn on him. It sounded like one of the cases I was given to review."

Too much information given to a first timer. "If you still have that file out, give it to me in the morning. I'll take a look at it."

"Yes, sir. Good night."

He waited until she was at the office door before saying, "Detective? One last question."

4

Charles Forrester focused on washing the dinner dishes while his wife, Aisha, dried and put things away. It was their custom to do the dishes together most nights, a time to share what they could about their respective days.

"Maybe I should wash the dishes tonight and you dry." Aisha's voice was quiet. It always was unless she was seriously angry or upset, but Charles detected the roughness underneath, the breaks that told him she'd used her voice too much today. Most people wouldn't realize her throat had been damaged when she was a girl—testimony to other kinds of damage she'd endured at the hands of a stepfather who objected to having to live in a house with a girl who couldn't pass for white. The bastard hadn't had any objections when he married Aisha's mother, hadn't said anything at all until the money from the first husband's life insurance ran out and he had to pay off his gambling debts on his own.

Considering her background, Charles still thought Aisha agreeing to marry him was a miracle.

"I'm fine doing the washing," he said.

She held out the plate he'd just handed her. "*If* you were washing."

He slipped the plate into the dishwater and washed it.

"You weren't there in body," she said when she accepted the now-clean dish, "but in spirit?"

They didn't have to say where *there* was. The Isle of Wyrd.

He held his hands above the dishwater, not even pretending to wash a dish. "Why do you say that?"

"There is a look in your eyes when you have to go there. And there is a different look when you have to send someone there." She hesitated. "Was it bad, this thing you sent someone to find?"

"My new detective lost the coin toss," Charles replied, scrubbing a pot as if he could erase what made him uneasy.

"But you don't send the new ones alone. And isn't the new detective a young woman?"

He nodded. "I was on the phone when they did the coin toss. Once it was done, I couldn't change the outcome without starting talk that I'm taking too much interest in her, giving her special treatment. The men have . . . reservations . . . about her being on the special investigations team."

"There are female police officers in all the other departments," Aisha said. "There are female detectives. Why is this different?"

"Because it takes balls to go to Wyrd. You have to be the right kind of *man* to cross the river and come back the same as when you went."

"Is she the same?"

Charles washed the last pan and emptied the water in the sink. "They told her too much, Aisha. *Showed* her too much. I don't know what it means when the Arcana are that accommodating. Yes, she appeared to be the same—this time."

Aisha studied him. "What else?"

"The first time I met Lucas Frost, he reminded me of my brother, of how Chad would have looked in his midthirties if he'd lived. Beth Fahey described a man who looked completely different—hair, eyes, skin, even a different height and build."

"Could it have been someone else claiming to be Lucas Frost?"

"No. It was the same man. It just brought home in another way that we don't know them, and even what we know might be an illusion. I think what Frost truly looks like is very different."

"If there is another call, will you send her back there?" Aisha asked.

Charles washed his hands and dried them on the dish towel before hanging it up. "I don't think I'll have a choice." He paused, then added, "I don't think they'll give me a choice."

5

He was known as Lucas Frost. Sometimes humans who dealt with him called him the Dictator because he was in charge of Destiny Park, and no one was allowed to challenge his decisions. Among his own, he was known as a Sorcerer King. He could manipulate the strange and uncanny, crush a person's fate, twist destiny, or even turn a person's world into a safe place or a nightmare.

Then again, so could all the Arcana to one degree or another.

Lucas watched the ferry leave the dock and head for the middle of the Fate River. The ferry wouldn't touch the human world, not now that the sun had set. No, the Ferryman was making this special journey because of a passenger who thought he was above the rules that governed Wyrd—a journey that would teach the human the price of trying to cheat the Ferryman.

The Ferryman's business was not his. The visitors who came for a little adventure, a little fun, had gone home or gone back to the hotel for dinner and whatever humans did for entertainment. Now it was just the Arcana in Destiny Park and the pavilion.

Lucas walked into the room where the Ladies Three ruled. After sunset, the most obvious physical change that indicated he was other than human were the antlers. They were small things, almost delicate when compared to a stag, but his were simply a sign of being from a different race, of being a part of the strange and uncanny in this world.

His wife, Justine, the Keeper of the Scales, looked at him.

"Well?" he asked. "What can you tell me about Beth Fahey?"

Justine looked at Zerah, her younger sister and Keeper of the Cards, then at Lysandra, her older sister and Keeper of the Fates, receiving a nod from each of them.

"As it has been since the Old Times, when our races first crossed paths, some members of the Arcana mingle with humans, live among humans, even mate with humans," Zerah said. "Sometimes offspring come from a mating."

"Arcana who live among humans tend to disappear," Lucas said.

Justine nodded. "Disappear, yes, but they are not forgotten because they bring a bit of strange to the human world, and if they stay in a place long enough, they create an anchor for the uncanny—a mostly benign connection."

Lucas studied the three sisters. "Your conclusion about Beth Fahey?"

Lysandra held up her pad of paper and turned it around for him to see the drawing.

Beth Fahey dressed as she had been that afternoon, looking into the still water of the ornamental lake. Looking at the delicate antlers revealed in her reflection.

This confirmed what he'd suspected when she had walked through the moon gate before entering the pavilion. "She's one of us."

"Yes," Justine replied. "Her heritage has been diluted by human blood and by living in the human world, but she is one of us."

6

"Do you know who I am?" Reginald Hampton III screamed as the Ferryman's crew tore off his clothes and held him down on the ferry's deck.

"You're a liar, a cheat, and a fornicator," the Ferryman replied. "You have more money than you could spend in three lifetimes, but you send men to threaten and beat people who are slow to pay their debts to you—and yet you try to avoid paying for services *you* want."

This *thing* standing over him looked somewhat human, but it wasn't. It *wasn't*. "Let me up. I'll pay the damn coin." Did they have any idea how much his suit had cost? As soon as he was on the other side of the river, he'd call his attorneys and raise such a stink that the Ferryman would have to cross the river in a rowboat, since that would be the only vessel he could afford.

Sue the bastard. Yeah, that's what he'd do. Call the newspapers and let them know how businessmen trying to make an honest deal were treated on Wyrd.

Not that he'd been trying to make an honest deal. He had a younger brother, Alistair, whose sexual excesses and unchecked spending were starting to interfere with *his* personal pleasures as well as getting in the way of potential business deals. He'd wanted information about how to curb Alistair's behavior without any of the splatter blowing back on *him.* And what did those bitches say? They said *he* would be the solution to the problem, but they wouldn't tell him *how.*

He'd had to pay five gold coins for them to tell him *that.* He'd be damned if he'd pay another gold coin for a ride back across the river on the ferry! He wouldn't have been on the ferry if the crew of his yacht had done their damn jobs and had the vessel ready, but his captain had told him that a minor but important repair had to be done before the yacht could go out again.

The Ferryman stared at Reginald, then shook his head. "The bargain between passengers and the Arcana is a coin. By refusing to pay for the ride across the river, you broke the bargain, so the price has gone up. You owe me more." He went down on one knee. "You owe me a year." He smiled and pulled out a knife. "During that year, you'll have no need of my ferry—or any other vessel—to navigate the Fate River and the waters beyond. But as your time approaches, you'll be drawn back here, closer to land, to give you a fighting chance to reach the shore."

The Ferryman held up a silver coin, then made a slice along one side of Reginald's abdomen, carefully making a pocket under the skin. Ignoring Reginald's screams, the Ferryman slid the coin into the slice. He made another slice on the other side of the man's abdomen and inserted five silvery scales to balance the silver coin.

One of the beings on the ferry handed the Ferryman a needle and black thread. Skin would tear before that thread broke.

As the Ferryman sewed up the two slices, Reginald began to gasp, began to change.

The Ferryman's crew lifted Reginald and tossed him over the side.

Gasping for air. Losing limbs. Changing.

As he hit the water, he thrashed, unaccustomed to having a tail and fins instead of arms and legs. Water flowed through his gills.

He was a fish? That bastard turned him into a *fish*?

He thrashed his way to the surface. The ferry was still there. The Ferryman looked over the rail and said, "If you can elude all the predators, you'll turn back into a man one year from today. If you can't . . ."

The Ferryman moved away from the rail. A minute later, the engine started, and the ferry headed back to Wyrd.

He tried to follow it. He would insist that they change him back into a man. He was Reginald Hampton III! He was *important*. If he disappeared for a year, what would happen to his investments, to the companies where he was a majority shareholder, to the wealth he'd grown after wresting most of the family's fortune out of the hands of his incompetent parents? Alistair would be trying to get his greedy hands on all of it.

Struggling to control an unfamiliar body, and no longer sure which direction he was swimming in, Reginald leaped above the surface of the water—and saw a sailing ship bearing down on him.

Where had *that* come from?

He twisted his body out of the way, but not enough. Not enough. The prow was going to hit . . .

His body passed right through the ship, as if it was some kind of hallucination. Or a ghost.

Just before he hit the water, he thought he heard someone on that ship yelling for help.

PART TWO

TRANSFORMATION

SEPTEMBER

1

Rachel Nightingale kept her head down and resisted the urge to look over her shoulder while she waited in the queue to buy passage on the ferry to Wyrd. There was no reason for anyone to look for her *here*. Alistair wouldn't think she'd have the courage to go to the Isle of Wyrd.

Her fiancé didn't understand that sometimes desperation could look a lot like courage—and she had been desperate for a long time. Not at the beginning. Alistair had been wonderful to her in the beginning, bragging to everyone that his lady friend was a beautiful best-selling *novelist*. He'd wined her and dined her and bedded her with care—until he persuaded her to move in with him. Then the slow erosion of her life began.

He said she needed to lose some weight. She was getting broad in the beam from sitting on her ass all day writing those "hack stories."

She couldn't go with him to his important dinner out of town because she had a deadline for some stupid book only marginally literate domestic staff would want to read? How could she be so *selfish*?

Why did she have to embarrass him by telling his associates she was reading some crap? Never mind that the wives of those associates were also reading that book, and she and the other women had been enjoying a lively discussion about the characters and storyline until he pulled her away from that group so that she could stand with him among a group of men who "joked" that a woman's proper place was on her knees.

When she pointed that out to Alistair when they got home, he'd dragged her into the bathroom and pushed her head into the toilet bowl, pulling her head up before she drowned.

She didn't have any friends. Not anymore. Alistair monitored her phone calls and her e-mails to her agent and editor. She set up another e-mail account, a secret one she used to stay in touch with them. She had a post office box in another part of King's Hill where she received her royalty statements and any contracts that might come in, although those were rare now. She hadn't written anything in two years because Alistair had insisted on reading her rough drafts and had brutally criticized her skills as a writer until she couldn't write a coherent sentence anymore, let alone a novel. The one time she'd tried to explain the writing process and why first drafts were *rough* drafts was the first time he'd hit her in the face and began telling people she was "clumsy."

He'd taken away her life and made sure she was too afraid of displeasing him to do anything on her own. He'd consumed most of her, but he still needed her because she had dug in and held on to one thing he wanted and she wouldn't give him.

He had made a couple of bad investments a few months ago and needed a fresh source of cash—and there were the royalties from her previous books, an influx of cash that came in twice a year. She and Alistair weren't married, so their finances had been kept separate.

Then he began pressuring her to add him as another person who could access her savings account and her checking account. He wanted access to her safe deposit box, accusing her of holding out on him when it came to putting in her share of the money for the upkeep of their luxury apartment—a new accusation, since splitting the costs had never been part of the agreement when he'd asked her to live with him. The lease was in his name. Nothing connected her to the place any more than the other women who had lived with him had been connected to the place. He used them up, then threw them out, because he was Alistair Hampton, one of the Hamptons from King's Hill, and that's what he could do with women.

She had some terrifying suspicions of what had happened to those other women, especially now that Alistair had escalated his campaign to gain access to her savings and the safe deposit box where she'd hidden her mother's jewelry and some cash.

Two nights ago, she had decided to run after Alistair slapped her around again for refusing to give him access to her money. She felt lightheaded and weak from hunger because he hadn't allowed her to eat for several days, and he took pictures on his phone every morning before he left for work—pictures of the contents of the fridge and pantry showing him all the food. She couldn't even take a swallow of milk or orange juice without him knowing—and punishing her for it.

This morning, she retrieved the five hundred dollars she had hidden in a box of tampons—about the only thing of hers she knew Alistair wouldn't touch—and packed a soft-sided overnight bag with the clothes she could fit into it, as well as her e-reader and charger. Her cell phone went into her purse. She turned off the phone at the last moment in case Alistair had someone monitoring her phone calls when he wasn't around.

She walked out of the apartment with the overnight bag and her purse, smiled at the man at the reception desk. As she smiled at the doorman, who wished her a pleasant day, she glanced back—and saw the man at the desk writing something in his book. Probably noting when she left and what she was carrying. But he didn't pick up the phone to inform Alistair that she had left the building.

She walked a block and crossed the street before hailing a taxi, giving the central branch of the King's Hill public library as her destination. She wasn't allowed to check out books that weren't on Alistair's approved reading list, but she went to the library a couple of times a week just to be among books—and to peruse the posters that offered phone numbers that could connect her to women's shelters in towns around the Fate River.

She walked into the library and waited until the taxi drove away. Leaving the library, she crossed the street to the small market and deli where she sometimes bought forbidden food. Today she bought a roll, a single-serve box of orange juice, and yogurt. She tucked the roll and orange juice into the overnight bag's side pocket and ate the yogurt at one of the high-top tables on the deli side of the store.

She wanted more, *needed* more, but she was afraid of getting sick if she ate too much after being empty for so long.

She lingered because now she had to decide. There was a small commuter ferry—a "river bus"—that traveled the Fate River, stopping at a few places in each town to pick people up and drop them off. The Fate was a wide, deep river with powerful, unpredictable currents. But it wasn't wide enough to hide the land on the other side of the water. The Isle of Wyrd.

Commercial vessels could anchor in Destiny Bay or dock at the Destiny Marina for a few hours while their crews off-loaded goods—or so she'd heard. It was risky to enter the bay without permission, but people *could* reach the island that way, and there were buses—or some kind of vehicles—that took passengers around the island. There was even some kind of train, but there were rumors that people who boarded that train didn't always arrive at their destination—or any destination at all. But if you needed help and were desperate enough to try to change your fate, there was only one place to go: the pavilion in Destiny Park.

Claiming she was doing research for a new book, Rachel had learned that much about Wyrd, just as she'd learned about the women's shelters.

She had to decide. Reaching the pavilion was the goal because Alistair didn't have any influence there.

God, she hoped he didn't have any influence there. But the moment Alistair realized she was gone, he'd send someone to hunt her down and bring her back. And once she was under his control again, he would break her down until she signed over everything she had. And then . . .

Then . . .

The river bus and any tourist boat that had a captain willing to chance entering Destiny Bay were run by men who were open to bribes or would buckle under threats—to say nothing of one of Alistair's people being on the river bus or another boat for some other reason and receiving the alert that she had bolted. Same with the land buses. Less likely, but someone could recognize her from the author photos on her books and have the bus stopped before she reached the Penwych docks—and the particular dock where *that* ferry crossed the river.

Taxi was the best choice. Still a chance of being stopped, but she had a story about bringing some gently used clothes to a friend who lived near the Penwych docks. No, not a friend. An acquaintance. Yes, that was better. She was doing a kindness for a woman down on her luck, but discretion was required and that's why she was traveling all the way around the Fate River.

She had studied maps of the towns that bordered the river, again claiming research, and she'd looked up residential areas on the library's computers, so she knew there was an apartment complex a block away from where the ferry to Wyrd ran.

Rachel hailed another taxi and gave the driver the address of the apartment complex in Penwych.

The cabby turned in his seat and looked pointedly at the diamond ring on her left hand. "You sure? Cops keep an eye on things around there because . . . well . . . just because. Still, wearing a ring like that might be a temptation."

"I'll be fine, thank you," Rachel replied.

"Suit yourself."

When the cabby headed into traffic and took the main highway that followed the river, Rachel slipped the ring off her finger and tucked it into a zip pocket of her purse. She wasn't worried about being mugged for the ring, although that was a possibility, but the diamond and setting were distinctive and easily identifiable, since Alistair had photos of the ring for insurance purposes.

She tried to act calm, tried to remember her cover story, tried not to look like someone who was running away from an abuser.

Alistair shouldn't know she was missing until he returned to the apartment that evening—assuming he didn't get in late because he'd spent time with whomever he was currently screwing. She felt sorry for his current mistress, but she hoped the woman would keep him occupied long enough.

When they arrived at the apartment complex, Rachel gave the driver the fare and a precisely correct tip. Nothing that would make her memorable.

The cabby would remember the ring, but she couldn't help that.

He didn't linger, didn't watch her go to one of the doors. Still, she waited until the taxi was out of sight before hurrying to the dock.

The ferry was unloading passengers when she arrived. She'd just made it. If she'd been a few minutes later, she would have had to wait for the ferry's next crossing, leaving her exposed on this side of the river.

She watched the people, afraid she might recognize someone—and be recognized in turn.

Groups of women walked off together, chatting about tarot and colors and strange vibes in the park. Other people, including a few men, walked off the ferry looking shattered, frightened.

Some people carried large totes; others had wheeled overnight suitcases, confirming that there was somewhere she could stay—provided she could afford the price of a room and a meal. The librarians had mentioned a hotel located near the entrance to Destiny Park, but they couldn't find any information about the cost of a room.

If she had to, she would find a place in the park to hide and sleep rough.

One librarian who had gone to the island on a day off did tell her that she would have to buy coins at a currency exchange booth since those coins were the only kind of currency used on the island.

When the last departing passenger reached the shore, the shutters on the currency exchange booth opened.

She was in the middle of the queue. The people around her were talking about tarot readings or having their futures revealed in the lines of their hands. She kept watching the people, kept waiting to hear a shout, kept bracing for a hand to grab her arm.

Five more people ahead of her. Four more.

Shouting behind her, but when she glanced back, it was two teenage boys doing some pushy-shovey until a male voice said, "The current is rough here. If you fall into the water, no one is going to go in after you."

The boys stopped fooling around.

Did that voice belong to another passenger? Maybe a regular who knew about the river? Or did the dock and ferry have its own discreet security?

Two more people. One more.

When she saw the person in the booth, Rachel blinked once, then busied herself with opening her purse and taking out three hundred dollars. Man? Woman? Young? Old? It was like her brain couldn't make a decision about what she was seeing.

She held out the money. "I'd like to exchange this, please."

The person stared at her. "You here for fun or something more?"

It was tempting to say "Fun." Didn't most people come here for a taste of the strange? But lying . . . "Something more."

The person took her money and gave her a stack of gold and silver coins.

"Gold is ten, silver is five," the person said. "Pay the Ferryman a gold coin. You'll see where. Next."

Rachel's hands shook as she gathered the coins. She almost dropped one stack on the dock and would have watched them slip into the water, but she managed to dump them into her purse, holding on to the one gold coin she would need when she boarded.

A covered black cauldron with a slot on the top and a sign that read PAY THE FERRYMAN. She dropped the gold coin into the slot and took an inside seat near the front of the ferry.

It was tempting to keep looking behind her, but she kept her head down and clutched her purse and overnight bag.

She didn't breathe easy until the ferry pulled away from the dock and headed for the Isle of Wyrd.

2

Lucas Frost completed his patrol of the part of Destiny Park visitors found interesting—or, to be precise, didn't find too strange and unnerving. There was more to the park if you knew how to find it—or were destined to find it—but no one had bought a ticket for any of the trains, no one had bought a ticket for the bus that traveled to the "neighborhoods" on the island. Since no one had come to the pavilion to report someone missing, that meant no one had been foolish enough to go through a moon gate without fully understanding what would happen, depending on the gate's intention at that moment.

Most of the moon gates within reach of determined visitors were transportation. They took a person from the park to the stations where tickets could be purchased for passage on a bus, train, or ship. Sometimes one of those gates took a person far beyond the park—and usually beyond any hope of returning unless you were one of the Arcana.

Some of the gates had multiple possibilities—like transformation. A kind of alchemy, changing one thing to another. Changing a person into something else.

Those who came to Wyrd came at their own risk as they searched for something beyond the mundane. Some parts of Wyrd could be benevolent in their own way, but usually people who looked for something other than a bit of fun crossed the river because of a deep need.

Lucas entered the pavilion and stopped at the arched doorway, puzzled by all the signs set out on one side of the pavilion—the side the visitors flocked to. OUT TO LUNCH. BACK IN ONE HOUR.

He walked into the room where his wife and her sisters did a different kind of business.

They were waiting for him.

"Someone is coming," Zerah said, her hand hovering above the cards she'd drawn from her chosen decks. "A desperate journey. Life or death."

"When?" he asked.

Zerah's hand moved over the cards. She selected another card and turned it over. "Now."

Meaning this person was on the ferry.

He looked at Justine. She looked at Lysandra, whose clouded eyes saw much and guided her hand as she sketched possible fates.

Lysandra closed her eyes. When she opened them, they were clear. She turned her sketch pad to reveal what she had seen.

A woman. Attractive, vibrant, holding a book in her hand. He couldn't read all of the title, but the author's name on the cover was Rachel Nightingale. That sketch blended into the same woman, dull eyed and looking like a walking corpse made of skin and bones. That sketch blended into the woman laid out in a coffin—and a date that was only a few months from now. Her destiny if she didn't do something to change it, if she didn't have the courage to embrace a different path.

Lysandra had revealed that path too. A dangerous one, and not without fear or pain. But a way to disappear for a while and, after an interval, return as someone else who would have a chance to live.

"Evil will hunt her," Justine said. "Evil that wears success and a three-piece bespoke suit and speaks pretty words to people willing to look the other way."

"I'll go meet the ferry," Lucas said.

"Tomorrow is soon enough for her to see us," Justine said.

"If she's being hunted . . ."

Zerah turned over another card. "The hunter has a hound. If the woman has courage, she will be gone before the hound crosses the river."

"I'll arrange for her to stay at the hotel for a day or two," he said. "And I'll ask Jack to stay there, too, and keep an eye on her."

Lucas strode out of the pavilion, reaching the dock a minute before the ferry arrived. Then he waited for the woman who had come to Wyrd to change her fate.

3

The problem with hiding in a seat at the front of the ferry was being one of the last people to disembark.

The rowdy teenage boys had tried to talk to her a couple of times, but Rachel pretended she didn't hear them, even when one of them called her a stuck-up bitch. They were apprentice abusers—or just immature boys. Either way, she couldn't afford to engage with them, even to defend herself in some way. There was always a chance one of them had a mother or an aunt who read her books, and he had seen—and might remember—her photo on the back cover.

Of course, she hadn't been so thin the last time she'd had an author photo taken.

She followed the boys out, relieved that there were a couple of middle-aged women between her and them. The women's chatter made it clear that they had come for a little taste of the strange—and an excellent lunch at the hotel.

She noticed the man at the end of the dock, eyeing each person as they passed him. The boys received a hard stare, but they were allowed to continue on their way. The two women received a nod that acknowledged them but didn't encourage any chat, not even to ask for directions.

On the other hand, the hotel was in plain view, positioned on a rise that overlooked a sandy beach. She couldn't see the pavilion the women had talked about.

The tall black-haired man who stood at the end of the dock was an alpha male—and a predator. He was the kind of man who made Alistair edgy, because Alistair's form of predator couldn't intimidate someone who was beyond dangerous.

Rachel ducked her head as she reached the end of the dock, hoping he'd dismiss her as uninteresting.

"Rachel Nightingale?"

A person can't be afraid all the time. She wanted to believe that, but she knew it wasn't true. She'd been afraid every waking moment for months now. Alistair didn't have any legal right to have her committed to an institution of some kind, but he implied he could pull the right strings and get her committed for being emotionally unstable, could force her into giving him power of attorney over her assets. Then he could leave her locked up somewhere while he spent her money and looked for his next victim.

A person *could* be afraid all the time, but right here, right now, she was going to pretend she was still the strong, successful woman she had been before she met Alistair Hampton.

She lifted her head and looked the man in the eyes. "Yes."

So much for bravery. Her throat closed up, choking her. One word was all she'd managed.

He took her overnight bag. "I'm Lucas Frost. Come with me." It was a command, not a request.

She followed him up the boardwalk and continued to follow him when he turned onto a dirt path toward the hotel. He had the bag with her clothes and all the worldly goods she couldn't stuff into her purse. "Are you some kind of security?"

"Why do you think that?"

"You knew who I was. Did Alistair send you?" If she reached the hotel and screamed for help, would anyone help her? Or would they all turn to this man, bending to his will?

"No one *sends* me," Lucas replied. "The Ladies Three saw that you were coming here and asked me to meet you when you disembarked. You'll meet them in the morning."

Was she supposed to know who the Ladies Three were? The librarian who had visited Wyrd hadn't mentioned them.

"Do you have a phone or other electronic device?" Lucas asked.

She couldn't see any point in lying. She'd been caught by someone who could turn Alistair into a smear under his shoe. "I have an e-reader and a cell phone. The phone is turned off. The e-reader can't be traced as long as I don't connect with Wi-Fi. Maybe not even then. I'm not sure."

"Give me the phone." Lucas held out a hand.

She wanted to refuse to give up her only way to communicate with anyone beyond this place, but she felt herself bend to his will. She opened her purse, then stopped walking because she couldn't walk and fumble through her purse at the same time.

He stopped and waited.

She found the phone and gave it to him.

"Does it have a password or a code to unlock it?" he asked.

"Yes." She told him her PIN.

"Is there anything on here that would be a danger to anyone else? Pictures? Phone numbers?"

Rachel shook her head. "I deleted all those things months ago. The only numbers are Alistair's cell phone, his office phone number, and the phone number for the central branch of the King's Hill public library. I do—did—research for . . . It doesn't matter. Nothing else."

"So if this phone is found in a location and given to Alistair, it won't tell him anything he doesn't already know?"

"No."

He started walking again. Rachel followed.

"There are a few rooms in the hotel that are very private," Lucas said. "You'll stay in that wing tonight, maybe longer. Stay in the room. Read your books. Order from the room service menu so that you're not seen by too many visitors. Make sure you order enough food. And get some sleep. Tomorrow you'll meet the Ladies Three, and you need to be strong, rested, and clear minded to understand your choices. My brother, Jack, will be staying in a room near yours to keep watch. You'll be safe."

"I'm not sure I have enough money to pay for a room at the hotel, and I can't use a credit card," Rachel said.

"We'll discuss the fees tomorrow once you decide what you want to do and understand what it will cost."

They reached the hotel. Lucas opened one of the glass doors.

"Why would you help me?" she asked.

"Sometimes we assist people who come here to meet their fate—or try to change it."

He took care of getting the room and escorted her to a solid wall that had been painted with a kind of forest-fantasy mural. Then he pushed one part of the wall, and Rachel heard a click as a door opened—a door so well camouflaged she wouldn't have found it on her own, since it just looked like the hallway ended there.

Halfway down the secret hallway, he opened the door to a room that was simple and luxurious at the same time. Restful to the eyes and mind.

Lucas opened the curtains. "There is a small balcony and a chair. You can sit out there if you'd like some air."

"Won't I be seen?"

He looked amused. "Yes, but not by visitors. This part of the park belongs to the Arcana and is private." The amused look faded into something feral. "But draw the curtains and don't look out after the sun goes down."

"In stories, telling the heroine not to look out would guarantee she would be overcome with curiosity and look in order to find out the secret."

"Your people's stories usually have the heroine seeing something that terrifies her but managing to escape and emerge victorious. In our versions of those stories, most of the time the heroine sees the truth and then goes insane or dies. Don't let curiosity waste your courage, Rachel Nightingale. Close the curtains after dark. Stay inside away from too many eyes. Tomorrow you will need all that you are in order to choose your future."

He set her room key on the dresser and left.

The room had a mini refrigerator and something that looked like an old-fashioned bread box to store non-refrigerated food. There were plates, silverware, and glasses, and a microwave to reheat food. No coffeemaker.

Her hands shook as she read the room service menu and called the hotel's restaurant to place an order—a sandwich and salad with a bowl of seasonal fruit. Foods that she could store in the fridge.

While she waited, she hung up tops and slacks, put the underclothes in a drawer in the dresser. She put her e-reader on the table next to the bed and tucked away her purse on the table's bottom shelf.

She prowled the room and bathroom. It had most of the amenities of a five-star hotel, but she wondered—and worried—about why a hotel would have a secret wing of rooms.

A knock on the door. Rachel stood frozen for a moment before she hurried to answer the second knock.

No security chain on the door. No peephole to see who was out there.

Swallowing against a suddenly queasy stomach, she opened the door.

The man who stood on the other side looked enough like Lucas Frost to be a close relative.

"I'm Jack." He held out a tray of food. "I'll be in the next room, keeping an eye on things. If you need help for any reason—need help faster than you would get by calling the front desk—just shout or pound on the wall. I'll hear you."

"Are you hotel security?" she asked, taking the tray.

"You could say that." Something about his smile made her think that his kind of security often ended with burying a body.

"Do I pay you?"

Jack shook his head. "The food has been added to your account." He looked at her. "Don't skimp. No matter what you decide, you'll need a strong body for what is ahead."

Rachel backed into the room. Jack closed the door, leaving her alone.

She was going to face some kind of ordeal. That much was clear. But not today. Today, in this room, she was safe.

4

Ted Ocampo followed Darren Palmer down another path in Destiny Park and wished he hadn't been chosen to be Dare's buddy today. He hadn't wanted to come to the island, and he didn't want to wander around this park looking for one of the moon gates Dare and his pack of bullyboys at school thought were so freaking cool.

But none of Dare's Doggs had been willing to cut class and take the ferry to Wyrd, so Dare had recruited Ted, who was one of Dare's favorite victims because he didn't have the guts to refuse to do anything Dare wanted him to do.

The place was seriously strange. It *looked* just like a gardeny park that his mom would jazz about, but . . .

That statue they passed a few minutes ago. It looked like a deer, except it had a man's torso and arms rising from the deer's body. The head was a stag's head with a rack of antlers. Ted had thought it was some freaking-ass statue that someone had created while on some serious drugs. Then it turned its head and stared at him as he walked past.

He tried to tell himself it was some kind of animatronic creature like movie studios built for special effects, but he knew that wasn't true. That thing was living and real—and watching them.

"Keep up, Tedious," Dare said. "If you get lost, I won't come looking for you."

"That woman on the ferry. Did you think she was hot?" Ted asked. The woman Dare had hassled, trying to get her to respond to sex talk, hadn't been *old*, but she'd been a lot older than them.

Dare gave him the "Are you kidding me?" face. "The stuck-up bitch who looked like she'd spent a few weeks at Camp Starvation? I wouldn't poke her with *your* dick, let alone mine."

Ted felt bad about bringing up the woman as a way to deflect Dare's attention away from him, but he thought Dare wasn't too far off with the Camp Starvation remark. Ted had a cousin who had some kind of big food issues and had looked like that woman. The adults in the family and their friends kept complimenting Molly on losing weight and didn't want to see that she was in trouble—like, mental trouble as well as looking like bones in a bag—until her body just gave up one day.

Nothing he could do about the woman. She was a grown-up and should be smart enough to look after herself.

Pushing thoughts of the woman aside, Ted focused on his own problem, which was how the freaking hell he could get off this island.

The paths meandered here and wandered there. Where were the freaking signs to tell you where you were going? Like, would it be too much trouble for the people running this place to put up a sign with an arrow to show you the way back to the pavilion? If there had been a sign, he would have slipped away from Dare and run back to the one place on this freaking island that was only a bit strange instead of seriously weird.

Maybe there were places that were close to normal on the island. After all, it wasn't *tiny*. He and Colin Forrester had taken the river bus all the way around the island one afternoon just to see it. Not that they'd seen all that much; the river bus hugged the side of the Fate River that was closer to the mainland towns, since that's where people got on and off in order to go to jobs or go shopping and whatnot. Colin said there were boats that hired out as water taxis that maybe would take you to Destiny Bay, but he'd heard there wasn't any touristy stuff around the bay. There was a beach and there were docks where fishing boats or supply boats could tie up, or whatever that boat term was—why would he know that shit?—but there wasn't anything *interesting* except the pavilion and the park on this side of the island.

"Score," Dare said.

Ted looked around. He'd been following blindly, lost in thoughts of escaping and going home without Dare and his bullyboys beating the shit out of him tomorrow at school.

In front of them was one of the moon gates. An arch made of stone with openwork metal gates that had a large butterfly in the center. The keystone had . . . symbols? He wasn't sure about that, but he was *certain* that he didn't want to push those metal gates open and walk under that arch. He was also certain that Dare would make him go first. Despite all his big-balls talk, Dare usually wasn't the first to do anything if someone else could be sacrificed.

He couldn't leave without Dare's permission, not if he wanted to survive this school year, but maybe he could make Dare *order* him to go away.

"You're a rat, Dare." Ted's voice carried. Not that there was anyone around to hear him and come over to check out what he and Dare were doing.

Dare pushed at the metal gates, which swung open over well-trimmed grass, each gate holding half the butterfly. Then he turned back and gave Ted that psycho smile that made the younger kids at school wet their pants. "Oh, yeah? Why is that, Tedious?"

"You told everyone that I felt up Melissa Stevens under her shirt."

"You wanted to, didn't you?"

Sure he did, but he hadn't *done* it. "I liked her, and now she won't even talk to me."

"Screw her," Dare said. "Come here and see what this moon gate is all about."

Something flickered on the keystone. Ted stared at it a minute. Was the symbol changing? He blinked. The symbols changed to letters.

Trans
porta
tion

Trans
forma
tion

Changing over and over, like the designation sign on a bus when it changes its route. Changing. Changing.

"Come *on*, Tedious," Dare said. "Do as you're told."

No fucking way. "If you're so curious, you go first." Bravery born of terror filled Ted. "Or are you chicken?"

"That's right, Tedious. I'm a chicken!" Dare tucked his hands under his arms and moved his elbows like wings. "Look at me! I'm a rat-faced chicken!" He danced around making clucking noises.

The letters on the keystone kept changing, changing: TRANSPORTATION. TRANSFORMATION. "Dare, you're too close to the gate."

"I'm a rat-faced chicken. Cluck, cluck, cluck." Dare kept moving his arms and doing some kind of dance. "I'm a rat-faced chicken!"

Dare danced under the arch—and disappeared.

Ted stared at the pile of clothes on the ground. Then he heard something scream. Not human and yet . . .

He raced around the gate. Something moved under the clothes as it screamed.

He took a step toward the moving clothes. Took two steps back as something freed itself from the T-shirt. It looked at him as it flapped its wings and screamed.

A rat-faced chicken.

"D-Dare?"

The thing flapped its wings. It opened its rat mouth and screamed.

Whump!

Something dropped from the sky. One big taloned foot landed on Dare's back.

Hawk? Eagle? Owl? How was he supposed to know? Whatever it was, it was almost as tall as he was. It looked at him and screamed, but not in terror. No, this was a challenge.

Ted didn't move. Couldn't move. The bird tightened its grip on its prey, which produced one final squeak as the bird's talons dug into flesh.

The bird flew away with its meal.

Ted stared at the bird and the thing that hung from its talons. He stared at the pile of empty clothes.

He fell to his knees and threw up.

Then he ran, blind to direction because the only direction he needed right now was *away.*

5

"Two came this way," Deerman told Lucas Frost as they studied the open moon gate.

"Only one set of clothes here." Lucas didn't look for a cell phone or a wallet that might hold identification. He simply put the clothes into the cardboard box he'd brought with him. Identification was a problem for the police.

"Someone was careless with destiny."

"Yes." Possibly more than one if the other youth he'd seen getting off the ferry that morning had gone through the moon gate when it offered connections to transportation instead of transformation. If that was the case, the boy could be anywhere depending on which train, bus, or boat he boarded.

Lucas raised a hand. The two sides of the gate slowly closed, the butterfly once more whole. He looked at Deerman and wondered, not for the first time, if that branch of the Arcana had intended to be a meld of human and deer, or if a transformation had gone wrong a long time ago.

"If you see anything else, let me know," Lucas said.

"By now, there won't be much to find."

Of course, he and Deerman were assuming this human hadn't been prepared for the change. It was possible that the boy was running in another form or hiding as he adjusted to a new shape. But more likely, if he transformed into some kind of prey form, all they would find were bones left from a predator's kill.

Lucas walked back to the pavilion. The moon gates were far enough away from the part of the park most visitors saw. Around the pavilion and the ornamental lake, humans could play at finding out their potential destiny, although what they were told was never *completely* play. When you went deeper into the park, embracing destiny was no longer any kind of game, and you couldn't be careless with words or intentions.

An archway in the pavilion that looked filled by a slab of solid stone shimmered as Lucas approached. He walked through the shimmer and stepped into an office that had state-of-the-art electronic equipment and looked like a CEO's suite.

Setting the box on a wooden conference table, Lucas walked to his desk and placed a call to Charles Forrester. "Captain. Send one of your men to the pier to meet the next ferry. We found some clothing that needs your attention. Detective Fahey isn't required for this pickup since there is no need to travel to Wyrd at this time."

"Understood," Forrester said.

Yes, Lucas thought as he finished the call and took the box of clothes to the ferry's dock. Forrester understood what he meant, which is why the police captain didn't ask any questions about the clothes.

6

Charles Forrester stepped out of his office as Castelletti and Fahey gathered around the large table where the team reviewed physical evidence or crime scene photos, setting out the material like it was pieces of a puzzle. And it was a puzzle, but often the picture showed the aftermath of a lethal event.

"Any problems, Kuhn?" he asked the detective he'd sent to meet the ferry.

"No, sir," Ian Kuhn replied. "The ferry was pulling in when I reached the pier. After the people disembarked, one of the crew got off and handed the box to me." He waved a hand at the box, which had the flaps folded to keep the top closed. "Wasn't sealed with tape, but I didn't check the contents. I figured you'd want us to do that here."

Forrester hesitated for a moment, tempted to send Fahey out on a spurious errand. He knew Lucas Frost was interested in Fahey—not in a sexual way, but something about the young detective had caught the Arcana's attention, and that was seldom good. But his team's investigations were always going to brush against the Isle of Wyrd because that was the reason for this special group of detectives, so Fahey had to come to terms with the truth or she'd burn out and transfer to another unit—or quit the police force altogether.

"Open it," he said.

Kuhn put on gloves, opened the flaps, and identified each item as he placed it on the table. "Sneakers, scuffed but fairly new. No socks. Plain T-shirt, medium blue. Briefs. Jeans." He emptied the pockets. "Cell phone. Four gold coins. Wallet with"—a hesitation—"a student ID."

Forrester studied the ID. "He goes to my son's school."

"This is a school day, Captain," Castelletti said. "A boy going over to Wyrd for fun or mischief isn't going to skip school and go alone."

Forrester nodded. "Call the school. Ask if any of Darren Palmer's friends didn't show up today."

Castelletti went to his desk to make the call.

"Should we contact his parents?" Fahey asked.

"Not yet," Forrester replied. "We don't know what happened to their son." He knew how he would feel if he received that call when the cops couldn't provide any answers, and having distraught parents charging into the pavilion and making demands wouldn't help matters.

Fate. Destiny. Whatever you wanted to call it, it could be a screaming bitch.

"The school will tell them Darren didn't show up today," Fahey said.

Castelletti returned. "All of Darren Palmer's friends were in school, but a boy who often received Palmer's attention—"

"Meaning he was bullied," Kuhn cut in.

Castelletti nodded. "That's how I heard it. Ted Ocampo also isn't in school. Could be sick. Could be faking being sick to get out of a test or to avoid Palmer and his friends. But . . ."

"I know him," Forrester said. "Ocampo and my son are on the school's swim team and sometimes hang out together."

He looked at Beth Fahey. The Arcana had told her too much, showed her too much. He didn't want to make an enemy of Lucas Frost, but he also didn't want one of his detectives going back to Wyrd thinking the Arcana were benign. They weren't—and neither was that island and how it worked.

"I wasn't told where the clothes were found." Forrester addressed his team, but he kept his eyes on Fahey. "However, based on my experience and some of the things I've seen, I'm guessing the boy went through a moon gate and was careless about his intentions. Moon gates only go in one direction. If Palmer went through a transportation gate and got on a bus or a train, he could end up anywhere in Wyrd." *And Wyrd was a lot bigger than that island. The boy could end up on a train or a bus that will let him off in another place that is a convergence of the uncanny. Or he could be on a train or a bus that never lets people get off until they have met the requirements of their intentions. Please, God, don't let that boy end up on a ship.* "He also wouldn't have shed his clothes in the park. However, if he went through a transformation gate, what he becomes will match his intentions. He will become something else."

Castelletti and Kuhn stared at him. They were seasoned detectives who had crossed the river and asked the questions that needed asking, but they didn't have the deeply haunted look at the back of their eyes that was a sign they had seen the after-dark truth about Wyrd. He had. So there were times when he had quietly crossed the river and dealt with the situations he suspected would break good men. Now? Something about Fahey's presence had changed the team's connection with the Arcana, and that changed what he *had* to share with his team about Wyrd. Even if they never saw the evidence, they all needed to know the reasons behind the cases that might never be solved.

"Can't he go through another gate and change back to who he was?" Fahey asked.

Forrester shook his head. "He would automatically change back if he specified a time limit to the transformation. 'I will be an octopus and live in Destiny Bay for one week.' If he spoke with intention—and survived any predators that might find an octopus an appealing, if surprising, meal—he would change back into the teenage boy he had been. If he didn't speak with intention . . ." He sighed. "The Arcana will search for Palmer in and around Destiny Park, and most likely, they will find him—or what is left of him."

"The other boy?" Castelletti asked. "Should someone cross the river and help with a search?" When Forrester said nothing, Castelletti added, "They *are* going to search for Ted Ocampo, aren't they?"

"No one on Wyrd is going to interfere with Ted Ocampo's fate," Forrester said quietly. "We wait until we are called."

Forrester walked into his office. He wasn't surprised that Beth Fahey followed him.

"They will call." She made the words a statement, not a question.

"Yes, they'll call."

"For us to pick up a body."

He nodded. "Hopefully only one."

7

A wave filled Ted's mouth with water at the moment he turned his head for a breath. He choked and coughed up river water, which forced him to stop. Which forced him to tread water and look around.

Which forced him to wonder what the freaking fuck he was doing in the river.

Then some part of his brain that had been numbed by terror woke up, and he remembered running away from the moon gate. Running and running. Looking for the pavilion or the ferry? Maybe?

When he reached the shoreline, it hadn't looked like the area where the ferry docked. He remembered standing there looking across the river and desperately wanting to go home. He remembered stripping down to his briefs because the Fate River had a strong current and waterlogged jeans would pull him under. He remembered . . . Had he sent a text to Colin before tucking his phone inside his sneakers?

He remembered wading into the water and setting off across the river. He was a strong swimmer, a member of Penwych High School's swim team, but even a strong swimmer didn't have much chance of getting across the Fate, especially at this time of year, when the water was turning cold.

"Hey!" a voice shouted. "Grab the ring buoy! I'll pull you in!"

A ring attached to a rope landed in the water in front of him and floated past until the rope was taut.

Kicking as hard as he could, Ted lunged for the rope and got one hand on it, then got an arm hooked into the buoy.

"Hurry up, boy, or the current will roll the dinghy right over you!"

Ted looked at the man who was hauling on the rope. The current was taking the dinghy, but it was taking him too. He swam toward the dinghy as the man hauled in the rope.

"I'll lean hard on this side and keep the rope taut," the man said. "You climb aboard."

Ted nodded. With one arm still looped in the buoy, he put both hands on the dinghy and surged over the side, landing in an awkward sprawl.

The man dropped the rope, set the oars in the oarlocks, and began rowing hard for the shore. The mundane, ordinary, kiss-the-ground-and-thank-God shore.

"Swimming in this river is a good way to get yourself killed," the man said.

"Yeah," Ted agreed, his teeth chattering. "It w-was stupid."

"But you were scared enough to risk it."

Ted nodded.

"That island." The man's mouth worked, but no words came out. "I hope you get to where you want to go, boy. I truly do."

Home. I want to get home. "I'm Ted Ocampo."

"Alan Naylor. Were you *there* very long?" He lifted his chin to indicate the island.

"Just today. I think just today."

Alan rowed, but the shore didn't seem like it was getting any closer. "I've been lost for a while now. Not sure how long."

He didn't know what to say, so Ted stared at the ring buoy. It looked old, and the name was so faded, he couldn't make out the words.

"Oh, God, no."

The look in Alan's eyes and the despair in his voice made Ted twist around to see what was there.

A three-masted schooner appeared out of nowhere and sailed toward them, but two of the largest sails had been lowered, so the ship approached them at a leisurely pace. A woman stood at the rail dressed in an old-fashioned costume that made Ted think of pirates. She looked at Alan, who moaned, then looked at Ted.

She touched two fingers to her temple in a kind of salute—and the ship sailed on as the crew hauled on the lines of the other two sails.

"They let me go," Alan whispered. Then he let out a shout of joy. "You are a good luck piece, Ted Ocampo. If you weren't with me, she would have hauled me back again. But that ship isn't your fate." He shuddered. "Let's get ashore before she changes her mind and comes back for us."

Alan applied himself to the oars, finally closing the distance between the dinghy and the land.

Maybe he'd gotten too much water in his eyes. Maybe he was in shock or something. Or maybe it was the day turning overcast, but Ted thought Alan looked older the closer they got to the shore.

"You want me to row for a while?" Ted asked. "I'm pretty strong." He was shivering and practically naked, so he might not look like he could lift an oar, let alone row against the river's current.

Alan shook his head. "Has to be me. Has to . . ." Lifting the oars out of the water, he pulled at a string around his neck and tugged a package out of his shirt. "Take this. Take it!"

Ted took the package. Some kind of heavy waxed paper folded and sealed with wax.

Alan started rowing again, but he was wheezing now. "There's a letter to my wife inside that package. Her name is Emma. The letter explains . . . I wasn't a good man, didn't appreciate what I had, always wanted more and thought I should have it, no matter the cost. I got into trouble with some bad men, and I went to Wyrd and made a bargain. I said, 'I want to get on a ship and disappear until all my enemies are gone.' That's what I said, and they fulfilled their side of the bargain. I just didn't know . . . I helped you. Didn't I help you, Ted?"

"Yes, sir. You did."

"Take that letter to the police. Emma may have moved, but they'll figure out how to find her and give her the letter. There's also a list of the men I ran with for a while until I got into trouble with them. The cops will want that too."

The shore was close. Rocky. No easy place to land the dinghy.

"Get that ring around you," Alan said. "I'll get as close to the shore as I can, but you'll still have to fight the river to reach land. The buoy should help you."

"What about you? If we tie the rope to the dinghy, once I get ashore, I can pull you in."

"I . . ." Alan looked like he was in pain. "I don't think I'm meant to reach the shore." He smiled. "But I got away from the ship, and you'll find a way to take that letter to Emma. That's good enough. Go now. I can't hold on much longer."

Ted wiggled the buoy over his shoulders until he looked like he was wearing a donut. He slipped the string around his neck to avoid losing the package. Then he went over the side—and discovered the water was chest high. The current tried to yank his legs out from under him, but he fought it, step by step, until he reached a rock he could grab as an anchor.

Slippery rocks. Couldn't get careless. A wrong step could break an ankle. Hand over hand. Climbing step by careful step.

Grass.

Ted hauled himself up the last few feet and collapsed for a moment before sitting up.

Alan Naylor and the dinghy were gone.

8

Charles Forrester approached the worktable where his team waited. "What have we got?" *The same thing we had an hour ago. Two missing teenagers and no way to know if we'll find either one of them.*

Darren Palmer's cell phone had been buzzing and chiming with text messages, but the phone was locked, and he didn't want to hand it over to the tech team just to read dozens of texts from Palmer's friends.

Then *his* cell phone rang. Seeing his son's number, he answered it. "Colin?"

"Dad?" The boy sounded concerned. No, more than that. Upset. "Do you remember Ted Ocampo?"

"Ocampo? From your swim team?" Forrester watched his detectives snap to attention. "What about him?"

"He sent me a really weird text, and he's not in school today. Neither is Darren Palmer, and his pack of bullyboys are acting strange, like they've been waiting for something to happen—and they're uneasy now."

That would explain all the texts coming into Palmer's phone.

Forrester made a writing motion. Ian Kuhn pushed a scratch pad of paper and a pen toward him. "Colin, I'm with my team right now. Would it be okay if I put you on speaker? We have reason to be concerned about a couple of boys from your school who may be missing."

A hesitation before Colin said, "Okay. Sure."

The high school was in the 12th precinct's district, not the 13th's. Colin would understand what it meant that Charles's team was investigating.

Forrester put his phone on speaker. "Read me the text."

"'Going to swim home. Clothes are on the shore. Phone is in my sneakers. My dad will shit bricks if I lose the phone.'"

"What time did Ted send the text?" Forrester heard his office phone ring. Beth Fahey rushed to answer it.

"This afternoon," Colin replied. "I was at swim practice and didn't check my messages until now."

"Okay." Another phone began ringing. Tom Castelletti hurried to answer it. "Anything else?"

"Yeah. This is the really weird part. 'Dare turned into a rat-faced chicken and was killed by a freaking big bird that had a woman's face.'" A shaky release of breath. "Dad? What should I do?"

"You told me. That's all you should do right now. Do you understand me, Colin? Don't tell anyone else about the text. Just go home. We'll talk about it this evening." And hopefully he could tell his boy that one of his friends survived whatever idiotic thing they had done on Wyrd.

Forrester ended the call. "Well?" he asked when Beth Fahey returned to her place around the table.

Tom Castelletti also returned, tipped his head toward Fahey, and said, "You first."

Fahey drew in a breath. "That was Captain Stan Wozniak from Lovecraft. A patrol car picked up Ted Ocampo. The boy was wearing nothing but briefs and was found lugging a ring buoy—the kind boats carry in case someone falls overboard. Ocampo says he has important information, but he has to talk to someone who has been to Wyrd so the cops won't think he's crazy."

"Fahey, you take this. Do you know which Lovecraft precinct Captain Wozniak works out of?" When she shook her head, Forrester added, "Kuhn, go with her. Castelletti? What have you got?"

"A couple of fishermen found a dead man in a dinghy," Castelletti replied. "The officers who answered the nine-one-one call are . . . spooked."

"You take that one. I'll make the call to Wyrd and see what assistance Lucas Frost can give us in locating where Ted Ocampo went into the river—and in finding Darren Palmer's remains."

9

Beth sat across the table from Ted Ocampo and Jeni Slown, the psychologist who was the welfare officer attached to this Lovecraft precinct. Someone had found some clothes for the boy, but he still looked cold and so very young. Except for his eyes. They were old now—and haunted.

"Ted? I'm Detective Beth Fahey. You have something important to tell us about what happened to you and your friend?"

"Dare's not my friend, but you don't say no when Dare wants you to do something. Except I did. I said no when he wanted me to go through the moon gate first."

"Okay. Tell me about that."

"You been across the river?"

Beth nodded. "I've been to the Isle of Wyrd. I was on official business, so I didn't have time to see much, but I've been there."

"Did you see a moon gate in the park?"

"No. Tell me about that."

"Dare—"

"That's Darren Palmer?"

"Yeah. Dare got this bug up his butt that he was going to figure out the secret of the moon gates, and I got tapped to skip school and go with him because none of his pack of bullyboys would do it. Dare is the alpha big balls, but even so, his pack must have known what he had in mind, and none of them would go.

"The pavilion was sort of lame—the kind of place my aunt would have jazzed over because she's into reading her horoscope and that kind of stuff, and the park had these gardens that my mom would have jazzed over." He paused. "The statues might have creeped her out. Anyway, the park is pretty big, so it took a while to find a moon gate." Ted braced his forearms on the table and leaned toward Beth. "There are signs when you enter the park. Rules. You know?"

She nodded. "I saw them."

"Bad idea to break the rules there, but Dare doesn't give a sh—doesn't care about following rules. He was giving me a hard time about not hassling this woman who was on the ferry, and I said he was a rat because . . . well, he said something about me and a girl I liked. Then he wanted me to go through the gate first, but the gate was doing this weird thing, like going back and forth between two choices."

"What were the choices?"

"Transportation and transformation. Those words kept appearing on the top stone."

"The keystone? Okay. Then what happened?"

"He started dancing around, saying he was a rat-faced chicken, and he was saying that when he walked through the gate."

Jeni Slown hadn't said anything up to that point. "Do you need to take a break, Ted?"

He shook his head. "He walked through the gate."

"And a rat-faced chicken came out the other side?" Beth asked.

Slown gave her a strange look, but Ted nodded.

"Then this bird creature with a woman's face dropped out of the sky and landed on top of him. Killed him. Flew away. I ran. First I threw up, and then I ran."

"Did you see anyone? Yell for help? Call anyone on your phone?"

Ted stared at Beth. "I ran. And then I was trying to swim across the river. Stupid. I'm a strong swimmer, but trying to cross the Fate with those currents? Stupid." He kept staring at her. "I might have texted Colin. He's a friend, and his dad is a cop."

Beth smiled. "Captain Forrester. My boss." Her smile faded. "You swam across the Fate River?"

Ted shook his head. "Wouldn't have made it if Alan hadn't pulled me into his dinghy. Hey, did you find Alan? He gave me letters."

Slown pushed a package across the table. "Ted told us he needed to give these letters to the police."

"Yeah," Ted said. "A letter to Alan's wife and a list of his enemies."

A dinghy. Beth tried to keep her expression neutral. "So Alan . . . rowed you . . . ? To the other side of the river?"

"Yeah. Oh! And there was a ship that freaked him out, but he said I was a lucky piece because I was in the dinghy with him and that's why they let him go."

"What kind of ship?"

"Tall ship with sails."

"A sailboat?"

"No, bigger, like a pirate ship with masts and sails, or one of those ships that sailed the oceans. You know? A woman—I got the idea that she was the captain—looked at us and gave a kind of salute. Can women be pirate captains?"

"Women can be anything."

"I guess."

A knock on the interview room's door before Ian Kuhn stepped in. Beth's cell phone rang at the same time.

"Excuse me," she said. "I have to take this. Castelletti?"

"I sent a photo to Ian," Castelletti said. "Ask Ocampo if he recognizes the man. I'll hold."

Kuhn stepped forward, showed her the photo, then turned his phone so that Ted could see it.

"Yeah, that's Alan." Ted looked a little puzzled. "He's dressed funny in that picture, like he was going to a retro costume party, but that's Alan."

"Last name?" Beth asked.

"Naylor."

"Ted just confirmed the man is Alan Naylor, who pulled him into a dinghy and helped him cross the river," Beth told Castelletti.

"Jesus walks on water," Castelletti muttered. "You can confirm we found Naylor. Don't tell the boy anything else."

"Like what?"

"Like Naylor's been missing for fifty years and was presumed dead. And now he is dead."

"Understood." Beth ended the call. She slipped her phone into her pocket and picked up the package. "We'll take care of the letters. Is there anything else you want to tell us?"

Ted shook his head.

Beth looked at Slown. "Unless you have something more . . . ?"

"No," Slown said. "I'll go with Ted when we take him home. Help smooth out the explanation of why he wasn't at school."

"My dad will kill me if I lost my phone," Ted said.

Beth smiled. "It's been reported. Someone will turn it in."

"I'm pretty sure it's across the river."

"Someone will turn it in." She hoped.

After Ted was escorted out of the room, Jeni Slown paused in the doorway and studied Beth. "Do you believe what he said?"

"Yes," Beth replied.

"All of it?"

"All of it."

"Why?"

"Because he and Darren Palmer went to Wyrd—and things happen there."

And the first chance she had, she was going to take the ferry to Wyrd and try to get some answers.

10

Charles Forrester set a file folder on the worktable, indicated the man standing next to him, and addressed his team. "I believe you all know Captain Stan Wozniak from Lovecraft."

Castelletti and Kuhn nodded. Fahey hesitated before nodding. Forrester took that to mean a formal introduction hadn't been made yet. Something he'd have to take care of before Stan left the building.

"Since police in Penwych and Lovecraft are involved in this investigation, Captain Wozniak looked into the list of Alan Naylor's alleged enemies."

"Not alleged," Wozniak said. "Naylor ran with a rough crowd for a while. Not the actual crime bosses that had been in some of the towns around the Fate River, but men who worked for those bosses. Then he made some bad decisions, acquired serious enemies, and disappeared without a trace. The people on the list Naylor gave Ted Ocampo? They're all deceased except for one, and he's in a facility that cares for Alzheimer patients."

"That's what he meant when he said Ted was a lucky piece," Fahey murmured.

"Detective?" Forrester asked.

"I read the letter Naylor wrote to his wife." Her shrug might have been an apology for opening private correspondence. "He went to Wyrd and made a bargain, saying he wanted to get on a ship and disappear until all his enemies were gone. Technically, one is still alive, even if the man can't remember Naylor. But Ted Ocampo was in the dinghy with him when the ship caught up to Naylor. I think the captain of that ship let Naylor go because he saved the boy from drowning—and because it wasn't Ted's fate to be on that ship."

Wozniak frowned. "No one on the river reported seeing a tall ship with sails. A couple of sailboats, but nothing like Ocampo described in his interview."

"One of the ghost ships," Forrester said quietly.

Wozniak gave him an uneasy look. "There is more than one?"

"There's more than one." Some of them were almost accidents, more like a careless intention that turned into a haunting. But if *that* ship was being seen on the Fate River again? Not good. "Anything on Emma Naylor's whereabouts?"

Castelletti lifted one hand. "Emma Naylor currently resides in an assisted living community in Barker. The impression I got from the eldest son, Alan Jr., is that certain people kept an eye on his family for a few years, but no one made a move against them. After the seven-year waiting period, Emma Naylor had her husband declared dead. Alan Jr. still lives in Barker. The younger son is out West somewhere. He's not big on communicating with his brother and mother, but he does send money every few months to help with his mother's expenses." He blew out a breath. "The man in the dinghy is definitely Alan Naylor, but Ted Ocampo identified a man who was in his late thirties. The man who was pulled ashore looked like this."

They looked at the photo Castelletti dropped on the table. An old man with a worn, lined face; scraggly hair, what there was left of it; threadbare clothes. Not a man who looked healthy enough to row a dinghy across the Fate River.

"Maybe he knew what would happen to him once he touched the shore," Kuhn said.

"Maybe," Forrester agreed. "Either way, Alan Naylor finally got home, and his family has some closure."

"What about Darren Palmer's family?" Castelletti asked.

"Anyone who goes to the Isle of Wyrd is taking a risk, and there is always a price. For most people, the price is nothing more than a few coins. For some, if they are careless . . ." Forrester sighed.

"You really believe a teenage boy turned into a rat-faced chicken?" Wozniak asked. "According to Ocampo's testimony, Palmer was a bully, and Ocampo was often on the receiving end of that bullying. Maybe Ocampo snapped but can't face that he killed another boy."

Fahey shook her head. "Ted told me what he and Darren Palmer did, what they saw, what Palmer said when he walked through the moon gate. I believe him."

"I'll call Darren Palmer's father and let him know his son went over to Wyrd and hasn't returned yet," Forrester said. "For now, that's all we can do."

11

After a lackluster dinner, Beth pulled out the banker's file box that held her fantasy art—the prints and sketches she had picked up at genre conventions during her teenage years, before Bonnie's strident opinion that the pictures were the devil's work and should be banned put an end to indulgences of any kind.

Personally, Beth found the "religious" pictures that covered Bonnie's walls, with their graphic illustrations of the torments of the damned or the equally brutal—and bloody—depictions of the suffering of the righteous, more disturbing than strange creatures living in meadows or woodlands.

For a while after she'd gone out on her own, Beth had felt some obligation to stay in touch with the woman who had let Beth live in her house after Beth's parents disappeared. But any attempt at conversation with the woman was full of complaints about Beth's stinginess and remarks shaped to wound because there was never anything else from Bonnie. The last time Beth refused to send money to pay off the woman's gambling debts, Bonnie tried to wreck Beth's career as a cop with a vindictive letter-writing campaign that claimed Beth was unbalanced and mentally defective because of her attraction to "obscene artwork." Beth stopped calling Bonnie after that—and stopped answering the phone when Bonnie's number appeared.

"Let it go," Beth muttered as she removed the lid on the banker's box and set it aside. "Bonnie didn't succeed, so let it go."

Easy to tell herself that, but despite what she knew rationally, the fear of what other people would think and say remained, because it was always possible that Bonnie would find someone in authority who would agree with her—or agree just enough to cause some trouble. As one of Beth's classmates at the academy had pointed out, just because an idea was wackadoodle didn't mean there wouldn't be people who agreed with it—especially if it provided an excuse to demean, hurt, or control another group of people. And Bonnie saw Beth as a cash cow she wanted to control.

As she lifted most of the prints and set them aside, it occurred to her that she could put anything she wanted on the walls of her own place. It wasn't like she was planning to have parties, and it was doubtful colleagues would drop by, see the artwork, and submit a "the girl is wacko" memo to the captain or someone higher up. Doubtful but not a certainty. She didn't know the men on the team well enough to feel certain of anything where they were concerned, and she wasn't willing to take that chance.

At the bottom of the box was an old sketchbook—the thing that Bonnie claimed was the reason for her attraction to perverted pictures. Beth didn't know where the sketchbook had come from, but she couldn't remember a time when she didn't have it. She hadn't looked at the drawings in years, not after the day Bonnie caught her looking at the sketches and threatened to burn the sketchbook.

Where had her parents been? Why couldn't she remember them?

She had stayed with Bonnie for weeks, sometimes months, at a time while her parents went away to "work things out." At least, according to Bonnie. But that meant she had lived with them at times. Then came the day when she was sent to visit Bonnie and never left the woman's house until she turned eighteen and graduated from high school—and received a substantial amount of money that had been held in trust. Bonnie claimed the money should be hers for taking care of Beth all those years, but Beth knew Bonnie had received sufficient money every month to cover any expenses connected to Beth.

Beth gave Bonnie a third of the funds from the trust as a kind of thank-you instead of letting the woman have control of all of it. Another bone of contention, but the money gave Beth a way to leave Bonnie's house for good and attend university before going into the police academy, after which she became a police officer and then studied for a detective's shield.

Beth sighed and focused on the present. The sketchbook.

She opened the cover and stared at the two words on the first page. She must have seen them before, but until a few days ago, they had had no context.

The Arcana.

She turned the pages, looking at each sketch with a different understanding. Could this be what the Arcana really looked like? A human-animal blend like a centaur, except this was a man's torso and arms blended with a stag's body and a stag's head. An emaciated female that looked like preserved skin and bones rising out of a lake and, touched by moonlight, changing into an alluring woman. Men and women that almost looked human except for the variety of horns on their heads. Delicate antlers on a male. Curved ram's horns on another. Spiraling horns that angled straight back over a female's head. Not all of them had pointed elfin ears, but many did.

Beth turned a page and stared at the bird woman that matched Ted Ocampo's description of the creature that had killed the transformed Darren Palmer. A bird's body about the size and shape of a harpy eagle, but the face was a woman's, despite the tiny feathers and the beak that could easily rend the creature's prey. Was this creature the basis of the harpy in folklore? Except harpies were supposed to have ugly female faces, and there was nothing ugly about the female in the sketch.

She looked at the rest of the sketches. Whoever had drawn these had spent time on Wyrd—or another place like it. She doubted one island was the source of strange for the whole world, but these sketches . . .

The last sketch was of three women. Not human, but their features indicated they were closely related. Behind them, sketched in so faintly the images looked like nothing more than a pattern on the wall, were a deck of cards fanned out around the first woman's head, a pair of scales above the middle woman, and a sketchbook and pencil floating near the third woman.

The Ladies Three. Probably not the ones currently working in the pavilion, but how could she be sure? Some of the sketches had a stylized *A* in the bottom right corner. If she brought this sketchbook to Wyrd, could they tell her the name of the artist? Could they tell her why it had been passed down to her?

What would it cost to ask the question?

Beth put the sketchbook and the prints back in the box, then tucked the box inside the closet.

As soon as she could, she needed to spend a night on Wyrd.

12

Charles Forrester arrived home almost on time and weary to the bone. He sympathized with Darren Palmer's father and understood the man's anger, but there was no use blaming anyone else for what happened. The boy had ignored the rules and warnings posted in Destiny Park and made a careless choice, thinking there would be no consequences.

The Isle of Wyrd was a place unto itself and wasn't governed by human laws or morals. People had been crossing the river for decades, maybe even centuries. The Arcana were not responsible for what humans did when they arrived on the island or the bargains humans chose to make, either with the Arcana or within themselves.

Darren Palmer's father was hurting. Charles sympathized. But spewing about retaliation and burning the ferry's pier or getting his gun and crossing the river to do what the cops didn't have the balls to do? That kind of action was suicidal at best.

The Arcana were very good at protecting themselves and their land.

He kissed his wife and held her close for a moment. "Smells good."

"Dinner?" Aisha asked.

"That too."

She leaned back and studied his face. "Colin is worried about a friend. Is that why you have that look in your eyes?"

"Two boys. Good news, bad news." He tipped his head. "Colin?"

"In his room."

"Do I have time to talk to him before dinner?"

Aisha nodded. "I think he's been waiting for you to get home."

Charles knocked on his son's door before walking in. Textbooks were open and fanned out at the end of the bed, a token effort toward doing homework since Colin was lying on the bed, staring at the ceiling, and there wasn't any indication that any assignments had been completed.

Not something Charles would argue about tonight.

Colin sat up and swung his legs over the side of the bed. Charles moved a couple of the books and sat beside his son.

"Ted made it home," Charles said.

Colin met his eyes for a moment before staring at the floor. "Is he okay?"

"Physically, yes. But he witnessed some things that I suspect will give him nightmares for a long time. Hopefully he'll get some counseling to help him come to terms with what happened."

"What about Dare? Darren?"

"He was careless, and he didn't survive."

"Did Dare really change into a rat-faced chicken?"

"There is no reason to doubt what Ted claimed he saw."

Charles studied his son's expression. A bit horrified, yes, but more than that, there was curiosity that would stifle common sense in the face of temptation. Or, being a fan of *Star Trek*, was it the allure of meeting a different race and being the person who could bridge the distance between their cultures?

He put a hand on the boy's shoulder. "Listen to me, Colin. People cross the river all the time, and they talk about Wyrd like it's a combination of a carnival and a park. If they're lucky, they don't see more than that. But Wyrd isn't a carnival. It's a convergence of the uncanny, and there is power there that our kind of people don't understand. Things happen there. Words and intentions have power there—and people can disappear for a very long time because of a flippant remark.

If you want to go to Wyrd, I will take you, and we'll explore Destiny Park together." He could almost feel the wheels of fate turning, possibilities realigning into a different future—a future without his son. "If you do cross the river with other boys, remember what I said about the power of words and intentions. You cannot afford to be careless when you're there—especially if you're around one of the moon gates that can take you somewhere else. But if you are threatened and in imminent danger, I would rather know you were lost but alive than to have someone bring your body back across the river."

Colin said nothing. As Charles pushed to his feet, the boy said, "You would really take me to see Wyrd?"

"Yes." *I should have known better than to offer. This was the boy who wanted to see dinosaurs at the history museum and was disappointed that there were only bones that didn't move; who wanted to ride the elephants at the zoo; who could spend hours watching the sharks at the aquarium—and who had wondered more than once if Wyrd was a way to boldly meet the unknown without needing a spaceship. Maybe what he can see on Wyrd during the daylight hours will satisfy his curiosity enough. Maybe.*

"Soon?"

Charles tried not to sigh. "I'll talk to your mom about what we have on the family calendar next month, and then you and I will pick a day to visit before the park closes until spring."

Aisha would have a few things to say about him making that promise, especially when she found out what happened to Darren Palmer, but she would realize that Colin going with his father would be safer than his going with a pack of teenage boys.

"It's time for dinner."

"Mom didn't give the dinner holler."

He smiled. "It was understood that dinner would be on the table when you and I finished talking. Besides, you know your mom's rule."

Colin sighed but stood up. "Come to the table while the food is hot, or eat it cold."

"Yep."

Aisha gave them both a look when they reached the dinner table, but she must have already had a talk with Jazz about not pestering Colin tonight because the girl chattered about her triumphs and failures at school that day.

The call didn't come until he was helping Aisha with the dishes.

"Hello?"

"Come to the pier at eleven p.m." Lucas Frost's voice had a depth that made Charles think of old-growth forests and primal places that held ancient truths and didn't welcome humans. "A vessel will take you across the river."

"Why?"

"Eleven p.m." Frost hung up.

"Charles?" Aisha asked when he tucked his cell phone into his pocket.

"I have to go out later. A meeting with Lucas Frost."

She looked alarmed. "Why?"

"I don't know." *But I can guess.*

13

The vessel was a small fishing boat with a motor and tiller on the back and a couple of boards across the width for seats. The pilot sat in the back next to the motor, saying nothing. A second individual held the boat close to the pier so that Charles could climb down a wooden ladder attached to the pier and come aboard.

Charles couldn't tell if the Arcana were male or female, since they didn't speak and their heads were covered with oversized hoods—a necessity when they dealt with humans after dark.

He pulled a watch cap out of his jacket pocket and put it on. The days in late September still held a hint of summer warmth, but the nights held a touch of winter.

"Where are we going?" he asked when it became apparent the boat wasn't heading to the dock on the Wyrd side of the river.

His companions didn't reply, but the answer became apparent when he saw a figure waiting for him on the sandy beach.

The pilot shut off the motor and tilted it out of the water as the front of the boat's hull scraped on the sand. The other Arcana jumped out of the boat and pulled it farther up the beach and gestured for Charles to jump out. He obeyed, landing in water up to his ankles, and moved quickly to reach the sand.

Lucas Frost wore no hood to hide the truth about what he was.

Charles tried not to stare at the delicate antlers that rose from Frost's head. He'd seen the antlers before, but the reminder that he was dealing with a different race of beings still unsettled him. "Mr. Frost? You wanted to see me?"

Frost withdrew a cell phone and slim wallet from a pocket of his leather jacket and held them out. "The boy made it across the river?"

Charles took the cell phone and wallet. He wasn't sure if Frost didn't know the outcome of Ted Ocampo's attempt to get home or if the Arcana leader was testing his honesty. "He made it across with some help." Charles pocketed the items. "Ted's clothes?"

"Let's call the clothing a finder's fee."

In other words, whatever had found Ted's possessions had use for the clothing and relinquished the other items in exchange.

Charles looked at the box at Frost's feet. Cardboard, but it looked like there was a plastic garbage bag inside. And whatever was in the bag smelled . . . funky.

"Apparently, the meat didn't taste enough like chicken," Frost said quietly. "That's why there was something left to find."

Charles swallowed hard. "Does he look human now?"

"No. But when your people do their tests, the meat will come back as being human—and it will match the human who ignored our rules when he went through the moon gate."

God have mercy on me. What am I supposed to tell Darren Palmer's father? How can I show him these remains and say, "This is what is left of your son?"

One of the Arcana picked up the box and put it in the boat, then stood by the boat, waiting.

"Something else, Captain Forrester?" Frost asked.

Even here on the beach, he had to choose his words with care. "Human children that age can be careless."

"Then they should stay away from Wyrd. Age has never been a criteria for meeting one's fate."

"I don't think Darren Palmer's father will see it that way."

Quiet anger, like fire burning beneath the ground until it bursts through a crack and consumes everything on the surface. "Then he should stay on his side of the river."

Warning? Threat? Both? Or an acknowledgment that Palmer's possible fates were already known to the Arcana, and it was merely a question of which path the man would choose.

"Mr. Frost." Charles took a step back. Nothing else for him to say.

"Captain."

Charles retreated to the boat and settled in the middle seat, the box between his feet. One Arcana pushed the boat off the sand and jumped in. The other Arcana started the motor.

They crossed the river, with the *putt-putt* of the motor being the only sound to break the silence.

Then a large game fish leaped out of the water next to the boat. Leaped. Looked. Twisted away from the boat as it fell back into the water.

Charles shivered. He was tired, unnerved. But for a moment, he had the fanciful notion that the fish would have leaped into the boat if it hadn't spotted the Arcana.

14

Already showered and dressed for the day, Rachel paced around the room and watched the early morning news on an Eastwood County TV station while she waited for room service to deliver her breakfast. She wanted to open the drapes and look at whatever part of the park was within view, but sunrise wasn't the same as full daylight, and she didn't want to get into trouble because she'd seen something she wasn't supposed to see. She didn't know what was supposed to happen next; she just knew that for the first time in a long time she felt safe when she fell asleep.

When she answered the knock on the door, Jack stood there holding a breakfast tray.

"I'll escort you to the pavilion in an hour," he said, handing her the tray. "Will you be ready by then?"

"Yes. Thank you." She didn't step back. "Am I dressed appropriately?" The business-casual pantsuit and silky T-shirt were the nicest things she'd brought with her, but that didn't mean they were appropriate or sufficiently classy. She could almost hear Alistair's sneering disapproval.

Had to shut him out. Had to erase him from her thoughts while she was here.

"Are you comfortable in those clothes?" Jack asked.

"Yes."

"Then they are appropriate for meeting the Ladies Three." He smiled. "Try to eat." His smile widened. "It's safe to open the drapes if you want to look outside—or sit on the balcony."

Rachel stepped back to allow the door to close. Was it common for people to be uncertain about when it was safe to look outside? Or did he understand the reason for her hesitation, that never-ending fear of being punished for doing the wrong thing?

Jack seemed friendly enough, but there was something . . . feral . . . about his smile. Like a lion walking past a herd of zebras when he wasn't hungry enough to hunt.

Shaking her head to dislodge the thought of being prey, Rachel carried the tray to the little table near the windows. Then she opened the drapes and opened the sliding balcony door halfway to bring in fresh air.

Birds singing. Women singing what sounded like a ritual chant or ancient song that came from another place, another language.

She used to like to sing, before she moved in with Alistair. She used to like a lot of things before she met Alistair.

"Focus on now," she muttered. "You need to take the next steps before Alistair sends someone to find you, because you won't escape a second time."

Which made her wonder—again—what had happened to the previous women Alistair had lured into becoming expendable property.

As she ate the vegetable omelet and buttered toast, she tried to clear her mind of thoughts about Alistair and think about herself. Her future mattered now. She didn't know if it was possible to buy a kind of witness protection from the people who controlled Wyrd. She had enough money in her bank accounts to hide for quite a while—if she could gain access to the money. How long could she hide and not contact an old friend or someone in her family or her agent and her editor? But if they could find her, Alistair could find her.

She ate some of the food, then worried that her stomach would rebel. Then she worried that Lucas Frost would think her ungrateful because she had wasted the food.

If she put a small portion of food on her plate and ate all of it, Alistair criticized her for pigging out. If she didn't eat everything on her plate, he criticized her for wasting food.

Stop it. Just stop thinking about him. Think about the life you want without him.

An hour after he delivered her meal, Jack knocked on the door.

"The ferry is making its first run to Penwych," he said as he led the way toward a door at the end of the corridor. "Usually, the only passengers arriving on the first run are people who work at the hotel or the food stands, but as a precaution, we'll go around the outside of this wing to reach the pavilion."

"If someone who is looking for me came on the ferry, the pavilion is the first place he'll look," Rachel protested.

Jack smiled. "Looking isn't the same as finding. Besides, the pavilion doesn't officially open until later in the morning. Seekers who come earlier don't tend to be looking for the entertainment side of what is offered there." He opened a door and stepped onto a wooden landing. Wooden stairs that looked like a series of waterfalls led down to a path that wound through a lush garden.

Rachel followed him, but a detail niggled at her. "You didn't lock that door. You aren't concerned about someone sneaking into the hotel?"

"No one except the Arcana can come into the hotel through that door without an invitation," he said quietly. When the path ended at a moon gate, he looked back at her. "It's quiet from this side, but you shouldn't try to walk through the moon gate to enter this area of the park unless you're prepared."

For what? She didn't ask because the moment they walked through the moon gate, she felt the difference. A park within a park? The plants and trees looked the same, but the *feel* was so different. Around the pavilion and the ornamental lake, the place felt . . . tamer.

Jack entered the pavilion and walked to the other end, where a table was set up to receive payments and allow patrons to turn the wheel and take the numbered discs.

"Did you exchange some money for the coins used here?" Jack asked.

"Yes." Rachel pulled several coins from her jacket pocket. "How much . . . ?"

"One gold coin in that box." Jack pointed. "Then take a bone disc."

"But . . ." She eyed the wheel.

"Bone disc. You're here to see the Ladies Three."

She put her coin in the box and took a bone disc.

Jack led her back to the other end of the pavilion. When they had walked past a couple of minutes ago, all the archways on one side were dark. Not just an absence of light, but she'd had the sense of a solid barrier. Now one of the archways was open, and the room was lit by overhead lights as well as the brightening sun.

She glanced at Lucas Frost and the woman standing beside him—a woman with short-cropped hair who was wearing a pantsuit similar to her own. But those two people couldn't compete with the three women who sat at the tables. One woman spread two decks of cards in a double arch on her table. One woman began sketching, although it was hard to guess what her clouded eyes might be able to see. The third woman, who sat between the other two, had a brass scale and weights made from a variety of substances.

Jack pointed to the first table. "Put the disc in the bowl and follow the instructions." He stepped away from her to stand next to Lucas Frost and the woman.

Rachel put the bone disc in the bowl. The woman handed her a wand made of wood and leather.

"Choose four cards from the top deck," the woman said. "Touch the cards with the wand. Choose with intention."

Intention. She wanted to hide. She wanted to escape. She wanted to be free. She wanted to reclaim the life she'd had before she met Alistair.

She hadn't realized she had tapped a card with each of those thoughts until the woman set the cards to one side.

"Choose three cards from the bottom deck," the woman said. "Choose with intention."

She wanted to regain the joy she used to feel when she was writing. She wanted to sing again. She wanted peace.

The wand tapped three cards.

The woman turned over the cards one by one. She offered no explanation of what the cards revealed, and Rachel couldn't see anything that would give someone else a clue about the meaning. The cards clearly meant something because the woman turned to the woman with the scales and nodded.

"Place something of personal value to you on one side of the scale," the second woman said.

Rachel automatically reached for the ring finger on her left hand, but she hadn't put the engagement ring on after arriving in Wyrd. Besides, the ring was valuable in monetary terms but had no value to her. She removed the ring she wore on her right hand—a gift from her grandmother. Its value came from sentiment and memories of time spent with the older woman.

She placed it on one side of the scale. The ring didn't feel heavy on her finger, so it surprised her to see that side of the scale sink almost to the tabletop.

The woman picked up a bone disc and set it on the other side of the scale. "You came here hoping to change your fate. Tell us what you desire, and be careful. Words have power here."

"I need to disappear, to hide in a way that Alistair Hampton can't find me. But I also want to reclaim the life I had before I met him—my writing, my friends, my family. I want the freedom to sing and be myself. I want to stop being afraid."

As she talked, Rachel watched the woman add various substances to one side of the scale, removing some and adding others until both sides were balanced.

The woman turned to the third woman, who stopped sketching and nodded.

"We will consider your request and give you a proposal in one hour." The woman removed Rachel's ring from the scale and held it out. "Walk around the park, but stay in sight of the lake. You'll be safe enough. The only predators here at the moment are the ones who live here."

Rachel slipped the ring on her finger, thanked the Ladies Three for their consideration, then walked over to Lucas and Jack—and wondered when the other woman had left the room.

"Should I check out of the hotel room first?" she asked.

"No," Lucas replied. "You'll need a quiet place."

She didn't ask why she would need it. As she walked around the ornamental lake and studied the statues that looked unnervingly real, she realized she would give these people anything they wanted if they could somehow manage to save her from Alistair and whatever plans he now had for her.

15

Lucas Frost walked up to the table where Justine balanced the scales that decided the price of the Arcana's assistance.

"She asks for nothing that would directly harm another," Zerah said, lightly touching the seven cards that revealed Rachel Nightingale's desires. "She asks to save herself; to survive; to thrive."

"Can it be done?" he asked Justine.

She considered each item that she had used to balance the scales and nodded. "If she has the courage, we can set her free."

"Her freedom will require flesh," Lysandra said, turning her sketchbook around for him to see. "Her enemy has great influence across the river. Everything must be done quickly if she is to succeed."

Lucas studied the series of drawings that showed the pathway to Rachel Nightingale achieving her desires.

Justine was right. The woman would need a great deal of courage if she was going to embrace this choice.

16

Rachel sat on a bench and studied the female statue rising up from the ornamental lake. Emaciated, dressed in rags, holding a lantern. A rock with a flat top rose up nearby, a perfect place to set a lantern. Was that the intention? To leave the lantern in that place to light the way for other women who needed to escape, who wanted freedom?

What others? And where would they come from?

There was power—and anger—in that emaciated form. There was power and beauty in the lake's other statue—a winged woman who stood atop a fountain that looked like a series of waterfalls that fell into the lake's water.

Opposite images and yet the same. Like seeing pictures of a forest before and after a fire. But with a forest, there was hope that the green would return, that what had been sacrificed to fire would begin again. A new start with new life.

Was she about to burn down her old life in order to create a new one?

When she spotted Jack walking toward her, she rose and moved to meet him.

"Ready?" he asked.

How to answer that when she didn't know what was ahead of her? "Ready enough."

He led her to a large office that must be part of the pavilion but hadn't been obvious when she walked past it an hour ago.

Expensive furnishings that she associated with a CEO's office filled one side of the room. The other side held a conference table. The Ladies Three sat on one side. The woman who had been with Lucas Frost earlier that morning sat on the other side.

Jack pulled out the chair next to the woman and indicated that Rachel should sit there. Then he pulled out the other chair and sat next to her. Was he acting friendly or acting as a guard?

Lucas Frost sat at the head of the table. "We have a solution that will give you what you said you desire, but you must understand that this is an all-or-nothing solution. You can't cherry-pick what you're willing to do. As much as we can, because some things cannot be known until they happen, we will explain now what has to be done and what it will cost. Until we take the first step, you are free to decline our help and disappear in your own way."

"If I decline your solution and try to do this on my own, will I survive?" Rachel asked.

The woman who had been sketching during that first meeting looked at her with eyes that were now clear and said, "I saw no line of fate that would keep you from being permanently harmed by the man you are fleeing from—except the solution we offer."

That was it? Do things their way or end up in an institution somewhere when Alistair caught her? Or end up in a shallow grave?

She should be more skeptical. But she wasn't. She was here because she'd already considered the usual ways to escape an abusive partner and knew they wouldn't work. Not against Alistair and his damn family name.

"What is your solution?"

"Transformation," Lucas replied. "You will become someone

else—something else—for one year. After that, you will return to your previous body. We will provide you with a new name and all the identity papers required to support that name."

"Even with a new name, if I contact anyone I know now, Alistair will find me," Rachel protested.

The woman who balanced the scales shook her head. "A year from now, Alistair Hampton will no longer be a concern."

How can you be sure? She almost asked the question, but she looked at the Ladies Three and *knew* they were sure, that they had seen Alistair's fate. Or at least a potential fate.

"During the year that the lines of destiny play out, you need to hide in plain sight in a place where you will be safe and where you will not be recognized for who and what you are," Lucas said.

"What if this takes longer than a year? Do I stay—"

"No." Lucas looked stern. "The bargain for transformation is for one year. Being something else longer than that can have severe consequences."

Hearing the warning, Rachel asked, "What do you want in return?"

Lucas gestured to the woman sitting beside Rachel. "You will know her as Ashley Laxton. She is one of the Arcana who handles the arrangements for these kinds of business transactions."

"You will know her as"—meaning she has another name among her own kind. Was that true for all of them?

Ashley Laxton folded her hands over the legal pad on the table. "Our fee for helping you in this quest is twenty percent of your current liquid assets, whatever that might be. We will close all your bank accounts, cash out any certificates of deposit in your name, empty your safe deposit box, empty any storage unit you might have in any of the towns around the Fate River. Liquid assets will be transferred to accounts belonging to the Arcana, which are beyond the reach of someone like Alistair Hampton. Everything that you value that we can move quickly will be moved beyond his reach.

"We will take care of you for that year, providing food, shelter, and safety. Before you take the last steps, you will contact the people involved in publishing your books, informing them that I will be your liaison for the next year, since you will be unable to contact them directly. I will take care of any transactions or approvals they require for your work." Ashley paused. "We will also need some of your flesh. How much will depend on how many places we need to be at the same time. We must be swift in collecting what belongs to you—swift enough that Alistair Hampton will not be aware of your actions until they are complete and our people have returned to Wyrd."

Rachel stared at the Arcana around the table, stunned. "Why do you need my flesh?"

"Humans have a saying, 'you are what you eat,'" Lucas said. "There is a branch of the Arcana who are able to temporarily assume the form of any flesh they consume. Females from that branch will take your place and remove all your belongings. How many females will be required will depend on how many places they need to be simultaneously."

What did it say about her fear of Alistair that having these beings take pieces of flesh wasn't as terrifying as crossing the river again and being in a town where Alistair or his minions could locate her?

"How much flesh?" At that moment, she couldn't remember the play where a pound of flesh was the payment for a debt. Was how much as important as *where* it was taken from?

"That will depend," Ashley replied. "Thigh muscles usually provide sufficient meat and can heal without loss of mobility if tended properly."

"When . . . ?"

"It must be done tomorrow," Lucas said. "You've been gone for a day already. Your enemy can't declare you missing and try to take your assets yet, but he won't wait any longer than he must. There were inquiries already by a private investigator who was searching for the emotionally disturbed wife of an important client. This PI talked to police a few days ago."

"We weren't married yet, but Alistair was already laying the groundwork for me to disappear," Rachel whispered. To disappear or be found dead in a seedy hotel in one of the towns along the river.

Alistair would talk to reporters about her depression and eating disorders that he had been helpless to change. Her delusions about people trying to hurt her, especially him. Would he mention that he'd been about to put her in an institution for her own good? Men used to do that all the time when a wife or some other woman became inconvenient.

Men like Alistair still believed they could do it and not be questioned.

Rachel looked at Lucas. "You said transformation, that I'll become something else. What?"

The woman who balanced the scales answered. "That will depend on you. Words have power here, Rachel Nightingale. Choose your intentions carefully because they will dictate what you become for the year you are with us."

Terrifying thought. Exhilarating thought. "What do I need to do?"

Ashley pushed the legal pad and a pen over to Rachel. "Today you provide information, and we plan. Tomorrow, we take action."

17

Lucas Frost met with Justine, Zerah, Lysandra, Jack, and Ashley in the Arçana's private section of Destiny Park. He looked at each of them and said, "What do we have, and what needs to be done?"

"She was clever," Ashley said, "which means it will be more work for us. But we can give the fate of some others an opportunity to balance the scales. Recently, three female bodies were found on the shore near Destiny Bay and have been a feast for many. Females from the branch of the Arcana that can transform through consuming flesh could make use of those bodies and accompany the Rachels who have the tasks that involve the most risk. I was told the remaining flesh of the three bodies is almost beyond use for transformation, but it will work for enough hours to complete the tasks. After the flesh is taken from them, the remains could be moved to a place on the other side of the river where humans will find them."

Lucas nodded. "That will allow them to be identified. Yes, we'll find a place for them on the other shore where they will be found."

"Two of the females will go with the Rachel who will return to the apartment, since that is the biggest task and the one with the most risk," Ashley said. "The three of them will pack up all the possessions they can carry—mostly clothes and toiletries and small things that are listed as having sentimental value, as well as the laptop and information about Rachel's work.

"I will go with another Rachel to her primary bank to assist in closing her accounts and having all the funds transferred into accounts controlled by the Arcana. We will also arrange to have any communication from the bank sent to Rachel Nightingale at a post office box that belongs to the Arcana.

"The third female will go with the third Rachel to the bank that holds her safe deposit box and another savings account. They will empty the safe deposit box and close the account, requesting a cashier's check, which I will deposit into one of our accounts. Then they will walk to the post office that is just down the street from that bank and arrange to have all the mail from the PO box forwarded to one of our mail drops.

"The fourth Rachel will go to the branch of the public library in King's Hill where Rachel Nightingale is known to spend time. She will turn on Nightingale's phone and make calls to a train station and a police station. She will leave the phone at the library for the police to find and head for the nearest river bus stop, then ride that vessel until she reaches the location where one of our boats will be waiting for her. Her transformation will be of the shortest duration. It won't matter if that Rachel is spotted getting on the river bus because the woman getting off the bus will not look the same."

Lucas considered the planning and the implications. The Arcana who crossed the river would be at risk. It was possible this Alistair Hampton would have hired men to kill Rachel Nightingale as soon as they saw her.

He looked at his brother.

Jack nodded. "Each Rachel and companion will be protected."

"We'll take the flesh for the Rachels tonight," Lucas said. "That will give Rachel Nightingale a little time to heal before her transformation tomorrow." He looked at Ashley. "The next step?"

"Rachel Nightingale has been making a list of the people who need to be contacted—names and e-mail addresses mostly. A few phone numbers that she had memorized." Ashley hesitated. "She has a storage unit that contains the extra copies of her books, as well as most of her business papers and her favorite books by other authors."

"Does she have the key to her unit?" Jack asked.

Ashley nodded.

"Then a Rachel isn't required. We rent a garage in Penwych and keep a van there that we use for hauling supplies. Some of our people will leave early in the morning to pick up the van and drive to King's Hill so that we're ready to open Rachel Nightingale's storage unit at the same time the Rachels are clearing out everything else. We'll load up as much as we can take in one trip and bring it to a storage unit we rent in Lovecraft."

"You'll look after our people?" Lucas asked his brother

Jack smiled, showing teeth. "I'll take care of them."

And anyone who came looking for Rachel Nightingale while Jack was keeping watch wouldn't be found for a very long time.

18

Rachel sat at the conference table, making lists, while four women sat across from her learning how to forge her signature. They didn't look anything like her except for being about the same height, but she was assured that no one would be able to tell the difference once the Arcana did whatever they did.

All of her banking information was in the notes section of her pocket calendar, but it was in code. A simple code, to be sure, substituting letters for numbers and numbers for letters, but she'd been able to fool Alistair because he'd told her every day for the past year that she was too stupid to be clever.

When she'd first met him, he said she was a brilliant novelist. Two years later, he called her a stupid hack.

Soon she would shed all the labels that cut into her life, her thoughts, her hopes, her dreams.

Once the four women had perfected her signature, they went up to her hotel room to study her clothes in order to select "costumes" that would mimic her clothing well enough to match the style of dress that people associated with her.

She had gotten so thin her bones showed through her skin. The women who were going to impersonate her all looked to be a normal weight and would never fit into her clothes. They weren't concerned about that. They assured her that they would look slim enough to fool most people.

While preparations were going on around her, Rachel wrote the e-mails she would send to her editor and agent, to her family and closest friends—at least, the friends who had been close to her before Alistair had isolated her from everyone who might help her get free of him. She assured her friends that she would be fine, but they wouldn't be able to contact her. She told her agent and her editor that she needed to disappear for a year and asked them to contact Ashley Laxton, who would act on her behalf.

She reviewed the e-mails with Ashley, then used an auxiliary computer in Lucas Frost's office to send them.

"You should get some rest now," Ashley said. "The Rachels are done looking at your clothes, so you won't be disturbed if you go to your room."

She would have liked to walk around the park, but the tourists had arrived, and she understood that if one person recognized her from a book cover photo or a picture of her with Alistair on a newspaper's society page, her effort to escape might end before it began.

She put on the oversized hooded jacket that Ashley took from the office closet. Leaving the office, Rachel followed Ashley and wondered how a secret wing of the hotel could be backed by lush gardens when the pavilion, the food stands, and wide sweeps of lawn were between the rest of the hotel and any kind of gardens.

"When are they going to take the flesh?" she asked.

"Soon," Ashley replied. "They want you to have a full day to rest and recover before the transformation."

"Have you ever done it? The transformation?"

"I have." Ashley held out a hand. "You need an escort to reach the hotel from this direction."

Rachel took Ashley's hand as they approached the moon gate and walked through.

"It didn't do anything," she said.

"Be grateful." A warning.

"If I'm going to become something else, how do I choose? *Do* I choose?"

Ashley released her hand and continued escorting her to the hotel stairs. "Don't try to choose a shape. Think about what you want to *be* when you're in that shape, what you want to have while you inhabit that temporary life."

"Words have power," Rachel said quietly. "Intentions matter."

"Yes."

When they reached Rachel's room, Ashley looked around, then checked the mini fridge. "You have water, juice, cheeses, and small containers of food you can heat up in the microwave. And there is some fruit on the table. Do you need anything else?"

Assurances that this plan would work, but that wasn't something the Arcana could give with absolute certainty, since some of the success of this scheme rested with her. "No. Thank you."

She picked at the food on and off all afternoon while she read a story in a series where she knew the hero and heroine would triumph over the villains and continue their adventures in the next book. If she couldn't concentrate enough to remember the names of any of the secondary characters, it didn't matter. Good would triumph over evil.

She just hoped she would emerge triumphant in her own story.

Quiet movements in the room. Not stealthy, just quiet.

Rachel opened her eyes.

A hand immediately pressed on the shin of one leg, and a woman said, "You shouldn't make sudden movements. Stay still while I turn on a light."

The woman turned on a lamp on the other side of the room. Soft light.

Rachel blinked. Nothing wrong with her vision. It had still been daylight when the Arcana had taken her down to the room in this wing where they "harvested flesh." She remembered being helped onto the table, and then . . .

Her hands moved over the covers close to her legs, but she hesitated to touch, to find out what she had sacrificed in payment for freedom.

"How long did I sleep?"

"A few hours." The woman approached the bed. "I'm Kia Dance. Do you remember me?"

"You were in the room."

"Yes. I'll look after you tonight and tomorrow until it's time for your transformation. Are you hungry? Liquids and light meals are recommended."

Was she hungry? She hadn't been until Kia mentioned food, but . . . "I need to pee first."

"I'll help you. We didn't have to harvest a lot of flesh, since the transformation of the women impersonating you doesn't need to last more than a few hours once it begins, but your legs will hurt, and you don't want to lose your balance and fall."

Kia pulled back the covers, helped Rachel sit up and ease her legs over the side of the bed.

"You have webbing between your fingers." Was that a rude thing to say?

"There are truths about the Arcana that can't be seen in the light of day," Kia replied. "Does that bother you? You're going to be living among us for the next year."

The throbbing in her thighs faded as she looked at Kia's hands and felt the excitement of learning something new. "Do all the Arcana have webbed fingers?"

"There are many branches on the Arcana's family tree. My branch has webbed fingers—and an affinity for water."

"Wow." It was more a sound made from an exhalation of breath than a deliberate word, but there was so much she hadn't understood about the Arcana—and now she would have a year to live among them.

Her bladder reminded her that she had more immediate concerns.

Her legs hurt again as soon as she stood up, and she was grateful for Kia's support as she shuffled to the bathroom to take care of business.

"Why the thick bandages?" she asked once Kia had settled her back in bed.

"We weren't sure what kind of patient you would be," Kia said dryly. "Some remove thin bandages in order to see the area where the flesh was harvested. Some ignore the necessity of staying quiet in order for the body to heal. Thicker bandages are a visual cue to rest."

"Does it work?"

Kia laughed. "Sometimes. I think you'll be one of the sensible people. Now, would you like some soup?"

19

A fishing trawler that couldn't be seen by any but the dying or the dead except at dawn and dusk dropped anchor in Destiny Bay. A small boat rowed by two Arcana males pulled up alongside. The men on the trawler hauled up the net that held the remains of three women.

"The Sorcerer King asks that you take these remains and leave them near a place called King's Hill where humans will find them."

"I can do that," the captain of the trawler said. "Any bounty for this favor?"

One of the Arcana males smiled, showing teeth that weren't yet masked by daylight. "The Ladies Three said there is a possibility of new crew members."

"Got a couple men here who would like to go but can't until there is a replacement."

"Then let's hope the humans are careless today."

The captain smiled. "I'll have my nets ready."

The two Arcana rowed back to the beach. The captain ordered his men to raise the trawler's anchor—and as dawn gave way to full day, one of the ghost ships moved up the Fate River, felt but unseen.

20

After an Arcana scout ascertained that Alistair Hampton was not in the apartment building, a driver pulled her shiny black car up to the curb of the riverside eatery where Rachel One and her two companions waited. The driver didn't work for the car service the Arcana usually used, but the woman owed the Arcana a favor.

"This shouldn't take more than an hour, so don't go too far away," Rachel One said as she slipped the engagement ring on the third finger of her left hand. "I'll call you when we're about to leave the apartment. It's important to avoid contact with the man who lives there."

"You're going to steal from some big shot?" the driver asked as she smoothly maneuvered the car through the morning traffic.

"We're not stealing. We're only taking what belongs to the woman who no longer wants to live with him."

The driver winced. "Fists?"

"And other kinds of harm."

"Do you know Lucas Frost?"

"We know him."

"Could you tell him I heard from my brother? He's settled in a neighborhood in Wyrd and is doing okay now. He's safe now."

"I'll tell him," Rachel One said.

The driver pulled up in front of the apartment building. "Wait until I open the door for you. The doorman will be watching and will expect it for anyone living in this building."

They waited for her to open the doors for them. Then she removed three large empty suitcases from the trunk, set the cases on the sidewalk, and raised the handles. Pulling the suitcases, the women strode to the door of the apartment building with a confidence that might have echoed what Rachel Nightingale had been like when she'd first moved in with Alistair Hampton.

The man at the security desk looked surprised to see her. "Ms. Nightingale! Mr. Hampton has been concerned about you."

Rachel One flashed him a smile that looked more feral than sultry, causing him to lean back from the desk. "Needed a little girl time with some friends."

They continued to the bank of elevators.

"Bibble babble, crotch and fire," Rachel One said quietly. Nightingale didn't think the security cameras could pick up sound, but just in case she was wrong, there was no reason to say anything that would be helpful to anyone.

The other women laughed, giving the impression that the girl time was going to continue upstairs.

Once they reached the apartment, the key Nightingale had provided fit into the lock on the door, and the alarm code hadn't been changed. Excellent.

"Let's get this done," Rachel One said when they entered the bedroom and opened the closet and drawers. She removed a folded piece of paper from her jacket pocket. "We take clothes, toiletries, and anything in a jewelry or trinket box. There are also a couple of favorite books on this list, as well as the laptop Rachel Nightingale used to write her stories."

"If the man hasn't already destroyed what she values most," one of the women said.

"What she values most is her life and freedom, and she'll have those things," Rachel One replied.

An hour later, they rode the elevator back down to the lobby. All three of them gave the man at the security desk a sassy smile, making sure the security camera caught their faces, and walked out of the building.

Their driver grunted a bit as she lifted the heavy suitcases, but she was efficient, and they were gone five minutes before Alistair Hampton's car screeched to a stop in front of the building.

21

At the same time that Rachel One and her companions walked into the apartment building, Rachel Two and Ashley Laxton walked into the bank that held Rachel Nightingale's primary accounts; Rachel Three and a companion walked into the bank that held the safe deposit box and a savings account; and Rachel Four walked up the steps of the main branch of the King's Hill public library and took a position next to a standing stone lion.

Rachel Two walked up to the counter, smiled at the cashier, and said, "I want to close all my accounts and transfer the funds to this account." She pushed the paper with the Nightingale account numbers through the slot in the glass shield, then the paper that contained the information for the Arcana account number.

The cashier's smile slipped. "All your accounts? Are you sure, Ms. Nightingale?"

"I'm sure," Rachel Two replied.

"Maybe you should talk to the manager?"

"Why?" Ashley asked. "My client is entitled to do whatever she pleases with her own money."

The cashier looked at the man quickly approaching the counter.

"Can we help you?" he asked.

"Mr. Danvers," the cashier said, "Ms. Nightingale would like to close her accounts."

"Why?" Danvers asked. "Is there a problem? Perhaps we should go into my office and discuss this before you make a final decision." He paused. "Have you discussed this with Mr. Hampton?"

Rachel Two gave Danvers a cold stare. "There is nothing to discuss. I want to close my accounts—*my* accounts—and transfer the funds to the account number I have provided. That you think a male companion should have any say with what I do with the money I earn is sufficient reason for me to move my money to another banking institution."

"I just meant . . ." Sweat beaded Danvers's upper lip.

"I've been taking care of my own finances since I was sixteen. That's half my life," Rachel Two said. "I can take care of them now."

Ashley gave Danvers and the cashier a sharp smile. "Perhaps you mistakenly believe that you should call Mr. Hampton to tell him his female companion is withdrawing what many of us would see as a considerable sum of money but would be petty cash to a man like him." Her eyes were cold, revealing a hint of what she was when the sun went down. "Be careful, Mr. Danvers. Fate—and business—can be a fickle thing. If word slipped out that you and this bank believe that men should be informed whenever a woman withdraws funds from her own private accounts—even men who have no legal or familial connection to the woman—what will happen to the bank's reputation if, after such a phone call, a woman is prevented from having the means to escape an abuser and ends up in the hospital—or the morgue? How many single women will want to leave their money in your bank and take that risk?"

Danvers paled as he stared at Ashley. "You wouldn't."

"Why not? While I don't know where they keep their money, I know of two women who wouldn't survive the next beating if you made that kind of phone call."

"But Ms. Nightingale is engaged to—"

Rachel Two held up her left hand. "Not anymore. I'm relocating to another city—for my health. I'm leaving within the hour."

"I see." Danvers pulled out a handkerchief and dabbed his forehead. "I see."

It didn't matter if he saw or not. The accounts were closed and the funds were transferred.

Rachel Two and Ashley Laxton were in an Arcana boat with Rachel Three and her companion, heading for the docks at Destiny Bay, before Mr. Danvers picked up a phone in his office—and almost made the call.

22

Rachel Four watched the man who walked past the library for the third time. The first time he walked past, she had been calling the train station and hung up before anyone came on the line. She didn't need to talk to anyone, just needed to have a call listed at the time when the other Rachels would be taking care of their tasks.

A human predator. She was sure Rachel Nightingale was the intended prey—which meant she couldn't delay the phone call to the police any longer.

"Penwych police, thirteenth precinct," a voice said. "How may I direct your call?"

"I need to speak to Beth Fahey." She made her voice sound breathless, tinged with fear. "Detective Fahey."

"One moment."

The man cruised past again, noted that she was on the phone, and kept going. Not far. Barely a few buildings down the street. He wouldn't try to grab her while she was talking to someone. No, he'd wait.

She wasn't worried about the human predator. He wasn't a danger to *her* unless he carried a weapon that could kill her from a distance. She didn't think that was the intention. Nightingale was needed alive until she could be raped of everything that mattered to someone—

first her money, then her freedom, then her life. So he would have to get personal, get his hands on her. One on one, that would be a mistake. But there could be more of Alistair Hampton's hirelings watching, prepared to assist the adversary she could see.

Then she spotted Jack Frost on the other side of the street, standing next to a building. She relaxed. Even if the human predator had a weapon, with Jack around, that man would become prey.

"This is Detective Fahey. How may I help you?"

"This is Rachel Nightingale." Breathless. Fearful. "I'm at the library, the main branch. There's a man following me. I'm afraid . . ." She gasped as if someone was rushing toward her.

"Ms. Nightingale? Are you inside the library? Can you stay within sight of other patrons or the librarians until we can reach you?"

Rachel Four turned away from the street and tucked the phone behind the lion's front paws where someone would find it. She didn't end the call; still heard Detective Fahey asking questions as she hurried down the steps. She dashed across the street and walked swiftly in the direction that would take her to the river and the river bus's nearest stop.

The human predator dashed across the street to follow her.

And Jack Frost followed him.

23

Beth's hand tightened on the receiver. "Hello? Can you hear me?"

Tom Castelletti and Ian Kuhn pushed away from their desks. Captain Forrester came out of his office.

"A woman in trouble," she said. "At the main branch of the library. She hasn't ended the call, but she isn't responding."

"In Penwych?" Kuhn asked.

Beth hesitated. "She didn't say."

"Hello?" A different voice. Younger.

"Hello." Beth pitched her voice toward friendly. "I was talking to a lady, but she's not answering. Can you see her?"

"There's no lady—just the library lion."

"Library lion?" Beth looked at the men.

"Main branch of the public library," Castelletti said. "In King's Hill."

"I'm not supposed to talk to strangers," the young voice said.

"Very wise," Beth replied, "but I'm a police officer, and I could use your help."

"Really?"

"Really. Could you take the phone inside the library and give it to one of the librarians? A police officer is on his way to pick it up. It's very important."

"Okay."

"You stay on the phone with me until you hand it over to a librarian."

"Okay."

"Casey!" A woman's voice, sounding irritated. "We have to go now. You have your books for the week."

"I can't, Mom! I have to give this phone to the librarian. The police said so."

"What police?"

"The one on the phone."

Sounds. Then another woman's voice. "Who is this?"

"This is Detective Fahey at the thirteenth precinct in Penwych. The woman who owns that phone may have been abducted a few minutes ago. We need you to take that phone inside and leave it with a librarian until we can retrieve it. Will you do that?"

"Abducted? A few minutes ago?"

"Ma'am, that's all I can tell you at this time. Please stay on the phone and go back inside the library until the detective and responding officers arrive."

"Yes. Yes. Come on, Casey."

More sounds. More voices. A woman identified herself as a librarian and promised to keep the phone under a counter until the police arrived.

Beth thanked her and ended the call.

Forrester looked grim. "King's Hill is in Westwood County, but anything that might be connected to Wyrd is within our mandate."

"We don't know this is connected to Wyrd," Kuhn said.

"Don't we? Fahey, go with Castelletti to retrieve the phone. The child and mother will recognize your voice, and that will help. Also, if the woman who initially made the call is running, she might hide from a male police officer."

"I know where that King's Hill branch is located," Castelletti said. "I'll drive."

"No, request the patrol boat to take you around the southern end of Wyrd. You'll reach King's Hill faster that way, and time is of the essence."

Beth looked at the three men. "Rachel Nightingale. Why did she call me? She specifically asked for me."

"Interesting question," Forrester replied. "Go. Get the phone. Find out what you can about Ms. Nightingale's reason for being at the library. Maybe someone has an idea about where she went—if she went voluntarily. I'll call the King's Hill police after you confirm that you're on your way back here."

"Yes, sir." Beth hurried to catch up with Castelletti. She waited until they were in the patrol boat and the officer at the wheel was heading downriver. Then she asked the question that had been bothering her. "Do you think we'll find anything? That we'll find her?"

Castelletti didn't say anything, just looked at the river. Finally, "I think we're meant to find something. That's why the call was aimed at you."

24

Rachel Four hurried down the street, glancing back every time she turned a corner.

The human predator followed her, making no effort to hide the fact that he *was* following her. He maintained the distance between them, running when she turned a corner and then slowing when she was in sight again. Playing with her.

She played with him, too, by taking what would seem to be wrong turns that led away from the river bus stop and would take them to a commercial area where businesses had loading platforms to receive goods from vessels on the river—an area of King's Hill that would have fewer possible witnesses if there was an accident or an abduction.

Because her task was the simplest one and she would be alone, Rachel Four had consumed just enough of Rachel Nightingale's flesh for a short transformation. She felt herself changing as she walked quickly down another street. The jeans and hooded sweatshirt she'd worn hadn't matched anything in Nightingale's overnight bag, but the Rachels had decided that it would seem like a costume that was being worn in an effort to hide, especially because the clothes had been baggy on the Nightingale body. Now, as she transformed back to herself, the clothes felt a little snug.

She was close to the river. She could see water beyond where the street ended. She could . . .

A hand grabbed her, yanked her around.

"You're coming with me, bitch."

"Who are you?" she demanded in a voice that held anger instead of the expected fear. "What do you want from me?"

He looked surprised. Confused. Must have been wondering how he could have lost sight of his intended prey. Then . . . "Where is she?"

"Who? Why have you been following me?" She tried to break away from him.

He seized her throat and squeezed. "You're going to tell me—"

As Jack came up behind him and slipped the thin steel blade coated in ice between the man's ribs and twisted it into a lung, Rachel Four lunged forward and took a big bite out of the man's cheek. She swallowed the flesh and smiled at the man as he gasped for air and saw her change into his own image.

"We'd better clean up and go." Jack sheathed his blade, which was no longer coated in ice.

After emptying the man's pockets and leaving the items where he fell, they each grabbed an arm and half dragged the dying man to the river's edge. A hard shove and he was in the water, caught in the currents.

Rachel Four, now looking like the man who had hunted for Nightingale, pulled off her shoes. The jeans were too short but fit the leaner male body well enough, and the hooded sweatshirt fit just fine. Only the shoes were suddenly too small, but the athletic socks were thick enough for her to walk to the river bus stop. Security cameras would see a man boarding the bus. The cameras weren't likely to show his feet, and even if they did, there could be reasons why a person wasn't wearing his shoes.

"You go ahead; I'll follow," Jack said. "You know where our boat will be waiting for us when you get off the river bus?"

She nodded. Then she looked at the river. "Do you think *he'll* find a boat before he drowns?"

Jack looked at her—and laughed.

25

Jeremy Swayne struggled to breathe, struggled to keep his head above water. His flailing hand touched coarse netting. Grabbed. Held on as he was hauled up to the deck of a fishing trawler like some stranded fish.

"Well, now, lads. That looks like a fine catch."

Jeremy gasped for the next breath. Still difficult, but not as bad as a minute ago when that bastard—whoever he'd been—had stuck a knife into him.

"My name is Jeremy Swayne. You need to get me to a hospital." Jeremy got to his feet, then staggered until he found his balance.

The burly, bearded man smiled at him. "I don't have to do anything. Besides, you're already past needing a hospital."

"I work for an important man!"

"As the captain of this boat, I guess I am an important man. You're either part of my crew now, or you go back in the water." The captain's smile widened, showing his teeth. "Only the dying or the dead can see this boat. You were taking your last breath when you grabbed hold of the net and we hauled you aboard. As long as you stay on this boat, you'll continue to take that last breath. The moment you leave, you're dead. So it's your choice. Take the place of a crew member who is ready to leave, or go back in the water now."

Jeremy looked at the men on the deck. Something about their pallor made him uneasy.

"Well, Jeremy Swayne?" the captain said. "Are you going to take your last breath with us for a while longer, or are we going to drop you into the river so you can eventually wash ashore somewhere?"

Had to be some kind of trick, but until the boat docked somewhere, he'd have to remain with these lunatics.

He reached into his trouser pocket, then remembered his killers had taken his cell phone, keys, and wallet with his identification. "This boat must have a radio. I need to contact my boss and tell him there will be a delay."

"Old boat," the captain said. "Some of us have been sailing since before such newfangled things were installed on boats. Besides, looking at that bite on your face, I'm guessing that plenty of people will see you onshore before you disappear."

He remembered the woman he'd followed from the library—the woman who had been Rachel Nightingale and then wasn't. The woman who, somehow, looked exactly like him before he ended up in the water.

Maybe he was already in the hospital. Maybe he was delusional from the stab wound. But maybe he wasn't.

"I'll stay for a while."

"Captain Flint?" a crew member said, his voice a mix of hope and weariness. "Is it my turn to go?"

Flint nodded. "If you're ready, Fletcher, then go and be at peace."

Fletcher said his goodbyes, gave Flint a salute, then vaulted over the side.

Jeremy hurried to the railing. The body floated alongside the boat before the current claimed it. The face, what there was of it, looked peaceful—and looked like a ravaged version of the man who had stood on the deck moments ago.

"He sailed with me for thirty years," Flint said. "He was finally ready to complete that last breath." He pointed at a man who approached them. "This is Carver, my first mate. He'll show you to your bunk."

"Do I need one?"

"Even the dying like to rest now and then."

When Carver led him belowdecks, Jeremy said, "I've killed men."

"Have you?" Carver smiled, showing a gold eyetooth. "Then you'll fit in with the rest of us."

26

Rachel Four had almost reached the crowd boarding the river bus when someone shouted, "Hey! Swayne!" The name meant nothing, so she ignored it while other people looked around.

"Jeremy!"

She looked at the man who stared at her. Ah. He knew the human predator. Good. An associate would be able to report seeing Jeremy Swayne board the river bus. Someone would either turn in the items left near the river, giving the police a place to investigate, or the items would disappear. Either way, confusion.

She gave the man a dismissive wave and boarded the river bus.

She disembarked at the third stop, waited until the vessel continued on its route, then boarded the small motorboat that would take her back to Destiny Bay.

"We're going around the other way," Jack said a minute later when he joined her. He held out a ball cap. "To the pavilion to report to Lucas and the Ladies."

She accepted the ball cap and lowered her head to hide her face. A pleasant journey on the water. "Did the others make it back?"

"I didn't hear about any trouble," Jack replied. "I expect that will come in another day or two—for the humans, anyway."

The motorboat pulled into its slip on the side of the beach reserved for Wyrd's residents. Avoiding the beach, she and Jack followed a path up to the grassy area in front of the pavilion.

Lucas looked at Jack, then at her, and said, "Not the same face you left with."

She smiled. "You know what they say about my branch of the Arcana: we are what we eat."

27

Captain Grace Russell gently put down her phone and looked at Markus Seibert, her senior detective. "Alistair Hampton claims that his fiancée, who disappeared a couple of days ago and is emotionally disturbed, returned to their apartment with two friends and cleaned out all the valuables. I'd like you to take a look at the apartment and talk to Mr. Hampton."

Markus frowned. "Wasn't his brother reported missing last week?" He studied her. "Since he's one of *those* Hamptons, shouldn't you talk to him? He would be expecting the most senior officer available."

"I have the wrong body shape to deal effectively with Mr. Hampton." Grace gave Markus the smile her team called her shark smile—but not when they thought she could hear them. "I interviewed Alistair when Reginald Hampton the Third disappeared. He made it clear that the best thing I could do for the investigation was to go down on my knees and give him some comfort."

Markus blinked. "And he didn't end up in the hospital?"

"I maintained my professional distance. I would prefer not to test my control a second time."

"Understood."

"Hampton also said that he tried to talk to the manager of the bank where, with Hampton's assistance, his fiancée had opened checking and savings accounts, but the manager refused to cooperate and insisted he could only talk to the police if we required it. Since Hampton is insisting that we require it, I'll find out what happened at the bank." *And find out what spooked the manager so much he wouldn't comply with a request from one of the Hamptons of King's Hill.*

Markus just stood in front of her desk, jingling coins in his pocket. "Hampton lives in one of those super-luxury apartment buildings with every kind of security. How did his fiancée and two of her friends clean out all the valuables? Where was the doorman and the guard at the security desk?"

"Find out," Grace replied as her phone rang. "In the meantime . . ." She picked up the phone. "Grace Russell." She raised her index finger, signaling Markus to wait. "Captain Forrester. What can I do for you? Ah. I see. Rachel Nightingale? The writer? I'll come to you sometime this morning. I have a couple of things to sort out first."

She finished the call and looked at Markus. "Rachel Nightingale placed a call to one of Charles Forrester's detectives at the thirteenth precinct in Penwych, asking for that person by name and claiming to be in danger. She was calling from the main branch of the King's Hill public library. His team retrieved the phone and are holding it at their precinct."

"You think there's a connection between the phone call and this theft of valuables?" Markus asked.

Grace sighed. "My mother reads the society pages, so I know that Alistair Hampton's fiancée is Rachel Nightingale. Which means these two things are definitely connected." She shook her head. "Something isn't right. A person can't be in two places at the same time." *Unless there is a reason Nightingale's phone ended up with Charles Forrester's team.*

28

Alistair Hampton blocked the doorway to his penthouse apartment. "Why do you have to come in and poke around my home? I reported a theft and *told* your superior who had taken the valuables—my fiancée and two women who must have forced her to let them into our apartment. All *you* need to do is find them."

Markus looked at the man standing behind Hampton. Took in the expression in the man's eyes, the way he positioned himself to have a clear shot at whoever was at the door. As tempting as it was to ask if the man had a permit to carry a concealed weapon, Markus kept his focus on his main target, knowing that his partner, Officer James Lamb, would be watching the other man.

"You reported a theft but won't allow the police to enter your home to ascertain that valuables were, in fact, taken." Markus kept his voice calm and controlled. "It sounds like you realized nothing was stolen but didn't have time to cancel the request for police assistance. I'll submit a report saying that you were mistaken."

"I am *not* mistaken!" Hampton shouted.

"We only have your word for that."

"Isn't that enough?"

"No, sir, it's not."

The man took a step forward and whispered in Hampton's ear.

Hampton huffed out an angry breath and stepped aside. "Come in, then. But don't make a mess!"

Markus and Lamb stepped inside. Big living area with furniture that looked expensive but uncomfortable. Lots of dust catchers on the shelves on either side of a fireplace, along with a few token books in leather bindings. No obvious empty spaces to indicate something small and valuable was snatched.

"This way," the man said, leading the way to the back of the apartment.

"And you are?" Markus asked when the man pushed open a door and stepped into the room.

"Martin Chandler, Mr. Hampton's head of security."

A bedroom suite. The doors to one walk-in closet were open; several drawers in a dresser weren't fully closed. The bathroom . . .

Markus took a quick look but stayed in the doorway. Something about the bathroom. "Did Ms. Nightingale have an office in the apartment? Since she's a well-known writer, I would expect her to have a work area and a computer."

Chandler gave him a hard look.

You don't like that we know who Hampton's fiancée is, do you? You don't like that someone else who knows her might disagree with Hampton's claim that she's emotionally disturbed.

"She and Mr. Hampton shared an office," Chandler said, clearly reluctant to provide even that much information.

"Officer Lamb, take a look at the office," Markus said. "Make a note of anything that is obviously missing."

Chandler gave him another hard look but escorted Lamb to the home office, leaving Markus alone to inspect the bathroom.

He stood in the doorway and told himself to look without expectation because *something* was off.

Where *wouldn't* a raging man look for some clue about the person or persons who had supposedly invaded his home with or without the help of his fiancée?

Two sinks and cabinets. His and hers? But one toilet. With the seat and lid down. Usual? Somehow, he didn't think Hampton would be that considerate.

Markus lifted the toilet lid. On the inside were two beautifully sharp thumbprints. He pulled out his phone and took a picture. Odds were good Hampton wouldn't let him bring in a crime scene unit to lift the prints.

He studied the prints. What had been used . . . ?

He opened one cabinet above a sink. Male body products.

The other cabinet was empty except for a small rectangular basket that held a makeup brush, charcoal eye shadow, a piece of paper, and an envelope. Nothing on the envelope, but the paper held two sharp thumbprints that he would bet matched the ones on the inside of the toilet lid. He'd also bet that the eye shadow that had been left behind had been used to make those prints.

Markus carefully slipped the paper into the envelope. He put the envelope and the eye shadow into his pocket, made sure the rest of the bathroom looked the same as when he entered, and returned to the bedroom moments before Lamb and Chandler returned.

"Anything?" Markus asked Lamb.

"A laptop appears to be missing from one of the desks," Lamb replied. "Looks like some files were taken from a desk drawer."

Markus looked at Chandler. "I assume Mr. Hampton has a home safe. Was anything taken from that?"

"No." Chandler bit off the word.

"So the only valuables taken belonged to Ms. Nightingale?"

"It looks that way."

Markus nodded. "We've seen everything we need to see." *At least in the apartment.*

Chandler escorted them out of the apartment and down to the lobby, trying to herd Markus away from the security desk.

Not a chance.

Markus showed the security guard his ID again and said, "You have top-level security in this building, and you have security cameras. I'd like to see who came in with Rachel Nightingale—unless you have a reason to obstruct a police inquiry."

The security guard hesitated, then glanced at Chandler.

Chandler's face darkened with anger. "I haven't had a chance to review the feed, so we'll look at it together."

"Much appreciated," Markus said. Before leaving the precinct, he'd taken a minute to find an author photo of Rachel Nightingale so that he'd know her if he saw her—and he would know if Hampton was lying about his fiancée being one of the women who had entered the apartment.

Markus and Lamb followed Chandler to the building's security room and viewed the morning's feed from the camera in the lobby. Rachel Nightingale and two other women walked in, each pulling a large suitcase. They looked like they flirted a little with the security guard on duty before making their way to the elevators.

"Fast forward," Markus said.

An hour later, the same three women with the same three suitcases walked out of the elevator, still looking like they were having a girl's day out. The two women with Rachel Nightingale looked up at the security camera—and smiled.

Markus looked at Chandler, who stared at the screen.

"Do you recognize them?" Markus asked.

"No."

"You sure?"

"Yes, I'm sure!" Chandler stormed out of the security room.

Markus pulled out his phone and took a picture of the three women on the screen. Then he looked the security guard in the eyes. "I didn't ask you to give me a printout of what's on that screen because that would put you between a rock and a hard place—the rock being Chandler and the hard place being the King's Hill police—so you don't need to say anything about me taking a picture on my phone before you could stop me."

The security guard nodded.

Chandler wasn't in the lobby when Markus and Lamb left the building. Markus waited until they reached their car before saying, "Your impression?"

"Clothes and jewelry are gone," Lamb said. "Also gone are a laptop and what I'm guessing were some important files. Three women arrive with suitcases and leave with the same number of suitcases.

Nothing belonging to Alistair Hampton was taken. Looks like his fiancée asked her friends to help her run away."

Markus nodded. "He claims she's emotionally unstable."

"Don't abusers usually say something like that?"

He sighed. "Yeah. They do. I'll call the boss and see how things are going at her end, and what she wants us to do next."

Alistair Hampton stared at the screen, at the faces of the two women who looked up at the camera and smiled. Then he turned on Chandler. "You said you took care of those bitches."

"I did." Chandler pointed at the screen. "That is *not* possible."

Alistair looked at the screen. "You'd better be right about that."

Maybe this was all a con. Had to be. The woman pretending to be Rachel had been too fat, and the other two women . . . Besides, one of Chandler's men had called and said Rachel had been spotted at the main branch of the public library and would be reacquired. But his fiancée hadn't been reacquired, and the police were sniffing around and might find out some things that were none of their business.

And where the hell was Jeremy Swayne?

29

Grace Russell studied the pictures of the two women that the bank manager, Mr. Danvers, had ready to hand over.

"You're sure this was Rachel Nightingale?" she asked.

"Of course I'm sure!" Danvers replied. "She is—or was—a good client, and I was very sorry to see that the other woman had influenced her to close all her accounts and move her funds to . . . well, I'm not sure where, but they did have an account number and the funds did transfer. *All* the funds."

"And you think this wasn't Ms. Nightingale's decision?"

"I'm sure of it. When I suggested contacting Mr. Hampton before Ms. Nightingale took such a drastic step, the other woman *threatened* me."

"She threatened you with bodily harm?"

Danvers hesitated. "No, she threatened my reputation, and the reputation of the bank."

Officer Laci Tower stared at Danvers. "Imagine that—a woman taking offense at being told she needed a man's permission to access her own money."

Tower by name, tower by stature. That Laci wore her hair in a buzz cut and had a deep voice added to her ability to intimidate just by standing there.

Amused by Danvers putting the teller between himself and Tower, Grace held on to her professional demeanor, but it was hard work.

"Not just any man, her fiancé," Danvers finally said, his voice defiant and a little squeaky.

"I'm not seeing a ring on her left hand," Tower said. "Do you see one, Captain? I remember seeing a picture of Rachel Nightingale when the engagement was announced, and she was wearing a *big* ring. You couldn't miss it."

"Did she say anything about that?" Grace asked.

Danvers didn't reply, but the teller tapped the ring finger of her own left hand and shook her head. Maybe Hampton was no longer a fiancé.

"So the woman with Ms. Nightingale threatened to smear your reputation if you called Mr. Hampton," Grace continued. "Do you want to tell us exactly what was said?"

Danvers claimed he couldn't recall exactly what was said, so Grace and Laci left the bank with a picture of the two women who had cleaned out Rachel Nightingale's accounts.

Laci's phone rang. Grace continued walking to the car, focusing her thoughts on the other woman in the picture. Something about that person had scared Danvers enough that he'd defied Alistair Hampton's attempt to get information about Nightingale's accounts. She needed to find out what that something was—and if it was somehow connected with the cell phone that was being held at Penwych's 13th precinct.

"Rachel Nightingale used to live in an upscale, artsy neighborhood in King's Hill," Laci said when she met Grace at the car. "Stands to reason she would have used a bank in the same neighborhood." She pulled up a map on her phone. "If a woman is looking to hold on to running-away money, she won't put it in the same bank that's used by the man she's running from, especially if she believes that man can influence the people working at that bank to spy on her and give him information about her accounts. And she's going to use a branch of that other bank that's convenient. Whatever mode of transportation she used, there is a bank and a post office within three blocks of the main branch of the library."

"Where her phone was found," Grace murmured. "All right, let's go with your hunch and check out the bank and post office. Maybe we'll get lucky."

Grace took the bank while Laci checked the post office.

Yes, Ms. Nightingale still came in often, since her royalties were deposited directly into her account at the bank. Yes, she had a safe deposit box, which she accessed this morning when she also closed out her account and requested a cashier's check for the full amount. There was some concern because Ms. Nightingale had gotten so thin and the staff had wondered quietly if she might be ill because she *did* mention to the teller that she was moving away for her health and that was the reason she was closing her account.

At Grace's request, the bank manager provided a picture from the security cameras of Rachel Nightingale and her companion, who was not the same woman who had been with her at the other bank.

She thanked the bank manager and teller for their help and left, meeting Laci at the car.

"Rachel Nightingale had a post office box and came in once a week to collect her mail—and she usually had a small carryall filled with books she was picking up from or returning to the library," Laci said. "This morning she collected her mail and filled out a change-of-address card, effective immediately. Her mail is being forwarded to a post office box in Lovecraft."

"Not Penwych?"

"You were expecting it to be Penwych?"

"Maybe." Grace's cell phone rang. "Markus? Anything? Issue a be on the lookout notice for Nightingale's companions. I'll meet you back at the precinct, and we'll review everything we know." She ended the call.

"Problem?" Laci asked.

Grace shivered and hoped there was a different explanation to Rachel Nightingale's behavior. "Probably."

30

Grace Russell studied the evidence laid out on the large table in what she thought of as the war room.

A picture of Rachel Nightingale with two women whose fingerprints were on file because they were "party girls" who had previous scrapes with the law but had wealthy patrons who sent expensive lawyers to make sure the girls didn't have time—or a reason—to talk to the cops.

A picture of Rachel Nightingale and an unknown woman whose body language made Grace shiver because there was something not quite human about her.

A picture of Rachel Nightingale with *another* woman at another bank.

A picture of the steps and the standing lions at the main branch of the King's Hill public library and notes from an interview with the librarian who had held on to the phone for the young detective from Penwych.

Four sightings of Rachel Nightingale *at the same time.*

Laci Tower approached the table and laid another picture at the end. "From another King's Hill precinct. Some workers taking a smoke break around the loading docks of a couple of businesses near the river spotted these items and called it in. The cops reported a blood trail leading from the items right to the river."

Grace studied the items in the picture. "A handgun but no holster. A cell phone. A wallet."

"Identification in the wallet is for a Jeremy Swayne," Lacy said.

"Any money in the wallet?"

"Several hundred dollars."

"Not a robbery, then. So where is Jeremy Swayne?" Not her puzzle to solve, thank God.

"Markus is escorting Detective Sheina Kali to the war room. She works in Jackson, and she claims to have information about our BOLO that she needs to share in person."

Markus and Detective Kali entered the room. After Markus made the introductions, Grace skipped to the main event. "You have some information about the women we're looking for?"

"I have a question about them," Kali replied. She opened her phone to a picture, then set it on the table facing Grace. "Why did you put out a BOLO this morning for women who have been dead for several days?"

Grace leaned over the table and stared at the picture of three bodies laid out on a dock. Then she looked at Kali. "Explain."

"This morning, we got a call from some men who were taking their boat out early and saw bodies tangled in old fishing net that had gotten caught on part of the dock. When our dive team retrieved them, we discovered three women who had been dead for several days. Lots of predation, and the Jackson medical examiner thinks they might have washed up somewhere and then were relocated to the marina in Jackson." Kali paused. "The divers said the net was secured to the dock, indicating that someone wanted them found." Another pause. "So why did you put out a BOLO now? They must have been missing for several days."

Grace turned the three time-stamped pictures showing Rachel Nightingale and her companions so that Kali could see them.

Kali stared. "That's not possible."

"We know," Grace replied, then thought, *Damn it. Damn it!*

"Are we going overland or by water?" Laci asked.

"Water. Contact the patrol boat." Grace studied Kali. Midthirties? Not new to police work, but . . . "How long have you lived in Jackson?"

"We moved here a few months ago," Kali replied. "My husband has a job at Jackson University. I've been with the Jackson police department for a couple of months."

"So this is your first experience with the strange?"

"I've earned my detective's shield, if that's what you're asking."

"That's not what I'm asking." *Better if Detective Kali gets her feet wet with me and my people instead of stumbling on her own.* "Inform your captain that you're coming with us to Penwych's thirteenth precinct."

"Shouldn't I tell him why?"

Grace gathered the pictures and tucked them into a folder. "As soon as you tell him you're going to the thirteenth precinct, he'll know why."

31

Flint, the captain of the fishing trawler, stared at Jeremy Swayne as the crew gathered to decide the man's fate. Carver and Skinner had already hamstrung the bastard and searched him for weapons, so Swayne wasn't going to be much of a threat to his men.

"Not even a day of taking that last breath, and you try to stick a knife in my back and take over my boat," Flint said.

"He doesn't deserve to keep taking his last breath," Skinner said. "He doesn't deserve a place on our boat, doesn't deserve the time to make amends."

Flint looked at his crew. He called them his men whether they had balls or breasts. They'd all managed to reach this boat before they'd taken that last breath, and he accepted them as part of his crew for as long as they needed to be there—or for as long as it took to find a replacement. The boat only took on so many, and it seldom went out with less. Now . . .

"If we let him go, we'll be a man short," Flint said, meeting the eyes of every one of his crew. "That means we'll need two before another who is ready can go."

"Better we wait, for however long we need to wait, than to have *that* with us," Carver said.

Murmurs of agreement.

Flint nodded. "Very well. We're almost at Susurration Sound. Carver and Skinner will finish the business there." He gave Jeremy Swayne a nasty smile. "Anyone who thinks to look for you won't find most of you, but we'll make sure they know you're gone."

32

Grace sat in the stern of the patrol boat, looking straight ahead. Sheina Kali sat beside her, watching the land on the port side.

"Is that the Isle of Wyrd?" Kali asked.

"It is." Grace refused to look at it, even from this distance. Some people looked at that island and saw nothing but another piece of land. For others—like her—there was a seductive, nightmarish beauty to the island that called to something in the deepest, most primitive part of the human mind—an invitation to remember things best forgotten.

That lure was the biggest reason she would never accept any promotion or advancement if it meant working in Penwych, the town that had a direct line to that island.

"My husband, Yaron, teaches courses in mythology and folklore,"

Kali said. "He wants to go to Wyrd, but not the tame part created for tourists. He thinks he can rent a boat and go to another part of the island and see what's really out there."

"Tell your husband there are other people who thought that way. If they were lucky, they returned to their side of the river alive and sane—or close enough to sanity that they could still live a passably normal life." Grace gave Kali a hard look. "There is only one safe way to go to Wyrd. You go to the pier at Penwych, you pay your fare to ride the ferry, and you visit the pavilion and the park—and you don't shrug off the warnings. If your husband needs proof of the dangers of going out on his own, I can give him the name of a facility that specializes in dealing with the mental trauma that occurs when someone is careless while visiting Wyrd. It won't be pretty, and he should consider if breaking the rules and going where he's not meant to go is worth spending the rest of his life in a facility like that—assuming he gets back at all. Not everyone does."

"If the people who inhabit the island are so dangerous, why are they allowed to stay there?"

Grace stood. Then she hesitated and looked at Kali. "Because they were here first, and because the strange ripples through the world. It's just concentrated here."

"Captain?" Markus said. "We're about to enter Susurration Sound."

Grace nodded and moved forward to join Markus and the pilot, needing to be close to her people. A moment later, Kali joined them.

"Once we get through the sound, we'll be back on the Fate River," Markus told Kali. "Then . . ."

Someone screamed—or tried to. It was a gasping sound, as if the person didn't have enough breath to convey the full measure of terror.

Then something—a man?—appeared out of nowhere, hit the water, and sank.

A moment later, a piece of driftwood arced through the air and fell into the water. It went under for a few seconds, then bobbed to the surface.

The pilot slowed the patrol boat.

"We're in the sound," Markus said. "Don't shut off the engine."

"I know," the pilot replied, idling the engine. "But I don't want to find out what will happen if we hit whatever is ahead of us. Do you?"

"That piece of wood," Grace said. "Can you snag it or push it out of the way so it doesn't foul our engine?"

Markus grabbed the boat hook. "I see it. I can . . . Shit!" After a startled moment, he hooked the piece of driftwood and brought it aboard.

The pilot kept his eyes on the water ahead of them. Grace, Markus, and Kali stared at the two hands secured to the driftwood with a piece of old fishing net.

"They look fresh," Markus said.

Grace stared at the water, refusing to hear the whispers that weren't really voices, that were nothing more than the odd sounds made by this water.

Look at that tall ship, Gracie! Isn't she a beauty, with all her sails catching the wind? I'd sure like to sail again one more time.

She had taken her father down to the river two years ago—a last outing for a dying man. He'd described that ship as it sailed past, had even saluted the woman at the wheel—and had laughed when the "pirate queen" had returned his salute.

He'd talked about a ship she couldn't see—a ship she had believed was a delusion.

He disappeared that night and was never seen again. The police who investigated concluded that he must have wandered back to the river and fallen in—or walked in, since they found his slippers near the edge of the water. She didn't argue with their conclusion. A man with only a few weeks—or days—left to live, making a choice.

She never told anyone that there were times since then when she heard his voice in the water of Susurration Sound. *I'm all right, Gracie. Don't worry about me. I'm just taking a last voyage. I'm all right.*

"Is it safe to proceed?" she asked.

The pilot nodded, gradually increasing the boat's speed.

Grace didn't take a full breath until they were out of the sound and headed up the Fate River to Penwych.

33

When he heard that Grace Russell and two other detectives were in the building, Charles Forrester pushed away from his desk to join his team and greet their guests. Russell had called him back and said that she had some information about Rachel Nightingale, and she was curious about why a Penwych detective had gone to King's Hill to pick up a cell phone. Since this could be Russell's case, he told Fahey to hold on to the phone for the time being instead of taking it to their tech team to figure out the PIN and find out what information they could glean from the device.

He glanced at his computer and was going to ignore the new e-mail that appeared, unwilling to delay hearing what had pushed Russell to come by boat to Penwych. When he saw the sender's cryptic name, he froze for a moment. Then he opened the e-mail from Lucas Frost.

The subject line read: *You will need this.*

The e-mail's content was a four-digit number.

No signature, which wasn't unusual. No other information, which meant he shouldn't need anything else to figure out what to do with the number.

Charles joined his team around the big evidence table, arriving at the same time one of the precinct's officers escorted his guests to the team's area of the precinct. Russell introduced Markus Seibert and Sheina Kali. Charles had met Seibert at area conferences. Kali was unknown—and looked as if she hadn't had an easy time on the trip.

Ian Kuhn set an old, folded blanket on the table. Seibert set a large evidence bag on the table—a bag that held a piece of driftwood and . . .

"Jesus," Castelletti said. "Are those *hands*?"

"We retrieved them on our way here," Russell said. "They appeared in Susurration Sound."

Charles heard the slight emphasis on the word *appeared* and knew what that meant.

Ghost ship.

"Men's hands," Fahey murmured. "Not Rachel Nightingale."

Russell gave Fahey a sharp look. "Not her hands, but Rachel Nightingale is the primary reason we're here. I'm hoping your people can pull fingerprints off the hands while they're still fresh."

"Of course," Charles said. "Kuhn? If you would oblige."

"Chain of custody?" Kuhn asked.

"Don't worry about it." He received sharp looks from the detectives from the other towns, but he suspected police procedure wasn't going to help any of them.

After Kuhn left with the driftwood and hands, Russell looked at Charles and said, "Tell me about the cell phone your people picked up at a King's Hill library."

Fahey set the cell phone, sealed in an evidence bag, on the table. "After calling the precinct and asking for me specifically, Rachel Nightingale left her phone outside the library. Hearing my voice, a young girl picked up the phone, and she and her mother took it inside, at my request. By the time Detective Castelletti and I arrived to retrieve it, the phone had shut down. Now it's locked."

"We'll have to get the tech boys to figure out the PIN," Castelletti said.

You will need this. "Try two zero zero seven," Charles said.

Fahey removed the phone from the evidence bag, turned it on, and put in the numbers. "It worked." She gave him a look that asked a question.

She wasn't the only one looking at him.

"Anonymous source." His voice warned all of them not to ask about the source.

"Did anyone see Rachel Nightingale?" Russell asked.

Fahey shook her head. "But the librarians know her. She comes in once or twice a week to do research for her next book or series of books. They had the impression that she was working on a woman-on-the-run sort of story because she'd asked for their help to pull information about women's shelters and witness protection. That sort of thing."

"Telling them she's doing research would be a good way to hide personal interest or intentions," Seibert said, looking at Russell.

"She said a man was following her, and she was afraid," Fahey said.

"No one else saw a man near her or acting in a threatening manner?" Russell asked.

Fahey shook her head again as she worked on the phone. "Why lead us to it? There are no texts, no photos. Only three phone numbers. Two are for Alistair Hampton: cell phone and office number. The other number is for that branch of the King's Hill public library. Two phone calls made this morning. One to the train station, and the second, a few minutes later, to us. To me."

"That establishes a timeline of when she was at the library," Seibert said.

Establishing a timeline. Or an alibi? That didn't explain why Lucas Frost sent him the cell phone's PIN or why Frost had the PIN in the first place.

"What's your interest in Rachel Nightingale?" Charles asked Grace Russell.

Russell opened a soft-sided briefcase and laid a series of pictures on the table. "This morning, Rachel Nightingale was seen at four places at the same time, packing up her personal possessions and closing her bank accounts. The two women who accompanied Nightingale to her apartment this morning are known to party with wealthy men, and we suspect another of Nightingale's companions also liked to party. The woman who assisted Nightingale in closing her primary checking and savings accounts is unknown."

Unknown by name, maybe, Charles thought, *but I suspect she came from the other side of the river.*

"However . . ." Russell nodded to Kali, who opened her phone and laid it on the table with a picture filling the screen. "The three women who liked to party were found at the Jackson marina this morning and have been dead for several days."

Charles felt his heart pounding but kept his voice matter-of-fact. "Anything else?"

"Possessions belonging to a man named Jeremy Swayne were found near the river this morning, along with a blood trail leading to the water. And then there are the dismembered hands we found." Russell took a deep breath and let it out slowly. "A person can't be in four places at the same time. Dead women can't be walking around helping that person pack up her possessions and close her bank accounts."

Were the hands deliberately dropped in front of a patrol boat for the police to find, or wasn't that a consideration?

Castelletti finally broke the silence that followed those words. "Someone is going to have to go to Wyrd."

"Not today," Kuhn said, returning to the meeting. "The officers who patrol around the docks just sent word that the ferry isn't running to Wyrd after two p.m." He looked at his watch. "No point in any of us trying to reach the island until tomorrow."

"The ferry is running one way?" Charles asked.

Kuhn nodded. "They're continuing to bring visitors back to Penwych but not allowing anyone on this side to board."

Charles considered—and discarded—a handful of things to say to the detectives from King's Hill and Jackson.

"I can send someone in the morning to see if any information can be acquired," he offered. After all, that was why his team existed—to cross the river and receive answers that no one else would be given. But this convergence of events? He had an uneasy feeling that Lucas Frost had already given him all the help they would receive from Wyrd.

34

Reginald Hampton III stayed on the edge of the feeding frenzy and gulped a chunk of flesh that floated nearby—and bit through a small fish that had darted too close, leaving its head and tail to sink to the bottom of the sound.

A sinking feast. He'd followed the rush of fish, large and small, hunger overwhelming fear of game fish as big as he was that would fight him over a meal—or fight him because they sensed, in some way, that he wasn't like them, wasn't natural. He was learning how to survive in this eat-or-be-eaten world, but catching food was a skill he hadn't mastered yet.

He swallowed another morsel that had been flung away from a bigger piece of meat. There were so many fish darting in and around the carcass, he couldn't see what it was. Another game fish? A shark or small whale that had swum into the sound and had been injured by a propeller? Whatever it was, he needed to get in there and grab a couple more chunks of meat before the thing sank deeper than he was willing to go.

Dangerous things lived in the depths of Susurration Sound.

The sound of a boat motor. Fish scattered. Reginald darted in before they regrouped—and saw what was left of a face he recognized.

Jeremy Swayne. Minus a shirt. Minus hands. Weighed down by a belt made of fish net filled with rocks. Sinking out of reach.

Reginald hesitated for a moment. Just a moment. Then hunger and an instinct not quite his own made the decision for him. He bit deep and gulped down another chunk of meat before swimming a safe distance away from the resumed feeding frenzy.

35

A small tent had been set up close to the nearest moon gate in Destiny Park—the tent a concession to Rachel's modesty.

She undressed, wrapped the knee-length cape around herself, then sat in the chair the Arcana had provided.

"Covered?" Kia Dance asked, standing outside the tent flap.

"Yes."

Kia entered the tent and carefully removed the bandages on Rachel's legs. "Your legs are healing well, but you'll need to stay quiet to let them finish healing. Lucas will want you to stay quiet for a few days anyway while you adjust to the transformation."

"How long . . . ?" Transformation. Being changed into something else in order to hide from Alistair.

"Moments. That's why it's so important to be clear in your heart and mind about what you want from this transformation, what you need."

I want to be free again. I want to sing again. I want to spread my wings and fly.

Perhaps a whimsical way of expressing what she wanted, but she couldn't think of a better way to describe what she wanted to gain from this year in hiding.

"Ready?" Kia asked.

Rachel stood and took a moment to make sure she had her balance. Then she nodded. "Ready."

She wished there was time to ask about this . . . ceremony, but she had a feeling any queries would be ignored. This was the business, and one of the mysteries, of the Arcana. Still, she clutched at the cape to avoid flashing Lucas and Jack Frost. Not that they might notice—or care. With them were the Ladies Three and Ashley Laxton.

Was it usual to have so many witnesses?

"Clear intentions," Kia whispered. "Heart and mind."

They had closed the park early just for this. Just for her.

Lucas stood next to the moon gate. He raised a hand and touched one of the stones. Metal gates with a large butterfly in the center opened—a pathway to a future.

Jack moved around to the other side of the gate, as if prepared to catch her when she passed through.

Lucas looked at her. "When you're ready."

She was terrified. She was excited. She was . . . hopeful.

I want to be free again. I want to sing again. I want to spread my wings and fly.

Rachel walked through the moon gate.

A moment of smothering darkness. Hands quickly wrapped cloth around her, securing her arms and legs.

"Easy, easy, easy," Jack said. "You're fine, just a little confused right now. That's to be expected."

"Let's get her home and settled," Lucas said as Jack set her inside . . . something.

Her body was firmly wrapped, but someone nudged the cloth away from her head just before a lid came down on a woven basket.

"The Nightingale became a lark." Ashley's voice. Pleased? Amused?

A lark? A *bird*? She was a *bird*?

I want to be free again. I want to sing again. I want to spread my wings and fly.

Words have power. Intentions matter.

Stunned by the truth that she had somehow made this happen, she remained quiet and didn't struggle while she was carried . . . somewhere.

The basket was set down. The lid opened. Before she could think to struggle, hands closed around her, lifted her. Held her against a chest so that she could hear a heartbeat.

"Who you are has not changed," Lucas said. "*What* you are? That has changed. You are a lark now, and you must learn to live in this body over the next year. This cage is not a prison. It is for your protection while you adjust and learn. It is a safe place for you to return to at night."

Jack opened the cage door. Lucas swiftly unwrapped the cloth that had secured her and set her on the bottom of the cage.

Jack closed and latched the door.

"Move slowly," Lucas said. "If you accept what you are now, you'll adjust to your new shape more quickly. Then you will sing again, and fly again—and be free again." He studied her. "Your new name is Rahele."

Lucas and Jack pulled up a large cloth that covered the back half of the cage.

"For some privacy," Lucas said, smiling.

A fluttering. Lucas held up his arm for the crow that flew over to them.

Rachel didn't know what to do. The crow looked so *big*.

"This is Faulkner," Lucas said. "He is like you—at least for now." He stared at the crow. "Do not open the door of Rahele's home. She needs time to adjust to her new body and could hurt herself if she comes out too soon."

The crow tipped his head this way and that. Then he flew out of sight.

Lucas sighed, but he didn't look angry or upset. "Faulkner means you no harm, but he is a bold and curious fellow. Don't let him persuade you to do something before you feel ready. On the other hand, he can show you a great deal about living in your new body if you're comfortable being around him."

Rachel wasn't sure what to say. Wasn't sure what she *could* say. She opened her . . . beak . . . and the sound . . .

She tried again, rather pleased with the sound.

"Singing already?" One of the Ladies, the one who balanced the scales, linked her arm with Lucas's. She smiled at Rachel. "You are safe here."

"We'll let you rest," Lucas said.

Rest. Yes. She would rest for a while before exploring her new home.

36

When Sheina Kali opened the door to her apartment and smelled food cooking, she knew it was going to be a difficult evening. Yaron talked a good game about being an equal partner when it came to household chores, but he always expected her to do the cooking and kitchen chores while he "unwound from a hard day"—unless he wanted something from her that she might not agree to. Then he was the solicitous spouse.

Hearing the TV in the background tuned to the news, she knew exactly what he wanted—and why.

"Hey," he said as he walked out of the kitchen and gave her a hug and a kiss. "I picked up that chicken dinner you like. From what I've been hearing on the news, I figured you could use a break from cooking tonight."

"I could, yes."

"The food will be ready in a few minutes. Come and keep me company while I finish up."

Sheina hung up her coat in the front closet and took her purse into the bedroom. After stowing her gun in the lockbox on the closet shelf in the bedroom, she returned to the kitchen.

Yaron smiled at her, but his eyes had that sharp interest that meant he would keep pushing for information about a case and for details he had no business knowing. If she didn't give in, he would sulk for the rest of the evening and give her the cold shoulder in bed. If she told him what would be public knowledge the next day, he'd still accuse her of holding out on him.

Before they moved to Jackson, he hadn't been interested in her cases or the grisly details of investigations. But before they moved to Jackson, Yaron hadn't been able to go down to this side of the Fate River and stare at the Isle of Wyrd.

They'd had good jobs where they lived before. Yaron was on track for receiving tenure at his old university, and they had talked about buying a house, maybe starting a family before they—meaning she—got too much older. She hadn't realized he'd been looking for another position until she came home one evening and he excitedly told her he'd been offered a teaching position in Jackson—and had accepted. He'd be teaching English—yawn—and the mythology and folklore classes that were his main focus and interest.

It wasn't until she looked up Jackson and realized it was across the river from Wyrd that she understood the reason for his excitement—and the reason he'd decided to relocate without discussing it with her. Fait accompli. It was his chance to study the strange and uncanny up close.

It hadn't occurred to him that the people who controlled Wyrd might not welcome him with open arms and grant him access to whatever he wanted to see. But saying no to Yaron just meant he had to push harder to wear you down—or it meant he did what he wanted and then gave you the choice of going along with him or shattering the life you thought you'd been building.

Well, tonight she did have something she could give him. She just hoped he would pay attention.

"I heard on the news about the bodies found at the marina this morning," Yaron said as he plated the chicken and lentils, put bread and butter on the table, filled the salad bowls. "Is that your case?"

Sheina poured water for both of them, ignoring the wineglasses on the table. "Yes."

"Anything interesting about the case?" he asked as he took his seat. "Anything . . . unusual?"

And there it was. What had begun as a keen interest in the uncanny was becoming an obsession, an addiction.

Sheina stared at her dinner as she remembered what she'd seen that day. "No, nothing unusual, unless you count my investigation connecting with a missing person case that involved the police in King's Hill and Penwych."

"Penwych? The thirteenth precinct?"

It figured he would know the significance of that precinct.

"Nothing unusual if you don't count seeing a body appear out of thin air and sink into Susurration Sound; if you don't count severed hands bound to a piece of driftwood; if you don't count women who were caught on security cameras this morning, walking around and doing God knows what else, being the same women the Jackson police pulled out of the water *at the same time.*"

Yaron shoveled in some food before asking, "Are the police sending someone to Wyrd?"

"Someone from the thirteenth's special team is going over in the morning."

He buttered a piece of bread. "How hard would it be for you to transfer to the Penwych police and get on that special team?"

Sheina shoved away from the table. "I'm not hungry."

Yaron blinked at her, perhaps realizing he had pushed her too far.

She reached into her jacket pocket and fingered the note. Would it help or hurt? "Before you go traipsing off to Wyrd and trespass in places you have no business being, you should check out this place and talk to the people there." She put the note on the table.

He opened the paper and studied the name and address. "What is it?"

"It's a place that takes care of people who got back after crossing the river and going where they don't belong."

She went into their bedroom and closed the door. After changing into sweats and thick socks, she curled up on the bed and tried not to think. Would Yaron look at the website for that place? Would he pay attention to the careful wording and read between the lines? People who went to Wyrd uninvited weren't the same when they came back—if they came back at all.

Yaron was gone the next morning before she woke up. She reported to work, did what she could to assist the investigation into the dead women and the missing woman. She ignored any calls from the university. They wouldn't be calling her if Yaron had showed up to teach his classes.

Home again, she heated up a bowl of soup for her dinner. She was still sitting at the table when Yaron returned. He looked pale and subdued—and resentful.

She waited.

Eventually he got up and heated a bowl of soup for himself.

"I went to that place," he said after he'd eaten a few spoonfuls. "You made your point. I'll teach my classes. I won't be impulsive." He finally looked at her. "Those people weren't prepared, Sheina. That's why they got in trouble. When I finally cross the river, I will be prepared to meet the uncanny."

She said nothing. But the next morning, she called her captain and took an hour's personal time. Then she went to a bank and opened her own checking and savings accounts. Yaron wouldn't notice. Paying the bills and balancing their finances were pesky jobs he always left to her anyway.

37

Beth Fahey sat at her desk with a large cup of coffee and a breakfast sandwich she'd purchased from one of the food trucks that set up every morning in a lot across from the precinct. Bonnie would have said she was being extravagant—or lazy—to be buying breakfast *and* lunch instead of bringing something from home.

It's my money, my budget, my decision, Beth thought, feeling defiant as she reminded herself that Bonnie Wilson no longer had any say in what she bought—or what she thought.

Today she wanted to get an early start and look over all the information they had accumulated about Rachel Nightingale's disappearance. Someone would have to go to Wyrd, and she wanted to be prepared because this investigation was *big.*

A joint investigation involving three of the six towns that were on the human side of the river. Was there a reason there were only two towns that bordered the Fate River in each of the three counties? Were those towns, and the people who lived in them, like canaries in a mine, providing a warning that ripples of the strange were about to touch human places before something went very wrong?

You're being fanciful, Beth scolded herself. And yet Rachel Nightingale had been seen in four places at the same time. Three of the women who had accompanied the Nightingales had been found dead that same morning—and had been dead for days. And a phone call aimed right at *her* assured that the 13th precinct in Penwych would be involved in the investigation.

Beth reviewed all the information Captain Russell and Detective Kali had provided. Rachel Nightingale had changed her address from a post office box in King's Hill to a post office box in Lovecraft. Was that significant? Or just convenient? If convenient, why?

While she ate, Beth accessed the files for people from the six towns who had been reported missing over the past year. Was there a pattern of multiple sightings of people who then vanished? Plenty of people went missing every year—and there were plenty of reasons why people disappeared. Surely not all of them had crossed the river and made some mistake or bargain while on Wyrd. Surely not.

Beth clicked through the files. Some senior citizens. Plenty of teens who were probably runaways who had taken a bus to some other part of the country. She'd come close to doing that herself a couple of times in her teenage years when Bonnie's verbal attacks had been particularly vicious. Yes, there were plenty of ordinary reasons for someone to walk away from a life in order to start a new one somewhere else.

She stopped clicking through the files when she came to a boy who went missing a few months ago. A handsome boy with an easy smile that didn't look quite genuine, and eyes that were already old and haunted. His family lived in Lovecraft, so Captain Wozniak was the contact listed on the file. According to the parents, the boy had left home one morning to go to school and never came back.

The look in those eyes bothered her, made her want to find some way to locate him and help him.

Beth printed the first page of the file. She had the printout folded and tucked into her purse before Tom Castelletti and Ian Kuhn showed up for work.

"Coin toss to see who goes to Wyrd?" Ian said.

"No, I'll go," Beth replied. "I've already reviewed all the material we have about Rachel Nightingale."

They looked at her.

"It's okay. I'll go," she repeated. "If Rachel Nightingale is hiding out at the hotel on the island, maybe she'll talk to another woman."

Captain Forrester walked into the team's area of the precinct as she gave that explanation for wanting to go. "And maybe she's so far away by now we'll never find out what happened to her."

He stared at Beth, who felt the last bite of her breakfast sandwich go down her throat in a hard lump. "Sir?"

"The call made from Rachel Nightingale's cell phone was aimed at you for a reason," Forrester said. "My receiving the PIN for that phone was aimed at this team for a reason. If you're the one going to Wyrd—"

"She is," Castelletti said.

"—you will confirm that Rachel Nightingale had been on the island at some point and had provided that information."

Beth nodded. "I can ask about the other women—"

"No." Forrester took a step closer to Beth's desk. "Those women were found, they were identified, and their families will have some closure even if the police in Jackson never find the person or persons

responsible for killing them. That's not our case, Detective. We were asked to inquire about Rachel Nightingale, and that is what we will do. If you can't stick to that, I will send someone else to Wyrd."

Stung by his tone—and confused by his refusal to have her ask about the other women—Beth squared her shoulders and said, "I understand, sir."

"No, you don't. You were lucky the last time you went to Wyrd and pushed for more information. You might not be as lucky a second time."

You think I'm not good enough to do this job? I am good enough. And I will find some answers.

Beth balled the paper from her breakfast sandwich and tossed it in the wastebasket. "I'd better get moving if I'm going to catch the next ferry."

"Officer Monkton will drive you to the pier," Forrester said.

"Good luck," Ian whispered as she walked past him and Castelletti.

On the way to the docks, Beth thought about the tone of Captain Forrester's voice and the look on his face. Was he reprimanding her for some reason? Or was he trying to protect her from something he already understood?

38

Rachel cowered at the bottom of the cage, wakened from an uneasy sleep when something huge landed on the top of the cage and began tearing it apart, pulling at the cover that gave her some privacy. Pulling and pulling and . . .

"Faulkner," Lucas Frost said as he walked up to her cage.

"Caw?" A sound that fit the words *"Who, me?"*

"Rahele still needs to be quiet today. Removing the cover isn't being helpful."

The pulling on the cover stopped. The crow looked down at her. "Caw."

Caw to you too, Rachel thought.

The crow pushed something through the bars. It fell, just missing her head.

A berry. Peace offering? Breakfast? Did larks eat berries? How would she know? Why hadn't she ever done any research about larks for one of her novels? Probably because she hadn't considered that a bird could be an active participant in a story.

If she had to spend a few months being around a crow, she might rethink that in terms of a plot.

"Good morning, Rahele," Lucas said.

Rahele. Yes. She needed to start thinking of herself by her new name. She liked the way he said the word—rah-HEEL.

Lucas gave Faulkner a stern look. "Do not pester Rahele today. Go back to your own house—or go outside and play."

When the crow flew off somewhere, Lucas opened the door of Rachel's cage. "He's friendly and curious and wants to help. Surprising, really, when you consider the condition he was in when he arrived here."

Condition? Someone else who had chosen an unusual escape as the only way out of a bad situation?

Lucas disappeared. Rachel walked to the open cage door, moving awkwardly as she adjusted to feet that were shaped very differently from the ones she'd had yesterday. She looked at the floor, which was a long way down. A long way to fall. Did her wings work?

When Lucas returned with a platform on a stand, she twittered at him.

He smiled. "Sorry, Rahele. I don't speak lark." He waited a moment. "I'm going to lift you out of the cage and put you on the platform. Kia will be here in a minute to make sure the places where flesh was harvested are healing properly and to put more salve on those spots."

She had to fight against the instinct to struggle when Lucas picked her up and set her on the platform. His hands were warm—and gentle—but being held usually meant danger. Didn't it? Or was it different for a lark?

Kia walked into the room. "Good morning, Rahele. How are you feeling today?"

Rachel twittered at the Arcana woman.

Kia was efficient in her inspection of the wounds and applying the salve. Then she packed up her first aid kit and said, "A quiet day at home. If everything looks good tomorrow, and you feel a bit adventurous, you can come out on a perch or platform."

Which were high off the ground. She should have asked if there was an instruction manual that came with a new form. Then again, the Arcana didn't know what form she would take, so they couldn't have prepared her for the changes.

Just as Lucas closed his hands around her to lift her back into the cage, Faulkner flew over to the platform. Suddenly Rachel was glad to be inside a nest made from Lucas's hands.

"Faulkner," Lucas warned.

Ignoring the man, Faulkner leaned toward her, holding something red in his beak. A piece of strawberry?

Rachel considered the offering. Birds ate fruits as well as seeds, right? And Lucas was there, so if she took a nibble of the fruit, he'd protect her from the big crow, right?

She stretched her neck out enough to reach the strawberry and take a tentative taste. Different taste. Different taste buds? She had a lot to learn.

She nibbled a little more, then withdrew to the safety of Lucas's hands. He returned her to the cage and secured the door. Then, with a sigh, he moved the platform so that it was in front of her door.

"Do not unlatch her door," Lucas said.

"Caw," Faulkner replied.

"I mean it."

"Caw."

"I won't be far away." Lucas left the room.

Promise or warning? Probably both.

Rachel studied Faulkner. Faulkner studied her. Then he balanced on one foot and stretched a leg and a wing. After a moment, he performed the same move on the other side.

Bird yoga? Rachel watched him do the sequence a second time before trying to imitate the moves. Legs were legs—sort of—but wings instead of arms? She would need to learn how to fly.

Faulkner flew off. He returned a minute later and shoved a raspberry between the bars of the cage, being careful to push it halfway so that it didn't fall into the sand at the bottom of her cage. When he flew away again, he didn't return, but she could hear him cawing somewhere outside.

She nibbled the raspberry and dozed—and thought that having a bird friend who knew where to find the berries might not be a bad thing.

39

Lucas made a quick patrol around the ornamental lake and the area of Destiny Park that was usually seen by visitors. The Arcana who were as still as stone during the daylight hours, and were mistaken for statues, were in their places, keeping watch.

Satisfied that all was as it should be, he entered the pavilion to see if Justine and her sisters had anything to tell him.

They did.

"Trouble is coming from an unexpected source," Zerah said, looking up from her cards.

"Trouble for who?" Lucas asked.

Lysandra turned her sketch pad around for him to see. "The lark and the crow."

Below the sketches of the birds was a sketch of Beth Fahey. "She is the source of that trouble?" Anger washed through him—and disappointment. "I expected better from her."

"She is young and doesn't yet understand what she is," Justine said. "Give her a chance to learn."

Lucas met his wife's eyes, then looked at the scales on her table. "And risk two lives?"

"No." She held out a bone disc that had the number 1 burned into it.

Understanding the decision made by the Ladies Three, Lucas approached Justine's table and took the disc. "When will the young detective arrive?"

Zerah selected another card. "She's already on the water."

"Then I'd better be at the dock to meet her."

Lucas strode out of the pavilion and up the stairs. He paused a moment to rein in his anger. A Sorcerer King's anger—*his anger*—could unleash uncontrolled veins of the strange on the other side of the river. That wasn't something he wanted happening right now. But if Beth Fahey was coming to Wyrd to do harm, she would learn how much a life could be twisted by a limited but *controlled* vein of the strange.

40

Was it a good sign or a bad sign that Lucas Frost was waiting for her when the ferry docked?

"Are you the welcoming committee?" she asked when she reached him.

"That depends on why you're here. This way." Lucas turned and strode up the boardwalk and then along the dirt path that would take them close to the cabins.

"I need to go to the pavilion," Beth said as she trotted to keep up with him.

"No, you don't."

There was a finality to those words that chilled her.

He led her behind the cabins to a set of stairs that ended at a wide woodland path. Following that, he walked for another minute before stopping in an alcove. Beth caught a glimpse of the ornamental lake—a small comfort since she had the unsettling feeling that she could be in another place or time, and Lucas's presence was the only thing keeping her grounded in the here and now.

"Say what you came to say, then leave," Lucas said.

Nothing friendly or tolerant about the words. This was a decree made by a ruler who allowed no challengers. Was this change of attitude the reason Captain Forrester had warned her not to ask about the other women?

"Yesterday, police from several towns along the river investigated some linked and puzzling cases involving missing persons," Beth said, feeling her way as if the words were thinning ice and one mistake might cause her to crash through—and not be able to surface.

Lucas said nothing.

"A woman named Rachel Nightingale called the thirteenth precinct and asked for me. She said there was a man watching her and she was afraid. She abandoned her phone while at a library in King's Hill. Now she is missing." Beth paused to see if there was any reaction from Frost. "People who care about her are worried about her."

"People who truly care about her already know they don't need to worry about her." Lucas's voice held the kind of cold that could burn, but he wasn't unleashing a blast at her. Not yet, anyway.

"Then why doesn't . . . ?" Beth thought about the precision of the words. Thought about a writer doing research on women's shelters and what that might mean beyond a story—and why women usually sought such places. "These people know where she is?"

"No. But they know she is safe—and out of reach of her enemies."

Enemies? "Her fiancé doesn't know where she is."

"As I said. She's out of reach of her enemies."

Beth considered all the things she wanted to know about yesterday's events and realized Frost wouldn't tell her about any of them. Not now. Maybe she could confirm one thing. "You were given the PIN for her phone?"

Frost gave her a look that made Beth feel like she was being dissected. "Rachel Nightingale was here. Now she is gone, and whatever was of interest to her enemies has vanished with her." He waited. "Something else?"

Beth hesitated. Then she opened her purse, took out the missing persons picture of the boy, and held it out to Frost. "Do you know anything about him? He's been missing for several months now. His family . . . They want to find him, bring him home."

Something feral and dangerous suddenly filled the alcove. Something that emanated from Lucas Frost. His voice held the timbre of primeval forests and forbidden places. "I'm sure they do want him back. It's hard to keep secrets hidden behind closed doors if one of the victims escapes."

Beth stared at him. Victims? "Do you know . . . ?"

Frost reached into his jacket pocket, pulled out a bone disc with the number 1 burned into it, and held it out to her. "You owe us three favors. This is the first. You will *never* again ask about Rachel Nightingale or this boy. Not here. If you're required to investigate, keep your investigations confined to the other side of the river. Don't bring them to Wyrd."

"If I can't oblige?"

"Then I will ban you from the Isle of Wyrd and make sure you never reach us again."

"You'll tell the people at the pier not to let me board the ferry?"

"Whether you're allowed on the ferry is the Ferryman's choice. I will make sure you never get beyond the beach, that you never get beyond any part of the island's shore. You will be banned, Beth Fahey, personally and professionally." Frost held out the disc again. "You made a bargain with the Arcana. Do you really want to find out what happens if you break it?"

No, she didn't.

Defeated, Beth took the disc. She folded the picture of the boy and shoved it in her purse. "Rachel Nightingale was afraid and called me for help—and I didn't get there in time." The words were a confession, an apology for overstepping boundaries.

Frost said nothing. Then he huffed out a breath. "Come with me."

He took another route, but in a couple of minutes, they were back in the area of the park within sight of the ornamental lake and the pavilion. Neutral ground. Limited safety—as long as a person obeyed the rules.

Frost didn't head for the entrance to the pavilion. Instead he walked toward what looked like solid walls until he was a few feet away. Then a solid archway became a doorway that led into a big room with windows that let in light and provided a view of the park. A big conference table was on one side of the room. The rest of the room looked like a CEO's office. Expensive. Expansive.

Frost walked to another arched doorway and went into another room. As Beth followed him, something in the doorway seemed to catch hold of her for a moment before letting her through. That *something* caused a momentary disorientation, had her seeing multiple versions of the room—had her almost seeing something so terrible it could break a person's mind. Then the room righted itself, and Lucas Frost watched her.

The room didn't have much in it beyond a square table that held a lot of little square pieces of wood. Did the Arcana play Scrabble? Or was this a similar game specific to Wyrd? She wished she felt brave enough to approach the table and look, but Frost hadn't invited her to explore, and she was on shaky ground with him.

In the next room, there were two large cages. The crow resting on a perch looked at her, cawed what sounded like a warning, hopped into one of the cages, and pulled the door closed.

The brownish bird in the other cage carefully shuffled along a low perch to put as much distance as possible between herself and the humans.

"This is Rahele," Frost said. "She is a lark."

"The herald of the morn," Beth said.

Lucas gave her a quizzical look.

Beth shrugged. "A line from *Romeo and Juliet*, a play by William Shakespeare. The lark is a songbird."

Now there was a dash of amusement in that look. "This play. It's well-known?"

"Yes."

"Ah. That could explain much." Frost studied the lark. "She was wounded but is healing well. In a couple more days, she'll relearn how to fly and be able to explore some of the park." He looked at Beth in a way that captured all her attention. 'Rahele' means 'traveler.'"

A message. Telling her what? To stop worrying, stop probing, because the answer . . .

Beth looked at the lark and felt awed—and chilled. If she understood him correctly, what he had told her was literally correct. Rachel Nightingale had visited Wyrd and now was gone. And Rahele, the traveler . . .

"It's a beautiful park," Beth said. "I'm sure Rahele will enjoy living here."

"We hope so."

She started to look toward the other cage, but stopped herself. If one had been human, could the other . . . ?

"Anything else?" Frost asked.

So many anythings, but she shook her head. "Thank you for your time, Mr. Frost."

"I'll escort you to the dock."

"Is there time to stop at one of the food stands before the next ferry arrives?" She wasn't sure if it was true hunger or anxiety, but she really wanted something to eat.

"There's time."

They walked out of his office, then around to the pavilion's entrance.

"Not a lot of business today," Beth said, noting all the seers who were waiting for customers.

"It's still early," Frost replied. "And you'll notice that the food stands are the ones doing a brisk business now."

Yes, there were plenty of people standing in lines for food and drink.

"That boy who caught your interest," Frost said. "Why him among the missing?"

Beth hesitated, but Frost had asked, and once she boarded the ferry, she would never ask about the boy again. "His eyes looked old and haunted. I just wanted to help him find a happy ending."

"If he were found, death would be his ending."

"You don't know that."

"You forget where you are, Detective. And you are not the only one who paid attention to his eyes." Frost lifted his chin. "If you want something to eat, you should get in line."

He walked away.

Beth bought a steak and cheese sandwich and a mug of hot chocolate. She sat at the end of a picnic table and listened to several women making cheerful plans to have their palms read and their astrological charts done.

The more playful side of Wyrd. But the other side . . .

The nightingale had flown away, leaving behind a lark, a songbird, a herald of the morn.

She had seen a glimpse of the other side of Wyrd.

Now she just had to figure out what she could safely tell Captain Forrester without getting herself banned from this place.

41

Detective Markus Seibert waited by the security desk and wondered how long Martin Chandler, the head of security for Alistair Hampton, would keep him waiting.

Not long, apparently.

The elevator doors opened. Hampton and Chandler strode toward the desk, Hampton one step ahead of his employee.

"You have news about my fiancée?" Hampton demanded.

"No, sir," Markus replied. "I'm here on another matter. Do you employ a man by the name of Jeremy Swayne?"

"He works in security," Chandler replied.

"Do you have any information about his next of kin?"

Chandler stared at him. "Why do you need to know that?"

A head of security should know exactly why a cop was asking, but Markus replied as if such a notification had never happened before. "I regret to inform you that Jeremy Swayne was killed. Some personal items were found near the river, along with a blood trail leading to the water."

"That's nonsense!" Hampton shouted. "An acquaintance saw Swayne boarding the river bus. There must be a mistake."

"There's no mistake. We identified remains through fingerprints that were on file." Markus took a small notebook and pen out of his pocket. "Has Swayne reported to work or contacted you since that sighting?"

"No," Chandler said, glancing at Hampton. "We haven't heard from him."

Markus nodded. "Which acquaintance saw him? And where? That could give us more information about where he died."

"Are you sure he's dead?" Chandler said.

"Not one hundred percent sure, no. However, his hands were secured to a piece of driftwood. They were retrieved by a patrol boat that was traveling through Susurration Sound. Considering the depth of the sound, it's unlikely that we'll find the rest of him."

"What about the women who were with Rachel Nightingale?" Chandler asked. "Do you have any information about them?"

"We've identified three out of the four women who allegedly were with Rachel Nightingale that morning," Markus said.

"Allegedly?" Hampton's face turned red with fury. "*Allegedly?* They were *seen*."

"Women with similar looks were seen," Markus countered. "Women who might have had a reason to impersonate individuals who had been dead for several days. The bodies were found at the Jackson marina that same morning, so the women we identified *couldn't* have been the ones who entered the apartment with Rachel Nightingale."

Hampton swore savagely. "It's that damn island. It has to be. We should bomb the whole fucking place and be done with it."

A classmate of Markus's had said the same thing once during a class at the academy years ago. The instructor had smiled and said, "The Hydra was a monster with many heads, and it had the ability to grow a new one if a head was cut off. The places that are a convergence of the uncanny are like the Hydra—you might think you can destroy one of them, but the uncanny just retreats and emerges somewhere else, and those places and what lives there are very dangerous when attacked. You can't kill the uncanny, gentlemen; you can only make it angry. And if it is angry, it will come after you—and the strange will absorb your life."

Markus looked at Chandler. "Swayne's next of kin?"

Chandler met his look, then nodded. "I'll get it for you."

"If Swayne is gone, that's regrettable," Hampton said when Chandler left to fetch the information. "But you damn well better put more effort into finding Rachel before you come back here asking for *her* next of kin."

Hampton stormed out of the building.

When Chandler returned, Markus thanked him for the information and turned to leave.

"You don't think you'll find her, do you?" Chandler asked.

Markus considered the question—and wondered if the Penwych detective going to Wyrd this morning would have an answer. For now, he said, "Until there is a body, there is always hope."

He walked out of the building. As he told Hampton and Chandler, three of the women who were with Rachel Nightingale that morning had been identified. The fourth woman was still a mystery.

He thought it was safer for all of them if she remained that way.

42

Charles Forrester studied Beth Fahey's pale face and asked the question that would have the most impact on his team. "Were you banned from going back to Wyrd?"

She looked startled—and scared.

"You wouldn't be the first, but if that's what happened, you'll need to put in a request to transfer to another team, either in Penwych or another town. I need people who can cross the river, Detective. Last year, there were four detectives on the team, but one man transferred to another precinct after an incident on the island. The other man is still on medical leave because he saw something that scared him so much, he hid under his desk for three days, crying. Even if he comes back to work, he'll never come back to the team. So I need to know if you no longer have the ability to cross the river."

"I wasn't banned," Fahey said. "But I was warned, and I'm forbidden to ask questions about some things."

"You pushed too hard." Charles let some of his frustration and anger show. "I warned you."

"Yes, sir." Fahey looked at the floor.

"Are you allowed to tell me what Lucas Frost said about Rachel Nightingale?"

She frowned and seemed to be sorting what she knew before deciding what she could say. "Rachel Nightingale had gone to Wyrd, and she did give her phone's PIN to Mr. Frost. She is gone now and not expected to return."

Charles blew out a breath. "I suppose we should inform her next of kin that she is officially considered missing."

"Mr. Frost." Fahey cleared her throat. "Mr. Frost said that those who truly care about her already know they don't have to worry about her."

Charles parsed that statement. Rachel Nightingale had disappeared by choice, and the people who mattered to her had been informed of her decision. They probably didn't know where she was or how to contact her directly—a man like Alistair Hampton could twist that information out of them—but someone would have the authority to handle Nightingale's intellectual property and the royalties generated from it. He'd bet a month's pay that whoever it was, that someone lived on the Isle of Wyrd.

"Did you ask about the other women? Is that why you were warned off?"

Fahey shook her head. "I didn't ask about them, but . . ." She withdrew a folded sheet of paper from her purse, opened it, and held it out. "I asked about him. That's when Mr. Frost became seriously angry."

With good reason. "Did you read the whole file before you made that inquiry?" Charles asked. "Did you pay attention to the medical part of that file?"

Stan Wozniak had sat in this office a few months ago and wrestled with a question—and wondered if he could live with the answer as a father, a cop, and a man.

"Clumsy? That kid isn't clumsy, Charles. Look at his medical file. Look at those burns!"

"Stan? Are you just venting, or are you asking for a favor?"

"If the kid is on this side of the river, I have to try to find him before he becomes another statistic. But if he got across the river, if he's somewhere . . . safe . . . or as close to safe as you can get, I'll go through the motions of looking for him."

Stan Wozniak was a good man and as solid and practical as they came. He had crossed the river once a few years ago—and he barely made it out of the pavilion before something unnerved him so badly he turned around and stayed at the dock until the ferry loaded for the return trip.

As a favor to Stan, Charles had crossed the river and asked the question about the boy.

"We don't need to find him if he's safe," he'd said.

And Lucas Frost had replied, "He's safe."

Charles stared at his young detective. The Arcana had taken an interest in her, had told her too much on her first visit to Wyrd. He didn't want to lose her, so he hoped she would understand the seriousness of Frost's warning. "Did you read the boy's medical file?"

"No, sir."

"I did. So did Captain Wozniak. That's why we know he's better off wherever he is. Do you understand?"

She hesitated before nodding.

"Write up your report with the information provided about Rachel Nightingale. Don't mention the boy."

Another hesitation. "I might know more about Ms. Nightingale, but I don't think I'm allowed to tell anyone."

"Then leave speculation out of the report." Now he hesitated, but it had to be said. "If your actions bring harm to someone under the Arcana's protection, they will come after you."

She turned away from his desk, then stopped. Not looking at him, she asked, "Do you ever get scared when you cross the river?"

"Every time," he replied. Then he added silently, *But I make the trip because I can, and there are many good cops who can't.*

When Fahey left his office and closed the door, Charles sat back and rubbed his hands over his face. He'd promised Colin that they would go to Wyrd and have a look around soon. One problem with taking a teenager on that ferry right now was Darren Palmer's father doing everything he could to stir up the people in Penwych—demanding that the ferry be shut down; demanding that the people running the ferry refuse passage to anyone under eighteen; demanding that the Penwych police create a barricade and turn away anyone underage who was trying to get on the ferry; demanding compensation for the death of his son. Demanding, demanding, demanding at any public forum, pushing his way in front of news cameras, trying to stir up a mob mentality.

So far, Edwena Bang, the mayor of Penwych, had held firm in her responses to Palmer's demands. The ferry was privately owned, as were the land and pier. Government officials couldn't shut it down. While the people running the ferry could refuse to provide passage to anyone, they were not obliged to turn away someone because of that person's age.

Finally pushed too far when she was leaving her office, Mayor Bang looked at Palmer and the news reporters surrounding him and said that parents were responsible for supervising their own children and shouldn't blame others if childish rebellions ended in tragedy.

That statement probably would cost her some votes in the next election, but it also probably saved the town from a hellish response.

That sailing ship might be a ghost ship, but the cannonballs fired from the guns were real enough when they hit anything on this side of the river.

Maybe he shouldn't have brought Darren Palmer's remains back across the river—especially in the shape they were in. Maybe he should have let people think that Ted Ocampo had killed a bully and then made up the bizarre story about a rat-faced chicken to explain returning alone—or to set himself up with an insanity plea when the body was found.

Ted didn't deserve to be labeled crazy, and Darren Palmer's family deserved the closure of having something to bury, even if there wasn't much left to the boy.

Don't stir up the Arcana, Mr. Palmer, Charles thought. *Just grieve for your boy and stop drawing attention to yourself. That kind of attention will only bring harm to everything it touches. It always does.*

OCTOBER

43

Rachel worked on strengthening her flight muscles. If she'd put in this much effort at the fitness center toward building up her shoulders and pecs, she would have looked like the Hulk's girlfriend. Only she wouldn't be green.

Her reward for such diligence was practicing her wing flapping on a low perch close to her cage.

"Think of it as training wheels," Lucas said when he encouraged her to let go of the death grip she had on his finger and step on the perch. "This perch is low enough to the ground that if you lose your grip, you won't fall far enough to hurt yourself—and you won't fly so high or fast if you do take off that you'll hit a wall or a window."

Yeah. Right. *Jumping off a cliff is perfectly safe. You probably don't even need that parachute.*

She wished Lucas could sell the idea a little better. And sure, the perch being low to the ground was a good thing—much better than having a parent bird shove you out of the nest or off a cliff face to encourage that first flight—but being this close to the floor, would anyone notice her before they stepped on her?

"I'm going to close the door between this room and my office," Lucas said. "We might have some visitors I'll need to see, and it would be better if they didn't see you or Faulkner."

She twittered at him.

"You'll be safe, Rahele." Lucas left the room and closed the door.

She trusted him, trusted the Arcana, so she would believe she was safe. She didn't have a mama bird or papa bird pushing her out of the nest before she was ready to fly.

But she did have Faulkner, who sashayed across the floor as only a crow could do. He stopped beside the perch and stretched his neck toward her.

What was dangling from his beak?

The dangling thing wiggled.

Twittering wildly, Rachel flapped her wings and forgot to hold on to the perch. She landed a few feet away.

Faulkner moved toward her.

Rachel tried again, flapping her wings furiously and flying a few more feet while she twittered for help. *Lucas, Lucas, Lucas!*

The door eased open just enough for Lucas to look around.

"You're flying," he said. "Well done." Then he looked at the crow. "Faulkner, I don't think Rahele is ready to eat a piece of worm."

Rachel flapped her wings and twittered to make sure both males understood that Rahele was *definitely* not ready to eat a piece of worm, that Rahele was *never* going to be ready to eat a worm or *any* kind of insect or crawly thing that other larks might choose to eat. Rahele was going to be a vegetarian lark.

But after she'd managed to get herself back on the perch and Lucas had gone back to his office, she watched Faulkner eat the worm—and her writer's brain, for one tiny moment, wondered what a worm tasted like.

44

After exchanging money for the coins used in Wyrd, Charles and Colin Forrester boarded the ferry and paid their fare. Colin chose to ride inside and slid into one of the seats midway up the cabin. Charles settled into the aisle seat next to his son.

Colin leaned against him and whispered, "Is the person who exchanged the money and told us the fare . . . ?"

Male or female? That was the boy's question. "I don't know," Charles replied.

"Why did . . . the person . . . ask if you were taking the ferry for personal reasons or for the police?"

"When we go over on police business, the fare is usually a silver coin."

Colin stared at him. "They charged you more because you're off duty?"

"Shh." The sound came out sharper than he'd intended, but you could never tell who might be sitting behind you or walking up the aisle and would overhear something best left unsaid. "The fees for some things have a set price, while the fees for other things, like the fare to ride the ferry, are flexible. You either pay the fee or you walk away."

"But that was ten dollars for each of us. Seems like a lot for a short ride."

A ride that can take a few minutes. Or a day. Or a year. Or forever.

A woman wearing enough perfume to make Charles's eyes water hesitated at the seat in front of him. He'd noticed her at the dock when she gave him a flirtatious smile, which he didn't return. He'd been standing behind Colin, letting the boy make his own exchange of money for coins, so the woman hadn't seen the boy—or hadn't realized they were together.

Now she looked at Colin's skin tone. It could have been a light tan that was the result of being out in the sun during the summer, but it wasn't.

The woman's face froze, and the look she gave Charles was no longer flirtatious. She deliberately went up two rows of seats before sitting down.

Another woman slipped into the seat in front of them and turned to look at them.

Charles felt a jolt of recognition. This was the unidentified woman who had accompanied one of the Nightingales to a bank. Sitting this close to her, there was no denying that she was Arcana. There was something about them that was unmistakable once you understood why a person made you feel like prey.

"It's fortunate that she didn't sit here," the woman said. "She's doused in so much scent you'd be hanging over the side of the ferry, gasping for breathable air, by the time we were halfway across the river."

She wasn't speaking in a loud voice, but her words carried.

The perfumed woman twisted in her seat. "You have some objection to my perfume?"

"Every living thing has an objection to your perfume." The Arcana smiled at the woman. It wasn't a nice smile. "They'll make you wash it off before they let you into the pavilion. But you already know that since this isn't your first trip across the river. Just like you know that the hotel won't let you in smelling that way, so your choice will be the public restrooms or the river."

"I don't need this crap." The perfumed woman stomped toward the back of the ferry, shoving aside people who were trying to enter the cabin. She gave Charles a particularly venomous look as she passed his seat.

"Why is she mad at you?" Colin asked, remembering to keep his voice down.

"He didn't defend her entitled right to asphyxiate the rest of us," the Arcana said cheerfully. She turned in her seat, opened her tote bag, and pulled out a paperback—a novel written by Rachel Nightingale.

Charles felt chilled. Coincidence? Or was she deliberately mocking him? Or offering him an opening to ask a question? She knew who he was; he was sure of it.

He thought about all the things he couldn't ask this Arcana woman, especially in a public place like the ferry—and he considered the one thing he could ask. As the ferry left the dock and started across the river, Charles leaned forward. "I heard that the people who truly care about her know she's safe."

No names, no specifics. None were needed. They both knew who he was asking about.

"Then you heard truth," the Arcana said quietly.

He would be satisfied with that.

Colin wondered what he was missing. Destiny Park was nice enough, with all the beds of flowers, the meandering paths that were sheltered by trees, and the little bridges that went over tiny creeks that spilled into pools of water; but it wasn't strange or scary. Okay, one of the statues in the ornamental lake had a spooky vibe, since the woman looked like she'd been locked in an underwater cave for years and years, wasting away but not dying and now finally reaching the surface to exact revenge on . . . Well, he wasn't sure, but if she was in a computer game, she would be one of the monsters you had to beat to escape and return home with the treasure.

In fact, all the statues gave him the willies because they seemed so real, like they might shift position any minute now or get up and go on a coffee break.

The truth was, the Isle of Wyrd and Destiny Park seemed a bit lame. A bit tame. At least the part Dad was willing to let him see. Looking for a moon gate was a big *no.* If it wasn't for what happened to Ted Ocampo and Darren Palmer, he'd follow Dad around for a while before campaigning to visit the food stands, which had looked pretty awesome. But Darren had died in some kind of weird-ass way, and Ted was still so freaked out, he was being homeschooled this year. Colin wasn't sure if that decision was because of Wyrd or because Darren's pack of bullyboys was blaming Ted for Darren doing something stupid and wanted some put-you-in-the-hospital kind of payback.

Colin and Dad returned to the area around the ornamental lake. He didn't know who to ask about finding the weird in Wyrd. Not Dad, who had been looking a little pale since he'd talked to that woman on the ferry.

Wyrd feels a bit tame? Then reframe. That's what Mom would have said.

He looked at the pavilion and the area around the lake. On an alien planet, this would be the safe place for visitors and diplomats to meet the native people, to sample some of the local foods, to participate in some activity as a gesture of goodwill. That's what Captain Picard would have done if he was leading a mission to meet a race that the crew of the *Enterprise* hadn't encountered before. Maybe the Arcana disguised themselves in some way until they decided the visitors could be trusted.

Was that what had spooked Dad about that woman on the ferry? Had he realized she was one of the Arcana?

Colin glanced at his father, who seemed lost in thought, before wandering over to the lake. The stonework that contained the water was waist high on him—a height that probably kept most kids from falling in or thinking it was meant to be a wading pool.

He leaned over, studying the water. So dark. Most ornamental ponds or lakes that he'd seen had the bottom painted a light color or a bright blue to make the water look pretty or to reflect the sky. This one?

"I wonder how deep it is," Colin said, feeling someone approaching on one side while Dad hurried up to him on the other side.

He looked up and . . . Whoa! When he'd approached the lake, the scary statue had been staring straight ahead. Now her face was turned toward him, and she was staring straight at him. How . . . ?

"That depends on which part of the lake you're measuring."

It took him a moment to look away from the scary woman's eyes and realize someone had answered his question. He turned away from the lake toward the man standing a few feet away—a man who looked ordinary, but the voice scratched at some primal memory, and if that man suddenly turned into a dragon or some other mythical beast, Colin would not have been surprised.

Dad might think he was foolish, but he was certain he'd just met one of the Arcana.

"Captain Forrester," the man said, sounding polite.

"Mr. Frost," Dad replied, sounding wary.

Frost looked at Colin. "The lake around the winged woman's fountain is a foot deeper than the retaining wall that is aboveground. The same is true for the other end of the lake, where the Guide of the Drowned rises out of the water and lights the way home for those lost at sea."

Colin shivered. Maybe it was Mr. Frost's voice, but he was almost ready to believe that scary woman holding a lantern *could* guide the drowned to the shore. "And the middle of the lake?"

"Ah, that's the mystery. It's said that the middle of this lake is so deep, it connects with Susurration Sound through an underground river, and at night you can hear the dead whispering a last message to the living." Frost smiled. "But no one is in the park after dark, so that's just a tale people like to tell."

Was it just a tale? Things weren't feeling quite so lame or so tame anymore.

"Have you visited any of the seers in the pavilion?" Frost asked.

Colin stopped himself from rolling his eyes. "Having someone read my palm and tell me I'll meet a tall dark stranger? Not really my thing."

"Colin." Dad's voice held the same warning as the time the family had been on vacation and Colin had almost stepped on a rattlesnake.

"I was thinking more of asking someone to read your cards," Frost said.

"Why?" Dad asked.

Frost looked at Colin, then at Dad. "Because knowledge can be the key to survival." He reached into his jacket pocket and handed Colin a disc. "No need to see the Ladies Three for this. Either of the readers on the other side of the pavilion can tell you enough, but I recommend Katherine Rose for this reading."

Frost gave them a nod and walked away.

Colin looked at the disc in his hand and felt like he was riding the craziest roller coaster on the planet. "What just happened?"

"Wyrd happened," Dad replied quietly. "Wyrd is about choosing your own fate—or trying to change it by having another choice revealed. The disc—and the suggestion—were given to you, so you have to decide for yourself about having the cards read."

"Is that guy one of the Arcana?"

"Yes. He's someone who never should be taken lightly."

"If he'd given the disc to you?"

Dad looked pale—and worried. "I would ask the woman Mr. Frost recommended to read the cards—and I would pay attention to what she said."

Charles accepted the mug of black coffee and took the chit that would give him another drink at that food stand. Two drinks for a silver coin. Two sandwiches for a gold coin. Simple math. No change required.

"You're worried?"

Charles turned and studied Lucas Frost. "You don't make idle suggestions, so yes, I'm worried about what the cards will tell my son."

"People come here all the time and have the cards read to show them possibilities," Frost said. "Some actually pay attention to that information and recognize when a particular moment of choice appears. Others, knowing a possibility might happen, step aside early enough that it never happens. And most are entertained by what is said here and never think about the words until the next time they cross the river—or until fate reveals itself. Will your son pay attention or shrug off what is said? His choice."

"Yes," Charles said. "His choice."

Colin thought it was kind of creepy the way Katherine Rose stared at him while she shuffled her deck of cards. It was like she was trying to see inside his head—or his heart.

Then she looked down and turned over the first card.

Mom had a friend who read tarot, so he'd seen a couple of the decks.

This deck didn't look like those. Then again, all he'd seen was the first card, which was a man kneeling with his head bowed. A hooded man with an ax stood beside him, and a young woman, flanked by soldiers, was hiding her face in her hands, as if she couldn't bear to watch what was going to happen.

"You will make a sacrifice to save someone close to you," Katherine Rose said. The next card revealed a moon gate. "That sacrifice may open up the opportunity to make a journey and escape your enemies." She tapped the moon gate's keystone. "Words have power. Pay attention to what the gate reveals before you choose."

The next card showed six men standing in a group, holding weapons, while the seventh man stood apart, unarmed. "Six enemies," she said. "Difficult odds, but you can prevail if you think—and remember."

"Words have power," Colin murmured.

"Yes."

The next card showed a man adrift in the sea, clinging to a piece of wood while sharks circled him. "Avoid the water—and the ship. You would not return from that journey."

"I came on the ferry with my dad," Colin protested. "You mean I can't get back home?"

She turned another card, which revealed a sailing ship. A real beauty. The kind of ship he wouldn't mind crewing for a summer. "Avoid this ship if you want to return home."

"Will this happen soon?"

She turned another card and shook her head. "After the next equinox."

Colin frowned at the card. The equinoxes were in the fall and spring, right? "So nothing will happen until spring?"

"The ferry will stop running at the end of the month. The park will be closed to visitors from across the river. Nothing I've seen will happen until the ferry is running again."

She turned the last card. It was a picture of a place. Not somewhere he recognized. Mountains in the background. What looked like a trading post in the foreground. "A safe possibility—if you remember."

Colin thanked her for the reading and left the pavilion to meet up with Dad at the food stands.

"You okay?" Dad asked.

"Yeah. It was interesting." Colin looked at the menu boards on the sides of the food stands.

"See anything you like?"

"Lots of things. I'm starving." He wasn't, but he knew saying it would amuse Dad and maybe get that worried look out of Dad's eyes.

"Then let's sample a few things before we head home."

Home sounded really good right now.

They ordered a couple of different sandwiches and split them to see which one they liked best. Colin ate more than his share of the order of fries, but Dad didn't notice. Well, they were superior fries, thick enough to have a crispy outside and still be tender inside.

Dad didn't say much on the way home, just gave him a long look a couple of times, as if he *wanted* to say something but didn't quite dare.

That was okay. There was a lot to think about. He hadn't thought to ask if he could use the camera on his phone to take a picture of the cards to help him remember. Probably wasn't allowed. Still, the one that he kept puzzling over was the last card. You would think a trading post would have some kind of sign for its name, but the only identification above the doorway was a hoofprint.

45

Rachel reviewed her personal to-do list. Feathers preened? Check. Breakfast seeds consumed? Check. Short flights around the room once Lucas Frost helped her down to the lower perch? Check.

Rachel fluffed her feathers and wondered what ordinary birds did with the rest of their day. Or were they content with preen, eat, and repeat?

And what was Faulkner doing in the room beyond the "bird room"? Based on the sounds, he was involved in *something*. Maybe he'd found some toys that a lark could play with too?

Rachel flutter-jumped to the floor and focused on not stepping on her own feet while she moved to where she could see some of the room beyond—the room that might have interesting things to do.

Faulkner was up on a wooden table, busy arranging objects that made a clacking sound. Wooden objects?

She walked up to the table. He paid no attention to her, which was unusual. She could have twittered at him to get his attention, but he probably would come down to the floor, and she wanted to see what he was doing.

The table was too high for her to reach with her current flying skills, but the chair, which was pulled away from the table, was about the same height as the low perch. She flew up to the chair seat, got herself repositioned to face the table, then flew up to the tabletop.

Faulkner was arranging little squares of wood that had letters and symbols. Like a Scrabble game, but it was obvious that these wooden pieces were handmade. Was this meant to teach birds human words, or was it intended as a way for birds to communicate with the Arcana?

Rachel focused on the message Faulkner had been forming.

FAULKNER

AND BIRD

ARE HUNGRY.

Rachel twittered loudly. Faulkner and bird? *Bird?* She wasn't *bird.* She had a name too!

Continuing to twitter loudly, Rachel knocked the *b-i-r-d* off to the side and found the letters she needed, while Faulkner moved out of her way, doing his best imitation of chastened crow.

r-a-h-e-e-l. Not bird!

Ashley Laxton walked into the room. "What's going on in here?"

Rachel twittered at her. Faulkner preened a wing feather.

Ashley looked at the message, then rearranged the *e* and *l.* "You had those two letters mixed up."

r-a-h-e-l-e. Yes. Much better.

"Wait there." Ashley walked out of the room.

"Caw," Faulkner said.

He sounded pretty pleased with himself, and Rachel had the sudden suspicion that he'd done this to show her that the bird room wasn't the only safe place.

Lucas Frost set aside the reports he was reviewing and decided to eat the hamburger and fries before they got cold.

There were signs of malice and danger across the river, but nothing had risen close enough to the surface for the Ladies Three to detect the source—probably because there was more than one source. Since the Arcana were about to close the park to visitors from across the river, the danger would stay across the river for a few months. But eventually, it would touch Wyrd, and Wyrd—and its Sorcerer King—would respond.

Ashley walked back into the room and opened a door in the credenza that filled a short wall in his office.

"What's going on in there?" he asked, using a fry to point to the room the Arcana called the playroom.

Holding a small plate, Ashley walked up to his desk, took a fry from his plate, and cut the fry in half. "Faulkner says he and Rahele are hungry."

Lucas looked at the fry. "Do larks eat fries?"

"I don't know, but crows do."

Lucas sighed. "Before Faulkner leads her into trouble, would you do some research about larks and find out what is safe for her to eat and what isn't?"

"Sure."

It was the way she grinned when she said it that made him wonder how much she already knew.

Ashley Laxton set the plate on the table and said, "Crows eat a lot of things that aren't typical foods for larks, so go easy until you know how your innards will react. You are a lark, but you're not just a lark. You have to remember which body you're in, and that it might react in ways you don't expect."

She returned to the other room.

Faulkner tore open one half of the fry, paused, then tore open the other half.

A steak fry, thick enough that it had a crisp outside with a soft middle. It had been her favorite kind of potato before . . . Before she allowed her life to be stolen by Alistair Hampton.

She waited, watching Faulkner. They couldn't blow on the fry to cool it enough to eat, but there had to be a clue for when it was edible.

Finally, Faulkner pulled off a bit of the outside of his half of the fry and ate it. "Caw."

Good enough. She happily tore into her share.

When they had eaten as much as they could, Faulkner arranged more letters.

FRY GOOD?

Rachel pushed aside the question mark and pushed a period in its place. She twittered softly.

FRY GOOD.

46

Albert Palmer poured the last shot of whiskey into his glass and swore. He told the wife to pick up another bottle, but what did the bitch do? Bought *food* for herself and that useless female brat. It would have been different if Darren was still here. The boy did need to eat, after all. But Darren was gone, and what that bastard Forrester brought back in a box and *garbage bag*! Police tests confirmed that the torn-up mess in the box was, in fact, what was left of Darren.

The boy had just been having a little fun, and *this* happened to him? It was that place across the river. Strange shit happened because of that place and the freaks who lived there.

How would Forrester feel if the freaks did something like that to *his* boy?

Palmer downed the last shot and let the thought simmer for a minute.

How *would* Forrester feel if the same thing happened to *his* son?

The ferry made its last trip across the river today, so it was too late to do anything until spring. But he could keep things stirred up over the winter, keep people remembering what was done to his boy and who was to blame.

In the spring? If he gave Darren's friends enough cash and got them stirred up for some payback, they would take the Forrester boy across the river—and make sure that what happened to Darren happened again.

PART THREE

BEGINNINGS AND ENDINGS

MARCH

1

As he did at this time every year, Charles Forrester called a meeting and waited while his team, including Officers Monkton and Reynolds, gathered around the big evidence table. November through February was the slow time for his team. There were still odd occurrences that were investigated in the six towns along the Fate River, and those occurrences might have had a touch of the strange. The uncanny didn't stop flowing through the world, after all. But Destiny Park was closed during those months—at least to visitors from the human towns—so the more serious, and frightening, encounters with the strange didn't happen over the winter. Now?

"We're past the spring equinox," Charles said. "The Penwych patrol boat reported seeing the Isle of Wyrd's ferry. Destiny Park and the pavilion open for visitors on the last week in March."

"So weird shit will start happening again," Castelletti said.

"It didn't stop happening this year," Kuhn said.

Charles glanced at Beth Fahey, who looked pale and didn't offer an opinion. He focused on the men. "Albert Palmer has been trying to stir up people for months, blaming the Arcana for his son's death. As soon as the ferry starts running again, I think he'll try to ramp up his efforts to get people to see the Arcana as an enemy to be eliminated—or isolated."

"*Can* the Arcana be isolated?" Fahey asked.

"It's doubtful," Charles replied. "People think the only way on or off the island is by boat. That's true for us." *Unless a person is very unlucky.* "It's not true for the Arcana. They don't need the visitors who come for entertainment or come to stay at the hotel. And people who go to Wyrd for other reasons will find a way to cross the river and make a bargain with the Arcana." He looked at each member of his team. "I think Albert Palmer is building up to something. Maybe a confrontation between his supporters and the visitors waiting at the pier for the ferry. We don't want Palmer's actions to embroil the whole town in an unfortunate incident, so stay alert and keep me informed of any information that might be passed along from other precincts."

He waited until Monkton and Reynolds left to resume their patrol and Kuhn and Castelletti returned to their desks. Then he said, "Fahey," and went into his office.

She followed.

"Rough night?" he asked. Fahey had been working for him for several months now. She was good at the job, but she was having a hard time fitting in. He didn't think she was a loner by nature; she just couldn't quite manage a social life. She tried, but something always seemed to get in the way. "Don't think giving me an answer is optional."

She stared at his desk. Finally, she said, "My parents disappeared when I was young, and I ended up staying with Bonnie Wilson, who was the neighbor next door. Someone paid her to look after me, so she wasn't letting me live with her out of the goodness of her heart. I stayed with Bonnie until I turned eighteen and graduated from high school. When I left, the money for my room and board stopped. I received a lump sum from that unknown source, which I spent on my education and a place to live while I was in college and attending the police academy.

"Bonnie has been a gambling addict for as long as I've known her. Even now, whenever she's pinched for money and owes the casinos, she'll call and use her combination of verbal abuse and threats to try to get me to send her money."

"Do you send her money?" Charles asked.

Beth shook her head. "I tell her I don't have any money, which is true. I have some savings as an emergency fund, but nothing close to what she wants."

Charles rested a hip on the corner of his desk. "You stayed with this woman all the years you were growing up? What about child protection services? Someone must have known your parents were missing."

Beth shook her head again. "Teachers seemed to think that Bonnie was an unofficial foster parent or a relative who had an arrangement with my parents. No one asked questions. I didn't truly appreciate how odd that was until I went to the police academy."

"She called last night? Wanting money?"

"Yes, she did. I said no."

"Does she threaten you, Beth? Because threatening a cop . . ." He let the sentence go unfinished.

"Not physical threats. Verbal poison, said with conviction. She just says things that people already want to believe. I haven't seen anyone who can successfully fight against that." She didn't quite look him in the eyes before she took a step back. "Sir."

Charles watched her walk out of his office before turning and sitting at his desk.

If Bonnie Wilson was telling tales about Beth, maybe that explained some of the isolation he sensed around his detective. But if Wilson didn't live in Penwych, that meant someone was keeping track of Fahey and supplying Wilson with information. A private investigator? Maybe. A couple of them had been making the rounds during the winter, asking about Rachel Nightingale. Or was one of those investigators using Nightingale as an excuse to hang around the 13th precinct and find someone willing to gossip about the cops on the special team?

However the information was being funneled to Bonnie Wilson, that wasn't his biggest concern. A child living with a neighbor for years and no one asking questions? He could think of one reason why no one had asked questions about Beth Fahey while she was growing up, and that made him wonder just how long the Arcana had been interested in her—and why.

2

As Beth turned the key in her apartment door's lock, the door across the hall opened.

"Hi, Mrs. Myers. How are you?"

"I'm fine, dear," Mrs. Myers replied. "A package came for you today. You weren't home, so I signed for it. Just a minute. I'll fetch it."

Beth unlocked the door and pushed it open. She hadn't ordered anything from a catalog or done any online shopping, so she couldn't imagine why she would be getting a package.

"Here you go." Mrs. Myers handed her a small box from a place called Medicine Magic & Specialty Teas.

"Thanks, Mrs. Myers."

Mrs. Myers smiled, as if waiting for some comment about the package. When Beth said nothing, the older woman wished her a good evening, went into her own apartment, and closed the door.

Beth entered her apartment and locked the door. Setting the package on her small kitchen table, she studied the return address. Then she turned on her laptop and did a search for Medicine Magic & Specialty Teas—and found no company with that exact name. And the return address? She couldn't find that either.

She carefully opened the package, making sure to save the return address, and found a small cardboard box inside. That box held three tea bags in separate containers that were numbered 1, 2, 3.

The instructions were specific. Use the teas in the numbered order to provide clarity in dreams and to access family memories.

A shiver ran down Beth's spine.

The only other thing in the box was a business card of sorts. No company. Not even a person's name. Just the letters *AdW*, like a person's initials. Like the person with those initials had no need for any other kind of identification.

On the other side of the card was a handwritten message: *These teas will not harm you.*

Maybe. Maybe not.

She stared at her cell phone for a minute, trying to decide which authority she should call for insights and information. Finally, she selected a phone number from her contacts list—a number that was on the special team's "need to know" list.

"Frost."

She hadn't heard his voice in months, but it was a voice a person wouldn't forget. "This is Beth Fahey. I wondered if you had heard of a company called Medicine Magic and Specialty Teas."

A long silence. "Why?"

"I was sent a package that held three tea bags and a set of instructions to drink them in a particular order."

"Was there anything else in the package?"

"A business card with the initials *AdW* and a note on the back that said the teas wouldn't harm me."

Another long silence. "Instructions that come from such a place are meant to be followed exactly. If you do that, you will come to no harm."

Beth hesitated, then said the words. "Is that a promise?"

"If that's the word you prefer, consider it a promise between you and the one who sent the package. He doesn't break a promise—and no one breaks a promise with *him*."

Her breath caught. "You know who this is?"

"Good night, Detective Fahey." He ended the call.

Beth set her cell phone on the table and blew out a breath. The package came from one of the Arcana? Probably, since Lucas Frost recognized whoever only needed to put his initials on a card for other Arcana to know who he was.

How long had the Arcana been aware of her? And why? Not Lucas Frost. He hadn't known anything about her until she went across the river to ask about a ghost gun. But had one of the Arcana taken an interest in her since she was a little girl? Why?

Beth looked at the package. Clarity in dreams.

Maybe.

No longer interested in dinner, she heated the water in the teakettle, then poured the water over the first tea bag. She steeped it for exactly the required time. Settling in to a comfortable chair in her living room, she slowly drank the tea.

The woman sat on a tree stump in a glade that had never been touched by a human hand, sketching something just out of the dreamer's sight. Something that made her smile.

Birds sang. Leaves sang their own kind of song when stirred by a breeze. A peaceful afternoon.

The woman put away her pencils and said, "Maxie, it's time to go."

A little girl rushed over to the woman. "Can I see your picture, Mama?"

"Of course you can."

And the dreamer, looking over their shoulders, saw a drawing of a mother and daughter—the mother sketching while the daughter danced with butterflies. Beneath the drawing were the names Maxine and Arianna Greenwood.

Beth woke with a start. Then she bolted into her bedroom and pulled out the box that held her fantasy art. That held the sketchbook. She'd looked at those sketches so many times, but . . .

No. That drawing wasn't among the sketches, but *some* of those sketches had a stylized *A* where the artist's name would be. A stylized *A* that matched the *A* in "Arianna."

Beth recognized Maxine Greenwood's name, but it couldn't be the same person. Could it? If the Maxine Greenwood who gave birth to her really was Arcana . . .

Was that the reason the Arcana were interested in *her*?

APRIL

3

Colin Forrester opened his locker to swap out a couple of books. One more class, then swim practice.

Over the winter, he'd been able to push that strange encounter with the card-reading woman aside and pretend everything was normal. It wasn't normal. Cops from the 12th precinct strolled through the school's halls at random times, paying attention to any physical scuffles between students—and paying special attention to the bullyboys who still called themselves Dare's Doggs as a tribute to their deceased leader.

He'd never been on the receiving end of the Doggs' bullying, probably because, unlike Ted Ocampo and the Doggs' other victims, he'd made it clear the only time Darren Palmer tried to push him that he would put up such a fight they would both end up in the emergency room—or in jail.

Now?

A few days ago, he heard a couple of girls talking about Destiny Park being open to visitors again, and he remembered the woman telling him that whatever was going to happen would happen after the spring equinox. A few days ago, Dare's Doggs began bumping into him in the halls, began saying things like "Your time is coming." Maybe he should have mentioned that to Dad or to one of the cops in the 12th precinct when they did a random check, but despite several talks in classrooms over the past few months about what constituted bullying, he wasn't sure shoulder bumps and a few words counted as bullying, since he'd felt annoyed rather than threatened.

Dad would probably have a few things to say about *that.*

But today he felt uneasy because something was going on. Dare's Doggs hadn't approached him, hadn't said a thing to him, but they'd been giving him the eye all day, following him between classes. That couldn't be good. He'd talk to the coach about the Doggs watching him. The coach would understand and make sure Colin wasn't alone in the locker room after swim practice, and Dad would tell him that smart beat bravado every time.

He felt someone come up behind him as he closed his locker. Felt something jammed under his ribs hard enough that he didn't dare take a deep breath. Not a knife. Didn't feel right to be a knife. Screwdriver? Maybe.

"You're going on an adventure with Dare's Doggs," Devl said, leaning into Colin. "You make a fuss or try to get away from us, we'll have some fun with your little sister like the Lovecraft pack had with that other girl. You know what I mean?"

"Yeah, I know what you mean," Colin replied, feeling sick. Everyone at Penwych High School knew about the freshman girl from Lovecraft High who had been beaten, raped by three older boys, then sliced up with box cutters. She had been an honors student. A happy, pretty girl who had joined all kinds of after-school activities.

The boys were in jail and would stand trial as adults. That was good, but the girl would never be the same.

"Leave that." Devl tugged at one of the backpack straps.

"You don't want to call attention to us?" Colin countered. "If teachers see me without my backpack during school hours, they'll start asking questions." He wasn't sure any of them *would* notice, but it sounded plausible, especially to someone like Devl, since teachers paid attention to the Doggs.

Someone must have kept watch to make sure the cops weren't around when Devl walked Colin out of the high school, keeping one arm around Colin's shoulders and that screwdriver pressed against his ribs. As soon as they were out of the building, Butch, Acid, and Stick—the other three Doggs—fell in around them and hustled him to Acid's car.

"Where are we going?" Colin asked.

Devl grinned. "Where do you think?"

Colin didn't have any trouble remembering what the card-reading woman had said. *You will make a sacrifice to save someone close to you.*

He wasn't sure he could save himself from whatever the Doggs had planned for him, but he'd do his best to protect Jazmin—and find a way to warn Dad that the Doggs had targeted Jazz in case he didn't make it back from this "adventure."

The person in the money exchange booth gave Colin a hard stare when he handed over thirty dollars, but didn't say anything except "pay the Ferryman one gold coin." Each of the Doggs exchanged fifty dollars and bitched about the price of the ride as they boarded the ferry. But they all dropped a gold coin into the pot. They pushed him into a seat and crowded around him, two behind him, one in front, and Devl beside him.

They were on the ferry, heading for Wyrd. The river would be between them and Jazz. As long as they were on the island, his little sister would be safe.

The black-haired man in the leather jacket wasn't standing at the dock watching visitors disembark, and Colin realized he'd been counting on Frost noticing them, maybe stopping them to find out what five teenage boys were doing on the island. This wasn't exactly a hotbed of excitement for teenagers, although most of the people at school wouldn't know that.

The Doggs kept close to him and headed toward the pavilion. Some kind of altercation near the food stands. Two guys mouthing off and gesturing—maybe protesting the prices? Then Frost and some other man showed up, and the guys backed off.

When Colin and the Doggs were almost at the pavilion, Devl shoved him toward the left. They went down the terraced lawn and entered the park, avoiding the pavilion and all the seers as well as the visitors coming to get a glimpse of their future.

They headed around one side of the ornamental lake. A minute later, Colin spotted the two guys who had been arguing at the food stands walking around the other side of the lake. One of them gestured toward a path that led through some of the flower gardens.

Devl led Colin and the Doggs around the lake and followed the same path. A couple of minutes later, they caught up with the two guys.

"This him?" one of them asked.

"Yeah," Devl said. "He's going on an adventure."

"We did a little exploring before you got here and know just the place to start that adventure."

Colin wasn't surprised when they ended up in a clearing that held a moon gate. After all, the card-reading woman had shown him at least some of this journey.

Words have power.

Except he didn't see any words on the keystone. Then Acid pushed the butterfly in the center, the two sides of the gate swung open—and words appeared on the keystone.

Transformation. Transportation.

Colin watched them change over and over. Maybe ten seconds between each change? Enough time if he was quick. Not transformation. God, no. He wasn't sure what kind of transportation he'd find on Wyrd, but that was a better choice than becoming . . . something else.

Devl grabbed one of his arms. Acid grabbed the other.

Devl said, "Let's see how your old man likes it when these freaks bring *you* home in a box."

Transformation. Transportation.

Colin watched the words on the keystone, bracing his feet and fighting the Doggs' effort to shove him through the moon gate.

The moment TRANSPORTATION appeared, Colin threw himself through the gate, dragging Devl and Acid with him. They hit the ground. Colin was up and running before the other boys realized what had happened.

A wide dirt path led toward a paved road and a one-story building in the distance. He ran past a sign with arrows pointing to various modes of transportation. Buses were straight ahead. The arrow for the train was angled, indicating another path, so people must board on the other side of the building, although Colin didn't see any tracks.

At the bottom of the sign was an arrow indicating the path to take to the ships.

Not the ships. The woman with the cards had warned him about the ships.

He heard Devl and Acid shouting, but they sounded farther behind him than he'd expected.

Bus or train? Bus or train?

He spotted a bus parked next to the station—a bus that hadn't been there a moment ago. Didn't matter. It was there now and hopefully leaving soon. He ran up to the counter.

An older man wearing a flannel shirt and suspenders looked at him. "Help you?"

Yes, help me. The man didn't look like he could defend himself against one Dogg, let along two, so Colin said, "I'd like a ticket, please."

"Where to?"

He almost said it didn't matter, except this was Wyrd, and everything mattered here. "I know what I need to find, but I don't know the name of the place."

Shouting in the distance.

Colin kept his eyes on the man, trying to appear polite and harmless.

"Two gold coins," the man said.

Twenty dollars for a bus ride? He didn't argue, didn't dare. He dug in the pocket of his jeans and pulled out the other two gold coins he'd acquired at the ferry's dock.

The man handed him a blank ticket.

"Where . . . ?"

"When you figure out where you want to go, the ticket will show you the name of the place."

"Thank you."

Shouting. Still in the distance—which shouldn't have been possible, since Devl and Acid were running after him and weren't going to let him get away—but definitely getting closer.

Colin approached the bus. It didn't show any destinations.

Words have power here.

Where did he want to go? Someplace safe. Someplace the Doggs couldn't reach. Someplace where he could contact Dad and warn him that Jazz might be in danger.

He repeated those thoughts, whispered the words that shaped the things he needed—and watched letters appear on the bus's sign and on his ticket: LLAM.

The bus's door opened. Colin bounded up the steps and hurried to find a seat. Plenty of seats to choose from. He took a window seat and slouched so he wouldn't be seen from outside. Of course, he also couldn't see when Devl and Acid reached the bus, but he'd take his chances.

A few other people boarded the bus. Adults going somewhere. Commuters? *Were* there commuters on Wyrd? Where would they be going in the middle of the afternoon?

Then Devl was there, leaping up the stairs, looking furious as he scanned the people on the bus. He charged toward the back of the bus, passing Colin without seeing him. Without . . .

Something strange about Devl. Like he was faded, not all there. Colin expected him to come charging back to the front of the bus, but he didn't. Wouldn't he look again at the people on the bus?

The bus's door closed, and the bus drove away from the station.

Colin waited and waited for Devl to drop into the seat beside him, but the Dogg never reappeared.

How could someone disappear inside a bus?

"Ticket?"

Colin blinked, straightened in his seat. The man was middle-aged and slim, with just a hint of a pot belly starting. A kind face that reminded Colin of the bus conductor in an old movie Mom liked to watch during the winter holidays.

"Ticket?" the bus conductor said again.

"Yes, sir." Colin handed him the ticket.

The bus conductor raised his eyebrows. "We don't see many people traveling to that neighborhood." He punched the ticket, then handed it back to Colin. "Hang on to this. You bought a ten-ride ticket, so you have nine rides remaining."

He hadn't realized he'd bought that many. Ten rides for twenty dollars wasn't a bad deal.

The bus conductor moved on, punching other people's tickets. Colin wasn't trying to eavesdrop, but he had the impression the other people were regulars. That seemed so . . . normal . . . and comforting.

Now if he could somehow avoid Devl until he reached this LLAM place.

Devl charged down the bus's aisle. For a moment, he thought he'd seen that asshole Forrester, but the image was so faint, like a reflection on a window.

Nothing. Fuck!

He turned around and headed back toward the front of the bus when he felt it move, saw it leaving the little station.

"Stop!" he shouted. "Let me off!"

A cadaverous old fart wearing some kind of uniform looked at him. "Do you have a ticket to indicate your destination?"

"No, I don't have a ticket," Devl snarled. "Let me the fuck off this bus!"

"This bus doesn't stop without a ticket or a turn of the wheel."

Instead of the side-facing seats or luggage racks that were in some buses, the conductor opened a set of wooden doors, revealing three wheels—the kind used for raffles or games of chance. Wheel of fortune, but smaller.

"Let's see what kind of journey you're taking," the conductor said. "This wheel determines the time." He spun the first wheel, then pulled a small notebook and pencil out of his jacket pocket. "Thirty-five years. Not bad. At your age, you should still have some years ahead of you when you get back to wherever you came from. The second wheel determines whether you're riding solo, or have occasional company, or a full load." He spun the second wheel. "Occasional. Better than solo for someone young."

Devl couldn't make sense of any of this. "Let me off this bus." He tried to sound menacing and dangerous. He was a Dogg, after all. But he was very much afraid that he just sounded scared.

"I will," the conductor said. "In thirty-five years."

"What's the third wheel for? You didn't spin that one."

The conductor smiled. "We don't spin that one until you're close to the end of the journey. That one determines where we let you off, geographically. We have found that passengers adjust better to the journey when the end of the trip remains a surprise."

No door closed. No curtain was drawn. But a wall of dark gray fog now stood between Devl and the front of the bus. No sign of the conductor or those wheels of chance.

Devl pushed at the fog. It gave a little. When he'd pushed his arms through up to his elbows, a voice behind him said, "It won't do any good. You'll work to the point of exhaustion, and once you're through that fog, you'll just find yourself at the back of the bus. Just a crazy-ass loop."

Devl pulled his arms out of the fog, turned, and looked at the man sitting a few rows back. He hadn't noticed him when he rushed up the aisle to confront the conductor.

"If you're like most of the passengers on this particular bus, you'll push through every so often for the first couple of years just to have something to do," the man said.

Devl took a seat on the other side of the aisle and one row up. He didn't know what this guy's angle was, but he didn't want to get too friendly with a stranger. "They have to open that . . . whatever . . . to bring in food and water, right?" He waved at the fog.

The man laughed. "You don't need food or water anymore. You don't need to shit or piss either. You're a ghost, boy, even if you're still among the living. All kinds of buses travel through places like Wyrd. You got on the wrong bus, and now you can't get off until your journey ends."

"The conductor said I was occasional. What does that mean?"

"You're like me. Sometimes you're the only one on the bus—or the only one you can see. Other times, you'll have the company of fellow passengers. An acquaintance of mine got the full bus, so for her, it's party, party, party. I see her occasionally, and she tells me things."

"Really?"

Another smile. "They got bored one night and tried to eat one of the other passengers. After a while, people get a little crazy. Makes me glad I ended up with occasional company."

"Fuck me," Devl whispered.

"You don't want me to do that."

Something about the words, about the way the man said them. Devl was sure this was someone who was more dangerous than any Dogg.

Acid reached the train moments before it started to pull out of the station. Just two cars? Not even a real train.

He grabbed a rail and leaped up the stairs of the first car. A few people there gave him a cold eye, the fuckers. Not seeing his prey, Acid hurried through that car and went into the other, passing through some gray, cobwebby barrier. He took a few steps forward, scanning the gray-looking people for Forrester.

Gray-looking people. Skeletons with skin. Some were dressed in old-fashioned clothes that looked worn out. Others wore clothes his old man might have worn as a teenager—and they weren't that far along in the process of becoming the mummy's stand-in. And one of the fresher ones . . . Hadn't that guy been featured on a cold case show recently? He'd gone on a killing spree, slaughtering three families in one night, and then disappeared.

This is where a killer disappeared to?

"Your ticket."

Acid turned around. The conductor looked like that Vincent Price guy who used to star in horror movies. "I didn't buy a ticket. I was just looking for a friend, but he's not here."

"We know." The conductor held out a rectangle of white cardboard with the number ninety-nine written on it. "This is your ticket. You must have done—or were planning to do—very wicked things to earn a ride this long."

"I have to get off the train."

"And you will—in ninety-nine years." The conductor looked at the other passengers. "It's quiet during the day. They don't reanimate until the sun goes down."

Reanimate? What the . . . ?

The conductor vanished. The piece of white cardboard lay on the floor at Acid's feet. He picked it up and shoved it in his pocket.

Then he found an empty seat next to an old woman who looked ready to fall apart—and wondered what happened to the still-living when the sun went down.

Butch watched Devl, Acid, and that Forrester prick stumble through the gate and disappear. What the fuck?

"That's . . ." one of the older guys said. Dare's father said these two guys worked with him sometimes and were part of the plan because they knew how to handle themselves. Seeing one of them backing away from the gate, Butch didn't think they had balls enough to be more than a distraction at a food stand.

"We're going after them because we're Dare's Doggs and no-fucking-body messes with the Doggs and walks away."

"Yeah," Stick said. "We're the Doggs!" He howled.

Butch looked at the two older guys. They weren't *old*, but they weren't in school anymore. Still, it looked like he was the alpha here. "Are you going to be Doggs or pussies?"

Heat in their eyes. Hands moving toward pockets in a way that indicated they might be carrying weapons. Switchblades most likely because he'd heard shit happened to anyone who tried to cross the river with a weapon more dangerous than some kind of sticker.

Butch howled. "We are the Doggs!"

Stick howled.

They rushed through the moon gate, with the other two guys right on their heels.

Yeah, Butch thought. *Prove you have balls.*

He tripped, tumbled, his legs suddenly trapped by his jeans. He kicked to free his feet from his sneakers, then got to his hands and knees. Except he didn't. He wobbled upright on four legs and stared at another scruffy beast that was staring back at him. Two more beasts were rolling and scrabbling, using teeth and claws to free themselves from the clothing they had worn moments ago.

We are the Doggs!

Now they were.

One of the older guys, a hind leg still stuck in the leg of his jeans, stumbled back through the gate, then whimpered when nothing happened. He ran through again in the original direction. Nothing.

There had to be *some* way to change back to human.

Butch clawed and pulled until he'd freed himself from all his clothes, then helped Stick. The two of them ripped and tore the clothing from the third guy, who was just sitting there staring at his front paws.

Definitely not worthy of being a Dogg.

The guy who had gone through the gate a couple of times without changing a fucking thing finally got rid of his clothes and was pushing at the gate to close it. Pushing and pushing.

That was a thought. Maybe the magic didn't work until the gate was closed again.

Nudging Stick, Butch went to the other half of the gate and put his shoulder against the bars to push and push and push.

Fucking gate wouldn't move. Not one inch. They would have to find someone who lived in this fucking place and knew how to change them back.

Butch headed toward the path they'd taken to reach this clearing. Stick caught up to him, but they had to circle back and nip the other two before one stopped whimpering and the other stopped staring at his paws.

They ran down the path toward the ornamental lake and the pavilion. Give some of those old lady visitors a scare that would have them wetting themselves. Yeah. They were the Doggs! Savage and wild. They could do whatever they wanted. Kill whatever they wanted.

Something stepped out of the trees just ahead of them. Butch stopped so fast one of the other guys ran over him before tripping.

The . . . thing . . . looked like that man-horse deal from mythology, except it was a man mixed with a deer—who was aiming a slingshot at them.

Butch snarled at the deer-thing. Four to one. Good odds in their favor.

Then Stick leaped forward. The deer-thing released the stone, and Stick was running away on three legs.

Before Butch thought to react, the deer-thing already had another stone in the sling, aimed right at him—and he realized he was alone, the other three dogs already running away.

Not knowing what else to do, Butch turned and ran to catch up to them.

Colin wasn't sure how long he'd been riding the bus. Other passengers had gotten on and gotten off. He'd checked his backpack to confirm he had a bottle of water and a couple of chocolate bars. Not what Mom would call a healthy snack, but it was better than nothing, especially when he had no idea what he would find when he got off the bus.

"Next stop, Llamalidia," the bus conductor called. He stopped at Colin's seat. "That's your stop. We'll be there in a few minutes."

"Thank you."

The conductor smiled and walked toward the back of the bus.

Colin closed his eyes and focused on breathing. Ever since he got on the bus, his cell phone had been searching for a signal. With any luck, the Llamalidia place would have cell phone service or a landline that could connect him to somewhere he could reach Dad.

A few more minutes. Just a few more minutes.

4

Lucas Frost patrolled the area of Destiny Park usually frequented by visitors, looking for the two human males who had made a fuss around the food stands. Arguing with the vendors and with each other about nothing. Either purchase the food for the stated price or don't eat. Simple enough. Except something had felt off about those males, as if they were performing to draw attention away from the dock just as the ferry arrived.

The ferry was heading back to the other side of the river to pick up the last visitors of the day, so he would wait to ask the Ferryman if anyone unusual had boarded this afternoon around the same time as that . . . ruckus.

Rahele and Faulkner weren't the only vulnerable humans living on Wyrd, and vengeance didn't have a shelf life—even among humans.

Lucas, we have a problem.

Lucas stopped at the far end of the ornamental lake. **Deerman?**

Four wild dogs were heading toward the visitors' area of the park. I encouraged them to run in another direction. An amused pause. **Slingshot and stone, aimed at the hindquarters of one of the dogs. Bruised a bone.** Another pause. **Maybe broke a bone.**

Lucas felt anger wash through him. **Wild dogs. Are you sure?** Almost an insult to ask Deerman that question. Fortunately, the other Arcana didn't take offense.

No kind of dog I've seen before. And nothing that comes from Wyrd.

Anything else?

Mia Skov told me she saw seven young males following a path that would lead to one of the moon gates. They seemed aggressive, so she remained hidden.

Mia Skov was from a branch of the Arcana that had an affinity for woodlands. She tended those areas of Destiny Park and kept an eye on visitors when they wandered toward the wilder areas of the park.

Seven young males. Four wild dogs. Where were the other three?

Ask your people to keep watch along the paths that would lead back to the pavilion and main visitor areas, Lucas said. **I'll fetch Jack, and we'll check the moon gate.**

Good hunting, Deerman replied.

One way or another there would be a hunt. He just didn't know what kind it would be.

After summoning his brother to meet him at the pavilion, Lucas stepped into the room where Justine and her sisters revealed the choices of fate that came with a price—and found Katherine Rose, one of the card readers, in a hushed discussion with the Ladies Three.

"Lucas, we may have a problem," Justine said.

"Deerman already told me about the wild dogs," Lucas replied. "What can you tell me?"

Justine moved her scales to make room at the front of the table, then nodded to Katherine Rose. The seer laid out four cards.

Seven males. Six with weapons; one standing alone.

A male on his knees; a hooded man with an ax; a woman weeping.

A moon gate.

A pack of dogs surrounding a kill.

"I was waiting for a customer when I felt compelled to turn the cards," Katherine Rose said. "The first three cards match a reading I did a few months ago for a boy. The fourth card is new."

A chill went through Lucas. Fate could be cruel. "What boy?"

"He came with a man you know."

Forrester.

Jack Frost walked into the room. "Something happening?"

Lucas nodded. "We need to check the moon gate." There was more than one moon gate in the park, but only one close enough to the pavilion for a visitor to stumble upon. Even that one required some effort to find. The others required a need—or the Arcana's assistance—to find them. "I'll ask Ethan to patrol the pavilion and grounds around the lake." He walked toward the dark archway that led to Ethan's armory, then stopped and looked at his brother. "Do you need a weapon?"

Jack gave him a sharp smile. "Not from Ethan."

Of course. Jack's abilities could freeze the edge of a leaf and make it sharp enough to slit a throat. He had no need for conventional weapons, although he usually carried a few of those too.

After confirming that Ethan would patrol the grounds, Lucas and Jack headed for the moon gate.

"Seven human males, but four wild dogs," Jack said after Lucas explained why they were going to look at the moon gate. "Three males unaccounted for. Best case scenario is we find them wounded around the gate and send them back across the river to their own healers."

"Best case," Lucas agreed. "The other possibilities could mean that Forrester never hears from his son again."

"Forrester. You like him."

"I do. He understands more of the truth about us and Wyrd than most of the humans who live around the Fate River, and he still has the courage to come here and deal with us. If he loses his son . . ."

Fate. Choices. It wasn't the Arcana's task to make a choice for a human, only facilitate that choice—if asked.

They approached the moon gate and spotted the torn clothing.

Jack swore softly. "They chose the form."

"Probably not intentionally." Lucas studied the clothing. "Fools."

"I'll go back to the pavilion and get a box."

"There's no time. Grab what you can. We'll take it to the Ladies Three and see what answers they can draw from the males' possessions."

Lucas gathered four pairs of jeans while Jack gathered the shirts and a couple of cell phones that had fallen out of pockets. They left the footwear for whoever might have a use for it and returned to the pavilion.

An empty cardboard box was waiting for them in front of Justine's table. Lucas and Jack dropped the clothes and phones into the box.

"I need whatever you can tell me about the possible lines of fate," Lucas said.

"There were seven," Zerah said. "You brought possessions belonging to four."

"That's all we have."

Justine studied him. "Did you look?"

Meaning, had he looked for identification that would confirm that one of the wild dogs that Deerman had seen was Forrester's son? "No."

"It's getting late," Jack said. "The sun will be going down soon, and the ferry will be making its last run across the river. I'll keep watch at the dock in case the other three boys find their way back there."

Lucas nodded, then went outside and around the part of the pavilion open to visitors. When he entered his office, he considered what he needed to do—and how he could do it without wounding Forrester.

He picked up his phone and made the call.

Beth Fahey was tidying her desk at the end of her shift when her phone rang. "Detective Fahey."

"Can you be overheard?"

Her breath caught. "Mr. Frost?"

"Can you be overheard?"

She heard temper in his voice. Something was wrong. She looked around just to be sure no one else had entered the team's area. "No. I'm alone right now."

"Captain Forrester. What is his son's name?"

Beth braced herself against her desk. "Colin. His name is Colin. Has something happened to him?" Of course something had happened. Frost wouldn't be calling the 13th precinct if *nothing* had happened.

"We don't know yet." A beat of silence. "Can you obtain a picture of the boy?"

Oh, God. "I should call Captain Forrester. He's gone for the day."

"No, you should not."

The words were a command. Later, she'd think about why she didn't question that he could give her orders. "There is a photo of his wife and children on his desk. I could take a picture of it with my cell phone and e-mail it to you."

He gave her an e-mail address.

"Will you let us know when you find out anything?" she asked.

"I'll call you."

She heard the emphasis on *you*. Her. Not Forrester. "I'll take that picture now and get it to you in a few minutes."

"I'll wait for it."

Beth ended the call and looked around. Still no one in this area of the precinct. She hurried into Forrester's office and almost dropped the photo in her haste to remove it from the frame so that she could take the clearest picture.

The first picture was Aisha Forrester and the two children. Then she tightened her focus to take a picture that was mostly Colin.

Rushing back to her desk, she forced herself to think. She didn't want it to appear like she was going behind her captain's back. She was in a way, but there was no need to alarm Captain Forrester or his wife when Colin might be on the ferry home and walk into the house a little late for dinner.

She sent the e-mail with the pictures to the address Lucas Frost provided—and to her work e-mail at the precinct.

Having done all she could do for the moment, Beth ran out to buy some food from the food trucks. She gave no thought to going home. Not now.

Returning to her desk, she unwrapped a sandwich and settled down to wait.

Lucas printed out the picture of the boy. He folded the paper several times to fit into the pocket of his leather jacket, then headed back to the moon gate. He didn't know who was ringing the bell that indicated the last ferry was boarding, but he nodded to the visitors who were chatting as they hustled to reach the dock.

No sign of young males.

Lucas reached the moon gate. Transportation. Transformation. Destiny could be shaped within those two words.

He pressed his hand against one of the stones in the gate. It was true that the gates only opened one way—unless you were Wyrd's Sorcerer King and had a special bond with the uncanny that made up the island. But even the Sorcerer King needed to take some care with a moon gate.

Transportation.

Lucas pushed the two sides of the gate open and said, "Stay in this moment until I return."

He walked through the gate and strode over the wide dirt path until it reached the paved road and the ticket station.

The stationmaster was from a minor branch of the Arcana and looked . . . safe . . . to the uninitiated.

"Something I can do for you, Mr. Frost?"

"Perhaps." Lucas removed the paper and unfolded it to reveal the picture. "Have you seen him?"

The stationmaster looked wary. "I saw him. Polite boy, unlike the one who came after him." He pointed to the picture. "This one bought a ten-punch ticket."

"Destination?"

"Don't know. The boy said he knew what he needed to find but didn't know the name of the place. I know he boarded a bus, but I was watching the other one running toward the station. Didn't like the look of that one."

"Did the other one buy a ticket?"

Grim delight in the stationmaster's eyes. "He did not."

Then that boy had boarded the wrong bus and wasn't ever going to be found—or he would return in weeks, months, maybe years. Even if he returned, he wouldn't be the same. Not after being a ghost.

"When the polite boy came up to the station, I could hear two more shouting," the stationmaster said. "One came here, like I said. I think the other went to the train station."

"Thank you. I'll check." Lucas refolded the paper and put it in his pocket.

"Are they important?"

"They were important to someone." Past tense, because there was only one train that let a person board without a ticket, and that train only let you off at the grave.

To be thorough, Lucas retraced his steps until he reached the path that led to the train station. The stationmaster there confirmed that a rude boy had boarded the train without a ticket.

Lucas headed back to the moon gate and walked through. He

pressed his hand to the stone opposite the one he'd pressed before—and the gate closed.

Transformation. Transportation. An unwanted fate if a person was careless.

Or maybe an unexpected destiny?

Two boys were definitely lost. The third? Lost, yes, but if the boy had really listened to what Katherine Rose had said when she read his cards, if he focused on what he needed before he got on a bus, he could be all right and might even find his way back.

It was possible. And *possible* was all the hope he could give Charles Forrester and his family.

Lucas returned to the pavilion and the room where Justine and her sisters saw the potential lines of fate.

"We weighed the possessions of each of these males and came up with the same conclusion," Justine said.

"Anger and vengeance began this path," Zerah said.

"If you want to give these males a chance to live, this is where the path ends." Lysandra held up her sketchbook.

A yard with a high fence. A man standing in the doorway, backlit from the room beyond. A street address in the town of Penwych.

"Mia Skov says she has darts that can be used in a specially shaped slingshot—darts that will put the wild dogs to sleep for capture," Justine said.

Lucas nodded. "They can't be allowed to stay on Wyrd. If we can capture them, we won't have to kill them. If they specified a time limit for their transformation, that I can't change. But if they went through without intention and we find them before they've spent a full day as wild dogs, I can force a change, and they'll go back to their original form when the sun rises."

If the Arcana didn't find the dogs in time and he tried to force a change after that first sunrise, the boys would cycle through the forms over and over until their bodies collapsed from the strain—or someone, terrified at seeing the legend of the werewolf come to life, killed them.

Ethan Sharpe entered the room with Jack Frost.

"No disturbances around the pavilion," Ethan said. "And I made sure there was no one left wandering in the park before the last ferry left."

"No young males were on the last ferry," Jack said.

"They wouldn't be." Lucas told them what he'd learned at the ticket station.

Jack blew out a breath. "More young humans going home transformed or not going home at all? That won't go down well with the people across the river."

"No, it won't," Lucas agreed. The Arcana didn't usually care about what did or didn't go down well across the river, but the fate of Forrester's boy changed things—because Forrester was connected to Beth Fahey.

Lucas gestured toward Lysandra's sketchbook. "The lines of fate for the transformed males. Can we deliver them to the police in their current form?"

The Ladies Three looked at one another and shook their heads.

"Every other line I tried to follow has the dogs killing humans before they themselves are killed," Lysandra said. "That fenced yard is the only chance they have of staying alive long enough to change back to human. But . . ." She looked at Justine.

"We saw nothing beyond that yard," Justine said. "Once they are delivered to that address, their fate is in someone else's hands."

5

Charles Forrester opened the back door of his house and walked into the kitchen. A workout at the gym had tired him in a good way, and he was ready to spend the evening with Aisha. The children, too, but they had reached an age where they were busy with after-school activities or friends, and quality time with them was usually when he was driving them to one place or another.

He didn't mind. They were good kids, and he loved them. Teaching them that adults needed "me time" was one reason he went to the gym after work a couple of days a week—but he usually scheduled those workouts on the same days that Colin had swim practice so that they could all sit down together for dinner.

He smiled at his wife and said, "Hi."

His daughter, Jazz, threw herself into his arms and held on while Aisha looked at him with eyes full of fear.

"What's going on?" Charles dropped his gym bag and held out a hand to his wife since his daughter was holding on to him as if her life depended on it.

"Colin didn't come home," Aisha said, hurrying across the kitchen to grab his hand.

Charles looked at the clock on the wall near the kitchen table where they had their family meals. "Is swim practice running late? Does he need me to pick him up from school?"

"He wasn't at swim practice," Aisha said. "The coach called to ask why he didn't show up. I've called Colin several times since talking to the coach, but his phone always goes to voicemail."

Charles tried to untangle himself from Jazz's grip without hurting the girl.

"And Jazz has something to tell you," Aisha added.

He put his hand on his daughter's head. "Honey? You know something about this?"

Jazz nodded. "Davie's brother said Colin cut his last class and left school with Dare's Doggs."

Rattled that Colin would skip a class, let alone leave school with Darren Palmer's gang of bullyboys, he almost asked who Davie was, but he remembered in time that a month ago, Davie had been Davinia Madison. Davie's parents hoped this was just a phase, but whatever the reason for the choice, he made an effort to use the correct pronoun whenever Jazz's friend came to their house.

Now he understood the fear in Aisha's eyes. Albert Palmer had been campaigning for months to have Wyrd outlawed in some way—as if that was possible. He'd blamed the police for not protecting his son, ignoring the fact that no town around the Fate River had any jurisdiction on the island. You went there at your own risk—and sometimes the risk was fatal.

But why would Colin go with Darren Palmer's friends?

A chill went through Charles. He could think of one reason.

He kissed his wife and released himself from his daughter's hold. "You two get something to eat. I'm going back to the precinct to see what I can find out."

He left the house and got in the car. Before he pulled out of the driveway, he made a call. "Colin, it's Dad. I need to know where you are. Call me as soon as you get this message." Since he didn't expect a return call, he called Kuhn and Castelletti and asked them to return to the precinct.

He hesitated, then made one more call to the precinct—and was told that Beth Fahey hadn't left for the day. Was his hesitation about calling her in with the rest of his team patronizing or practical? Or was he saving the one who had an affinity with the Arcana to help him deal with whatever was to come?

6

Beth Fahey returned from the women's restroom to find the whole special team gathered around the evidence table, including Officers Ben Reynolds and Jim Monkton.

She looked at Captain Forrester's pale face and thought, *What does he know?*

"Fahey," Forrester said.

"Captain."

Forrester looked at the team, studying each face—except hers. "This isn't by the book, but I'm asking for your help. My son missed swim practice and hasn't come home. He was last seen leaving the high school with some of Darren Palmer's friends."

"You think Al Palmer put them up to abducting Colin?" Kuhn asked. "Maybe paid them to . . ." He stopped.

Plenty of calls about domestic disputes had been logged for the Palmer residence even before Darren Palmer's death, so it wasn't a big leap to think Palmer might want some payback against the man who had brought what was left of his son home from Wyrd.

Maybe she could have a quiet word with the captain before things went beyond the team.

"Is Colin still young enough for us to put out an Amber Alert?" Castelletti asked. "Or maybe a BOLO."

"There's no point in an Amber Alert or a BOLO," Beth said. "He's not on this side of the river."

They stared at her. She saw a fierce anger building in Forrester's eyes—and she couldn't blame him. She'd known something was wrong and had kept silent. "Lucas Frost called."

"And?" The quiet voice warned of an anger going down to the man's core.

"He wanted to know your son's name, and he asked for a picture. I . . . used . . . the photo on your desk, took a picture with my cell phone, and e-mailed it to him."

"You didn't call me."

"He told me not to."

The anger began to rise and spill over. "Since when do you take orders from Lucas Frost?"

"I . . ." *Don't know.*

Her cell phone rang. She noted the tremor in her hands when she took the phone out of her pocket. She was sure the rest of the team noticed too. "Fahey."

"Detective."

"Mr. Frost." She looked at Forrester. "The captain and the rest of the team are here. Should I put you on speaker?" *Please, say yes.*

Frost released a breath that almost sounded like a sigh. "Yes."

Relieved, Beth pressed the speaker button and set the phone on the table.

"Captain Forrester," Frost said.

"Mr. Frost," Forrester replied. His voice sounded calm. His hands were tight fists pressed against the table.

"Seven young males crossed the river this afternoon. It appears that the intentions of six of them were not . . . benign." A long pause. "Transformation or transportation. You know how some of the moon gates work, Forrester."

Forrester flinched and closed his eyes, as if he couldn't bear to see the people around him—or see their pity.

"Four of those young males transformed into wild dogs," Frost continued. "Your son is not one of them. We have their clothing. We'll deliver it to the dock on your side of the river when the ferry makes its first run tomorrow."

"I could come over tonight and help you look for Colin," Forrester said.

"No."

"I know what you are, Frost!"

"Yes, you do. And that is why you are going to stay on your side of the river. The Arcana are hunting tonight. We have determined the only place where we can take the wild dogs where they will have a chance to survive. If we can capture them and deliver them to that place on your side of the river before the sun rises, we can turn them back into their human form."

Forrester's voice broke. "Colin?"

"Transportation. Your son eluded his captors and bought a bus ticket. He told the stationmaster he knew what he needed to find but didn't know the name of the place. Unfortunately, when the name revealed itself and Colin boarded the bus, the stationmaster was distracted by the boy pursuing your son and couldn't tell me Colin's destination. Your son made a choice, Forrester. Hold on to that."

"It doesn't mean he can come back."

"No, it doesn't. But he considered what he needed to find, and that means there is a possibility that he'll find his way home." Another pause. "The two boys who pursued him should be considered lost for good. The one who took another bus may return, but he didn't purchase a ticket, so there is no way to tell when and where he'll return.

The boy who boarded the train without a ticket . . . There is only one place that particular train lets off passengers."

Beth looked around the table. When no one else said anything, she asked, "Where?"

"Graveyards," Frost replied.

Forrester let out a shuddering breath. "What can I tell my wife?"

"Your son was not careless in his choice, so there is hope. I have to go. The hunt has begun." Frost ended the call.

Forrester walked into his office. Beth followed him and watched him put the photo of his family back in the frame. After she'd sent the picture to Frost and began her vigil, she'd forgotten that she hadn't restored the photo.

"You should have called me," Forrester said, not looking at her.

"All I could have told you was that Lucas Frost wanted to know your son's name and wanted a picture of him. Would that have helped?"

"No." He looked up. "You still should have called me." He hesitated. "But I understand why you didn't. I might have done the same in your shoes."

"Is there anything I can do?"

"Go home. Get some rest. Report back at five a.m. The team needs to be ready to respond to whatever happens when the sun rises."

7

Colin Forrester stepped off the bus and stared at the sign on the building in front of him. No words to indicate where he was; just that hoofprint he'd seen when the woman had read his cards, as if that was all that was required.

He tried his cell phone. No signal. If the building was a store of some kind, hopefully they would have a landline.

He put one foot on the bottom step, then stopped and looked around. The air smelled . . . different. The land looked different. When he and Ted Ocampo had ridden the river bus for its whole journey around the island last year, he didn't remember seeing mountains. Maybe he was somewhere in the interior of Wyrd? But even then, mountains were kind of hard to miss.

Wherever he was, he needed to find a phone.

He entered the building and thought the interior looked like photos of old-time trading posts. Except . . .

The individual standing behind the counter next to an old-fashioned cash register was a llama standing on its hind legs. Or else it was a bipedal species of llama that shaved off its fur—or whatever it was called when it was still on the animal—and then . . . Would these beings shave off the fur and then use it to weave clothing for themselves? Because the llama was wearing a long vest that had different colors and patterns.

"Mmmm?"

Colin blinked. It sounded like a question—and that reminded him that he had to find a way to call Dad. "Hello. My cell phone isn't getting a signal." He held up the cell phone. "Do you have a landline I could use to call my dad? Landline? Phone?" He raised his hand next to his head, thumb and little finger extended, in the sign that meant "call me."

The llama looked at his hand and raised its own hoof-hand up to its ear. "Mmmm?"

The hoof-hand had a familiar shape, but Colin didn't think if he gave the creature a Vulcan salute and said "Live long and prosper" it would understand the joke.

A human woman walked up to the counter from the back of the store and said, "I'll take care of this."

Colin watched them communicate with some kind of sign language before the llama wandered off to do . . . something.

"What's your story?" the woman said. "Not many people can reach this place."

"I'll tell you everything, but first, can I use your phone? I have to call my dad. He's a police officer in Penwych. A town on the other side of the river?"

"I know where it is."

That was something. "I need to tell him my sister could be in danger. She's only twelve." When the woman didn't respond, he added, "Please."

"If the danger is imminent, you're probably too late," she said. "This is Llamalidia. It's a . . . neighborhood . . . in Wyrd. There are no phones, no internet."

Colin sagged against the counter.

"Where did you start out?"

"Destiny Park. Some bullyboys were trying to shove me through a moon gate. I went through when it said "Transportation" and bought a ticket for the bus. I thought one of those boys got on the bus, too, but after he passed my seat, I didn't see him again."

"You think these boys are a danger to your sister?"

"They said if I didn't go with them, they would rape her. They didn't use those exact words, but that's what they meant."

"How many of them went through the gate when you did?"

"Two that I know of." He looked at the woman. "There were six of them."

She looked at a windup clock on the counter and nodded. She reached under the counter and pulled out two sheets of stationery, two envelopes, and two pencils. "It will be a few days before the bus comes by again, but the mobile library will be here within the hour."

"Could I hitch a ride on it?" Colin asked.

"No. Your presence could disrupt the route, and you and the librarian might never be seen again—at least not in any part of Wyrd that either of you would recognize. What you're going to do now is write a letter to your father telling him you're all right and you're safe. You can't tell him where you are. It's forbidden. No one across the river is allowed to know about this place, and the Arcana exact a huge payment if that rule is broken. Make sure what you tell him is something you would be okay having your mother read. But before you do that, tell me the names of the boys who threatened you and pose a threat to your sister. I will send my letter to the Sorcerer King, and he will get the information to the proper people."

"Who is he?"

"He is the ruler of Wyrd."

"Is he dangerous?"

"He is . . . annihilation." She blew out a breath. "Give me those names and let's get these letters written."

Colin wrote his letter, assuring his dad that he had escaped the bullyboys and bought a bus ticket for one of Wyrd's neighborhoods and was safe. When the woman approved what he'd written, he folded the letter into the envelope and addressed it to Dad at Penwych's 13th precinct.

The woman finished her letter and sealed it in an envelope addressed to the Sorcerer King, care of Lucas Frost at Destiny Park. On both envelopes, she added the word *Urgent.* She also added a postage stamp to each envelope.

"Whoa," Colin said. "Those stamps are . . ." He couldn't think of a word an adult might understand indicated something outstandingly unusual.

The woman picked up both envelopes. "Come on. The mobile library is here."

When they walked outside, Colin noticed the line of Llamalidians waiting for the mobile library, including small beings that must have been children. All of them looked shorn, and all of them either wore a wrap that went from waist to knees or a long vest.

One of the small ones approached him. It tapped its chest, then held out a hoof-hand.

"That means hello," the woman said.

Colin shaped his fingers to imitate the hoof-hand and repeated the gesture.

Hoof-hand circling the face. "Mmmm?"

"Name?" the woman interpreted.

"Colin."

The youngster scampered back to the adults.

"I'm Tia Downing," the woman said.

"Thank you for your help."

"We all do what we can." She hailed the woman who opened the library's doors.

More signing had the Llamalidians patiently waiting for admittance.

"Tia." The librarian gave Tia a big smile.

"Rya. This is Colin . . . Forrester? There are urgent messages that need to reach Destiny Park." Tia held out the envelopes.

Rya took the envelopes. "It will still take time. I can't change my route."

"But some places on your route have a more direct line to the park—and to Lucas Frost?"

Rya nodded. "It will still take a couple of days."

When Colin made a wordless protest, Tia put a hand on his shoulder and said, "That will do."

"I'd better take care of getting books exchanged."

"Stop in for a bit of food before you go," Tia said.

When the librarian returned to the mobile library, the Llamalidians began entering to return books and find something new.

"The Llamalidians use drums to communicate between the family groups in the neighborhood," Tia said. "Letters are the only way to communicate to any place beyond these borders."

"Is the librarian like you?" Colin asked.

Tia shook her head. "I'm human. Rya Hedden is half Arcana. We come from different places, but we're here because we don't belong on the other side of the river. I needed a simple life. I needed peace. I found it here among these people."

"I needed a safe place the bullyboys couldn't reach, and a place where I could contact my dad."

"Then you found it, even if it's not exactly what you imagined." Tia smiled. "Rya can issue you a temporary library card. You should pick up a couple of books since you'll be here a few days no matter how things shake out."

"This place doesn't feel like it belongs to the geography around the island."

"The uncanny has many anchors in the world."

Colin thought about that. "So the Isle of Wyrd is kind of like the TARDIS? It's bigger on the inside?" He wondered if Tia would understand a *Doctor Who* reference.

A moment of silence before she snorted a laugh. "Kind of like that, except there are neighborhoods instead of rooms."

"Cool."

He and Tia got in line and waited their turn to borrow books.

8

Lucas, Jack, Ethan, and Deerman studied the remains of a young doe. Bad enough to see what the wild dogs had done to the animal. If they'd done that to one of Deerman's people, there would have been no way to bring the transformed humans back across the river alive without starting a fight between branches of the Arcana.

"They raped her," Deerman said. "They caught her, severed the tendons in her legs, and raped her while they ate her."

"As wild dogs or humans, that makes no sense," Jack said.

"No, it doesn't," Lucas agreed. "But it's the human inside the dog's body that made that choice." What did that say about what these males had done, or would do, to their own kind?

"We've been hunting these beasts for hours, and we're near the edge of the park now," Ethan said. "If the wild dogs go into one of the neighborhoods, it will be harder to find them—*if* we can find them."

A convergence of the uncanny attracted the strange in the world, like a magnet attracted iron filings. Someone long ago had called those clusters of places "neighborhoods," implying that there were differences, either geographical or cultural, when a person crossed a boundary. But the convergences were more complicated than that. They were more like a patchwork quilt made up of static neighborhoods, which were anchored to a particular convergence, and roaming neighborhoods, which shifted their locations during the spring and fall equinox.

If the wild dogs left the park, they would end up in a static neighborhood that bordered the park. If that happened, there would be no chance of finding them in time to change them back to human. If that happened, the dogs would kill again and again until they, in turn, were killed by whatever beings lived in that part of Wyrd.

"They still think like humans. If they somehow manage to go through a moon gate that allows entry into our part of the park . . ." Ethan continued.

The Arcana's residential area of Destiny Park held no predators—except the Arcana themselves—so the young there didn't fear any wildlife that ventured into their area since the animal could be a member of the family.

"This savaging of a female is part of what is driving them," Jack said. "They liked it."

Lucas turned to his brother. "Your point?"

"If we're going to catch them, we need bait."

Mia Skov's branch of the Arcana was the inspiration for woodland sprites in human art and literature. As Lucas and the other males took up a position around the small clearing, Mia wandered, using one hand to pick wild violets and other flowers that nestled in the grass that various animals in the park kept cropped. She sang as she moved around the moonlit clearing—and she kept the special slingshot and dart ready in her other hand.

Something's coming, Deerman said.

Lucas couldn't tell if the wild dogs knew the Arcana males were there and just didn't care or if they didn't understand that predators could also be prey. The dogs' attention was focused on Mia, and they burst into the clearing so fast, they were halfway to the Arcana female before Lucas and the others could raise their slingshots and take aim.

Mia raised her slingshot and shot her dart into the leader before she sprang out of the way.

Lucas also targeted the leader while Jack, Ethan, and Deerman took down the other three. After hours of searching, bringing down the dogs had been fast and simple.

They readied another dart as they approached the wild dogs. The dogs twitched as the Arcana approached, but whatever sedative Mia had concocted would keep the dogs contained long enough.

"We need to move if we're going to take these males across the river and deliver them to that fenced-in place before sunrise," Lucas said. Then he called to Ashley Laxton.

The acquaintance who has a van and owes us a favor says there is a police cruiser sitting near the pier, she told him. **If he parks there to wait for you, the police will ask questions. He says there is a boat launch connected to a river park not far from the ferry's pier. You can bring a boat in there without being seen.**

All right. I know where that is.

They had to wait for the Arcana who was bringing the pony and cart that would haul the dogs to the shore, aware of the passing of time. Getting the dogs across the river and to the fenced yard before they recovered from the sedative didn't give them much leeway. Leaving the dogs anywhere else would bring death to at least one human as well as the dogs. The Ladies Three had seen that possibility.

From the pony cart to the beach, where one of the smaller motorboats belonging to the Arcana waited. From the boat to the van on the other side of the river. From the van to the address Lysandra had seen when she sketched out the possible lines of fate.

The back gate was locked, so Lucas, Jack, and the human who owed them a favor lifted each dog and lowered it over the fence, back legs first. Just before he released each one, Lucas, as Wyrd's Sorcerer King, sent his power and his intentions through each dog to assure they would transform back to humans when the sun rose.

The driver of the van—a man who had seen the truth about the Arcana—returned Lucas and Jack to the boat launch and the boat waiting for them there.

Upon their return to Wyrd, Lucas sought a rocky area of the shore and laid out four muslin bags that held fur and a little blood that he'd taken from each wild dog.

"We, the Arcana, reject your presence on our land," he said quietly as he touched each bag and opened himself to be a vessel for the uncanny. "You will find no welcome, no succor on our shores or from our people. If you come onto our land again, the dark places will take you."

Lucas stood on the shore, scenting the change in the air. The sun would rise soon. No point going home and disturbing Justine's sleep. He would stretch out on the floor in his office and get what rest he could.

When the sun rose, someone would discover four naked boys in their yard. Hopefully that person would call the police. Hopefully those boys would tell the police the names of the two boys who wouldn't be coming home at all.

9

Butch jerked awake and struggled for a moment to get his four legs to support him. He gave himself a good shake, then nudged Stick and the other two guys who were slowly coming around.

He remembered having fun, running through the park, chasing down females and ripping flesh from that still-living prey. And then . . .

The little female who should have been so tasty hit him with something that knocked him on his ass. Bitch. And then . . .

He gave himself another shake and looked around. Where were they?

He caught a scent in the air, heard a quiet whine.

A bitch in heat. What could be better?

Stick came up beside him, sniffed the air, and growled.

Yeah. What could be better?

Albert Palmer jerked awake to what sounded like a war in his backyard.

Dog fight. And the pedigreed bitch he'd recently bought—a bitch that had just come into heat and was ready to be bred to a champion—was yelping. Almost screaming.

How the fuck did dogs get over that fence to go after his bitch?

Albert grabbed the gun he'd tucked into the drawer of the bedside table and hurried through the house to the back door. He'd put his useless wife and the female brat on a bus to Lovecraft yesterday so they could spend a few days with the wife's equally useless sister. Which meant she wasn't home to wring her hands about him not securing the gun properly when their children were in the house. Well, there weren't any children in the house now, were there? There wasn't the son, the child that mattered.

He unlocked the back door, flipped the switch for the outside lights, and stepped out into that war.

Four fucking dogs tearing at his pedigreed bitch. *Ruining* her, since he wouldn't make any profit from any pups that came out of her from *them*.

One of the dogs noticed him and stopped savaging the bitch. It stared at him and snarled—a sound that Albert thought held triumph and vicious glee.

He released the safety and shot the bastard twice, dropping it where it stood.

The other three dogs abandoned the bitch and lunged at him.

He shot them, too, firing and firing until he almost emptied the magazine. One of the dogs still twitched, but it would be dead soon.

Albert walked over to the bitch and looked at her. She whimpered. Too far gone to save, not far gone enough to die quickly.

He shot her in the head, ending her misery and his investment.

Hearing multiple sirens and cursing the neighbors who must have called the cops on him, he went inside, removed the magazine from the gun, and set both on the coffee table in the living room. Figuring he had a couple more minutes before he had cops banging on the door, he hurried into the bedroom and pulled on jeans and a T-shirt.

Returning to the front of the house, he unlocked the door and walked out with his hands up as armed police officers spread out and approached the house.

Shit. They'd brought enough fire power to level the whole fucking street.

"I have a right to defend my property," he said in a loud voice. Loud but civil, because he was sure they would side with him once they saw what those dogs had done to his bitch.

"You were firing at an intruder?" a female cop asked.

"Four of them." Who was the insane fuck who thought it was a good idea to let bitches be cops and carry guns? "They're in the backyard."

"Step away from the house."

He took a few steps down the front walk. A cop eased around him and went inside.

"The gun is on the coffee table," he shouted over his shoulder. "It's registered."

The cop returned a minute later and said, "Detective? We have a problem."

Cops converged on Albert and handcuffed him. The female holstered her weapon and went inside.

She returned a minute later with a strange look on her face. "Sir? You said there were four intruders. Can you describe them?"

"Dogs. You blind or something? I shot four dogs that were savaging a pedigreed bitch I purchased a few weeks ago. She was so torn up, I had to put her down."

Another strange look. "Come with me."

Cops held on to him as they walked through the house. The female cop opened the back door and stepped out. Albert followed her, ready to tell her what he thought of cops who couldn't figure out the obvious.

Then he looked and almost knocked down the cops holding him in his effort to back away. "No. I shot four dogs."

"Have you been drinking, sir?" the female cop asked. "The nine-one-one call came in just before sunrise. The light . . ."

"Don't tell me what the fuck I saw!" Albert shouted. "I shot four dogs. *Four dogs!*"

"You shot what you may have believed were dogs, but you killed four boys."

Albert stared at Butch, at Stick, at the two young guys he'd recruited from work to help him . . . "Where's Forrester's boy? Where is he? He was with them."

"We should continue this down at the precinct," the female cop said. "You'll be able to contact your attorney at that time."

"Where is he?" Albert shouted as the police escorted him to a cruiser. "You ask Forrester! You ask those freaks across the river."

Before the cops drove him to the precinct, he had the satisfaction of seeing the female cop shudder.

10

Beth Fahey walked into the team's area of the 13th precinct promptly at five o'clock in the morning. The food trucks didn't arrive that early to set up and start their business, so she made do with the last cup of coffee in the pot in the break room and started a fresh pot for the next people to report to work.

Captain Forrester wasn't in yet. That surprised her. Then again, he probably hadn't gotten much sleep after telling his wife that their son was lost somewhere on the Isle of Wyrd.

Ian Kuhn and Tom Castelletti walked in, carrying mugs of coffee.

"Did you set up the fresh pot?" Kuhn asked, lifting his mug.

Beth nodded. She stared at her desk phone, willing it to ring, wanting to hear from Lucas Frost that the wild dogs had been captured and were secured somewhere in Penwych—and that the Arcana had found Colin Forrester.

Captain Forrester walked in and looked at her. She shook her head. The men knew Lucas Frost would call *her* rather than any of them, and no one was willing—yet—to ask why that was so.

She was glad they didn't ask, since she didn't have an answer.

A phone finally rang, but it wasn't her desk phone or her cell phone. Castelletti answered it, listened, and promised that members of the team would get there as soon as they could.

Forrester stepped out of his office. "Well?"

"Detective Amanda Gibson from the twelfth precinct needs our help," Castelletti said. "Armed response teams arrived at Albert Palmer's residence shortly after sunrise because neighbors called nine-one-one and reported hearing gunshots. Palmer came outside, unarmed, and informed the police that he'd shot four dogs that were killing his bitch."

"God, no," Kuhn breathed.

Castelletti kept his eyes on Forrester. "Detective Gibson found four young, naked human males dead at the scene from multiple gunshot wounds."

Forrester closed his eyes.

"Palmer mentioned your son, Captain, and the . . . people . . . across the river," Castelletti continued. "Detective Gibson would like us to look at the crime scene and provide . . . insights . . . before she returns to the twelfth and questions Palmer."

Another phone rang. Kuhn answered it.

"Fahey and I can liaise with Gibson, Captain," Castelletti said. "It's better if you steer clear of the Palmer residence."

"Agreed," Forrester replied. He looked at Kuhn. "Was that Frost?"

Kuhn shook his head. "A woman's voice, but someone from over there. She said the first ferry will be crossing the river soon, and we should send someone to pick up the possessions of the transformed boys."

"A few minutes, maybe less," Beth said. "If the dogs had been a little slower to attack Palmer's bitch, if Palmer had been a couple minutes slower retrieving his gun from the lockbox and loading it, he would have stepped out after sunrise and seen the boys instead of . . ." She couldn't finish it.

Had the Arcana known this would happen? Or was this a moment when five individuals made choices that determined their fate? If she asked, would Frost tell her?

"Come on, Fahey," Castelletti said. "Let's go talk to Detective Gibson."

"Why choose me?" she asked when they were driving toward the Palmer residence. "Kuhn has more experience."

"Because Lucas Frost didn't call me or Kuhn or even the captain when the shit hit the fan over there yesterday. He called *you*. I'm not real comfortable with that. Neither is Kuhn. You seem a little too friendly with the Arcana for anyone's comfort." Castelletti glanced at her as he pulled up behind an unmarked car. "But you get answers, and you get assistance the rest of us don't get." He shut off the car and turned to look at her. "And I'm guessing that what you *don't* get is nightmares about what you see when you cross the river—unlike the rest of us."

No, she didn't get nightmares, Beth thought as she followed Castelletti up the front walk. But last night she'd drunk the second serving of the special tea and dreamed about Maxine Greenwood as a teenager—and almost saw the reason why someone had given her Arianna Greenwood's sketchbook of drawings of the Arcana.

Beth listened to Detective Gibson's report. She looked at the four boys and the dog that was actually a dog. All dead.

"Palmer didn't indicate he knew any of the intruders," Gibson said.

"He knew them," Beth replied quietly. Before they'd met Gibson, Castelletti had told her to take the lead on this. "What goes around comes around."

"Meaning what?" Gibson didn't look pleased to be talking to the special team's junior detective.

Castelletti gave Beth a sharp look of warning, but Beth was focused on explaining the path that had led to senseless killing. "Albert Palmer blamed Captain Forrester for Darren Palmer's death, even though the boy chose to go to Wyrd and chose to go through a moon gate—and he was killed within moments of his transformation, so there was nothing anyone could have done to save him. Yesterday afternoon, four teenage boys rode the ferry to Wyrd with Colin Forrester. They must have been joined by two other young men because there were seven young males involved in what happened. Four of those boys went through a moon gate and were transformed into wild dogs. We don't know yet why that form was triggered. The Arcana who look after Destiny Park were going to capture the dogs and bring them back to Penwych to what they believed would be a safe place where the boys could transform back into humans at sunrise."

"Sunrise." Gibson blew out an angry breath. "Just a couple of minutes, and things might have been so different here. But we still have to identify these boys."

"Their possessions are being sent over on the first ferry," Beth said. "A detective on our team is picking them up."

"This is your case," Castelletti said. "We can take the first look for identification, since you'll be busy questioning Palmer, or we can deliver the box to your team at the twelfth precinct if you prefer." He waited a beat before adding, "The high school is in the twelfth's jurisdiction."

"Yes, it is." Gibson frowned. "You said there were seven young men. We have the four who changed into dogs. What happened to the other three?"

Beth looked at Castelletti. He looked at her, offering no help—not because he wouldn't give it if she needed that help, but he didn't want to say the words.

"Two of those boys chose . . . unforgiving . . . modes of transportation, and it's unlikely that they will be seen for years, if they return at all."

"And Captain Forrester's boy?"

Beth drew in a shaky breath. "Missing. The Arcana are looking for him, but it's the Isle of Wyrd. There's no guarantee they'll find him."

"God," Gibson said. "So you have no idea who the missing boys are?"

Beth tipped her head toward the bodies that were being removed from the yard. "We were hoping they would tell us when they . . ."

Gibson nodded. "You know there is going to be a shitstorm over this. I'm aware of what Albert Palmer has been saying about . . . *them* . . . and this will give other people a reason to say he's right."

"Who persuaded those boys to go to Wyrd to do whatever they'd intended to do?" Beth asked. "Who paid them to go there?"

"There's no proof," Gibson argued.

Yet was the word that hung in the air.

"The Arcana are supposed to see people's fate, aren't they?" Gibson continued. "Why didn't they stop those boys from going through the gate?"

"Why didn't God stop those boys from getting on the ferry?" Beth countered.

"God doesn't interfere with our choices because we have free will!"

"Free will." Beth nodded. "I think the Arcana believe in that too."

11

Colin Forrester loved his first full day in Llamalidia. Sure, he felt anxious when he thought about his parents waiting for some word from him, but this was like being on a mission for Captain Picard and having his shuttle make a forced landing on an unfamiliar planet and then discovering a race of people almost no one else knew about—and a place that was a quarter turn to the left of reality as most humans knew it.

There was a kind of bunkhouse for seasonal workers who came to assist the Llamalidians with shearing, but Tia lived above the trading post and was letting him use her spare room as long as he followed the rules that were part of the deal of living in this land.

Plumbing was primitive, and water, which was a gift of the rainy season, was important enough to be rationed. Humans were allowed quick showers twice a week. The other days, you had a basin of water and a washcloth to wash your face, your armpits, and your privates.

The water from the washbasin and the shower was collected and used in the toilet to wash the solid waste through some pipes down to something called the sludge quarry—which was fortunately way downwind most of the time and not a place you wanted to visit in high summer.

The Llamalidians understood that he was a juvenile human who was far from home and whose education did not include their civilized language. Their children, called cria, were curious about him and invited him to play some of their games. So he played with the cria and began learning how to communicate in the Llamalidians' language while he observed their culture and daily life. Determined not to be a freeloader, since he wasn't sure how his being there impacted Tia's supplies and rationed goods, he also made an effort to help out at the trading post by sweeping the floors, wiping down shelves, and restocking goods—just like a good young officer would do while he waited for rescue.

He wasn't sure how much time he would have here, so he wanted to do and see and learn as much as he could. And despite the worry it would cause his parents, part of him hoped the bus that would be able to take him back to Destiny Park wouldn't arrive for a few days.

12

Charles Forrester didn't pay much attention to the radio station's local news segment until the editorial.

"The uncanny, the strange, the powerful currents of fate, are all around us. People go to practitioners in their own towns to have tarot cards read or have their palms read. They are looking to bring their intuition into the realm of conscious thought. They choose to do this, just like some people choose to ride the ferry and visit the Isle of Wyrd. They choose to go across the river knowing that most of the island is dangerous and potentially fatal to anyone who disregards the warnings. If someone enters the tiger enclosure at the zoo, despite all the warnings and ignoring all common sense, we should not blame the tiger if the person is killed. We should not blame the people living on Wyrd for tragedy that is not of their making."

"Captain?" Castelletti stood in the doorway of Forrester's office. "Detective Gibson is here to see you."

Charles turned off the radio. Albert Palmer's claiming the four boys he killed were dogs when he shot them was the hot story in local news—and fodder for all kinds of reports and speculation. Did Palmer have a mental breakdown after the death of his own son and blame his son's friends for not going with the boy on that fateful trip to Wyrd? Or had he known what he was doing when he shot those boys and was now using a diminished capacity defense as a get-out-of-jail card?

Or was he telling the simple truth?

"Detective Gibson," he said when she walked into his office.

"Captain."

"Have a seat." He offered her coffee or tea, which she declined. "What can I do for you?"

"Using the items in the box of possessions you sent to my team, we were able to confirm the identities of two Penwych High School boys who were part of a 'pack' that called themselves Dare's Doggs. The other two boys, who were older and out of school, worked for the same construction company as Albert Palmer. Coworkers confirmed that Palmer and those two went out drinking after work several nights a week and had been doing so for the past few months."

"He denied knowing any of the boys who were in his yard."

"He did," Gibson agreed. "However, when she returned from visiting her sister in Lovecraft, Mrs. Palmer identified the boys who were her son's friends, saying they'd been to the house often. She didn't know their actual names; she knew them as Butch and Stick. She said there were two others, Devl and Acid. She thought they were a bad influence on Darren."

Charles sat back. "Why are you telling me this? I'm under orders to stay away from any investigation involving Albert Palmer because he may directly or indirectly be responsible for my son's disappearance."

Gibson gave him a sour look. "I have questions, and I'll have to talk to those *people* to get the answers." She hesitated. "I have to go to Wyrd, and I'd like one of your detectives to go with me since they have experience dealing with . . ."

The Arcana, Charles thought. "Have you talked to any of the Arcana before?"

"No."

But someone who mattered to you had crossed the river—and wherever that person's fate had taken them, it hadn't ended well. "Do you intend to ask about the missing boys?"

"Yes. I also want to see this moon gate and determine if there was some negligence on *their* part that allowed those boys to get turned into dogs."

"Your prejudice will taint all your transactions with the Arcana," Charles said. "It would be better if you gave us your questions, and we'll go over and get the answers."

Gibson shook her head. "I don't want answers that have been filtered by someone who is sympathetic to them. I want to ask the questions and hear the answers. Damn it, Forrester, we have four dead boys and two others whose parents are calling every hour asking if we've found them yet." She closed her eyes and took a couple of breaths. "I'm sorry. Your son is missing too. I haven't forgotten that."

"But I'm not calling you every hour looking for answers." Charles sighed. "I'll send Detective Fahey with you."

"I'd prefer someone other than your junior detective."

"Your hostility toward the Arcana is unmistakable. That being the case, they won't talk to you, let alone answer questions for a police investigation. You want answers? You need Fahey. They'll talk to her—or overlook your rudeness because she's with you."

Gibson stared at him. "What's her deal with them?"

"The same as every member of my team," Charles replied. "We can go to Wyrd and come back in one piece. That's a vital requirement when you're a cop because we don't go over there for entertainment."

Or for reasons that are far more desperate than entertainment.

He considered the other inquiries his team was currently investigating. Nothing urgent. Locating Rachel Nightingale was an ongoing investigation and had been for months, but that was Grace Russell's case. So was finding Reginald Hampton III, who was still listed as missing—or finally listed as missing, since his family and the administrators running his businesses were now admitting that he didn't usually drop out of sight for this long.

"I can send Detective Castelletti along, too, if that makes it easier for you," he said. "But if you don't take Fahey, it will be a wasted trip."

"Fine." Gibson paused. "Thank you."

Charles pushed away from his desk, escorted Gibson out of his office, and gave Fahey and Castelletti their assignment.

13

Lucas Frost strode into his office and looked toward the large table where Ashley Laxton sorted the mail that came from Wyrd's various—and varied—neighborhoods. Some people wanted to stay in touch with those they had left behind. Others wanted supplies not easily found wherever they were currently located. All the mail went through Destiny Park and was sent on to post offices across the river. Mail sent from a person in the human towns to a resident of Wyrd was delivered to one of the Arcana's post office boxes—usually the ones in Penwych or Lovecraft. It was collected and then brought to the park for distribution. A letter going to a neighborhood in Wyrd might arrive in a couple of days, or it might take a year, depending on how often someone or something was able to reach a particular place—and that often depended on the intentions of the sender and receiver.

He stopped when Ashley held out two letters. As he walked over to the table and took the letters, he could feel lines of fate lightly touching, possibly changing what might come.

One letter was addressed to him. The other was addressed to Captain Forrester.

Ferryman, he called.

Frost?

If you see any police officers around the pier on the other side of the river, tell them I need to see one of Forrester's people as soon as possible.

The young female who doesn't fear the strange?

Not surprising that the Ferryman had noticed her. *All* the Arcana Beth Fahey had come in contact with had noticed her because she wasn't like the rest of the police—except Forrester. But even he wasn't as easy about being here as she was. Then again, she had an ancestor who had been Arcana—a truth it wasn't yet time for her to know, according to the Ladies Three. **Yes, tell them I need to see Beth Fahey.**

He opened the letter addressed to him. From Tia Downing? She wouldn't send a request for supplies to *him*, so what . . .

He skimmed the letter for the general sense of her message, then read it again carefully. He didn't think Forrester's girl child was in danger. Not anymore. But the boy couldn't have known that when he arrived at Llamalidia. Since the boy had written to his father, why had the warning come through Tia, along with the report of how—and why—Colin Forrester had gone to Wyrd? Unless . . .

Colin wrote a letter that could be shared with his mother, while Tia had sent information that was strictly for the police captain? Considering the content of Tia's report, that would make sense.

Setting the letters under a paperweight on his desk, Lucas left his office to patrol the park and check on the food stands—and wait for the ferry's return.

14

Beth Fahey didn't know why Detective Gibson was so against her or why the woman was so against the Arcana when she admitted that she'd never gone to Wyrd. Which didn't mean she hadn't crossed paths with one of the Arcana. The multiple Rachel Nightingales were proof that people could interact with the Arcana and never know it. But this simmering anger wasn't going to net any answers. Not from someone like Lucas Frost.

There were sawhorses at the land end of the pier. People queued up and waited while the ferry arrived and prepared to take on passengers.

Beth had drawn money from the team's petty cash box to cover the anticipated fare for the three of them. As she stepped up to the booth and exchanged the money for the coins used on Wyrd, a man walked down the stairs from the ferry's wheelhouse. He was large and dark in a way that made her think of deep water and sea graves.

"Beth Fahey." A voice like heavy surf.

She didn't doubt for a moment that she was looking at the Ferryman. And she didn't doubt for a moment that she should be . . . careful . . . around him. "I'm Detective Fahey."

"Lucas Frost wants to see you." The Ferryman looked at Gibson and Castelletti. "They are with you?"

"Yes, they are." *Be careful. Stay respectful.*

"Come aboard. There is no fare required today for the crossing to Wyrd."

Which didn't mean they wouldn't be charged double for passage to get home.

He waited until the three of them were on board before returning to the wheelhouse.

Gibson walked into the ferry's cabin, slipped onto a seat, and turned her face toward the window.

Beth sat on the seat behind Gibson, letting Castelletti sit with the other Penwych detective since Gibson seemed to find his presence less objectionable.

Why did Frost want to see her? If he'd found out something about any of the missing boys, why not call her or Forrester? Unless he had something physical that a detective from the team needed to bring back to Forrester.

Whatever turns the wheels of the world, please give us some good news about Colin Forrester.

Once the ferry reached Wyrd, Beth and the other two detectives waited until the visitors disembarked before they left the ferry and walked toward the pavilion. Since he'd asked for her, Beth was surprised not to see Lucas Frost waiting for her.

Then they reached the top of the low rise. Beth looked back at Gibson, who was studying the food stands and hotel on the right and the cabins on the left. In the middle of the grassy space, Lucas Frost stood behind the large moon gate.

Beth shifted her direction toward the gate—and the Arcana's leader.

"Detective Fahey," Frost said. "You and Detective Castelletti don't need to go through the moon gate. But you . . ." The look in his eyes was cold and hostile when he focused on Gibson—a look that matched hers. "You *will* need to walk through the moon gate."

"Why?" Gibson said. "What will it do to me?"

"Nothing. You came seeking answers. What I see when you walk through the gate will determine if we will provide any."

"If I refuse?"

"Then you should go back to the dock and wait until the ferry makes the return trip across the river," Frost replied. "My business is with Detective Fahey, not with you."

The look Frost gave Beth felt like a silent command—and made her wonder, again, why it felt natural to take orders from this man. When he began to walk away, she swung around the moon gate and started to follow, ignoring Castelletti's quiet cursing and Gibson's sputtering.

"Wait," Gibson called. "I'll walk through the damn gate."

Frost turned around but didn't come closer to the gate.

Beth joined Frost and watched Castelletti swing around the gate, shooting her a look that was part wary, part pissed off.

She couldn't blame him. He was probably wondering, if push came to shove, if she would have his back or Frost's.

She wondered the same thing.

As Gibson walked through the moon gate, Beth thought she saw a faint light coming from some of the runes carved in the back of the stones. It was too faint for her to be sure it was something uncanny and not god fingers coming through the clouds and hitting the stones to create that illusion.

Lucas Frost wasn't pleased with whatever he saw on the stones, but he said, "You may ask the Ladies Three your question." He headed for the pavilion.

"I might have more than one," Gibson said, raising her voice.

Frost didn't answer, and he didn't slow down.

"What should I expect?" Gibson asked, turning her head slightly to direct the question to Castelletti.

"I don't know," he replied. "I've never dealt with the Ladies Three, never talked to anyone but Frost when I've had to come here for an investigation. Fahey? Do you know?"

"They set a price for what you want," Beth said as they began walking down the steps that led into the pavilion. "If you agree to pay it, they'll answer your question—or provide the service or material you require." She added the last part when she remembered what the use of a ghost gun and three bullets cost Gerry Palowski.

As soon as they entered the pavilion, Beth went to the table, put a gold coin in the box, and took one of the bone discs. She had an uneasy feeling that Frost wouldn't have told Gibson how to start a bargain with the Ladies Three, and that made her wonder if the Arcana were going to ask for something they already knew Gibson wouldn't pay.

They walked into the room where the Ladies Three conducted

their business. The three women glanced at Beth and Castelletti before giving Gibson a cold stare.

The woman with the cards selected two decks, shuffled them, spread out the decks in two arches, then selected some cards—but didn't invite Gibson to make any choices.

This isn't the way it's supposed to work when you ask them for something, Beth thought. *What's going on here?*

The woman Beth thought of as justice because she balanced the scales between want and payment looked at the woman with the cards, then looked at Gibson.

"You come under false pretenses," Justice said. "We've already given Captain Forrester and his people the information we have about the human predators who made bad choices. They are gone for the foreseeable future. Use whatever words you use on your reports when someone disappears." The woman paused. "Now ask the real question you came here to ask."

"What is the price for the answer?" Beth asked when she realized that Gibson wouldn't think to ask.

Justice looked at Beth. "That she never comes back to Wyrd for any reason."

God, they really don't like her.

"I don't have a question," Gibson snarled. "But I'll give *you* an answer. You want to know why I hate you? Because my mother came here, got taken in by your flimflam bullshit, and a few weeks later she killed herself."

Silence. Then Frost said, "What was your mother's name?"

"Angela Gibson."

The woman with the sketchbook put it aside, opened the pocket doors behind her part of the room, and disappeared. She returned a few minutes later with a sheet of drawing paper. She turned the paper around to reveal the sketches, and said, "Angela Gibson."

The paper held several sketches that spilled into one another, but the three that held Beth's attention were the gravestone with Angela Gibson's name, her birth and death dates, and the number seventy; the hand with a distinct scar near the base of the thumb pouring a powder into a glass of clear liquid; and the ghostly image of a woman who looked like an older version of Gibson standing behind the gravestone.

Frost said, "Your mother didn't kill herself."

Gibson collapsed. Beth and Castelletti caught her arms and eased her to the floor.

A chair was brought, and they helped Gibson into it.

"Mom's stepbrother had a scar like that on his hand," Gibson whispered. "He . . . killed her? Why?"

"If she knew or guessed, she didn't say," Justice replied.

"She'd gone to a reader on your side of the river," Cards said. "Whatever she learned from that person gave her warning—and brought her to Wyrd to make a bargain with the Arcana."

"She bargained for the full measure of her years, regardless of her age when she died," Justice said.

Beth stared at the gravestone and calculated Angela Gibson's age when she died. Then she looked at the ghostly image—and understood. "She bargained to become a ghost, didn't she?"

"A spectral being who could protect what she loved the most." Justice looked at Gibson.

Castelletti pulled a packet of tissues out of his pocket and gave them to Gibson, who stared at the sketches as tears ran down her face.

Gibson pulled a couple of tissues out of the pack, wiped her face, and blew her nose. "My mother rearranged her finances after coming here, tied up a lot of her money in a trust for me, revised her will. All the burial arrangements were prepaid, and there wasn't much left of her money when she . . . died . . . because most of her liquid assets had been given to a couple of companies for 'services rendered.' I couldn't find out what those services were, and her lawyer didn't know."

How much did it cost to become a ghost? Beth wondered.

"When the house and other physical assets were sold, her stepbrother and I received the proceeds as our inheritance," Gibson said. "An equal split. By the time all the bills were paid, it wasn't much—and no one told me about the trust until I received the letter from the lawyer on my mother's seventieth birthday." She studied the sketches, focused on the one in the bottom left-hand corner. "She was sixty-seven when she died. Two years later, her stepbrother died in a horrific car accident—although there was some question that it was an accident. There was no reason for the car to be traveling at those speeds on a rain-slick road unless the driver put his foot all the way down on the accelerator."

"Except . . . ?" Beth asked when Gibson hesitated.

"Except he was still alive when the EMTs and rescue vehicles arrived, and he kept telling them that he had seen Angela. He had broken into my apartment and taken a piece of jewelry she had given me years ago, and she wanted it back. That's what he said with his last breath: he had seen Angela." Gibson wiped her nose again. "Funny thing was, someone *had* broken into my apartment that day. The jewelry box on my dresser was open, and the good jewelry was scattered over the top of the dresser, but only a brooch with a broken pin was missing." She hesitated. "They found it in the wreckage."

Gibson looked at Frost. "She looked out for me those three years she would have had if he hadn't . . ."

"When we make a bargain, we keep it," he said.

Gibson let out a watery laugh. "Mom watching over me. Well, that might explain the man I was dating who ran out of my apartment without getting dressed and was arrested for indecent exposure. Turned out he was a bit of a con artist when it came to women. If he'd looked into the bathroom mirror and saw my mother looking back . . ." She shook her head.

"You have your answer," Justice said. "Our associate will escort you to the hotel, where you can consume a restorative beverage while the other detectives have their meeting with Lucas."

Beth stared at the woman who entered the room. She was certain no one would offer a name. She was also certain this was the unknown woman who had accompanied one of the Rachel Nightingales to a bank to close all of Nightingale's accounts.

After Gibson left the pavilion with her escort, Frost led Beth and Castelletti to his office. Going to his desk, he picked up two letters and handed them to Beth.

Beth looked at the letter addressed to Captain Forrester and shivered. She unfolded the other letter.

"Shit," Castelletti said, reading over her shoulder. "That explains why Colin went with Dare's Doggs, but how is he able to make contact with us?"

"As it says," Frost replied. "He bought a bus ticket and made a choice—and landed in a neighborhood where communication with Destiny Park is possible. The two boys who pursued him . . . Their intentions decided their destination, which is why they are unlikely to return. Not even as ghosts."

"Is communication with that neighborhood possible in both directions?" Beth asked. "Can Captain Forrester send a letter to his son?"

"Send it? Yes. Will the boy receive it?" Frost shrugged. "It depends."

"On what?" Castelletti's voice had sharpened—and was matched by a sharp look from Frost.

Words have power, Beth thought. *Intentions matter.* "Did you need to see us for anything else?"

Frost looked at Castelletti and said, "No. Nothing."

Castelletti jerked as if he'd been slapped. Then he slowly let out a breath. "I'm sorry if I sounded . . . brusque. We've been worried about the captain's son."

"Understandable."

Which wasn't the same as being forgotten—or forgiven.

Castelletti walked out of Frost's office.

Beth took her time tucking the letters into her purse. Then she looked toward the door that led to another room and said, "How is Rahele doing?"

Frost got a peculiar look on his face. "She is teaching the crow to write poems."

Oh. "Well, that's better than teaching him to write limericks."

Frost stared at her.

Mischief bubbled up inside her, impossible to resist now that she could bring Captain Forrester *some* news about his son. Beth gave the ruler of Destiny Park a cheeky curtsy and said, "Good day, Mr. Frost."

His face looked stern, but she thought she detected a hint of amusement in his eyes. "Good day, Detective Fahey."

Beth hurried out of Frost's office and caught up to Castelletti on his way to the hotel to fetch Detective Gibson.

They didn't talk during the return ride across the river. Maybe because no one knew what to say about the revelations regarding

Gibson's mother. Maybe because no one knew how Captain Forrester would react to the information that his daughter had also been targeted by the bullyboys known as Dare's Doggs.

Maybe because no one wanted to say "what goes around comes around" as it applied to Albert Palmer and what happened to the boys he had sent across the river.

15

"Detective Gibson got an answer," Castelletti had said. *"But not the answer she expected. We escorted her back to the twelfth precinct. She was still shaken up when we got off the ferry on this side of the river."*

Now Charles Forrester stood around the large evidence table with his team, waiting for the rest of the report. Because there was more. Something had happened on Wyrd. The way Tom Castelletti was distancing himself from Beth Fahey told him that much. He'd talk to Tom privately. If his people couldn't work together, investigating the strange would be even more dangerous.

Fahey withdrew two envelopes from her purse. She handed one to him and said, "This one is private."

Charles's breath caught when he recognized Colin's handwriting. His hand trembled as he accepted the envelope, and it took every ounce of discipline he had to stand there with his team instead of locking himself in his office to read his son's message.

Fahey held out another envelope. "The team should know about this."

He looked at the envelope. "That's addressed to Frost." *And to the Sorcerer King.*

"Yes," she replied, "but it was intended for both of you." She hesitated. "For you as a police officer."

Charles opened the letter and braced a hand on the table as he read the report. "Who's Tia Downing?"

"Don't know," Castelletti said. He glanced at Fahey, who shook her head.

"Captain?" Ian Kuhn said.

Charles handed him the letter and looked at Castelletti and Fahey. "You both know what it says?"

They nodded.

Kuhn finished reading and whistled. "Your boy has backbone, trying to save his sister by making that choice."

Hold it together. There are still things we need to do.

Pulling Jazz out of school wasn't one of those things, although he wanted to do exactly that. God, how he wanted to do that.

"I called the high school and made some inquiries," Kuhn said. "The bullyboys known as Dare's Doggs were Darren Palmer and his four friends. It's unlikely that there is anyone else connected with . . . this . . . that would aim that kind of attack on your daughter."

"It also sounds like your son went through the moon gate before the four boys who were turned into dogs," Castelletti said. "He didn't know they were no longer a threat to his sister."

If Albert Palmer hadn't shot them just before sunrise, they still could have been a threat to her, Charles thought. *They could have carried out their "mission" against my family.*

"Captain?" Kuhn said. "What do you want us to do?"

"We could pick up your daughter after school," Fahey said. "Make sure she gets home okay."

He almost agreed. "I appreciate the suggestion, but she might see it as bad news about her brother." He hesitated. "Maybe Monkton and Reynolds could do a drive-by when her school lets out and just keep an eye on things."

"I'll tell them," Castelletti said.

Charles walked into his office. He wasn't surprised when Fahey followed him.

"I don't know what your son's letter says, but Lucas Frost told us that communication can go both ways." She looked at him. "He also said that how long it takes for a letter to arrive depends on the intentions of the sender and receiver." She looked startled. "I'm sure he said that, but I don't remember *hearing* the words. Maybe I inferred it."

Or maybe you somehow heard something the rest of us couldn't hear.

He gave her a long look. "Something happen between you and Castelletti? Something I should know about?"

She shrugged, an uneasy movement. "He thinks I'm too friendly with the Arcana—and maybe wonders who I'll stand with if it becomes a question of them or us."

I don't wonder, Charles thought. *I know you won't stand with us. I don't know why that's true, but I know it's true. I just hope we never have to put that truth to the test.*

"The team needs you, Beth," he said quietly. "I've never seen the Arcana take to any of us the way they take to you. They show you more, tell you more. They haven't shown you everything yet. You don't have the look in your eyes that tells me you've seen the truth about the Arcana that gives other cops nightmares—but I don't think that truth will give *you* nightmares." He paused. "If other members of the team give you any trouble, I want to know. Understand?"

"Yes, sir."

He hoped she did. "Close the door on your way out."

When he was alone, he sat at his desk and opened his son's letter.

Dear Mom and Dad,

I'm okay! I got away from the bullyboys, bought a bus ticket, and I ended up here. I can't tell you where because not telling is one of the rules. But I'm safe, and I have a place to stay while things get sorted out. I'll write again soon, but I'm not sure how long it will take for you to get a letter. Mail delivery is way different from what it's like across the river. Everything is different—and it's kind of cool.

Give Jazz a hug from me.

Love you.
Colin

Charles let out a shuddering sigh. His boy was safe. Knowing that much eased a pressure in his chest and would relieve Aisha's worst fears too.

"It's kind of cool, huh?" Coming from Colin, that could mean a lot of things, but what it meant most of all was that, for the moment, he was safe.

Whether Colin would be able to get home was a different question.

Using his cell phone, he made a call.

"Frost."

"It's Forrester."

"Did you receive the letters?"

"I did."

"Is your daughter safe?"

"She is." *Is my son?* That was a question he couldn't ask. "I wanted to clarify a couple of things about sending a parcel to Colin's . . . location. I imagine he could use some spending money and other things."

A thoughtful pause. "Send over your parcel. We'll try to get it to him. He's not on a main bus route."

Charles didn't ask for more information because he knew Frost wouldn't provide it.

He ended the call and sat back, elated and exhausted. Aisha would be disappointed that they couldn't bring Colin home, but they weren't burying their son and they weren't going to wonder for years if they would ever hear from their boy again. Colin was *somewhere* that was connected to the Isle of Wyrd, and he was with someone who had cared enough to write and send a report and a warning.

He had to be content with that. If he had any hope of keeping a line of communication open, he had to keep his intentions focused on being content with that.

16

The sensation of cobwebs brushing bare skin had Captain Flint scanning the river—and seeing the *Bonnie Lass* slowly sailing toward the *Last Breath*. The black skull-and-crossbones flag wasn't flying, so Sheridan Gray wasn't on the hunt for someone, but she was steering her ship close enough to his fishing trawler to make things very interesting. Except the river was as still as glass, and he suspected that was the Pirate Queen's doing. They were both Arcana who had a connection to water, but Captain Gray came from a major branch of their kind—and was more dangerous because of it.

Captain Flint. Even using their psychic communication, her voice was a siren's song. Not like some of her sisters, who used their songs to lure foolish men into being their lovers until the men were withered and spent. No, Sheridan Gray offered sanctuary and a different kind of life to women—and men—who would have used a razor or a bottle of pills to escape an abuser. Freedom from despair often birthed rage, and her chosen crew was fierce when they were hunting.

She also took on passengers who had made a bargain with the Arcana at Destiny Park, but she was strict about people working for their passage and completing the bargain that had been made.

What did she want with him and his boat?

Captain Gray?

I understand your crew is a man short. I have someone who has sailed with me for two years. He's a good man, an honorable man, but now he is near his last breath. Sailing on the* Bonnie Lass *was a wish fulfilled. He has one other wish. I can't help him, but I think you can, because you and I touch the Isle in different ways and for different reasons. Would you take him?

She'd sent him crew members before. After all, the *Last Breath* was often the final stop in a person's journey. **We're down a man, so I'll be pleased to take him.**

"Carver," Flint called to his first mate. "New crewman coming aboard from the *Bonnie Lass*. Ready the lines."

As lines were tossed across the narrow space between the vessels and secured, Flint shut off the trawler's engines while the *Bonnie Lass*'s crew lowered the remaining sail. A gangplank was secured between the vessels.

Wing Kei Lee, Sheridan Gray's first mate, escorted an older man to the gangplank, then walked behind him, protective. When the man took that final step and his feet were on the deck of the *Last Breath*, Lee retreated to the *Bonnie Lass* and helped another woman haul in the gangplank and untie the ropes.

The older man saluted. Gray smiled, and Wing Kei Lee bowed in farewell.

Sails were raised, and the *Bonnie Lass* went on its way.

Flint turned to the man, aware that the other members of his crew gathered around. After the unpleasantness with Jeremy Swayne, they were understandably cautious about welcoming someone new.

"I'm Flint, captain of this boat."

The man held out a hand and smiled. "Patrick Russell. I'm grateful to be here, Captain Flint. Grateful to have a little more time on the water and . . ." His voice faded.

"What is it you'd like that you're not sure you can have?" Flint asked.

"I was dying." Russell gave Flint an odd little smile. "Still am, but I had two wonderful years sailing on the *Bonnie Lass*, and that was longer than I would have survived on land. Now the end is close, and I wish there was a way to get a message to my daughter, Gracie. When I boarded the *Bonnie Lass*, I didn't realize there wouldn't be a way to say goodbye. Gracie deserved a proper goodbye."

"That's your wish?"

"That's my wish."

Flint looked at his crew. All of them nodded. Most of them had been with him long enough that there wasn't anyone left to remember them—or anyone they wanted remembering them. But this man . . .

"Write a letter to your daughter. We'll get it to Destiny Park. Someone there will see that it reaches her." And perhaps, if Wyrd's Sorcerer King was willing to help, there was one other thing Flint and his crew could do to fulfill that wish.

"Thank you," Russell said. His eyes widened as a large fish leaped out of the water next to the trawler. "Gracious! That's a trophy fish for sure."

"He may be caught someday, but not by us. We have an agreement with the Ferryman not to lower a net or a line when that one is near."

He saw a question in Russell's eyes, but the man had learned enough about Wyrd and its ways not to ask.

After Carver led Russell below to settle into the bunk that would be his until it was his turn to take that last breath and leave the trawler, Flint scanned the river.

I won't lower net or line to catch you until your debt to the Ferryman is paid, Flint thought as he watched the fish leap out of the water well ahead of the trawler. *But I know who you are. Some of my crew took that last breath because of you. If you're still in the water when that debt is paid, I'll be coming for you—and not to add you to my crew.*

17

Charles Forrester packed the rolled T-shirts for a second time. Or was it the third? Another pair of jeans. A pullover sweater. Socks. Underwear. Shorts. Chinos. Windbreaker. A variety of clothes to fit the weather in an unknown place. He hadn't found Colin's spring jacket, so he had to figure the boy had been wearing it to school the day the bullyboys took him to Wyrd. Had Colin been wearing it when he crossed the river, or would someone at the school find it in the boy's locker? He'd have to arrange to have Colin's locker cleared out so that he could bring the boy's things home—for the time being.

He looked at his wife. Aisha watched him pack the suitcase, a mix of hope and horror in her eyes. She had spun between wanting to pack every article of clothing Colin owned to wanting to send nothing more than would fit into a backpack, as if the size of the suitcase would determine how long their son would remain lost in some piece of Wyrd.

Not lost, Charles reminded himself. Tucked away, yes. But not lost. Colin had sent a letter home, and that had to mean something.

Maybe being tucked away was the safest thing for Colin right now. After months of Albert Palmer agitating to have something done about Wyrd, the uproar over the four boys he killed and the two that were officially listed as missing wasn't going to die down soon. He and Aisha were keeping a close eye on Jazz to make sure she wasn't being bullied or otherwise bothered by children at her school. A couple of her friends stopped talking to her, stopped going to the movies with her or any of the other things girls that age did. But Davie was at the house every day, doing homework with Jazz and coaxing her into practicing dance routines that had Charles biting his tongue because they sounded more like elephants pounding on the floor than twelve-year-old . . . people. Although, based on a nature show he'd seen recently, elephants were actually quiet when they walked.

"All his favorite clothes," Aisha whispered when Charles reached for the sweatshirt she'd been hugging since he'd begun packing the suitcase this time. "What if it gets lost? You said they can't promise it will be delivered."

"Then we'll buy him new clothes," Charles said gently.

"What if he comes home and the suitcase hasn't arrived yet?"

"Aisha." He gathered her in his arms and held on. "Beth Fahey called Lucas Frost and asked about the weather in that part of Wyrd. He told her to figure on hot days and chilly nights. We're packing the same way we would if he was at summer camp. He has a place to stay. He'll have food. The woman who reported Colin's whereabouts to Lucas Frost seems like a solid individual."

"We don't know anything about her."

He knew a couple of things about Tia Downing. She had been in the military, had served honorably—and had disappeared after her enlistment was up. "We'll send Colin his favorite clothes to remind him of home. We'll add the toothbrush and dental floss—and a couple of paperbacks of his current favorite series."

"E-reader?" Aisha asked, finally releasing the sweatshirt so that Charles could pack it.

"Fahey said there is no electricity where he is."

"No . . . ?" Aisha stared at him. "He's a *teenager.* How is he going to survive without texting? Without the internet? Without . . ." She waved her arms to indicate all the things kids Colin's age swore they couldn't live without.

Charles laughed. "Maybe when he misses those things enough, he'll find his way home."

18

Lucas Frost met Charles Forrester at the hotel. A man with a suitcase walking into the hotel wouldn't attract attention. A man hauling a suitcase into the pavilion? People would notice, and even a casual remark said to the wrong person at the wrong time could have unintentional consequences.

Lucas looked at the large suitcase, then at Forrester. The police captain was the only one of his team who habitually wore a uniform. Today he wasn't dressed for work, had known not to call attention to himself that way.

"What are your intentions?" Lucas asked. "Are you thinking you can take that suitcase to where your son is now and somehow find your way home?"

He saw the conflict in Forrester's eyes. The man wanted to do just that. Another man might have made that choice, and the Arcana would not have interfered with whatever fate came from that choice. But Forrester had seen enough of Wyrd to know what might happen.

"What are the odds that I could actually reach the place where Colin is staying and get back home to my wife and daughter, with or without my son?" Forrester asked.

"Long odds," Lucas replied. "If that is your intention, I hope you provided your wife with all the information she'll need to live without you."

"That's what I thought." Forrester placed a hand on the suitcase. "So my intention is that this suitcase containing my son's clothes and a few of his personal possessions reach him in a timely manner. I exchanged some money for the coins used on Wyrd and tucked those into the suitcase so that he'll have spending money. I also tucked in some stationery and envelopes to encourage him to write. He's a teenage boy, so we should be grateful we heard from him at all, but it would ease our hearts to hear from him now and then."

"A person's fate is his or her own, but the Arcana can assist in some things," Lucas said. "Like adding my intention to yours that the suitcase finds the correct destination with alacrity."

"Thank you." Forrester studied him. "Is there something I can do for you?"

"We'll call it a favor." Lucas removed an envelope out of his jacket pocket and held it out, along with a sheet of paper. "Instructions. The timing is critical because it will happen only once in that place and at that time."

Forrester's eyes widened when he saw the name on the envelope. "What is supposed to happen?"

"Closure."

19

Charles Forrester changed into his uniform and was about to check in with his team when Tom Castelletti stepped into the doorway.

"Detective Gibson is here to see you," Castelletti said.

"Send her in."

The woman who walked into his office looked haunted. That look was the reason there was a special team of police officers who assisted the six towns around the Fate River when an investigation indicated a connection with Wyrd.

In Amanda Gibson's case, Charles thought she had more reason than most to look haunted.

"How are you?" he asked when they were seated.

"My mother was murdered by her stepbrother and was a ghost who tried to protect me for the last three years of her existence." She tried to smile. "I'm having trouble coping with that."

"Can you sleep?"

"Not really. The dreams are . . ." Gibson shivered. "Anyway, I've taken a leave of absence—a few weeks to get some counseling, to think about things that happened during those years in light of what I now know. Another detective in the twelfth precinct will be handling the Albert Palmer investigation—or as much as he can investigate. He may contact you." She took a deep breath and exhaled slowly. "I also wanted to let you know that officers will be patrolling at the high school, middle school, and grade school for the remainder of this school year. Some of the boys who died or are missing have siblings who might react badly to what has happened and want to blame someone else for their brothers' bad choices."

"I appreciate you telling me." Gibson wasn't the first who had told him about the patrols to reassure him that his daughter would be as safe as possible. "Are you going to stay in Penwych?" After a brush with Wyrd, some officers stayed on the job but wouldn't go near the river. Others found jobs in towns far enough away that they could pretend the Fate River and the Isle of Wyrd didn't exist—and didn't realize that denying the existence of a place that was a convergence of the uncanny didn't mean they couldn't brush against the uncanny somewhere else.

"I'm going to a luxury resort with a couple of close friends and get away from everything. They are people I trust, friends I can talk to about . . . my mother. About that place." Gibson stood, preparing to leave. Then she hesitated. "Any news about your son?"

"He's safe, but his location is unknown."

"A bit like witness protection."

"Yes." Except Charles had hope that they would hear from Colin, that he would come home someday.

After Amanda Gibson left the team's area of the 13th precinct, Charles sat at his desk and placed a phone call to Grace Russell.

20

Grace Russell parked her car and walked to the dock reserved for police patrol boats—and wondered what was going on with Charles Forrester that he wanted to meet her here. The police dock was located at a waterfront park, which was officially closed at this hour.

"Should I bring my officers?" she'd asked.

"No. This is personal."

She saw the lights and heard the motor of the Penwych patrol boat. Standing at the land end of the dock, she waited for Forrester to disembark.

"Captain Russell," Forrester said when he reached her.

"Captain Forrester. What's this about?"

Forrester removed a piece of paper and a small high-powered flashlight from his coat pocket. After studying the paper, he looked around. "We need to take that path along the river."

"Why?"

The flashlight didn't illuminate his face enough for her to see his expression. "Closure," he said.

Did she trust him? He was a colleague, and she believed he was a good man, and she relied on his skill to deal with what came out of Wyrd. But it was that connection with the place and, more, the people there that produced that kernel of doubt—especially when someone from that team asked for something . . . unusual.

Forrester used his flashlight to locate the path. Then he looked at her.

Nodding decisively, she followed him. She was armed, after all. Then again, he probably was too.

Grace pulled out her own flashlight so she wouldn't be dependent on his. They walked in silence for a few minutes. Forrester seemed to be looking for something specific, since he consulted the paper a couple of times.

"Here." Forrester stepped off the path and crossed a grassy area between the path and the large rocks that bordered the river.

The sky had lightened. Almost dawn.

After a moment's hesitation, Grace joined him at the river's edge and noticed how he scanned the river. "What are we looking for?"

Forrester pointed. "That."

Grace looked where he pointed—and saw nothing. And then . . .

Faint at first, as if seeing something shrouded by fog. Except there was no fog on the river, no mist. Nothing to obscure vision. She didn't hear a motor, but moment by moment the boat took shape, became solid. And she saw . . .

"Gracie!"

The voice. So loved. So familiar. But it couldn't be. "Dad?" she whispered.

Patrick Russell waved his arms over his head to draw attention to himself, to the boat that couldn't possibly exist.

"Gracie!" Patrick called again.

"Dad?" *How . . . ?* "Dad!"

His smile lit up his face, lit up the sky. He grabbed the arm of the man standing next to him and pointed toward the shore with his other hand. "That's my girl! That's Gracie!"

"Dad!" He'd disappeared two years ago. She'd never thought she would see him again. And with everything the doctors had told her at the time, she never thought she would see more than his corpse—if it was ever found. But there he was, waving at her.

"I love you, Gracie! I love you!"

She swallowed a sob. Not sorrow. Maybe that would come. For now, the tears were from joy. "I love you, Dad!"

The boat came abreast of their position on the bank. The man who seemed to be the captain touched two fingers to his cap in a salute. The other men and women who stood around Patrick either took off their caps and held them over their hearts or raised a hand in greeting. All of them were smiling—but none of them smiled more than Patrick Russell.

As the sky lightened and the boat passed their position on the bank, it began to fade. Then it was gone as if it had never been.

"They say the living can only see a ghost ship for a few moments at dawn and dusk," Forrester said quietly. "You needed to be at this spot at this time to see your father. To say goodbye."

Grace scrubbed the tears off her face. "Goodbye? But if it can be seen . . ."

"I was told this is a one-time deal. That's why it was important to get you here."

She looked at him. "Closure."

Forrester nodded. "Several of the Arcana arranged for this to happen. For your father. For you." He paused. "You will owe them a favor." Before she could protest, he added, "Like the favor I did this morning by making sure you were here." He removed an envelope from his coat pocket. "I was asked to give you this."

It was light enough now that she could see her father's handwriting on the envelope.

She wanted to tear it open and read whatever message her father had written, but she wanted—needed—to be alone when she did that. "Thank you."

"You're welcome." Forrester studied her. "Did it help?"

Grace thought about that for a moment, then nodded. "He looks so happy. I remember . . . I remember the day before he disappeared. He'd been given weeks to live, and I'd brought him to the park to see the river. He always loved the river, had always said sailing on a three-master was at the top of his bucket list." She wiped away more tears. "He saw one that day. Was so excited to see it sail past. I didn't see it. I thought his illness was affecting his mind."

"The dying can see the ghost ships," Forrester said.

"That night, he slipped away from the care facility and disappeared. I guess he found . . ." What had her father found? Something.

"Well," Forrester said. "I need to get back to Penwych. Will you be all right?"

Grace nodded. "I'll walk you to the dock. My car is near there."

Going back to the dock, they walked in a silence that was more companionable than the silence that had surrounded them on the way to her meeting.

"Has your team heard anything about Rachel Nightingale?" Grace asked.

"Nothing," he replied. "My impression is that she chose to disappear."

"It would be nice to know we're not waiting for another body to wash ashore." She thought for a moment, then decided that what she was about to tell him was hardly private, given what the senior police officers in King's Hill were calling the Hampton Three-Ring Circus. "There's a lot of infighting within the Hampton family and with the officers and boards of directors of the companies controlled by Reginald Hampton the Third. Alistair Hampton is trying to take control of at least some of his brother's assets, but he's being challenged by Reginald's ex-wives—there are two—as well as numerous cousins who probably aren't even a footnote in Hampton's will. No one can make use of the Hampton wealth that had been under Reginald's control until we find him, one way or another.

"Alistair Hampton can't afford his current lifestyle. I'd heard he attempted to grab control of Rachel Nightingale's literary assets, claiming they were his now because he and Nightingale had been engaged. The publisher refused to cooperate."

"Go figure," Forrester said dryly.

Grace almost asked him if the Arcana were the ones who had control, but it was better not to have an answer. Markus Seibert, her senior detective, checked in with Alistair Hampton every few days, more to find out how much emotional gasoline the man was throwing on the family bonfire than to tell Hampton anything.

She watched Forrester board the Penwych patrol boat before returning to her car, getting in, and locking the doors. Then she carefully opened the envelope that contained her father's last message to her.

Gracie,

So much to say and not much time if this letter is going to reach you.

The last time we were at the park together? I saw that sailing ship and wanted the chance to sail on it. And I did, Gracie. I went down to the river the morning after, and the ship was anchored, as if waiting for me, and two of the crew rowed a dinghy to the shore and asked if I wanted to sail with them.

I had two wonderful years on the Bonnie Lass*. Two years of adventures. Dangerous, sometimes. But I was a dead man walking, so danger doesn't have much hold on someone like me. Doesn't have much hold on any of us, really.*

I know how much time the doctors had given me. I had more, and I lived and enjoyed every day I was on the water.

But the end is coming, and my one regret is I never said a proper goodbye to you, my darling girl. Captain Flint says there might be a way if someone called the Sorcerer King agrees to help. If I had the chance to see you, then help was given. If not, Captain Flint promised to get this letter to you.

No tears, Gracie. Not for me. I hope you have a long and wonderful life. I hope you know I'll always love you.

Dad

P.S. A man named Alan Naylor was a member of the crew. He started fretting about going home, but he hadn't fulfilled all of the bargain he'd made with the

Arcana, and the captain of the <u>*Bonnie Lass*</u> *wouldn't let him go. He took a dinghy and escaped last September, and the captain released him from his bargain because he saved a boy from drowning in the river. I hope Alan managed to make it home.*

Grace folded the letter and put it back in the envelope. Senior officers in the six towns on the Fate River knew about the man who had rescued the teenage boy and was then found dead, an old man who had been touched by the weight of his years. He hadn't quite made it home, but his reappearance had given his family closure.

Tucking her father's letter into her purse, Grace started her car and drove to the King's Hill precinct where she worked.

21

When he heard the *beep beep* of a horn, Colin Forrester set aside the broom he was using to sweep the trading post floor and went outside. Tia had said there weren't any cars in this Wyrd neighborhood, and it wasn't the day for the mobile library to show up.

A bus like the one that had dropped him off in Llamalidia pulled up to the trading post. The door opened, and the driver said, "I've got a delivery here for someone named Colin Forrester."

"For me?" Colin approached the bus but hesitated to step on board to pick up the delivery. He kept his bus ticket tucked into the back pocket of his jeans as a kind of talisman—an unspoken promise that he would, somehow, be able to get home someday. But Tia had mentioned a couple of times that if you weren't focused on where you wanted to go, you could end up somewhere that would be forever—

and the forever places often had a nightmarish quality to them. Or so she'd heard.

The driver looked past Colin to Tia, who also approached the bus. She studied Colin for a moment, then looked at the driver and shook her head as if conveying a message, adult to adult. Nodding, the driver swung out of his seat and pulled a big suitcase from the cargo racks. He tipped it onto its side and set it on the middle step.

Tia reached for the suitcase while keeping her feet firmly on the ground of Llamalidia. She swung it off the bus and told the driver, "We're good here. Thanks for the delivery."

The driver looked pointedly at the suitcase. "Someone has a connection with Destiny Park." Retreating to his seat, he closed the door, and the bus continued to its next destination.

"What did he mean by that?" Colin grabbed the handle on the suitcase and tried to lift it—and almost dropped it on his foot, surprised by the weight. What the heck had Dad packed that weighed that much?

Tia lifted the suitcase and walked into the trading post.

The Llamalidians, who were coming to the trading post to exchange their woven vests and scarves for items Tia had stocked—or would stock if there was enough interest in an item—now hurried behind the two humans to see what the Colin Boy had received.

Tia set the suitcase down in front of the back counter and looked at Colin. Then she looked at the Llamalidians, including the four juveniles and the seven cria who had accompanied the adults. "You sure you want to open this here and not in your room?"

He couldn't imagine his parents sending him something . . . weird, but he sidestepped the question by asking one of his own.

"What did the bus driver mean about having a connection with Destiny Park?"

Tia lifted the two identification tags. The one in Dad's handwriting simply said, "Colin Forrester, c/o Destiny Park, Wyrd." The other said, "Expedite delivery to Colin Forrester at Llamalidia Trading Post. LF."

"Lucas Frost," Tia said quietly.

"The guy in charge of Destiny Park," Colin said just as quietly.

"Yeah."

Given the weight of the suitcase, he wouldn't have been surprised to find it half-filled with bricks, but it was tightly packed with clothes, the next two books of a series he was reading, a pouch of coins, and . . .

He saw one of the juveniles take a small box out of the suitcase, and hurry over to another part of the trading post, followed by the other three juveniles.

Teenagers, Colin thought, ignoring that he fit into the same category. Whatever it was, he'd get it back. The adult Llamalidians would make sure of it. They were pretty strict when it came to bargaining and fair exchange.

He focused on the neatly rolled clothing. "All right!" He stripped off the T-shirt that had been rinsed out but hadn't been given a proper washing since he'd arrived. Tia had offered to loan him a T-shirt, but he quickly realized that her wardrobe didn't have much to spare. Besides, he was pretty sure they weren't the same size.

He unrolled one of the T-shirts in the suitcase and pulled it on. The cria hummed, a sound filled with curiosity. Their hoof-hands, which were far more flexible than he'd thought, pinched the T-shirt fabric, then pinched their woven vests.

Colin did a quick count of the cria, then unrolled another T-shirt and held it up against one of them. It—because he'd not looked at their privates for a definite answer of he or she—raised its arms.

He grinned. "This would go under the vest."

The cria undid the vest's fasteners, dropped the garment on the floor, and raised its arms again in imitation of what Colin had done when he put on the T-shirt.

Colin put the T-shirt on it and helped it back into the vest. "Very nice!"

The other six cria dropped their vests and approached with their arms up to get a T-shirt. Well, he'd still have a couple left for his own use, and they really did look cute wearing colorful T-shirts that fell almost to their knees.

A commotion in the part of the trading post where the juveniles had gathered for their secret whatever. Colin rose to his feet. Tia pushed the top of the suitcase down and partially zipped it before turning to deal with the juveniles.

Colin headed toward them. Some kind of pushy-shovey over . . .

He stopped. Stared. What the . . . ?

The juveniles were wearing unrolled condoms over their ears.

He heard Tia, coming up behind him, snort out a laugh.

A condom was a condom was a condom, but one juvenile was having trouble getting its booty unrolled and tried to grab one from a friend.

"Wait a minute," Colin said as he reached them.

Hums and groans. Ears went back in warning as the two juveniles faced each other.

Colin stepped between them, putting his hands out to keep them apart. "There's no reason—"

Spit.

Spit.

Colin looked at the green gobs of spit that covered his clean T-shirt. "Geez! That is *gross*!" Not to mention that it *stank*.

The adults converged on the juveniles. Angry hums and sharp hoof claps.

The juveniles, chastened, followed the adults out of the trading post, signing *sorry, so sorry*.

They weren't the only ones who were sorry.

One adult Llamalidian herded the cria outside.

Tia set a bucket beside Colin. "You want some help getting that shirt off so you don't make things worse?"

"I can do it," Colin wheezed as he gingerly took off the T-shirt, holding his breath when his face got close to the green globs soaking into the fabric.

"Dump it in the bucket. I'll use some of the stored gray water for the first rinse, then give it a proper washing with the rest of the clothes." She studied Colin and sniffed. "And you can have an extra bucket of water for your shower."

"Tomorrow is my day to shower," he said.

"I'm changing the schedule. Now go out and wash before everything in the trading post starts to smell."

Colin stared at her. "Why would my dad put . . . *those* . . . in the suitcase?"

"Well, you're old enough to be interested, aren't you?" She waited a beat. "Besides, your mother might have packed those. Moms can be practical, and are well aware of the consequences that can come from being careless."

"You're just messing with me."

"Maybe. And I'll keep messing with you until you don't stink like green spit. Now go. I'll take the suitcase up to your room."

"I'll need clean clothes."

Tia went back to the suitcase, opened it, removed a set of clothes, looked at him, and said, "I'll put these on the bench just outside the shower."

Because if he took them now, they'd be stinky. "Thanks."

He used three and a half buckets of water, but he used extra soap to wash his chest. He sniffed himself and was pretty sure he smelled clean by the time he was done. He toweled off and dressed in a pair of old, soft jeans and an equally soft T-shirt. The jeans were a little too warm for that time of day. He'd have to see what else his parents had packed.

And he really hoped there weren't any more unwanted surprises.

An hour later, Colin had changed into a pair of shorts and was examining the items that weren't clothes or toiletries. He appreciated the books, was glad he didn't know what his parents were thinking when they packed the condoms, and really appreciated the Wyrd coins.

Tia had said there was a neighborhood that was a mostly human town where you could get a burger and fries and a milkshake from the diner—foods that didn't exist in Llamalidia. That neighborhood also had a drugstore, a grocery store, and a bookstore, as well as a two-screen movie theater. No telling what the movies might be or how long ago they'd been released, but the people who lived in that town didn't seem to care about that. There was also a bed-and-breakfast where a person could stay over if they missed the bus—or if they wanted to spend an extra day away from wherever else they were.

Since he had money now, maybe he and Tia could go there one of these days and he could treat her to a meal and a movie as a thank-you for letting him stay with her until . . .

Colin reached into the suitcase and removed the photo in its simple frame at the same time Tia knocked on his door.

"Your family?" she asked, looking at the photo.

He nodded. "Mom, Dad, and my sister, Jazmin. We call her Jazz."

"Do you miss them?"

He hesitated. "I will." Being in a strange new place hadn't lost its excitement, even if the chores were *so* familiar. He remembered watching a *Star Trek* episode with Dad and saying how it would be wicked cool to visit a strange world, and Dad saying that once the excitement subsided, he suspected the day-to-day tasks of finding food and water, making clothes of some kind, and building and maintaining living quarters would be pretty much the same everywhere—and everywhere fathers would be reminding sons to take out the garbage.

Dad wasn't wrong about that, but taking care of the day-to-day tasks in Llamalidia hadn't lost its shine yet.

Colin looked at Tia. "What would happen if I stayed a while longer? Like a foreign exchange student—without the exchange." He could imagine the reaction if a juvenile Llamalidian showed up at Wyrd's dock with a suitcase and a note pinned to its vest asking to be taken to Charles Forrester, 13th precinct, Penwych.

"There are reasons why people choose not to live among their own kind anymore," Tia said quietly. "But you're too young to make that kind of choice. And you have family who would miss you. That makes a difference." She thought a moment, then shrugged. "Foreign exchange student? That fits. Let's say twelve weeks at the most. That would give you time to absorb enough of the culture to write a decent report for your commanding officer." She smiled because she, too, was familiar with *Star Trek*.

So he might have mentioned a time or three in the past couple of days that interacting with another race and forming friendly ties was his geeky fantasy, and how he was actually doing that.

Tia's smile faded. "After that, you need to focus on getting home."

"Okay."

Tia laid a book and a notebook on his bed. "I don't know who created this primer of the Llamalidian language or how long ago it was made. There are only a few copies stored here at the trading post. Seems to me you should have one. It will help speed up your skill with the language. The blank notebook is for the daily notes you will need when you write up your reports."

"Thanks." He reached for the primer.

"The Llamalidians are downstairs. They want to talk to you."

Colin placed the photo of his family on the wood dresser, left the primer and notebook on his bed, and followed Tia downstairs.

Sorry. So sorry, the adult Llamalidians signed.

His face burning, Colin accepted the seven unrolled condoms and the still-rolled one that had been the reason for the commotion. He shoved them in his pocket and tried not to think about them.

The adults signed and hummed too fast for him to get a sense of what they were saying.

"They appreciate the gifts you gave the cria and would like to give you gifts in return," Tia said.

Two of the Llamalidians held out beautifully woven vests.

Rubbing his hands on his shorts to make sure they were clean, Colin touched the vests. Surprisingly lightweight and so soft. Made sense in this warmer weather.

He almost accepted the vests as a way to sweeten the sting of his wanting to stay a while longer. Then he thought about it and stepped back.

A sad hum from the Llamalidians followed by a groan.

"The vests are wonderful," Colin said, glancing at Tia, who nodded and began to translate even though most of the Llamalidian adults understood human speech. "But if I sent them to my mom and sister, other humans would ask questions about where to buy them. That might cause trouble?"

More hums that sounded like agreement. Colin Boy came from a place where the vests would be too unusual.

Colin looked at the scarves displayed on a rack and the basket that held skeins of yarn. He pointed to them. "Scarves are worn in my neighborhood. They would be welcome gifts."

He selected three long scarves. When he understood the exchange was for an equal number of items to match the T-shirts he'd given the cria, he pointed to the skeins of yarn, Tia helping him explain that his mother liked to make things from yarn and would be happy to have them.

Pleased that he was sharing these items with his family herd, the Llamalidians left the trading post to go about their business.

"You did well," Tia said as she put together a box and carefully packed the scarves and yarn. "I wear T-shirts, too, but I never thought to exchange them for the yarn or clothing, since I know what a T-shirt costs outside of Wyrd and what that yarn costs. I guess I'll place an order for T-shirts and see if there's continued interest."

"Maybe colored ones?" Colin said, glancing at the shoulder of her white T-shirt.

She thought for a moment, then nodded. "That could be the attraction."

He got the feeling that she didn't think that was the reason, but he didn't ask.

"You should think of what else you want to put in the box before I seal it up for shipping," Tia said.

"Like what?"

She stared at him. "Like a letter letting your folks know you're doing a foreign student exchange deal and why you're sending them scarves and yarn?"

"Oh. Yeah." And he should ask Mom to send him more T-shirts for his own use.

Later that evening, Colin paged through the language primer. The printing and binding weren't like anything he'd seen before, but whoever created the primer showed how hoof-hand and ear position equaled a human phrase and how to reply given the human body's limited range of movements. Basic questions and answers, beautifully illustrated. And sketches of the Llamalidians' daily life that helped match the phrases to an activity!

Tia had said the trading post had been a fixture in this neighborhood for a long time, and she was just the latest person to run it. Had the artist who created the primer been someone who needed to step away from their own place and people for a while?

Colin looked at the stylized *A* in the right-hand corner of the daily life sketches and wondered if he would ever know who the artist had been—and why that person thought making a connection with another race of beings was so important.

22

Beth Fahey tried to push her feelings of horror and disgust aside while she typed the report of the team's latest investigation. Not that the incident actually fell within the parameters of the team's investigations. She and Ian Kuhn had driven to the town of Carter in Northwood County to review the information the detectives there had about a murder where a python was the murder weapon.

Or would it be considered manslaughter? Not for her to decide. What she had told the Carter detectives—and Kuhn thankfully backed her up—was that the incident had nothing to do with the Isle of Wyrd or its residents.

Captain Forrester came out of his office. He didn't look like he'd slept much in the past few days, and she understood why. There was no way to know if the suitcase he'd sent to his son had reached the boy. Even Lucas Frost didn't know for sure, but he'd pointed out that people across the river—meaning the humans—expected overnight deliveries and instant communication these days, and those were two things that didn't happen in Wyrd.

Frost did promise to send word if he heard anything from Colin Forrester or Tia Downing.

Forrester approached Beth's desk, joined by Ian Kuhn.

"Anything we need to deal with?" Forrester asked.

"Doesn't appear to be," Kuhn said.

"No," Beth said.

Both men looked at her. Kuhn wanted to be more cautious about drawing a line under the possibility of Wyrd being involved. He'd said as much on the drive back to Penwych. He also pointed out that they didn't know enough about how moon gates worked to be sure this wasn't like the other recent incidents.

It wasn't like those other incidents. And the team did know enough about the moon gates—or they would. She'd made the phone call and asked Ashley Laxton when the woman answered Frost's office phone.

Beth drew in a breath and tried not to sigh. That phone call would be another reason why the team had become uneasy working with her.

"We weren't able to talk to the family directly, but this is what the detectives in Carter were able to put together," Beth said. "Chloe Peterson was at a sleepover at a friend's house a few days ago. Late night, lots of giggles—and some playing around with what was described as 'sympathetic magic.' That is, putting the energy of a wish into an object so that something will happen."

"Words have power. Intentions matter," Forrester said. "I could see someone connecting sympathetic magic to Wyrd if they didn't understand how bargains were made with the Arcana."

Beth nodded. "The next time the older brother tried to pressure her into 'being a good girl,' Chloe screamed at him that he was a snake, which gave him the idea of borrowing a friend's pet python and putting it in her bed to make her think he really could turn into a snake.

"Fortunately for Chloe, she'd taken to sleeping in a hidden storage space inside her closet, hiding from her brothers. Unfortunately, the other brother, who came home very drunk after being out with his friends—none of whom are anywhere near the legal age for drinking—decided it was his turn to visit his little sister and got into Chloe's bed."

Beth sighed. “The python squeezed the life out of him. The parents found him in the morning when Chloe emerged from her hiding place and started screaming.

“When the detectives questioned why the brother was in his younger sister’s bed, it came out that Chloe was being sexually abused by both of her brothers—something her parents vigorously denied even after the girl was removed from the family home to protect her from the surviving brother.”

Kuhn said, “The detectives wanted to know if this was a transformation.”

“It wasn’t,” Beth replied sharply. “The brother who put the snake in Chloe’s bed is alive and well, and had spent the night at a friend’s house in order to claim he had no idea how the snake got into Chloe’s bed. Besides, moon gates don’t work that way. A person can’t transform another person.” That wasn’t quite true. Some of the Arcana *could* transform a person into something else without needing a moon gate, but a human telling someone he’s a snake wouldn’t do anything except, perhaps, make a person feel like they were defending themselves against an abuser. “No teenagers have been on the ferry since the last incident with those boys, and no children have been on the ferry, alone or with an adult. Since Carter is located at the north bend of the Fate River, I suppose someone could have taken a boat and landed somewhere on Wyrd, but it’s long odds that they would have found a moon gate and gotten back out.”

“How do you know that?” Kuhn said.

“She asked,” Forrester replied quietly, studying Beth.

“Yes, I asked,” Beth acknowledged.

“So did I, and I didn’t get that much information,” Kuhn said.

“Let it go,” Forrester warned. He looked thoughtful. “What we have is a sexually abused girl who did some 'magic,' in the hope of turning one of her abusers into a snake. We have that brother putting a snake in her bed, either to scare her or kill her if he thought she might tell someone who would believe her about the abuse. And we have the other brother getting into her bed and passing out, not realizing he was in bed with a python, which killed him. Does that cover it?"

"Yes, sir," Beth said.

"All right," Forrester said. "Mayor Bang wants me to give her a report about this in person. Penwych has the only official place to cross the river and visit Wyrd, so she's feeling some heat about continuing to make the island accessible to people on this side of the river."

"Captain?" Tom Castelletti walked into the team's area of the precinct. "There's a package for you coming in on the next ferry. Officers Monkton and Reynolds are currently patrolling the area. Do you want them to pick it up and bring it here?"

Beth watched Forrester pale and knew they were all thinking about the last time the Arcana delivered a box to the police.

"Yes," Forrester finally said. "Have them bring it here." He walked out.

"I'm getting coffee from one of the food trucks," Castelletti said. "Either of you want anything?"

Beth shook her head.

"I'll join you in a minute," Kuhn said. When they were alone, he looked at Beth. "I like you. I do." He wagged a thumb toward the door to indicate Castelletti. "But sometimes we wonder if you're on the wrong side of the river."

When she was alone, Beth braced her head in her hands. Then she sat up, looked around the empty room, and finished typing her report for the Chloe Peterson investigation.

23

When he got home, Forrester set the package on the kitchen table. He'd opened it at the precinct, in case there was something inside that he didn't want Aisha to see, but he hadn't opened the letter addressed to them both.

"Where's Jazz?" he asked when Aisha joined him in the kitchen.

"In her room, doing homework with Davie." She looked at the box. "Charles? Is something wrong?"

"This came for us." He opened the box and stepped aside.

Aisha picked up one of the scarves. "This is gorgeous work. And so soft!" She wrapped it around her neck and stroked one end.

"There are two more scarves and . . ."

"Oh," Aisha breathed as she lifted one of the skeins of yarn. Then she looked at the symbol on the brown paper wrapped around the skein to keep it tidy. "Oh!"

"They're from Colin." Charles watched his wife. The symbol had looked familiar, but he hadn't been able to place it.

"How much money did you tuck into the suitcase?"

He frowned at her. "Why?"

She held up the skein. "There is a specialty yarn shop in Barker and one in Lovecraft. I'm on the mailing list for both of them. When a shipment of this yarn becomes available, their customers are notified. You place an order the minute you see the notification, and there is a four-skein limit."

"I gather it's expensive," Charles said. Browsing yarn shops and making things for friends and family was a passion for Aisha, and he'd never asked about the price of her purchases.

"It's expensive," she confirmed.

Charles opened the letter. "Let's see what Colin says about it."

Dear Mom and Dad,

The suitcase arrived. Thanks for sending the T-shirts. I ended up giving a few of them to the children in the community where I'm staying. They were a big hit since no one had seen material like that—at least not with colors and pictures. The people here feel it's important to exchange gifts, so they gave me these scarves to send to you, and I thought Mom would enjoy having yarn that's made here.

Could you send more T-shirts in my size for me and also in a size or two larger in case other people in the community would like to have one? In colors. White doesn't attract interest.

Also, please don't send any more ear coverings. Tia says since they aren't made from a material that is native to this place, they fall under the "pack in, pack out" category of items for disposal.

"Ear coverings?" Aisha muttered. "And what kind of material . . ." She blushed.

"Is that why you asked me to pick up a box of condoms when I was sure we had an unopened box in the bedside table?" Charles asked.

"He's on his own, and a teenage boy . . ." She ran her fingers over the yarn. "I didn't want him to do without birth control if he found himself in a situation where he should use it."

Aisha had done such a good job of tucking that box into the suitcase, he hadn't noticed it when he packed the half-full box from his drawer. But ear coverings?

"Do you recognize the symbol?" he asked.

"We think it indicates that the yarn comes from llamas or alpacas, or a combination of both. It's a unique blend, and there is *no* information about the manufacturer." Aisha looked at him. "You think this is where Colin ended up? But . . . He's somewhere on Wyrd. Isn't he?"

"He's someplace connected to the island." He looked at the letter.

I don't want to worry you, but being in this place is a chance that won't come again. Tia said I can stay for twelve weeks as a kind of foreign exchange student—learning about their culture and their language and living a different kind of life. Like a young Starfleet officer on a diplomatic mission.

I really want to stay. Even if I had to come home tomorrow, I wouldn't want to go back to school. Not until the other bullyboys have been sorted out. And I have a feeling that Devl and Acid aren't going to be able to come back at all. A lot of hard feelings might get stirred up if I come home soon and they can't. I'm safe here. I really am. So I'm going to stay for a while, and then I'll focus my intentions on reaching Destiny Park.

I love you both. And Jazz too. I hope she likes the scarf.

Colin

"Twelve weeks?" Aisha's breath caught. Then she wiped the tears from her face and pulled her shoulders back. "I'll go to the school tomorrow and explain that Colin is finishing up the school year as a cultural exchange student, and will make up the rest of his classes when he returns."

"I'll go with you and clear out his locker," Charles said.

"I can do that."

He smiled. "Teenage boy, remember? He might be embarrassed by what I find, but his mom seeing something he'd prefer she didn't see?"

"All right, we'll both go." She hesitated. "He doesn't know about the other boys."

"I didn't see any reason to tell him." Charles held his wife close. "He's out of reach but not out of touch. The suitcase reached him; his gifts reached us."

"I think I'll use some of the yarn to make a scarf for Davie. He's the only friend who has stood by Jazz."

"As Jazz has stood by him."

Aisha kissed him, then stepped back. "If you would put the box in my craft corner, I'll get supper started."

Charles took the box to the family room and left it in Aisha's craft corner.

Condoms as ear coverings.

He did a quick scan of the bookshelves in the room and found the children's book *Animals Around the World*. He flipped through the pages until he found llamas. He studied the ears. Then he closed the book, tucked it back on the shelf, and returned to the kitchen to help his wife make supper.

24

Late that evening, Beth turned the pages of the sketchbook filled with drawings of the Arcana—drawings she suspected had been made by Arianna Greenwood, the woman she had seen in a vivid dream.

She hadn't gone to Wyrd on her day off to stay at the hotel and wander around Destiny Park. She'd wanted to bring this sketchbook and show it to someone at the pavilion. Lucas Frost, maybe, or the Ladies Three. Maybe they could help her fill in the missing blanks of her childhood before she had ended up living full-time with Bonnie

Wilson. But she'd been wary of being seen as too "friendly" with the Arcana, wary of the schism that was forming between her and her colleagues because she received more information from the Arcana than they did.

Beth closed the sketchbook and put it away. Even now, she was afraid of being honest about the things that pulled at her, resonated with her. If the police who were trained to deal with Wyrd thought that she was strange or unnatural, what sort of future did she have?

Maybe Ian Kuhn was right. Maybe she was living on the wrong side of the river.

25

"You said you loved me. You said if I gave up my people and went with you—"

"Your people are fucking strange!"

"—you would take care of me forever. And now you're going back on your word?"

"You have horns, Maxie!"

"I'm half Arcana."

"Fucking horns growing out of your head!"

"You knew what I was before you asked me to go away with you. Why do you sound so shocked now? You've seen them every night you enjoyed having me under you."

"And you didn't enjoy it?"

"Not as much as you wanted to believe."

"Laura has no complaints about me!"

"Does she know you won't walk away with the money my people provided to support us?"

Silence.

"What changed between us?"

"You got pregnant!"

"You got me pregnant."

"It's bad enough that we can't go out after dark without you wearing some ridiculous scarf on your head, what are we going to do with a kid who has horns?"

"The horns might not show, even in moonlight or starlight."

"I'm not taking a chance of being saddled with a kid like that. Either get rid of it now or pawn it off on someone else later, but we're not keeping it."

"Then you keep nothing that comes from me."

"Maxie, wait. Maxie!"

"There were complications during the birth because of the mother's unusual heritage. The doctors couldn't save her, but they did save the child. When she was admitted, your mate listed you as the child's father and gave the hospital—and me—your last known address. It took us a few days to locate you, but your daughter is ready to go home." A pause. "Your mate wrote you a note while she was in labor. I promised to give it to you once I located you."

"I don't want the fucking note, and I don't want the kid."

"I suggest you read the note before you decide, but know this: Right now, I represent Maxine Greenwood's branch of the Arcana. If you don't take your offspring from this place and take proper care of her, the Arcana will twist your fate until you are caught in an insatiable desert of misfortune—and there you will stay for the full measure of your life."

"Is that a threat?"

"That is a promise."

"A baby? What are we supposed to do with your ex's baby?"

"Look . . ."

"And what does this mean? 'Your fate was sealed when you turned away from me. Your continued existence—and the existence of your whore wife—now depends on how well you take care of the child you planted in me.'"

"For fuck's sake, Laura, how am I supposed to know? She was probably high on whatever drugs they give women when they're pushing out a kid."

"What's with the package?"

"It's a book and an old, worthless ring. I was told they have to go with the kid, always. Or else."

"Or else what?"

"Look. It's not like she'll cost us anything. Maxie's family will provide for the kid as long as we take care of her and as long as the book and ring stay with her."

"I don't know. We're just scraping by with what I earn, and you . . ."

"I'm looking for work, babe. You know I am. But this money? It's more than enough to take care of a baby. More than enough for us to take some of those trips we'd talked about."

"Lugging a baby with us to the romantic hot spots in Europe?"

"We can leave the kid with Bonnie."

"The religious nut next door?"

"If she thinks we're fostering a kid out of the goodness of our hearts, she'll help."

A long pause. "How much money?"

Beth Fahey fought her way out of the dream, freed herself from the tangled sheets, and stumbled to the bathroom to splash cold water on her face.

What the hell? This wasn't like the first two dreams she'd experienced after drinking the special tea. This dream of accessed family memories was a series of scenes where she couldn't see the faces of the people involved; could just hear the voices, like she was listening from the other side of a partially open door.

Unless her subconscious was just shaping a story to explain parents who were more absent than present, always going on trips and leaving the child with the next-door neighbor.

How often had she considered purchasing one of those home DNA kits to see if she could find out anything about the people she had believed to be her parents? How often, after she became a cop, had she chickened out of doing the test? How many times had she told herself that it didn't matter?

And it didn't matter. Not anymore. Not in that way. But there might be another reason for the fixation she'd had for the dark-eyed, black-haired boy who'd gone missing almost a year ago.

Had her own photo ever appeared on a missing person flyer?

Charles Forrester walked into the special team's area of the precinct and headed for his office. He came in early most days since Colin's disappearance, wanting—needing—to check his e-mail and any physical post that had been brought up from the mailroom overnight. Foolish to expect another letter so soon. Even more foolish to think the timing of the suitcase sent and the package received in return was a consistent measure of delivery. Outside Destiny Park, he wasn't sure Wyrd had a consistent measure for anything.

He'd be glad when this school year was done. He had vacation time coming, and he'd already talked to Aisha about getting away from Penwych and the river, going to some vacation spot where they would be unknown and could simply *be* again. Catch their breath and their balance. Maybe they could invite Davie to go with them. The . . . boy . . . also might benefit from being away from expectations.

Spotting Beth Fahey at her desk, Charles stopped to see what she was working on.

Missing persons?

"Detective?"

She almost jumped out of her chair, so focused on whatever was on her screen that she didn't notice him. "Captain."

"Did something come in last night?"

"No, sir. I'm just . . ." She trailed off, clearly reluctant to explain.

"A nationwide search from"—he leaned over her shoulder to read the dates—"almost twenty-five years ago? Who are you looking for?"

She turned her head and looked at him. "Me."

Easing back, he sat on the edge of her desk. "You?"

"I had a strange dream last night. It was like listening to a drama on TV, with a mother dying soon after childbirth and the father and his wife taking the child but not really wanting the child. So they frequently leave her with a neighbor while they go on trips. Then one day they don't come back, and the child ends up living with the neighbor, who everyone assumes is the child's aunt."

"It sounds a lot like what you told me about your life. At least the part about being taken in by a neighbor. Are you still getting phone calls from that woman, asking for money?"

"Sometimes, but I don't answer the phone when I see her number."

"So you had a dream that provided a narrative for your earliest memories."

Beth hesitated, then nodded. "There is no way I could know what was said or what happened before I was born, but when she was angry, Bonnie would say my foster parents abandoned me because they'd discovered I was 'unnatural.' It sounded like *she* believed the people I thought were my parents weren't actually my biological parents."

"Any evidence to substantiate that possibility?"

"The name on my birth certificate matched the name of the man I believed was my father, but the mother's name was listed as Maxine Greenwood. She must have been my biological mother but not my father's wife. It's just . . . Lately I've been feeling like I might be on the wrong side of the river."

Charles sighed. "You're a valuable—and valued—member of this team, Beth. Your affinity with the Arcana has closed some of the distance between us. Personally, I don't think I would have found out as much about Colin's situation if you weren't here, despite my having what I like to think is a cordial relationship with Lucas Frost. Make no mistake: the Arcana can be as brutal as they can be kind, but either way, they usually don't care what happens to us. They may facilitate our choosing a particular path to our fate, but they aren't concerned with the outcome."

"Our choice, our responsibility," she said.

"Yes." He hesitated. "I'll talk to the men. I'm sure they don't realize that their comments can be hurtful."

"Maybe it's hurtful because I think they might be right."

He touched her shoulder. A light touch. A moment's contact. "If you feel you can't stay at the thirteenth, talk to me before you decide. Please?"

She nodded.

Hearing voices, Charles stepped away from Fahey's desk. "Close those files now and focus on what we have to investigate today."

Her computer screen was clear when Castelletti, Kuhn, Reynolds, and Monkton walked into the room.

Nodding to his men, Charles went into his office to check his e-mail. Nothing from Lucas Frost, which meant no news about Colin. He'd take that as a good sign.

MAY

26

Lucas Frost reviewed the reports of people crossing the river and entering Wyrd at other parts of the island. The Arcana had created Destiny Park as a neutral place where humans could visit, ask for assistance, or simply brush against the strange and still get home. These reports indicated that four humans had landed on other parts of the island over the past few days and made the mistake of going beyond the shore. They were spotted by Arcana, who reported the sightings to him—and then the humans disappeared, either by entering one of the neighborhoods or by walking through a moon gate. Some of those humans might return to the shore if they had wandered into a benign neighborhood; some might reappear in some other uncanny place in the world. And some might be nothing more than a memory.

So far he hadn't received a visit from Charles Forrester or his team about the missing people, but sooner or later, he would.

The humans were getting too complacent, too careless—and they wanted to blame the Arcana for that carelessness instead of owning that their choices set them on a path that might swallow their intended fate—and end their lives.

He looked up when Faulkner flew over to his desk, strutting toward the mug that Lucas used to hold pens and pencils—a mug that said WYRD IS WHERE IT'S AT. It was a gift from Justine and her sisters. Ashley Laxton said it was a big seller in the hotel's gift shop.

He watched Faulkner select various pens and pencils, dropping the discards on the desk until the crow found a new, unsharpened pencil with a pristine eraser and flew away with the prize. Listening to the twitters and caws coming from the next room, he gave Mia Skov and Ashley Laxton a long look as the two women entered his office.

"I'll look," Mia said, moving silently to the doorway of the next room. After peering around the corner, she returned to stand near Lucas's desk. "I guess Faulkner using the eraser to hold down one key makes it easier for Rahele to hold down another key and save their current work."

"Which is?" Lucas asked.

"'Ode to a Worm,'" Ashley replied.

"Keys?" Lucas stared at the women.

Ashley shrugged. "We were getting tired of being called away from our own work to record the new verse of whatever Rahele and Faulkner were working on, so I set up a laptop we weren't using in the office and opened the word-processing program for them."

"It was that or buy a lot more sets of lettered squares to give them enough letters for their longer creations," Mia said.

"They've been pecking out poems for a few days now and having a good time." Ashley's smile faded before it took shape. "Are you concerned that someone will realize they aren't birds in the truest sense? I could take the laptop away."

"No," Lucas said quietly. "It's almost time for Faulkner to leave. Let them play for the days that are left." He handed the reports to Ashley, who read them and handed them to Mia.

"If these humans had landed at Destiny Bay, they might have had a chance, since the Arcana who work around the bay would have warned them to turn back," Ashley said. "But coming here unprepared?" She shook her head. "I'll watch the news for a few days and make notes of anyone reported missing."

Nodding, Lucas took back the reports, put them in a file folder, and tucked the folder into a drawer in his desk, where it would be handy when the police crossed the river to make inquiries.

27

Acid stared out the train window at land that didn't look anything like home.

Where the fuck was he?

He shifted in his seat and looked at the passengers on the other side of the aisle, grateful that no one had claimed the seat next to him—yet. Most of them were skeletons with skin, mummies without the wrappings—until nightfall. They didn't flesh out when it got dark, but they did come alive. It had freaked him out the first few nights, watching all these corpses stir and stretch and get up and walk around, talking to one another. A few of them—the fresher ones—acknowledged his presence. A couple of them tried to make small talk, asking where he got on the train. When he told them to fuck off, they stopped trying to talk to him. As the days passed, he wished he hadn't been such a prick, because there was nothing to do but stare out the window.

Acid felt the train slow and realized it was pulling into a station. Or stopping, anyway.

When the train stopped, one of the almost-corpses made its way to the back of the car, shaking a few hands and saying goodbye to some of the other people. Then it stopped, seemed to steady itself, and left the train.

Acid waited, but the guy didn't come back—and the train pulled out of the station.

Could it be that easy? Just walk to the back of the passenger car and get off when the train stopped?

According to his watch, it was two in the morning. He looked out the window. Looked and looked, but he didn't see any lights from a station or a town or, hell, even a pit stop of any kind. And yet the train had stopped, and someone had left.

The conductor came by for the first time in days. At least, it seemed that way.

"Last stop before dawn," the conductor said.

Then he said a word that might have been the name of the town or the station or something else entirely. It wasn't a name Acid recognized, but . . .

He'd been on an *island* when he'd gotten on the train. They had to be going round and round because there weren't any bridges connecting the island to the other side of the river. So round and round and never *that* far from home, no matter what words the conductor used.

That meant that all he had to do when the train reached another station was walk to the back of the car and leave with any other passengers who were getting off at that stop.

28

Colin washed his face, gave the rest of his body a quick sponge bath, then brushed his teeth using the water he'd set aside for drinking and good dental health. Brush and floss daily—or at least while the floss Mom had sent lasted—because there were no dentists in Llamalidia who knew anything about human teeth, and someone with a toothache might not be able to focus their intentions well enough to reach a place that had the right kind of dentist.

Today he and the cria of the appropriate age were having their first lesson in weaving. What the Llamalidians made from their own fleece provided them with the income to purchase supplies that weren't easy to find in their neighborhood—if they could be found at all. He still didn't know if this place provided "isolated evolution" like he'd seen on nature shows, where a species evolved differently because it couldn't be reached, or if the land called Llamalidia was part of a bigger country that was somehow connected to the Isle of Wyrd. It had to be some kind of secret. Otherwise, the existence of the Llamalidians would be all over the news.

Regardless of his current geographical position, he thought Mom would get a kick out of him learning to weave well enough to make a set of place mats for the kitchen table.

29

There were some batshit, crazy-ass people on the bus. Devl wasn't sure if they had started out batshit and crazy assed when they boarded, but they were now.

Nobody had disrespected him when he'd been part of Dare's Doggs. Now? How many times had he been told he was the youngest person on the bus? How many ways had it been implied that he must be truly stupid or truly evil to have ended up riding on the ghost bus at his age? What really fried his ass was it didn't matter if he was riding with one other person or a dozen, everyone thought he was one thing or the other. Except, maybe, the guy he'd met the first day on the bus. *That* guy didn't seem to give a damn that Devl had been a member of a gang that had been feared at Penwych High School, and he didn't mind being on his own with no one to talk to. He always had a thick book—a thriller or some other shit—or a couple of newspapers he'd picked up from who knew where that still had untouched crossword puzzles.

What kind of badass read thrillers and did crossword puzzles? You would think the guy would pull out a big knife once in a while to prove he *was* a badass.

Unless the guy did that at times when he was riding with whoever else was on this bus.

The conductor, whom Devl hadn't seen since the bastard had spun those wheels and told him how long he'd be stuck in this hell ride, stopped at his seat.

"We don't usually grant a night off until a person has been riding the bus for a few years, but we've never had someone as young as you . . ." He stopped and considered. "Well, there had been a few, but youngsters grew up faster in those days and were considered adults before they reached your age. Regardless, it has been decided that you will be given time off the bus when we reach our next stop."

"How much time?"

"That will depend on you. Think carefully about where you want to be when you step off the bus, so you'll be ready."

Devl sat back and smiled. Oh, he knew exactly where he wanted to be, especially if he didn't have much time.

30

Rachel knew something was wrong the moment Lucas Frost stepped into the room where she and Faulkner had been using a laptop to write some poems. Was there a rule that birds who weren't really birds couldn't use a computer? No one had said anything. In fact, Ashley Laxton had supplied them with the laptop, and she would have said if there was a rule that prohibited its use.

"Faulkner," Lucas said quietly.

Faulkner ignored the man and kept pecking out letters. But the crow suddenly had trouble spelling, and autocorrect was filling in with interesting choices.

"It's time, Faulkner," Lucas said. "Tomorrow you'll make the transition and move on to a new life."

"Caw!"

Lucas shook his head. "No delays, no exceptions. You made a bargain with us. It's time to complete it."

Rachel stared at Lucas. Transition? New life? Faulkner was *leaving*?

"Remember to save your poem," Lucas said. "We'll print out a copy for each of you." He stepped back into his office.

Rachel sidled over to Faulkner until her wing touched his. The warmth of a friend. Why hadn't anyone warned them sooner that this would be their last day to spend time together?

What was she supposed to do on her own?

31

Acid stepped off the train and hurried behind a nearby tree in case anyone bothered to look at who was getting off that nightmare. How had he ever thought it was an ordinary train that had pulled into the station on Wyrd? It had an unearthly sheen, like fog shrouding metal, softening the shape without making it disappear. Or *would* it disappear when the train left the station? *This* station. After all, he was on an island, so every station had to be a Wyrd station.

The train pulled out. Acid watched it go. He remembered two passenger cars behind the engine when he'd boarded to look for Colin Forrester. Now there were three cars. Did that matter? Couldn't matter.

The train disappeared. Once he was sure that no one on the train could see him, Acid stepped away from the tree and looked around. He didn't see a station, a platform, a sign telling him where he was. He didn't see any fucking thing. Except gravestones.

He saw rows and rows and rows of gravestones.

Why were train tracks going through a cemetery?

Wait. Hadn't the conductor said something about cemeteries? He'd been pissed off about being trapped on the train and hadn't paid attention.

Turning in a slow circle, Acid finally spotted a man digging near one of the stones. Maybe that guy knew where they were and how he could get back to Destiny Park.

He walked fast and didn't seem to get any closer to the man with the spade. Did people still dig graves? Didn't they use machines and shit like that to dig a hole?

"Hey!" Acid shouted.

The man turned and raised a hand in greeting before focusing on making neat cuts in the sod. When Acid got close enough, the man said, "Did you get off the train too?"

"Yeah," Acid replied. "Had enough of that ride. Decided to skip the rest."

The man gave him an odd look. "How long were you supposed to ride?"

"That joke of a conductor said ninety-nine years. Can you believe that?"

"How long had you been riding?"

"A few days." Acid was sure it wasn't more than that. Pretty sure it wasn't. Although it had felt a lot longer.

The man was quiet. Then he said, "You're going to have a long journey if you want to get home."

"I need to get to Destiny Park. I'll catch the ferry home from there."

Another hesitation. "Destiny Park? Where were you when you boarded the train?"

Something wasn't right about the way the man looked at him. "On Wyrd."

The man sighed. "A very long journey."

"It's a fucking island. If there's a cemetery, there has to be a town around here, right?"

The man shook his head. "The train only lets passengers off at the graveyards—and your grave is your only destination." He pointed to the big stone with the family name and the smaller stones on either side with individual names. "I'm almost home," he said softly. "Don't have to dig down far. Just enough to reach the ground that is meant to hold my bones."

The guy was spooking him. "Destiny Park?"

"Pick a direction." The man gave him a sad smile. "You got off too soon. You have to locate the cemetery where you belong if you want your family to find you." He waved a hand. "In this place, every cemetery that is and was in this world is connected. When you get off the train, there is nothing else. Just graveyards. One flowing into the next and into the next and on and on. Some have monuments, some have simple crosses, some have stones set flat in the ground. All the cities of the dead." A puzzled look. "Your ticket should have told you when it was time to depart."

"Didn't buy a ticket."

"Ah. That explains the length of your ride." The man sighed. "There will be signs when you pass from one cemetery to another. If you don't recognize the language, you've strayed too far from your home and need to choose another direction." He set the edge of the spade into the sod. "Now, if you will excuse me, I want to finish this task and go home."

"That's it?" Acid demanded. "That's all you'll tell me?"

"What else is there to say? You left the train too soon. Now you must search for your home or someplace close enough that you will be found."

Acid stared at the man. "But you got on the train at Wyrd too."

"No. A place like it, I think, but not there. The places that are a convergence of the uncanny . . . Those places abide by different rules." The man resumed digging.

Acid watched the man for a minute, then walked back to the tracks. He'd follow those because they had to lead somewhere.

They had to.

JUNE

32

Beth glanced at the clock on the bedside table and swore mildly. If she didn't leave in the next minute, she'd miss her bus and be late for work. Captain Forrester would cut her some slack because she'd been coming in early or working a bit late since Colin Forrester's disappearance into Wyrd, but colleagues noticed when a cop didn't show up on time for her shift—especially when she was still considered the newbie on a special team that made other cops uneasy. The team that crossed the river and dealt with the Arcana was *needed*, but you had to be a little bit . . . odd . . . in order to do the work and not go doolally, right? And she didn't need anyone whispering that Forrester was playing favorites because she was the only woman on the team—and a young woman at that.

She'd just opened her front door when her cell phone rang. Feeling rushed, she answered it without checking the identity of the caller. "Hello?"

"I need money."

Beth felt her heart constrict. She should have known she wasn't going to dodge these calls forever. "I don't have any more money, Bonnie. I told you that the last time. And the time before that."

"You do have money. And you owe me."

"I don't owe you anything. I gave you some of the money I received when I turned eighteen, and that's more than you were entitled to since you were sent money every month I lived with you."

"Barely enough." Bonnie's voice was low and harsh. "Barely enough for what you cost me to keep you."

"More than enough," Beth countered sharply. "You bought my clothes from thrift stores while you wore designer labels and left me on my own without any food in the house while you enjoyed an overnight at a casino."

"You were strange. I had to get away from you once in a while."

"If you've run out of money because you're gambling again, that's not my problem," Beth said. "I haven't lived with you for years, so you can't use me as an excuse for your addictions."

"I'm not addicted to anything!" Bonnie screamed.

"Religion and gambling. Don't all the holy men you have pinned to the walls of your house have something to say about gambling?"

"Send me the money. Twenty thousand."

"I don't have that kind of money."

"Then you'd better find it. If you don't, I'll let some people know your secret, let them know why you're so attracted to abominations like the ones in that book you've kept all these years."

Beth pressed a hand to her stomach. She knew better than to let Bonnie realize that an emotional bomb might hold a kernel of truth, but she couldn't stop herself from saying, "What secret?"

"Send the money, or people will find out how unnatural you really are." Bonnie ended the call.

Beth sagged against the doorframe. Bonnie couldn't have any proof that would confirm Beth's heritage one way or the other. Could she? No. She would have used it before now if she had anything. Unless . . .

I guess it's time to cross the river and ask the Ladies Three a question.

33

The stench woke Devl from an uneasy sleep. Pushing himself upright on the bus seat, he gagged as the stench intensified. Had he shit himself? Yeah, he was pretty sure he'd filled his jeans. And . . . was that *blood* on his shirt? And why was it so fucking cold on the bus?

He remembered being given time off the bus, remembered being able to choose anyplace he wanted to visit. And when he stepped off the bus, he walked into the kind of bar he'd fantasized about, where the rough-looking man tending bar didn't ask his age or want any kind of ID, where there were full-on strippers and women who let you bang them against the wall and didn't whine about a man enjoying himself without using a condom. Even the fight where he whupped a couple of men almost twice his size was everything he could have asked for, even if he ended up busted up himself.

He remembered a sharp, sledgehammer blow to his guts, remembered hurting like he'd never hurt before. Remembered dragging himself back on the bus before he passed out.

The conductor set two large buckets of water in the aisle next to Devl's seat. Two large plastic trash bags were draped over the seat in front of him, along with a set of clean clothes.

Devl looked at the conductor—and wondered why the mix of pity and contempt on the man's face made him so afraid.

"Strip out of all your clothes and put them in one of the trash bags," the conductor said. "We'll burn them when we reach a disposal site. But keep your wallet or any other identification that will be useful to authorities. Use one of the buckets of water to wash yourself. The other bucket is to wash the seat and floor and everything else you soiled. If two buckets of water doesn't get rid of the stink, I'll be back with more water. You'll be riding alone until you've cleaned up the mess you made."

"Can't you close some of the windows? It's freezing in here," Devl whined.

"Just because you're alone doesn't mean the bus doesn't have other passengers. They don't want to be around you—and most of them don't mind the cold." The conductor turned away.

Devl started to cry. "I don't want to be here. I wanna go home." That was something he wanted with everything in him. "I wanna go home!"

The conductor turned back and stared at him with cold eyes. "We gave you a chance to leave the bus and go anywhere you wanted to go. We gave you the chance to go home, but you chose to go to a place where you could drink and fuck and fight. Where you could indulge yourself in a bar that exactly matched where you wanted to be."

"I didn't know it was my only chance to go home! I didn't know!"

The conductor didn't speak for a long moment. Then, quietly, he said, "Maybe it was your destiny to die in a bar fight far from the place you called home. Maybe you just met your fate sooner rather than later. Either way, it's been decided to reduce your time on the bus. The next time you leave, you'll be close enough to where you came from that someone will know how to find your people."

"I don't . . . I don't understand."

That pitying look again. "You managed to drag yourself back on the bus before you died. If you hadn't, you would have been stripped of any useful possessions and buried in an unmarked grave so that no one in that bar would be blamed for killing you. Now you're riding with us as a true ghost, your spirit tethered to flesh only as long as you remain on the bus. If you truly want to get home, you won't try to leave."

The conductor vanished.

Devl stripped out of his soiled clothes. He stared at the wound in his belly—and remembered the man ramming the sharp edges of a broken bottle into his gut and twisting the bottle to cause the most damage.

Death wound. He'd stumbled out of the bar and stumbled onto the bus, vaguely wondering why no one had pursued him, why no one seemed to notice the bus sitting there with its door open.

No one had noticed because the bus wasn't meant for them. They weren't ghosts. Not yet anyway.

Devl cleaned himself up, then cleaned up the seats and the floor before putting on the clothes that had been left for him.

At some point, the buckets of dirty water and the garbage bags filled with his clothes and the soiled rags disappeared. At some point, windows on the bus began to close as the stench of death faded.

But Devl still felt cold—cold as the grave, his grandma used to say—and he wondered if he would ever feel warm again.

34

Sheina Kali wasn't surprised to find the note on the kitchen table. Yaron's obsession with seeing the "truth" about Wyrd had grown over the past few months. It was only her constant reminders that if he went exploring before he handed in final grades and left his students hanging, he could kiss the job at Jackson University goodbye—and most likely his career as well. His verbal abuse had gone from nasty to savage, mostly because he knew she was right, and her being right messed with his plans.

In the end, he finished up the school year and handed in his grades for one simple reason: he couldn't find anyone who was willing to take him across the river to any spot on Wyrd that wasn't one of the two places permitted by the Arcana—namely, Destiny Bay or Destiny Park. Even the couple of men who said they were willing to drop him off anywhere he wanted—for a few thousand dollars paid up front—weren't willing to hang around for a few hours while he explored, and said flat out that if he caused any kind of fuss while he was there and had the Arcana paying attention to the shore, they weren't going to risk their lives or their boats to return and pick him up.

But Yaron must have found someone, because he'd left a three-word note: *I have to.* As if that said anything, justified everything.

Couldn't he have spent a few more moments to add *I'm sorry*? Or *I love you*? Maybe that wasn't true anymore. Maybe she was just useful to him for the extra income, for taking care of the house chores, for sex. Maybe she was the only one who still thought love mattered.

She didn't know the man who rang the doorbell later that evening, who sounded so apologetic as he explained that he worked at the university and had a boat, and had reluctantly agreed to take Yaron across the river. Yaron had promised to be gone two hours at the most, and he had waited for three hours. Then he began to draw too much attention and got nervous, so he returned to the marina—and now he was here because Yaron was still across the river, and he hoped Yaron would find his way home soon.

She thanked the man for telling her and closed the door. But was she closing the door to her house, the door to her heart, or the door to her life as she'd known it?

She needed some help, and she needed advice—and she needed to keep this as quiet as possible in her own precinct, at least until she received that advice.

Struggling to remain calm, to be a cop and not a wife, Sheina called Captain Grace Russell at King's Hill.

35

After confirming that she was scheduled for two consecutive days off, Beth called the hotel at Destiny Park and booked a room for an overnight stay. The hotel had a website of sorts—a single page that provided basic information—a phone number, room rates, and a mention that the hotel had a restaurant, a spa, and a fitness center.

In the months she'd been working in Penwych, she hadn't found any other credible information about the Isle of Wyrd. Apparently, the only people who had phone numbers for any of the Arcana worked on Captain Forrester's team, which was the most likely reason why police in the other towns—and other precincts in Penwych—called Forrester when they had to deal with something that looked connected to the strange or uncanny.

Feeling like a trap was slowly closing around her—a trap that would consume her life because it was only a matter of time before Bonnie lashed out in an attempt to extract more money—Beth dithered over what to take with her to Wyrd. It was just an overnight, for pity's sake, but . . .

She finally decided she would look like any other woman who couldn't leave home without packing a dozen extra outfits that she wouldn't need. Pulling out a small wheeled suitcase and a large soft-sided bag that was *meant* as an overnighter, she packed several sets of underwear, clean pajamas, a fresh pair of jeans, T-shirts, a couple of sweaters, and her toiletries, along with two of her favorite comfort-read paperbacks. The wheeled suitcase also held a tailored pantsuit and her favorite dress in case the hotel restaurant was a dress-up kind of place. She added semi-opaque tights, pumps, and a shawl in case the restaurant was chilly. Her e-reader and chargers went into the cushioned pocket designed for protecting electronic devices.

Underneath the clothes, she carefully packed the sketchbook that held drawings of the Arcana and, hopefully, held some kind of answer to her own past.

Checking and double-checking that she had everything she might need, Beth squeezed in two more paperbacks—new ones she'd been saving for a rainy day.

With nothing else to do, she set her alarm and tried to sleep.

The next morning, Beth tried to reason with herself. The hotel check-in time wasn't until early afternoon. But other guests must arrive early to walk around the park and get their cards read or whatever else they did. Surely the hotel had a secure room to store luggage just like hotels did on this side of the river. If she couldn't get an appointment to see the Ladies Three until tomorrow, what would she do with herself all day?

Explore. Breathe. Simply be without feeling . . . other.

Would that be true?

Wasn't it true?

In the end, she waited in line for the first ferry—the one that mostly held people employed by the hotel or park, and the people who worked at the food stands. She scanned the men and women who chatted with one another about sports or the latest miniseries on TV—casual friends who might not connect otherwise but made this trip across the river almost every day.

Spotting a patrol car, Beth looked away, hoping she wouldn't be recognized. She held her breath, waiting to hear the *bloop* of the siren or someone shouting her name—or worse, one of the officers getting out of the car and coming over to ask what she was doing.

Then one of the ferry's crew removed the sawhorses at the end of the pier, and people began making their way to the money exchange shack and the person who set the price for a ferry ride.

Beth sighed with relief and moved with the rest of the people to exchange her money and pay her fare.

She didn't look back to find out which cop had spotted her and would, no doubt, report her to Captain Forrester.

36

Lucas opened the door of Rachel's cage, put his hand in with his fingers extended as a perch, and said, "Enough, Rahele. I know you miss Faulkner, but he would be the first to tell you that you're wasting the opportunity to experience being in a different body if you just sit in the cage day after day. Kia Dance offered to stay with you this morning so that you can spend time outside. She'll be here in a minute. You have months before your own transformation back to human. You had the courage to make this choice. Now have the courage to live it."

She didn't step up on his fingers to come out of the cage. Had it been a mistake to give her a few days to feel sad about the loss of her friend? When the Arcana were looking after more than one human who had made a transformation, most of the time the forms weren't harmonious enough to get along and were kept in separate areas of the park. He'd like to think that Rahele's curiosity about her new form would have engaged on its own, but she'd had Faulkner to lean on rather than having to try anything by herself.

Frost.

Lucas withdrew his hand from the cage, alert to potential danger. *Ferryman?*

The police female is on the ferry. With luggage. Not police business. I thought you should know.

I'll meet her at the dock.

He wasn't surprised that Beth Fahey would come to Wyrd to spend some personal time, but . . . luggage?

He nodded to Kia Dance as she walked through the door that led to the Arcana's private part of the park, then headed for the public section of the pavilion. He glanced into the room where the Ladies Three dealt with the visitors who came for more than entertainment—and froze for a moment when he saw the look on his wife's face. He strode across the room, stopping when he reached Justine's table. "What is it?"

Lysandra turned her sketch pad so that he could see her drawing. An older woman at the top of the page, her face twisted with ugly emotions as she threw lightning bolts at a tower that had split with the force of her fury. Falling from the tower was Beth Fahey, her expression fearful yet defiant. Lysandra had lightly sketched the proof of Beth's heritage rising from the young woman's head.

"A life torn asunder," Lysandra said.

Zerah held up a card that showed Death riding a dark horse. "Endings and beginnings."

"If Beth Fahey asks, we will tell her what we can," Justine said. "We will show her the truth." She paused, then added, "And we should offer her sanctuary, even before she asks, so that she knows the possibility exists."

"All right," Lucas replied. "We'll know soon enough what she seeks. She's on the ferry."

He walked out of the pavilion and reached the dock just as the ferry arrived. Many of the people who worked at the hotel and the food stands were three-season workers. From spring through fall, the Arcana provided assistance or information to the humans across the river. Winter was the fallow season when his people tended to their own business. Oh, the hotel was still open with a reduced staff, and a couple of the food stands, whose owners lived on the island, opened for a few hours each day and carried a limited menu. But the people who came for a reading—or came to use the internet—were residents of Wyrd, not visitors from across the river.

Summer was a busy time of year, both for legitimate visitors and for fools who thought they were knowledgeable enough to ignore the rules that gave humans a little protection when dealing with the uncanny.

As for Beth Fahey, he would find out soon enough what brought her to Wyrd on the day that Justine and her sisters foresaw the woman's life being torn apart.

37

Beth saw Lucas Frost at the end of the dock. Well, what had she expected? She was usually here in her capacity as a detective, so she shouldn't be surprised that the person in charge of Destiny Park would want to know what she was doing on the island—especially since she hadn't called ahead to let him know she was coming.

He eyed her suitcase and her soft-sided bag.

"The hotel's website didn't say anything about a dress code for eating in the restaurant, so I came prepared," she said by way of greeting.

"I see." He looked amused. "I'll mention that to the hotel's management. It might keep the ferry from sinking under the weight of visitors' luggage."

"Ha ha."

He reached for the wheeled suitcase. Her hand clenched around the handle, a physical reaction to needing to protect what was inside. What if the suitcase rolled off the dock and into the water? What if . . . ?

"You brought something precious with you?" Frost asked.

Beth nodded. With an effort, she released her grip on the suitcase's handle.

Frost lowered that handle and lifted the suitcase by the other grip. "I won't be careless with it."

"I'm staying at the hotel," she said as she followed him from the beach to the path that led to the hotel.

"Really?" His voice was dryer than dust.

"I guess you figured that out."

"The second piece of luggage was a clue."

She stifled a laugh.

"Would they let me store my stuff somewhere until the room is ready?" she asked when Frost opened the hotel door for her.

"If necessary," he replied.

It wasn't necessary. A room was available, and the woman on the desk was quick to point out that Beth would only be charged for the one night. Taking her key, Beth followed Frost to the second-floor rooms.

He set her suitcase beside her door and stepped back, watchful.

Beth hesitated, then turned to look at him. "I need to make an appointment to see the Ladies Three."

Frost nodded. "Come down to the pavilion when you're ready. They're expecting you."

Chilled by the words, Beth nodded.

"Go in," Frost said quietly.

She opened the door and pushed the wheeled suitcase inside. "In an hour?"

Frost gave her a look she couldn't interpret. "I'll tell them."

Beth closed the door and leaned against it. An hour from now she might have some answers, but did she really want them?

38

Charles Forrester looked away from his computer monitor when Tom Castelletti knocked on the doorframe of his office. "Problem?"

"A patrol car making an early sweep around the river spotted Beth Fahey at the pier, waiting for the ferry. He thought we should know." Castelletti hesitated. "She had luggage."

Charles leaned back in his chair. "There is a very nice hotel across the river, not to mention a well-maintained park. Maybe she wanted to get out of her apartment for a day."

"Why go there?"

Hearing something in Castelletti's voice, Charles said, "Why not?"

"There's been talk about how friendly Fahey is with the Arcana. With her going over there when she has time off . . . Which side is she on, Captain?"

"Are we taking sides now, Tom?"

"Not yet, but sooner or later, someone is going to ask about her."

"If they do, refer them to me." Charles studied his senior detective. "I'm going on vacation next week with my family. I'll be away for two weeks, and you'll be in charge of the team. Are you going to have a problem working with Detective Fahey?"

"No, sir." Castelletti retreated—for the time being.

Charles pressed his fingers against his temples to ease a sudden ache. Sweet Jesus, since when did success make a person suspect?

Whenever the wrong person was successful.

Aisha and Jazz needed time away from Penwych and the daily turmoil the families of the dead boys continued to stir up. Never mind that Albert Palmer had shot those boys. The Arcana were being blamed for not preventing the boys from crossing the river and doing whatever they did while on Wyrd.

Like not allowing someone on the ferry would prevent a person from crossing the river and going ashore to face God only knew what.

Well, according to the Arcana, a person crossing the river and entering Wyrd came to face their destiny or try to change their fate.

His phone rang. "Forrester."

"Charles? It's Grace Russell."

"How are you, Grace?"

"I'm doing okay. I still miss my father, but seeing him that last time, it's different now. Better. What about you? Any news about your son?"

"Not recently." He could feel her hesitating. "Something wrong?"

"Do you remember Sheina Kali, a detective in the Jackson police force? Her husband, Yaron, is an English professor at Jackson University, with an interest in mythology, folklore, and the supernatural."

Charles knew where this was going, but he gave her time to get there. "So why is a police captain working in King's Hill calling to tell me this?"

"Because the damn fool convinced someone with a boat to take him across the river so that he could explore on his own and see the real island instead of the tourist trap." Grace's voice was sharp with annoyance. "That was a few days ago. Sheina wanted to keep it quiet for the first couple of days in case her husband made it home on his own—and because what cop wants to admit her spouse is idiot enough to ignore every warning he'd received about going anywhere in Wyrd except Destiny Park? Hell, Charles, even I warned her." Now she sighed. "At this point, she's filed a missing person report, which is being distributed to all the towns around the Fate River. I wondered if you'd heard anything from across the river."

"Lucas Frost hasn't contacted me to say they'd found someone, but I can call and ask if the Arcana have spotted anyone who looks out of place."

"Will he give you a straight answer?"

"It depends on whether or not the person wants to be found." He waited a beat. "Is Detective Kali sure her husband didn't take a boat somewhere else?"

"Did he skip out on her? I don't think so. They moved to Jackson last year because he'd been hired by the university, and they seemed happy with their respective careers and with each other. I don't think he's using Wyrd as a way to deliberately disappear. Besides, the man with the boat went to Kali's house that first evening and told Sheina he'd taken Yaron to Wyrd."

"I'll make the call and let you know what I find out."

"Thanks, Charles."

Ending that call, Charles dialed Lucas Frost's office number.

"Frost."

"It's Charles Forrester."

Silence.

Are you wondering if I'm checking up on Beth Fahey? "I just received a report of a man who went ashore on your side of the river and has been missing for a few days. He's the husband of a police officer in Jackson. I wondered if you'd heard anything on your end."

"Near the end of May, four people came ashore where they shouldn't have," Frost replied. "Three men and one woman. They've all disappeared into the neighborhoods. If any of them found and used a moon gate, that person could be anywhere by now."

Four people missing since May, and no one reported it? That would make Yaron Kali the fifth person—and the only one reported missing. "Could I send you the man's details?"

"You can send them."

There was a curtness to Frost's answer that troubled Charles, but asking if there was a problem probably overstepped the line of civility he had established with the Arcana leader. "Thank you."

Maybe this was a poor time to go away, but he'd learned years ago that if he allowed himself to feel that no one else could do his job, there would never be a good time to go away and give his family his undivided attention—and give himself some rest. He'd put in for this vacation time months ago, timed for the end of the school year. And the very reasons it was a poor time to go away were the same reasons he *needed* to get his family away from Penwych and the river . . . and Wyrd.

39

Hugging the sketchbook, Beth walked to the pavilion. Entering the building, she put a gold coin in the box on the "admissions" table and took a bone disc. Then she walked into the room where the Ladies Three named the price required when a person wanted the Arcana's assistancc.

She put the bone disc into the bowl on the first table. The woman who reads the cards silently offered her a wand before spreading two decks of cards in arches.

Words have power. Intentions matter.

"Choose three cards from the first deck, two cards from the second," the woman said.

Beth had intended to move the wand over the entire arch before choosing the first three cards, but the wand jerked in her hand like a divining rod, tapping cards.

The woman moved the cards out of position but didn't turn them over. "Two more."

Again, the wand seemed in command, since Beth couldn't resist the tug toward two cards.

Was it supposed to do that? The wand hadn't acted like that the first time.

The woman turned the cards over.

Beth stared at the cards. What did it mean that she'd chosen a person in a cell, then a cell with the door torn off the hinges, and a bridge partially destroyed by fire. The two cards from the other deck looked like the Tower from a tarot deck—and Death.

The woman behind the scales said, "What have you brought for your side of the scales?"

Turning away from the cards, Beth laid the sketchbook beside the scales. "This."

The woman opened the sketchbook and studied several drawings. Then she looked up and looked past Beth, who suddenly realized Lucas Frost had come in and was standing behind her.

"Where did you get that?" Frost asked.

Beth held out her hand to show them the old ring. "The sketchbook and this ring are the closest things I have to family heirlooms."

"Ask your question," the woman said.

"Don't you have to tell me what it will cost?"

"Not this time. Ask."

Hard to breathe. Once the question was asked—and answered—there was no turning back. "Who am I?"

A weighted silence.

"You will join us for the evening meal," Lucas Frost finally said. "You will have your answer then."

Beth looked at the woman who balanced the scales. The woman nodded. She looked at the woman who had been sketching since she walked into the room.

That woman closed her cloudy eyes. When she opened them, they were clear. "What needs to be said will be said after the evening meal. Will be said in moonlight, in starlight. Until then, walk the safe paths in the gardens. You know which ones they are."

Beth reached for the sketchbook, then glanced at the cards that had been revealed—and hesitated. "Is there somewhere I could leave this for safekeeping? Just for a while."

"I'll take care of it," Lucas Frost said.

Nodding, Beth left the room and turned toward the archway that led into Destiny Park. She would walk the safe paths in the gardens. She would eat lunch at the hotel. And she would wait for the answer to her question.

Lucas waited until Beth had left the pavilion. Then he looked at Lysandra, who turned her sketchbook to show him and her sisters what had been revealed.

Destruction. A sacrifice of some kind, but he couldn't tell from the image if it was supposed to be physical or emotional. Perhaps both. He could see clearly—they could all see clearly—who was going to be sacrificed. But not why.

"Tonight we will tell her what we know," Justine said. "Once she has her answer, her destiny is her own."

"Yes," Lucas agreed. "Her destiny is her own."

40

After dithering about what to wear, Beth finally chose the green handkerchief-hem dress and hoped it was appropriate for a dinner with the Arcana. Hoped she wouldn't look too out of place. Hoped . . .

She didn't know what she hoped for.

A knock on the door. When she opened the door, the woman on the other side smiled at her and said, "I'm Kia Dance. That's a lovely dress. Did you bring a shawl? It might get cool later in the evening."

"I have a wrap." Beth fetched it, then slipped the strap of the small clutch over her wrist—a convenient place to carry a couple of tissues and her room key.

Beth closed the door, confirmed that it was properly locked, then followed Kia.

"This way," Kia said, turning in the opposite direction of the wall sign for the lobby. She walked to the end of the corridor and the mural that filled the wall.

Beth didn't see a handle of any kind, although there could have been one. She was too busy staring at the webbing between Kia's fingers.

Noticing Beth's attention, Kia said, "Water Arcana," as if that explained everything.

Maybe it did.

A door opened in the wall. Kia gestured for Beth to go first. Once they were both on the other side and the door closed behind them, Beth looked around—and saw nothing that looked different from the other side of the door, but the air *smelled* different.

"This is the Arcana's side of the hotel," Kia said.

Did that explain the growing sense that she was in another place?

Kia opened a door at the end of the corridor. "Watch your step on the stairs."

Not a metal fire escape, which would have made sense. These wooden stairs were more like a Gothic representation of a series of waterfalls than something as basic as stairs.

Beth paused when she saw the moon gate.

"That leads to the public area of the park," Kia said. "If you go through the gate from this side, you can't get back to the hotel or your room without going around to the public side."

"If I stay on this side of the gate?"

"Then you can return to your room using the stairs."

And try to figure out how to open a door that had no handle.

The flagstone path wandered through flower beds that, even in moonlight, seemed to invite her to touch, to rest, to breathe.

Kia pointed to a shallow water feature. "Birds gather there to drink and bathe."

"Is Rahele allowed to come out and fly around and bathe there?"

"Yes," Kia replied. "Although she lost her crow friend recently and is feeling too sad to come out on her own. She will, in time."

"Her friend died?"

Kia stopped walking and gave her a puzzled look. "No, he didn't die. He had to return to his own form and begin the next part of his journey. But that journey isn't here."

They continued to an open-air pavilion with walls made of fine netting. Several tables were set for a meal. Various kinds of lanterns and candles in glass globes lit the pavilion and the tables, the flickering light making everything look soft and a little unreal, like a fantasy.

That's what she first thought when Lucas Frost turned around and looked at her. A fantasy. The delicate antlers rising from his head were proof that the Arcana weren't human. The look in his eyes was a warning that he was a power that should not be taken lightly.

She looked past him to the women coming up to join them. Looked at the various shapes of antlers and horns—and realized she'd seen all these variations in her sketchbook.

The Arcana. The masters of the uncanny.

She also realized that something had settled inside her, and the faces of the people around her no longer shifted or looked out of focus. She saw them for who they were.

"Sit with us," Lucas Frost said. "You've met Ethan Sharpe. And you've met my wife, Justine, and her sisters, Zerah and Lysandra. Have you met my brother, Jack?"

"I would have remembered if we had," Jack said.

Those words might have sounded lightly flirtatious coming from another man, but Jack Frost was stating a fact, and his smile was sharp and feral—a predator sizing up potential prey.

Seated between Lucas and Jack, Beth felt relieved when Ashley Laxton took a seat opposite her. Kia Dance and a woman named Mia Skov also sat at their table.

Given the placement, Beth had a feeling that this was the high table, and she wouldn't be sitting there if she wasn't a guest.

At first the talk flowed around her as servers offered platters of various meats and vegetables. Some things she recognized. Other things she'd heard of but had never tasted.

At one point she found herself in an animated discussion with Ashley and Ethan about a mystery series she enjoyed reading and stopped seeing the horns and other markings that made the differences between humans and the Arcana so obvious.

Lucas said little and seemed preoccupied. Did the leader of such a place feel alone even among his people?

After the meal, the Arcana left the pavilion in groups or alone until the only people left were Justine and her sisters, Ashley, Lucas, Jack, Ethan—and her.

Justine stood and looked at Beth. "It's time for your answer. Come with us."

Beth followed Justine past quaint cottages and rambling buildings that could house a dozen families. All were made of wood and stone and blended in so well, she wondered how many other buildings she had passed and hadn't seen.

Finally, they came to a stone sculpture that looked like the trunk of an ancient tree that had been cut to the perfect height to hold a large stone bowl filled with water. Filled with moonlight reflected in the water.

Justine pointed. "Stand there—and look."

Moonlight and water and . . .

Beth gasped. She raised her hands, an involuntary move to touch the antlers that rose from her head. Her hands felt nothing. She took a step back and looked at Lucas.

"Mine are real," he said quietly. "Moonlight and starlight reveal our true nature. That's why visitors aren't welcome after dark. Yours are a kind of ancestral memory."

Beth stepped toward the stone bowl of water and stared at her reflection. "I've seen my reflection at night, even reflected in water. I've never seen *those.*"

"You've never been standing on Arcana land."

Would Lucas and the others know the names Maxine and Arianna Greenwood? If they did, was *she* ready to know about that branch of the Arcana? Not yet. Tonight, it was enough just to have confirmation that the dreams brought on by that special tea were true.

Justine stood on the other side of the stone bowl. "What this tells us is that you are one-quarter Arcana. That's why the antlers don't physically manifest and why your heritage is only revealed in this way." She looked at Lucas. "And that's why there is something else you need to see."

Justine led them back to the hotel and walked through the moon gate.

"It's all right," Lucas said when Beth hesitated. "Kia will see you back to the public side of the hotel. Her difference is less obvious to any human guests who are staying tonight."

One side of the carved wooden doors that secured one of the pavilion's archways slid into the wall. They all followed Justine into the room where she and her sisters assisted people who wanted to meet—or change—their fate.

Lysandra walked over to her table and picked up the sketchbook she used while supplicants asked for whatever they wanted and heard what it would cost. She removed a sketch and held it up for all of them to see. "Do you know this woman?"

Beth stared at the drawing and shivered. "Her name is Bonnie Wilson. I don't think there was any legal document assigning her as a foster parent or my legal guardian, but after my parents disappeared, I lived with her until I turned eighteen. Someone sent money every month for my upkeep. When I turned eighteen, the money Bonnie received for taking care of me stopped. She liked to gamble, and when she couldn't pay her bills, she would call me and try to guilt me into sending her money."

"Did you send her some?" Lucas asked.

"For a while, I did send her a little money whenever she threatened to tell the police academy that I was strange and unstable." Beth smiled bitterly. "I think the correct term is 'smear campaign.' I doubt Bonnie had any proof about my heritage except the sketchbook and the ring, and I doubt she understood the significance of either, but she had the ability to find a person's weakness and exploit that vulnerability. She did it with me every time she reminded me that there had to be a reason why my parents left one day and never came back for me. When I was older, I recognized that she used the same gaslighting techniques on other people. She liked sowing discord. But with me?" A sigh. "Well, she wasn't wrong about me, was she? I worked very hard to become a police officer and then a detective, but I've always felt I had to hide a part of myself from my colleagues—and now I know why."

"A life torn asunder," Lysandra said. "That is what we read as her intention."

Beth nodded. "She called recently, wanting money. She said she knows my secret. People in Penwych are already upset about the Arcana's alleged involvement in the deaths of the four boys who were killed by Albert Palmer and the two boys who are still missing. Once an accusation is made that a detective on the special investigations team isn't fully human, there will be a public outcry and demands for *every* police officer to take a DNA test to prove he or she is human. It won't matter if everything Bonnie says is a lie, because it will be what enough people want to believe, and that will end my career as a cop. Captain Forrester's team is already being criticized. He doesn't need my problems on top of that."

And his daily worry about his son.

"What humans often forget is this: if you try to change or damage someone's fate, you also change or damage your own," Justine said.

Beth sighed. "At least I'll be prepared when it happens."

"Come with me," Lucas said.

It wasn't a suggestion or a request. Beth went with him and didn't try to break the silence as they strolled around the ornamental lake until she noticed the empty pedestal. "The statues are missing."

"Not missing," Lucas replied. "They're off duty—and probably hunting."

She heard a dark edge of approval in his voice.

"We are what we are, Beth Fahey, and we make no apologies for that. We were here on this land long before the humans built their towns along the river. If they didn't want to deal with us, they could have gone elsewhere or stayed away from us. They chose to build their towns and chose to touch our land—and us. To mate with some of us. And sometimes they learn the cost of breaking a bargain with us."

They circled the lake and headed back to the pavilion.

"There are a couple of things I want to show you in the morning," Lucas said. "We'll consider obliging me to be the second favor you owe the Arcana."

"All right. I can check out of my room after breakfast."

"There's no need for that. The room is for your use until you're ready to catch the ferry."

Authority. Command. And something else, something more. Something dangerous.

"Thank you."

Lucas nodded. "There's Kia. She'll take you back to the hotel."

"Good night. I'll see you in the morning." Were those words considered a bargain among the Arcana? She wasn't sure.

A life torn asunder. Nothing she could do about that tonight. Even if she called Bonnie and agreed to pay the twenty thousand dollars she didn't have, the threat would always be there. Even if Bonnie made something up just to cause trouble, a DNA test would provide all the proof needed that Beth Fahey wasn't completely human.

Lucas walked back into the pavilion and joined the others who had waited for him.

"Fire burns away the old, but it also makes room for the new," Zerah said, holding up a card.

"Are you going to show Beth Fahey the possibility of the new?" Jack asked.

Lucas nodded. "Tomorrow." He looked at them, his most trusted counselors. Power swelled inside him, wanting to burst free. "I want to know everything there is to know about Bonnie Wilson, especially which branch of the Arcana paid her for looking after Beth Fahey—and why."

He'd seen the stylized *A* in the corner of one of the sketches in Beth's book and knew of only one person who signed her drawings that way. If Beth was descended from Arianna Greenwood, he could guess which branch of the Arcana had been watching her for most of her life. The why? He wasn't sure he wanted the answer to why.

41

After looking over the impressive breakfast buffet, Beth settled for scrambled eggs and toast, hoping the simple food would settle a stomach made queasy by a sleepless night and nerves. Fate wasn't a narrow road lined with high walls. There were turnoffs and turnarounds. And sometimes there were unexpected sinkholes or mudslides that could alter a person's choices. Her first trip across the river was because of a man purchasing the use of a ghost gun to shoot three people. His fate was sealed when he pulled the trigger, but he could have had a different life if he'd changed his mind and returned the bullets and the gun.

Choices could make a difference, but she didn't think whatever choice *she* made would change the fact that Bonnie was going to do something that would tear apart the life she'd built. It didn't take a great leap of logic to understand that the kernel of uneasiness most of her colleagues felt about her would contribute to her life being torn asunder.

A man approached her table, his plate piled so high with food the slightest shake of his hand would start an avalanche that would spill over the table and onto the floor.

"May I join you?" He didn't wait for an answer, just set his plate on the table. Since the foods at the top of the pile were already starting to slide, maybe he realized he didn't have time to hear her reply.

"I'm waiting for someone," Beth said. Had she seen his face before? Not on a missing person flyer but somewhere else connected to the police?

"He's not here now." The man smiled before shoveling food into his mouth.

"How do you know I'm waiting for a man?"

"You don't look like someone who plays for the other team. I'm Richard." He chomped on a sausage. "And you are?"

"Someone who enjoys quiet time with her breakfast."

Richard looked at the scant amount of food on her plate. "Not much of an appetite. Love affair gone sour?"

"Do you have a business card, Richard?" Beth pushed aside her plate. "A licensed private investigator would carry business cards." If she was wrong about his profession, he'd correct her, but she didn't think she was wrong. Spotting Ethan Sharpe and Jack Frost walking toward her, she raised her voice. "Or are you just a snoop who is here to cause trouble for someone?"

He smirked. "Wouldn't you like to know?"

Ethan stood behind Richard's chair. Jack came up on the side of the table, blocking any chance of escape.

Jack gave Richard that sharp, feral smile. "We want to know, and you're going to tell us."

"Or what?"

"Or you will have a new job title: tethered goat." Jack looked at Beth's untouched food. "He's waiting for you."

Beth pushed away from the table. She gave Richard a long look, then hurried out of the hotel's restaurant. She paused in the lobby to send a note to her precinct e-mail, detailing Richard's physical description. He was smart not to provide a last name. It would make it harder to find him, especially if he didn't live in any of the towns around the Fate River.

Then again, maybe it wouldn't be hard to find him if she started looking in the town where Bonnie now lived.

Keeping his hands beneath the table, Jack opened the camera app on the cell phone. He raised his hands and took a couple of quick pictures of the man who had sat down at Beth's table without an invitation, ignoring the man's squawked protest.

The man—Richard—put his hands on the table as if he were going to leave. His eyes widened. He sank back into the seat.

"My friend is holding a short, very sharp blade," Jack said. "If you try to leave again or cause any fuss while we're talking, he'll slip that blade between a couple of vertebrae and sever your spine. It will be done so fast, you won't even have time to feel the blade pierce the skin. Do you understand?"

"You can't . . ." Richard sputtered.

"Can't what? Kill you? Of course we can. But we don't *have* to kill you this time, as long as you answer our questions. The Ladies Three have considered your presence here and set the price: one year of your life for every lie you tell while you're talking to us. I don't know the measure of your years, but I hope you don't tell so many lies that you end up expiring face-first in what is left of your breakfast." Jack smiled. "Tell us why you targeted the young woman sitting here, and who else is on your list of targets."

"You didn't sleep," Lucas Frost said as he led Beth toward the cabins on the other side of the pavilion from the hotel.

"I had a lot to think about." Did she look that haggard, or was he just very observant?

"Here is something else for you to think about." Lucas unlocked and opened the door of the first cabin—a one-story building that was larger than the other cabins. "This is our information center. It has phones, two computers for sending e-mail and accessing the internet, even a ham radio. It provides the Arcana with the ability to communicate with people and companies on the other side of the river. It also provides communication with the neighborhoods that also have such things."

"I thought your office did that."

"My office is *mine*. This is . . . communal. The building also holds two meeting rooms, which could also function as offices. The other cabins that are visible are for visiting families or people who want a place to stay that is more economical than the hotel."

If she'd known that was a possibility, she would have inquired about using a cabin. She didn't want to know what the hotel bill would do to her credit card. But . . . families?

"If whatever is coming changes circumstances so much that you can no longer do police work on the other side of the river, you can come here and work for me," Lucas said. "Even if it doesn't change things so much, you have that option."

Beth stared at him. "To work for you? Doing what?"

"The same thing you're doing now. Investigating when problems occur between the Arcana and humans. Being someone who can talk to the police and speak their language when they're looking for information. Helping visitors when conflicts arise."

"So I would commute every day?"

"No. You would live here."

Something in his eyes, in his voice, made Beth uneasy. Like he was offering her a bolt-hole. Like he suspected she would need one.

"I could live here in . . . ?"

"I'll show you."

They left the communications cabin. Behind the row of cabins were picnic tables and chairs beneath the trees. There were even a couple of hammocks. Beyond that area was a gate so cleverly disguised she didn't see it or realize there was a path leading to another part of the park until Lucas opened the gate and led her to a well-maintained path. They walked for several minutes until they reached a large clearing that looked like a woodland fantasy combined with mundane practicality.

The cottages here weren't in a row. They seemed to grow out of the land, connected by mulched pathways that all led to a sunny area where raised beds held a communal garden.

"The people who live in these cottages work in the hotel or run a food stand or work in the pavilion," Lucas said. "Most are like you—part Arcana. Two of the cottages are currently vacant. You could choose one as your residence. It would be most convenient for you to live within the boundaries of the park, but there is another place on Wyrd where humans have made a home. I'll show it to you. It requires taking a shuttle."

The shuttle was the same kind of vehicle that car dealerships used to transport customers to work after customers brought their cars in for service. This one was black and had "Shuttle" painted on the side doors.

Lucas pulled the side door open and gestured for Beth to get in.

"I'm waiting for Katherine Rose," the driver said. "She reserved a seat last night. I'm dropping her off at the library."

"The library will work for us, and we're not in a hurry," Lucas replied. Then to Beth, he added, "Katherine Rose works in the pavilion. She reads cards, although not like the Ladies Three. She is mostly human, but she feels more comfortable living on this side of the river."

A woman rushed up to the shuttle, handed her tote bag to Lucas, then climbed in and took a seat in the second row. "Thanks for waiting for me."

Lucas closed the side door, and the driver headed out on a road that might accommodate two cars if the drivers didn't mind sharing paint.

Lucas looked at the words on the tote bag and sighed. "Really, Katherine Rose?"

"Hey, Wyrd is where it's at," Katherine Rose said brightly.

"Where did you get the bag?" Beth asked.

"The hotel gift shop. They're selling coffee mugs, too, and pads of notepaper that have that saying. There is talk of doing T-shirts."

Lucas sighed again, handed the bag to Katherine Rose, and made the introductions.

"You're with the police?" Katherine Rose asked.

"Yes," Beth replied.

Katherine Rose leaned forward and touched Beth's arm. "He's all right."

"I'm sorry?"

"The boy is all right. I looked this morning." She hesitated. "I've looked a couple of times each week. The boy connected to the police is all right. He'll be coming home soon." Another hesitation. "But maybe not all the way home."

What did that mean? "Two other boys went missing at the same time. Did you see anything about them?"

Katherine Rose said nothing. Then she whispered, "Specters make their homes in the graveyards of the world."

Chilled, Beth didn't know how to respond. She turned to Lucas. "Where are we going? Besides the library."

"We're going to Wyrd's Teeth," Lucas replied. "It's a piece of land that runs from Destiny Bay to the Fate River. It's one of the static neighborhoods." He looked at her. "You've looked at a kaleidoscope? You've seen how the colored pieces shift and change? The places in the world that are a convergence of the uncanny are like that, and pieces shift during the spring and fall equinox, the two days of the year when the light and the dark are balanced. But some of the pieces in each place are anchored to that place and are constant, are stable. Destiny Park is one of those places on the Isle of Wyrd. The Teeth is another, along with a few other neighborhoods. The rest get shuffled to another place of convergence. Some come back here at the next equinox; others never do."

"So Colin Forrester could be lost forever," Beth said.

"No," Katherine Rose replied. "He'll be home before the next equinox."

"We've reached the Teeth," Lucas said.

Beth halfway expected jagged rocks and something gothic and menacing. What she saw were clusters of small houses arranged in various geographic shapes around a central area. She spotted small ponds and waterfalls as part of the garden features. It all looked lovely. Welcoming.

"Why call this place the Teeth?" Beth asked.

"If you were looking for sanctuary, would you go to a place with that name?" Lucas asked in return.

"No."

"Which is exactly why the first humans who settled in this part of Wyrd gave it that name. And also because this land is located where the teeth would be in a human skull. There are three hundred houses on this entire strip of land, plus buildings that hold a variety of businesses. The people who choose to live here are here because they needed to disappear. Not from the law but from people who would do them harm. Some people live here for a while before going back across the river—or they choose to travel to another neighborhood and leave everything in their present life behind. Some stay for the rest of their lives."

Beth thought about Richard. Had Jack discovered if the man was a PI or just a snoop? Was she the target or was he here looking for someone else? "How many people know about the Teeth?"

"The most vulnerable residents don't live near either end where the businesses around the bay and the river interact with people on the other side of the water—people who might recognize an individual and tell someone else."

The driver pulled over. "We're here, folks." He looked back at Lucas. "I was going to make the circuit and pick up anyone who wants to go to the park. That will take about an hour."

"An hour is enough time for us," Lucas said. He opened the shuttle's side door and offered a hand to Katherine Rose and Beth to help them down.

A bus that had MOBILE LIBRARY painted along its side was parked next to a building that didn't look much bigger than the bus. As Beth studied the small building, someone inside turned the CLOSED sign to OPEN and opened the door. A woman carrying a cardboard box stepped out and said, "Good morning."

Lucas turned to Beth. "Beth, this is Rya Hedden. She handles the mobile library and brings books to residents in the static neighborhoods, as well as to some places that are temporarily connected to Wyrd. Rya, this is Beth Fahey, a detective who works in Penwych."

Rya gave Lucas a questioning look. He nodded.

Rya handed the box to Lucas, who carried it into the bus. She said, "I won't be making the circuit that includes Llamalidia for a few more days, but when I get there, is there any message you want me to deliver to Colin?"

Beth blinked. "You know Colin Forrester?"

"I've met him," Rya replied. "He takes out three books every week. Mostly thrillers, mysteries, fantasies, nonfiction about the natural—and unnatural—world. No 'girly' books. He's currently learning to weave and is making a set of place mats for his mother. But that's a surprise." She studied Beth. "He asked about graphic novels, but I don't know what those are."

"Comic books," another woman said as she stepped out of the library. She held out her hand. "Betsy Richens. I look after the library here."

Beth shook the woman's hand as she cataloged some features: late forties, appeared to have some nerve damage to one side of her face, and needed a cane.

"Graphic novels are more than comic books," Beth said.

The three women looked at her with interest that was now sharper than just being curious about someone new.

"You know about them?" Betsy asked.

Beth nodded. "I could pick up a few at a bookstore in Penwych and drop them off at the pavilion the next time I cross the river."

"We'd appreciate that," Betsy said. "We've got a newcomer who's just settling in to one of the houses. He's young and might enjoy books like that." She looked at Lucas, who stepped up to join them. "We appreciate the donation of the Rachel Nightingale books—and having a copy of each book for the library and the mobile library."

Rya nodded. "She's a new author for a lot of the neighborhoods, so the books are in demand."

"I'll see if I can get more copies of her books," Lucas said.

"Appreciate it."

Katherine Rose smiled. "I'd better exchange my books before the shuttle comes back. It was nice to meet you, Beth. Stop by the pavilion sometime. I'll read your cards."

"I'll do that." She wasn't sure she would. She had a feeling that Katherine Rose might see too much in the cards. Then again, some warning of what was coming might be better than being blindsided.

"Let's walk," Lucas said.

"Do they ever swap tasks?" Beth asked. "Betsy taking the mobile library and Rya minding the library here?"

"No. Rya is half Arcana. That heritage helps her keep the bus on its established routes and not take an unwanted turn in a neighborhood. Betsy is human. It wouldn't be safe for her to try to reach some of the places Rya can visit."

"Lucas!"

Hearing the shout, Beth turned toward the sound.

A boy about eleven or twelve years old—a boy with curly black hair and fear in his dark eyes—stared at her. Giving Lucas a panicked look, he bolted for one of the houses.

She recognized that boy from the missing person flyer. "That's—"

"You didn't see him," Lucas said firmly.

"But he's—"

"You. Didn't. See him."

Feeling like she was standing on the edge of a cliff, Beth squared off against Lucas Frost. "He's afraid."

"Of you, not me."

That cliff edge crumbled a little. "I wouldn't hurt him."

"You're police. Telling anyone he's here could destroy him. He disappeared for a reason, Beth. He's safe here, protected here, and he will make his own fate. Over there? If you make his whereabouts known and he's forced to go back to what he'd escaped, will you put flowers on his grave and tell him you're sorry you were part of the reason his life ended?"

"Do you know it will end?" she whispered.

"What Justine and her sisters saw is the reason we gave him this choice."

"He's just a boy."

"His eyes are old."

Beth looked around. The buildings looked quaint, and maybe the people living here didn't have the newest whatevers. She focused on a red box. "Telephone boxes?"

"There is a telephone box located every couple of blocks. There is no internet here, no Wi-Fi," Lucas said. "And most houses don't have a telephone. The businesses do. Residents make a call at the box. Anyone who wants to send or receive e-mail comes up to the park and uses the equipment in the communications cabin."

Half listening to Lucas, Beth thought about a young boy on his own. "I guess people don't have much access to junk food here, so he'd have to eat nutritious meals."

"He's quite self-sufficient. Even if he wasn't, the people here help each other. He'll be all right."

"Tell him . . . Tell him I didn't see him officially."

"I'll tell him. Let's walk a bit more, then head back to the library to catch the shuttle."

After walking for a few minutes, Beth said, "Not much vehicular traffic." None, in fact.

"Not many vehicles," Lucas replied. "Most people walk or ride a bicycle—or take the bus." He pointed to a small horse-drawn double-decker bus coming toward them.

Life here moved at a different pace than in towns across the river. "How did you get all the copies of Rachel Nightingale's books?"

"She had extra copies in storage and offered some of them for the libraries."

"You can speak lark?"

Lucas just smiled.

42

"Forrester."

"This is Jack Frost. Check your e-mail."

Charles closed his eyes for a moment before opening his e-mail program. He could deal with Lucas, but Jack scared him to the bone. Lucas was a predator—and a ruler. He was also a civilized man in his own way. Jack was a stone-cold killer.

He opened the attachments and studied the photos of a man. "Who is he?"

"His name is Richard. He was at the hotel this morning sniffing around Detective Fahey. He said he was a private investigator and was just hitting on a pretty woman. We think his claim of being an investigator is true. His reason for targeting Beth? That lie will cost him. Things are in motion, Captain. We thought you might like a photo of this man to show around her apartment building, see if he's been stalking her."

"You think that's likely?"

"We do."

That wasn't good any way he looked at it. Someone stalking a cop? That was pure trouble. Someone foolish enough to cross the river and attract the attention of an Arcana like Jack Frost? That was a death wish.

He'd promised Aisha and Jazz time away from Penwych. He couldn't back out of that. "We'll look into it. Could you tell Lucas that I will be on vacation starting next week? My family needs some time away from . . . everything. Tom Castelletti will be in charge of the team while I'm away, if there's anything you need from us."

"I'll tell him."

Charles ended the call, printed several copies of the photo, and handed them to his team.

"This isn't one of the people who went walkabout in Wyrd," Ian Kuhn said. "We're coming up blank on all of them, including Detective Kali's husband."

Tom Castelletti looked uncomfortable. "Maybe Fahey could ask for advice about finding these people since she's over there already."

Charles nodded. "I'll check with her before she catches the ferry back to Penwych. This man"—he pointed to the picture—"is possibly stalking Detective Fahey. I believe her apartment building is in Amanda Gibson's precinct, so check with her people before you start knocking on doors."

"Ex-boyfriend?" Kuhn asked.

"Jack Frost think he's a PI."

"Nothing we can do about the missing people, so we might as well talk to Detective Gibson about this mystery PI," Castelletti said.

Once his men were on their way, Charles returned to his office and called Beth Fahey—and received no answer.

43

No internet, no Wi-Fi, and no cell phone service in Wyrd's Teeth, Beth thought as she listened to the two voicemail messages from Captain Forrester. The first one was a "call me" message. The second held a sharp edge of concern.

"Captain?"

"Are you all right?"

Whoa. "I was in a part of Wyrd that doesn't have cell phone service. I checked my messages as soon as I got back to the hotel." Technically true. After leaving Lucas Frost, she'd stopped at one of the food stands and enjoyed coffee and a meal while she thought about what she'd seen—and about Lucas's job offer. It wasn't until she'd gone back to the hotel room to pack her things that she thought to check her phone, since she was still off duty. "Did something happen?"

"Do you know the man who is stalking you?"

Beth frowned. "Have you confirmed that he's stalking me? I'm pretty sure he's a PI. I'm not sure he has a license. He came across as sleazy."

"A couple of people living in your apartment building recognized him, said he'd been hanging around for a few days. There's a community playground nearby, and one of your neighbors did report him to the police, thinking he might be too interested in the children."

"I didn't see him until this morning." Beth exhaled slowly. "I think he was hired by Bonnie Wilson. She wants money and threatened to cause trouble if I didn't pay her."

"So he followed you to Wyrd. That was a mistake."

Beth wondered for a moment if the police somewhere along the Fate River were going to find another body. "I'll catch the next ferry back and report in."

"No, it's still your day off. Just be careful. Don't second-guess your instincts if something feels off."

In other words, consider Richard NoLastName a threat.

"I just said it's still your day off, but I'd like you to do something officially. Detective Kali's husband, Yaron, went exploring on Wyrd and is missing. When I tried to ask Lucas Frost about him yesterday, Frost's response was cool bordering on cold. Maybe he'll be more forthcoming with you."

"I'll ask him." Feeling the call was about to end, Beth weighed what she could say without saying too much. "Sir? I met someone this morning who saw Colin recently."

"Someone at Destiny Park *saw* him?"

"No, not at the park. She runs Wyrd's mobile library, and he's staying at one of her stops."

She listened to Forrester breathe as the man tried to sort out what he could say in return. If someone had a vehicle that could reach that place, why couldn't Colin come home? Well, he was coming home soon. But how soon was soon?

"Did this person say anything about him?" Forrester finally asked.

"He's doing all right." She hesitated, then added, "He's learning how to weave and is making place mats for his mother—but that's a surprise."

She heard Forrester's strangled laugh. "He's having what he would call a *Star Trek* adventure."

"Yes, sir, I think he is."

"Thank you."

"I'll ask about Yaron Kali."

"Let me know when you're on the ferry. I'll send a car for you."

He ended the call before she could say it wasn't necessary. Maybe it was necessary—or at least prudent if the man who approached her that morning really was a stalker or someone sent by Bonnie to keep tabs on her.

Beth finished packing, then went down to the reception desk. The woman on duty assured her that the room was hers for as long as she needed it.

As she walked back to the pavilion, Beth scanned the area around the food stands, then the dock. If she worked on this side of the river, would she be the one standing at the dock assessing the people getting off the ferry? Seeing Lucas would have more impact, but maybe that was the point of his making the job offer. Maybe he needed to step back and be more remote in order to do *his* job of protecting everyone in Destiny Park. And everyone in the Teeth? And how many other places in Wyrd?

She walked past the archways for the diviners of one kind or another and heard someone call her name. Beth approached an archway, then stepped inside the room when Ashley Laxton gestured for her to come in.

Katherine Rose sat behind the table, studying the cards.

"You didn't ask for a reading, but I was curious," Katherine Rose said.

"I'm guessing those cards confirm what I was told yesterday: my life is about to be torn apart."

Katherine Rose nodded. "Someone will begin the destruction of your life with the destruction of things you value. Move them. Hide them."

"How soon?" Ashley asked.

Katherine Rose turned over another card, then looked at Beth. "You have a protector on the other side of the river. It will begin when he is out of reach."

"Captain Forrester is going on vacation next week," Beth said. She couldn't think of anyone else in Penwych who would qualify as a protector.

Think. Think of Gerry Palowski and the possible life he could have had—the life that had vanished because he chose to use the ghost gun.

She had been warned by the Arcana that her life would be torn apart and items she valued would be destroyed. But no one had taken action against her yet. There wasn't one concrete piece of evidence that she was in physical danger, despite the certainty that Bonnie would be the reason this chapter in her life would end. Until some action *was* taken against her, she wasn't going to be a coward and flee. Moving to Wyrd was going to be a choice to move toward a new life rather than running away from her old one.

"These things that are important to you," Ashley said. "How soon could you get them packed?"

"I never unpacked most of my things when I moved to Penwych. I just stacked the boxes against a wall." She tried to smile. "No room for extra stuff in a furnished studio apartment."

Ashley stared at the cards. Then she nodded. "A couple of hours during the day would be enough time. We'll call in a favor and get the use of a van. There are storage facilities in Penwych where . . ."

Beth shook her head. "Things can be stolen from storage facilities if someone follows me and knows which lockup I rented. Could those boxes be stored over here?"

Ashley and Katherine Rose exchanged a look. "You're going to take the job?" Ashley asked.

"Yes. Until I move to Wyrd, I'd like to store my things where they will be within easy reach for me and not within reach for anyone else. I guess I should talk to Lucas about that."

"No need."

Meaning Lucas had already given his people instructions where she was concerned.

Ashley handed Beth a slip of paper with a phone number. "I think you'll know when the trouble starts. When that happens, call me. We'll arrange a time and move everything you want to save. I'll get

Jack and Ethan to help us haul boxes. We'll bring a pizza and call it a decluttering party. Your neighbors won't think twice about it—or they'll think enough about it to mention it to the police if the police are called in."

Beth tucked the paper into her pocket. "I need to talk to Lucas about one other thing before I head . . . across the river." *Home* didn't feel like the appropriate word now.

She found Lucas in his office, talking to Jack. The men gave her a long look, and Beth wondered if the Arcana had a way of communicating with each other that wasn't known to humans.

"Do you want to look at the available cottages and choose one now?" Lucas asked. "Or we can store your possessions in a private room at the hotel. They will be secure there."

"The hotel room would be better for now," Beth said. "I have to give two weeks' notice and work out the time. I'd rather not dump that on Captain Forrester just before he goes on vacation. I'll wait a couple of days, then hand my resignation letter to Detective Castelletti." *Who will be glad to see the back of me.*

Jack smiled. "I gather Ethan and I are helping you and Ashley move your things."

"That's the plan."

They waited. Finally, Lucas said, "Anything else?"

Beth drew in a breath and let it out slowly. "I'd like to talk to you about Yaron Kali."

44

Devl slowly became aware of his surroundings. This wasn't the same as waking up. This was . . .

Dead people. He was on a bus full of dead people. A few of them still looked normal, like the scary guy he suspected was not really dead and on the bus for some other reason, but the majority of the passengers weren't really . . . lively . . . until dark.

The conductor approached him. From where? The guy just seemed to appear and disappear.

"The bus's next stop will be a station close to your starting point. You will be required to leave."

"What will happen to me when I get off the bus?" Devl asked.

"You will be found, and your family will be notified." The conductor disappeared.

Home. He was going home.

Devl started to look at his belly, then turned to stare out the window. The last time he looked at the wounds made during that fight, he knew they were bad and getting worse. There were little wormy things crawling around in the wounds. If he got home in time, his folks would get him to a hospital and the doctors would clean him up and sew him up. He would be okay . . . if he got home in time.

Hours later—maybe days later—he heard the conductor say, "Next stop, Lovecraft."

45

Charles Forrester came around his desk when Captain Stan Wozniak appeared in his office doorway.

"Stan." Charles smiled and held out a hand to his friend. "What brings you to Penwych?"

"I have some information that you should have. I thought it was better to tell you in person since it's going to add to the shitstorm that's been raging about the Arcana since those four boys died."

He didn't want to know about any of this today, but if Stan had driven over from Lovecraft to tell him something, he owed the man the time to listen—and then make it clear that assistance would come from other members of his team. "Good thing you showed up today. Aisha, Jazz, and I are leaving tomorrow morning for a two-week vacation."

"Oh? Where?"

"A resort a couple of hours away from here. Hiking trails, horseback riding trails, swimming, tennis, and whatever else Aisha and Jazz want to do. A friend of Jazz's is coming with us." Charles stopped, then added, "I have some information for you, too, although I don't know if it's relevant to you right now."

Stan's smile didn't reach his eyes. "You first."

Charles gestured toward the visitor's chair before he took his seat behind his desk. "In the past few weeks, five people crossed the river and landed at various points on Wyrd. The most recent person is an English professor working at Jackson University. I didn't find missing person reports for the other four. Maybe no one realizes yet that they are missing—or maybe no one cares enough to report the person to the police."

"Or maybe they landed on Wyrd, came to their senses, and went back home."

"Possible but unlikely. Apparently, there is a 'neutral zone' around the island that extends for about fifty yards inland."

"Are your kids big on *Star Trek* reruns too?"

Charles nodded, but he didn't feel lighthearted about using the words. "That's pretty much what it is, Stan. Neutral ground the length of half a football field. If you aren't focused on what you're looking for when you leave the neutral zone, the odds are good that you won't be coming back because whatever else is on that island will swallow a person whole unless they are very, very lucky—or it's part of their destiny to be there."

Stan stared at him. "I don't think any of us have ever heard about this neutral zone. How reliable is your source of information?"

"Solid." After a minute's silence, Charles said, "What have you got for me?"

Stan seemed uneasy. "Have you heard anything about your son?"

Wary now, Charles nodded. "Someone had seen him recently and passed along the message that he was doing all right."

"One of the other boys who went missing at the same time turned up early this morning in one of Lovecraft's cemeteries."

"What the hell was he doing . . ." Charles sucked in a breath. "Dead?"

"Yes." Stan looked down at his hands, then met Charles's eyes. "It looks like the boy, who went by the name of Devl, got into a bar fight and was stabbed in the abdomen multiple times with what the coroner speculates was a broken bottle. The wounds weren't immediately fatal, for reasons the coroner can't explain, but they were the cause of death. However . . ."

Charles pushed away from his desk and left his office. He returned with a glass of water.

"Thanks," Stan said, taking the glass and drinking half the water. "According to the crime scene investigators, the evidence suggests that the boy left one of the roads through the cemetery, then stumbled a few yards before collapsing next to a grave. We haven't found a connection between the family name on the gravestone and the boy, so we think that's just as far as he could go." He drank the rest of the water. "Except the coroner thinks the boy died several days ago."

"No sign of being carried or dragged to that spot?" Charles asked.

"Nothing like that. And no indication there was anyone with him. We found a bar coaster in his jacket pocket that said 'Devil's Den,' with an address. We located the place. Christ almighty, it's not even on this side of the country. How did he get there?"

"He got on a bus in Wyrd, and he got off at a place that must have a sufficient concentration of the strange and uncanny that the bus would stop there," Charles replied wearily. "He must have lived long enough to get back on the bus, and then . . ."

"Then he got off for the last time at a cemetery in Lovecraft and collapsed after taking a few steps?" Stan rubbed his forehead. "Are we saying there's a *bus stop* for the dead located at that cemetery?"

"We're not saying anything. We don't *know* anything." Charles sat back in his chair. "The press will be all over this, and the anti-Arcana crowd will be howling about the police not finding the boy who is still missing. If simmering anger reaches a flashpoint . . ."

"It won't take much at this point," Stan agreed. "If the people in Penwych and the other towns turn against them, what do you think the Arcana will do?"

"The truth? We have been living across the river from them for generations and still have no real idea what the Arcana *can* do, let alone what they *will* do under those circumstances."

Stan rose. "When you leave tomorrow, turn off your phone, have the rest of your family turn off their phones. Don't watch TV. Leave the resort's number if someone has to contact you, but don't make it easy for them to 'keep you informed.' Get away from this, Charles. Get away while you can."

Sound advice, Charles thought after Stan left. He just hoped he could follow it.

46

"Mama, that ghost took my sandwich!"

"Don't be silly. Ghosts don't eat sandwiches."

"He did take it! And I'm *hungry.*"

So am I, kid, Acid thought as he hurried away. It was tempting to wolf down the sandwich while he walked, but he didn't want to swallow wrong and choke.

Could he choke? What was he now? Kids could see him; adults couldn't. There was always a place in a cemetery to find water, but the sandwich was the first food he'd been able to acquire in days.

He slipped behind a large headstone and took a big bite of the sandwich. It didn't taste like much. Either the kid's mom didn't know how to make a good sandwich, or he was losing the ability to taste anything.

He'd passed through cemeteries whose names he couldn't pronounce. He'd passed through cemeteries where the most recent dates on the stones were from two hundred years ago. He felt like he was being whittled down, layer by layer, becoming a little more insubstantial every day.

Maybe the kid was right. Maybe he'd started turning into a ghost the moment he'd boarded that damn train.

Finishing the sandwich, Acid continued walking. He kept the

tracks in sight. They were the only touchstone he had, the only way to keep from being thoroughly lost among the dead.

The only way to find the train again and hope it might take him home.

47

Waiting for the weather forecast, Beth half listened to the morning news while she finished getting ready for work. She had spent the weekend reviewing her possessions. There were plenty of things, like her winter clothes, already stored in banker's boxes, so the review was for deciding what else to pack up and what to leave behind so it didn't *look* like she had moved out. She had the file box that held all her important papers hidden in a banker's box, and she'd used a set of bath towels as packing material. Her checkbook was in her purse. She'd culled her books, packing only her favorite comfort reads along with the new books she'd binged on when she went to the bookstore for a couple of collections of comics she enjoyed, along with graphic novels she hoped would be suitable for a young boy. She'd packed her second set of bedsheets and a quilt that made her feel good when she cuddled under it to read. She figured she could do without those things for a couple of weeks while she worked out her two weeks' notice, then . . .

"And I have proof! D-N-A proof that one of the detectives working in Penwych isn't a true human."

Beth spun around and stared at the TV. Stared at Bonnie Wilson's furious—and triumphant—face as she stood on the steps of Penwych's courthouse. Below her was a crowd of people waving signs that read AL PALMER WAS RIGHT! and WEED OUT WEIRDO POLICE!

It didn't matter how Bonnie had connected with the anti-Arcana people whom Albert Palmer had gathered after his son died. It didn't matter whether anything she said was true. There were people in Penwych who wanted to cause trouble, who wanted an excuse for violence—and Bonnie had just provided it.

"She's a half-breed spawned by those weirdos on the island," Bonnie shouted. "Who knows how many other public officials are contaminated like that? If this was my town, I'd find out fast how many of the police who *investigate* crimes connected to that island are really human."

The reporter stared at the camera. "Upon hearing the accusations made by Bonnie Wilson, who claims to have been a neighbor of Detective Beth Fahey when Fahey was growing up, Mayor Edwena Bang said she would have her most trusted officials looking into Ms. Wilson's claim. Of course, that begs the underlying question: Who *can* be trusted now?"

Shaking, Beth picked up her cell phone and called the number on the slip of paper she had tucked into her purse. "Ashley? It's started."

"How soon can you have your things packed?" Ashley asked.

"They're already packed."

"We'll be there around lunchtime. Take a long lunch, just in case we need a little more time."

No point mentioning that she might be packing up her desk at work. Her name was out there, and any detective who worked with her could be tarred with the same brush. At the very least, every member of the team could be required to submit to a DNA test to prove they were pure human.

And if they took that test and found out they weren't pure human? Would this become a kind of witch hunt where an accusation could tarnish a person's life—or worse?

Beth turned off the TV, left her apartment, and prepared herself for whatever would happen when she reached the precinct.

48

Standing in Captain Forrester's office, Tom Castelletti gripped the phone's receiver and listened to the controlled anger in Mayor Edwena Bang's voice as she asked questions he couldn't answer. That *none* of them could answer. Except, perhaps, the detective who hadn't reported for work yet.

"Captain Forrester is on vacation, but if you can produce a court order to have it done, I can get DNA collected from every member of the team," he said. "We have an accusation, mayor, without any proof. This woman could be a nutjob that came here to cause trouble, and whatever DNA she claims to have could have come from anywhere or anything." He winced as he listened to her response to *that*. Apparently calling a woman of a certain age a nutjob was not politically correct—even if it was accurate. "Yes, ma'am. I understand. We'll expect Detective Gibson's team and give them our full cooperation."

He hung up and stared at Ian Kuhn.

"We're fucked?" Ian asked.

"We're fucked. A court order is already in the works. Gibson from the twelfth precinct is coming in to take DNA samples from everyone on the team, including Monkton and Reynolds. They'll take a sample from Captain Forrester once he returns from his vacation." Tom scowled. "We're not supposed to contact him because he might do a runner."

"You're joking."

"No, I'm not. Where the hell is Fahey?"

"She walked in a minute ago."

"Then let's get some answers." Tom headed out of the captain's office, with Ian right behind him.

Beth folded the letter and slipped it into an envelope before looking up at Tom Castelletti and Ian Kuhn.

"Did you see the news?" Castelletti asked.

"I saw it," she replied.

"Anything you want to tell us before detectives from the twelfth show up to take samples of our DNA?"

"Yes." Beth took a deep breath and let it out slowly. "Bonnie Wilson is a liar, a manipulator, and a gambling addict. After my parents disappeared, I lived with her until I was eighteen. Then I got out and kept my distance as much as I could because the woman is toxic."

Beth took another deep breath and kept going before either man could interrupt. "But what she said is true: I am part Arcana. I found that out a few days ago when I went to Wyrd."

"Shit," Kuhn said. "Did *they* know? The ones across the river?"

"Before I did their little test? I don't know. It doesn't matter now. They didn't know how, they didn't know when, but they saw that Bonnie was going to tear apart my life. And she has." Beth picked up the envelope and held it out to Castelletti. "My letter of resignation. I'll work out my two weeks' notice."

Castelletti took the envelope. "I'll let human resources and the higher-ups know about this." A beat of silence. "Your name is all over the news. If we get called to investigate something that seems connected with Wyrd, other cops aren't going to want you there."

"I know. I'm taking a couple of hours of personal time for an appointment that I need to keep. Otherwise, I'll hang around here today for whatever questions people want to ask. Then I'll see what I can do about finding Yaron Kali."

Castelletti nodded. "Anything else?"

"Yes. The timing. A PI approached me while I was at the hotel on Wyrd, but he was held by hotel security and escorted to the ferry. If he's working for Bonnie, part of his assignment might have been to let her know when my boss wasn't going to be available for a few days."

The phone on Kuhn's desk rang. He answered, listened, and hung up. "Detective Gibson is on her way up to take those DNA samples."

Castelletti looked uncomfortable. He tapped a finger against Beth's desk. "I'm sorry it came to this. Truly sorry."

Beth tried to smile. "So am I."

49

Beth heard the rattle of the security chain on her neighbor's door. She unlocked her own door but looked over her shoulder and smiled at the old woman peering at her through the narrow opening. "Hi, Mrs. Myers."

Mrs. Myers fussed with the chain, then opened her own door. "Is everything all right, Beth? You don't usually come home in the middle of the day."

No need for security cameras in the public areas of the building when you had a neighbor like Mrs. Myers.

Before Beth could think of an answer that would satisfy, she heard the voices of people coming up the stairs. A moment later, Ashley, Jack, and Ethan headed for her.

"We brought pizza," Jack said.

"And ale," Ethan said. "But it's the ginger kind because we all have to work this afternoon."

Ashley flashed a smile at Mrs. Myers. "We're having a decluttering party. Beth helped the three of us this weekend as we packed up the extra bits and pieces in our places. Now it's her turn."

"Not much room for storage in a studio apartment," Mrs. Myers said.

"No, indeed," Ashley agreed.

Jack gave Beth a nudge. "We're on the clock, girl. Let's get to the pizza and packing."

Beth wasn't sure what sort of smile Ethan had leveled at Mrs. Myers, but the woman blushed before retreating to her own apartment.

"I've already packed up my things," Beth said.

Jack found the dishes and brought them over to the tiny dining table. "Good. More time to eat." He opened one of the bottles of ginger ale and held it out to her.

Ashley studied the living area, then the bedroom alcove and tiny bathroom. "You've left some things."

"I didn't want it to look like I'd moved out if the building manager needed to come in for something," Beth replied. She set the bottle on the counter in order to hold the plate and eat a slice of pizza.

Ashley took out her cell phone and began taking pictures of the bookshelf and other parts of the room.

Beth almost admitted that she'd already done the same thing—taken pictures of the books and other items she was leaving as stage setting. Why? She wasn't sure, especially since the books she'd bought as replacements were packed in the boxes that the Arcana were going to store somewhere.

"My laptop and e-reader are in one of the boxes," she said. "They're fully charged, but I'd like them to be handy, if that's possible."

"Show me which box, and I'll make sure it doesn't get buried when we get the boxes into storage," Ashley said.

"That's all the music CDs you own?" Ethan asked as he examined the handful of discs beside the CD player.

"The rest are packed. The ones I left behind are ones I don't listen to anymore."

Ethan gave her a long look. Then he unplugged the player and set it on top of the banker's boxes.

Beth ate because she was hungry and because she didn't want the Arcana to think that their being there had killed her appetite. The truth was, watching them examine her living space, she had the impression that on their own, they would have stripped the place of every single thing they could identify as hers—and they could have done it within an hour.

Had they done that when they'd helped Rachel Nightingale disappear?

The pizza had been devoured and most of the boxes had been carted down to the borrowed van well before Beth needed to return to work. As Jack picked up the last box, Beth said, "Jack?"

He turned toward her and waited.

"Is there a way to look for people who have gone missing in Wyrd?"

He gave her a long look. "Not for outsiders, but there are ways—if searching for them would be a step in fulfilling your own destiny. You couldn't go alone. But if that's what you want to do, I'll talk to Lucas. He'll decide. If he agrees, pack three or four changes of clothes, along with nightwear and toiletries. These kinds of searches are rarely quick and easy."

"Okay. Thanks."

Jack left. Beth locked up her apartment and returned to work—and needed the help of uniformed officers to get through the anti-Arcana protesters who had assembled in front of the precinct.

Bonnie Wilson listened to Beth's cell phone ring. Oh, she'd stirred up trouble good and proper for that little bitch. There were reporters—*important* people—panting to hear what she had to say about Beth Fahey. She was going to be on TV tomorrow morning, and what she said would depend on . . .

Beth's voicemail message kicked in. Well, that was fine. She didn't really want to talk to the girl. "I want thirty thousand dollars now, or the story I'll tell about you will *crush* you."

She ended the call, satisfied that Beth would find the money. The girl just needed the right amount of incentive.

Bonnie's cell phone chirped its little tune. The caller was unknown, but that didn't matter. So many people wanted to talk to her now. "Hello?"

"Bonnie Wilson." The male voice sounded cold and full of a violence that turned Bonnie's bowels to water. "You betrayed your side of the bargain you made with us. Payment is now due."

The call ended.

Bonnie dropped her phone and hurried to the bathroom. After dumping her soiled underpants in the waste basket and washing up a bit, she opened a bottle of whiskey from the minibar to steady her nerves.

They knew where she lived. They knew she was here. Maybe it had been foolish to go on TV, but she'd never thought they knew what she looked like or that they would track her to *this* town.

She'd had a losing streak at the casino. Her credit cards were maxed out. The overdraft on her checking account was at its limit too. She'd expected Beth to buckle in order to keep her precious status with the police, but the girl had refused to buckle. Which meant Bonnie couldn't pay for this hotel room, couldn't buy a ticket on anything that would get her out of this town. Couldn't do anything. And she sure as hell couldn't pay those bastards—whoever they were—anything either. After all, you couldn't get blood out of a stone.

Except . . . Maybe *they* could.

Beth thanked Ian Kuhn when he dropped her off at her apartment on his way home. The protest in front of the 13th precinct had swelled during the day, led by the fathers of the boys Al Palmer had shot and killed. She didn't think Palmer was lying when he said he'd shot four dogs that were savaging one of his bitches, but blaming the Arcana wasn't going to help anyone.

Then there was the boy who had been found dead in a cemetery in Lovecraft. And the boy who was still missing. And the five people who made the choice to go to unsupervised parts of Wyrd and disappeared.

All those people made *choices*, but someone was going to be sacrificed for their poor judgment—and she knew who that someone would be.

Beth did a quick search of her apartment, checking closets and the shower stall in case someone had gotten in. She even checked under the bed. She checked the locks on her windows and double-checked the locks on her door.

Finally convinced that she was as safe as she could be, she yelped when a call came in on her cell phone.

"Jack says you want to search for the people who came ashore and then disappeared," Lucas Frost said.

"Yes. I gave Detective Castelletti my resignation letter today and said I would work out my two weeks' notice, but I'm not sure the precinct is going to want me there."

"I saw the news about the protesters."

"The protesters are going to hassle the people who want to take the ferry over to Destiny Park."

"That's their choice."

Something about the way Lucas said the words made Beth shiver.

"If the police have no use for you in Penwych, then pack what you'll need and cross the river tomorrow to begin your search."

"I'll do that. If I'm not on the ferry tomorrow, I'll let you know."

"Be on the ferry tomorrow, Beth. Wyrd is not the only place that is a convergence of the uncanny, and things are in motion."

"Okay. See you tomorrow." She ended the call, pulled her suitcase out from under the bed, and packed everything she could fit into it because she wasn't sure she would be coming back.

"Do you have her?" The voice on the phone was old and cold and filled with the kind of power and violence that could make the earth itself shiver.

It was a voice Lucas knew well.

"She'll be crossing the river tomorrow," Lucas replied. "She'll be searching some of the neighborhoods for some missing people."

"She'll be safe?"

"She'll be with Jack. She'll be as safe as she can be while she meets her fate." Each place that was a convergence of the uncanny had a Sorcerer King. The one calling him tonight was probably the most powerful among them. "Is Beth Fahey connected to your branch of the Arcana?" *To our branch of the Arcana?*

"No. But she came from a branch of someone who was once dear to me."

He'd suspected that much. The Greenwood and de Winter branches of the Arcana were like summer and winter—one balanced the other. But he had wondered if the interest in Beth Fahey was more . . . personal. Thankfully not.

"You are willing to let these humans meet their fate in whatever way they choose, regardless of the inconvenience to the Arcana."

Most of the time, that was true, Lucas thought. *But not always.*

"I am willing to snap the thread that measures out their years when humans betray a bargain made with us," the voice continued.

"That is your choice."

"Yes, it is. And no stain of that choice will fall on you."

"Do you want regular reports about her?"

"Will I need them?"

"No."

"Then I will leave her in your hands."

Lucas ended the call and sat back in his chair. He watched Justine and her sisters enter his office and stand on the other side of his desk.

"Is Beth coming soon?" Justine asked.

"Tomorrow."

"Good," Lysandra said.

"Why is that good?" Lucas asked. He felt unsettled by the phone call, so his voice was sharp.

Lysandra looked at Justine, who said, "She'll be needed here."

50

At first light, Beth called the number Ashley had given her and discovered it was the number for Richens Car Service, not a taxi. The person who answered the phone sounded a little sleepy but also seemed to be expecting her call.

Was this how it was when a person worked for the Arcana?

The car that pulled up in front of her apartment building was a shiny black sedan. The driver wore a black suit with a white shirt and black tie. He greeted her, stored her suitcase in the trunk, and opened the back door for her.

"My instructions are to drop you off at the thirteenth precinct, then wait for you," the driver said. "Is that correct?"

"Yes. I won't be there long. Then I need to catch the first ferry over to Destiny Park."

"Very good. There are bottles of water if you'd like one, as well as some nibbles."

"The water is enough," Beth replied, taking one of the small plastic bottles.

Richens. Thinking about the woman who ran the little library in Wyrd's Teeth, she wanted to ask if there was a family connection, but remembering *why* people lived in Wyrd's Teeth, she appreciated the need to be very careful. "I didn't ask about payment."

He met her eyes in the rearview mirror for a moment. Assessing. "They have an account with us. We were told to add your name. Anytime you need a ride in Penwych or need to go to any of the other towns around the Fate River, you can call us. We try to have one car available for flexible assignments—the rides that aren't prebooked."

"How did you come to work for them? If that's not too personal a question."

Another assessing look. "They saved one of my aunts. My father's sister. That was twenty, twenty-five years ago. A bargain was struck to get her out of a bad situation and keep her safe."

Beth thought about Betsy Richens, who had a noticeable limp and needed a cane. Who had some nerve damage to her face that could have come from a severe beating.

"Do you ever get to see her or have any contact? Or is she in witness protection?"

He was wary now. "There are ways we can get together once in a while."

Better not to admit to anything about the ones who needed to disappear—especially if there was still the possibility that someone wanted to do harm. "I'm not trying to pry. I met someone recently who lives in a closed community. I liked her. I'm glad to know she can stay in touch with friends."

He pulled into the parking lot behind the 13th precinct. "Do you need your suitcase?"

"No."

He got out of the car and opened the door for her. "I'll park and wait for you here."

"Thank you. I shouldn't be long."

Tom Castelletti was in before her, looking like he hadn't had much sleep.

"You're in early," he said as he studied her. "I gave the commander your letter of resignation. He didn't have any trouble taking it, but he's not sure about you working out your two-week notice. You haven't been here long enough to have any time coming to you that you can use in lieu of the notice, but he's going to talk to human resources. After yesterday, the powers that be aren't thrilled to have a precinct under siege because of one junior detective."

"I have a way to fix the problem." Beth held out her gun and holster. When he didn't take it, she laid it on the big table where they reviewed evidence. "The Arcana have agreed to help me with the search for Yaron Kali and the other people who recently went to Wyrd and disappeared, but I'll need to be over there to accomplish anything. I can't take a weapon with me. I can lock it in a drawer in my desk, or you can take it. Whichever you prefer."

"How long will you be gone?" Castelletti asked.

"Three or four days. A car is waiting to take me to the ferry. I'll go over today and start the search."

"You'll report in?"

"When I can. There are places in Wyrd that don't have cell service—or phones of any kind."

"I'll authorize you going over to participate in a cooperative effort to search for the missing people. That way you'll be officially on duty . . ."

"But out of sight," Beth finished.

Castelletti nodded. "I'll secure your weapon until you get back."

"I'd better get going."

"Good hunting."

On her way out, she nodded to Ian Kuhn, who was on his way in. No one else greeted her, and she couldn't blame them. Bonnie's accusations had smeared all of them at the 13th.

As the car headed for the ferry's pier, she wondered if that had been Bonnie's intention. And she wondered how everyone's fate might change because of it.

51

Colin stepped out of the trading post. The language lessons were still interesting, and the weaving was interesting because Mom would be excited to hear about it when he got home, but the chores he did at the trading post were leaning toward boring now that the excitement of being in Llamalidia was wearing off.

Then he noticed Tia Downing standing near the road, looking at the sky in a way that made him uneasy. "Tia? Is something wrong?"

"Storm's coming."

"The sky looks clear."

"Not that kind of storm." She turned toward him. "You need to leave while there's still a chance of you getting home, so you finish up and pack up today. Tomorrow we'll take the bus to the town I told you about. We'll eat hamburgers and fries and see a movie. The day after, you'll get on a bus for Destiny Park—and you'll stay focused on *needing* to reach the park."

"What's happening?"

"I've told you Wyrd isn't the only place in the world that is a convergence of the uncanny, and each of those places has a Sorcerer King."

"Gender prejudice."

That made her smile. "Not really. Some of them are female, but all of them are called kings." Tia rubbed a hand over her short hair. "Llamalidia is a neighborhood that moves between two convergences, and when that happens, the Llamalidians and I are safe in both of those places. But sometimes something stirs things up in a way that provokes the Sorcerer Kings, and then it's like surviving a bad storm and being tossed onto an unfamiliar, and potentially dangerous, shore. Usually, the Sorcerer King who rules over Wyrd can hold his own against such disturbances, but if someone stronger is trying to shake up the world—or alter the fate of a lot of people—it can be bad for all of us. That's why you need to get to a place that is anchored in Wyrd, a place where you can reach your home and family."

Colin rubbed his chest, trying to ease muscle tension. "I'd better get to my lesson. At least I'll have one place mat finished today to bring home to my mom."

Tia went back to looking at the sky.

Colin hurried to reach the cria and tell the adults he was leaving tomorrow. He should have had weeks left to live among the Llamalidians. Since that couldn't happen, he was going to say goodbye to his friends and then focus his intentions on getting home.

52

Beth wasn't sure what Jack Frost meant when he'd told her to bring what she would usually use during a workday, but she filled her large purse with a travel kit of toiletries, her wallet, tissues, and a paperback. If asked, she would explain that it was something to read during her lunch break.

She had no idea if she would get a lunch break once she officially started working for the Arcana.

She'd been given a room in the private wing of the hotel. The banker's box that held her laptop and e-reader was stored in the closet. All her other things were in a secure storage space in the hotel so that she could take her time choosing which cottage she wanted for her own.

But that was something she would consider after this assignment. Right now, she had to meet Jack at the pavilion.

The Ladies Three weren't in their room yet, but Jack was there, standing near the dark archway that led to the armory.

"This way," Jack said, leading her into the room that held cases of weapons that had been used for centuries and still couldn't be traced.

Ethan stood behind one of the cases and gave her a careful study. "Your police weapon. Nine millimeter?"

"Yes, but I didn't bring it," Beth replied.

"Wouldn't do you any good here if you did," Jack said. "But for what we're doing, you need a weapon, and it's better if it's one you're comfortable handling."

"Nine mil it is." Ethan opened a case and took out a gun and a clip. "Full clip, but there isn't a round in the chamber."

Beth shook her head, thinking of the man who died after firing three bullets from one of these ghost guns. "I can't."

"Yes, you can," Ethan said. "The Ladies Three have decided that there is no cost to you for the use of the gun, and the cost of every bullet you use is one day of your life. However, if you fire the weapon in self-defense or to protect someone else, there is no cost at all. Since you'll be going with Jack, it's unlikely you'll need to draw your weapon, but Lucas requires that you have one, just in case there's trouble." He holstered the weapon and handed it to Beth.

She took it and attached the holster to her belt. It felt like her police issue weapon, but it felt like something else too. Something more. She wondered if she would need to bring it back at the end of the day, or if it would return to its spot in the case on its own.

Leaving Ethan, Jack headed back to the hotel, giving Beth a look that made her think he saw her as a frisky puppy he was saddled with for a day.

"Have you eaten?" Jack asked.

"Not hungry." She'd been too unsettled to eat much since she saw Bonnie on the news.

A huff of annoyance. "Put something in your belly before we go, and take care of any personal things you need to do. Today we'll be driving on the road that circles Wyrd and checking the static neighborhoods, so there should be places where we can stop to eat and eliminate"—Beth felt her face heat, but she realized Jack wasn't being crude; he was providing information he felt she needed—"but the distance between them can be farther than you would expect."

"Right. When do you want to leave?"

"In an hour. Someone will show you the way to the vehicle we'll be using."

Beth learned there were plates with covers that residents and staff used when they wanted a private meal, so she made her selection from the hotel's buffet and added a mug of hot chocolate instead of coffee. Back in her room, she ate while she considered what she was doing—and why.

She wanted to do one good thing while she was still on the police force in Penwych. And she wanted to show the leaders in Wyrd that she could do the job they needed her to do.

She wanted to find Yaron Kali. She wanted to bring *someone* home.

And she wondered if Jack held the same, if opposite, prejudices about her that her colleagues at the 13th precinct held, and thought she was a little too human to be useful.

53

"Rahele?" Lucas called.

Rachel ignored him. She was out on the perch instead of sulking in her cage, wasn't she? She was cleaning her feathers like she was supposed to, wasn't she?

Lucas had no right to give her a disapproving look just because she still felt sad.

"You have a letter," Lucas said.

Probably from her agent. Apparently, an author disappearing boosted book sales, and there was talk of new cover designs for her books and various "first in a series" sales. Ashley reviewed all of those e-mails, as well as sending a "Rachel is doing fine" weekly report. It wasn't like in TV cop shows where a photo was sent with the person holding a newspaper to show the date for proof of life. She could imagine the reaction from people if a picture was sent of her in *this* form standing on top of a newspaper.

"It looks like it's from Faulkner."

Faulkner sent her a letter?

Rachel launched herself off the perch and flew into Lucas's office. She hadn't been flying in place or flying outside for several days, and realized the exercise phrase "use it or lose it" also applied to flight muscles. She aimed for Lucas's shoulder but didn't have the height. Smacking into his arm, she got her nails into the fabric of his shirt and, using nails and beak, climbed up to his shoulder, twittering excitedly.

Lucas jerked his head. "You don't have to twitter so loud. Your head is right next to my ear."

She preened a few of his hairs as an apology, then pressed her head against his cheek.

"Would you like me to read it to you?"

She twittered softly. In her current form, she could read typed text or the block letters she and Faulkner had used before Ashley set up a laptop for their poetry efforts, but it took effort because bird's eyes weren't really built for reading.

"'Dear Rahele,'" Lucas read. "'I'm not being cheeky. Miss Betsy says this is the proper way to begin a letter to a friend, and she knows about stuff like that.'"

Oh really? Luring Faulkner into a "friendship" by dangling knowledge in front of a curious crow? The hussy.

She realized Lucas had stopped reading. Probably because she'd been twittering her opinion in his ear.

She preened a couple more of his hairs in apology, then poked him with her beak to encourage him to continue.

"'She takes care of the library here and has offered to help me find books about things I want to learn. And she is going to teach me cursive. That's not swear words but a fancy kind of writing.'"

Okay, maybe not a hussy. This Betsy person sounded more like a favorite aunt. Or a grandmotherly type who would look after Faulkner and bake cookies. Yes. Much better.

"'I can't tell you where I am, but I wanted you to know that I'm safe. I have my own little house, and I'm looking into finding work because everyone needs to contribute something to the community. I might even be able to get a puppy, which would be a lot of work but would also be fun. I hope you're taking daily flights around the safe part of the park and having fun being a lark. The world looks so different when you're in a winged form, and you'll never have this chance again because humans can only do this once. It would be a shame to waste the time you have to be something else.

"'Your friend, Faulkner.'"

His printing was a little wobbly, even her bird eyes could see that, but that could be because he was still learning to use hands and fingers again. His words made her think. He sounded younger than she'd expected, and yet . . . experienced. And his assurance that he was safe was a sharp reminder that Rachel Nightingale wasn't the first person the Arcana had helped to disappear. Faulkner, too, had had his reasons for making that choice.

Lucas folded the letter and slipped it back into the envelope. "I'll put this in the file box with the other papers we're keeping for you."

Rachel rubbed her head against his cheek, then sidestepped to the end of his shoulder before flying back to the room with her perch and cage.

When Mia Skov came to give her some supervised outside time, she hopped on the woman's hand instead of needing to be coaxed. Receiving Faulkner's letter had lifted a heaviness that had weighed her down. He was right. She should store up sensations and experiences while she was in this form. She might never write another book to publish, but she would write again.

Maybe Rahele would write some stories about a crow who solved crimes with the help of a human detective.

With that thought in mind, Rachel flew and twittered and poked around in the grass.

But she still refused to taste a worm.

54

Geographically, it made no sense. The Isle of Wyrd just wasn't that big, and driving on a road that went through the static exterior neighborhoods of the island shouldn't take a full day. They had stopped at three static neighborhoods—which was a word that didn't remotely resemble what she had seen—to stretch their legs and ask about the missing people. When they reached a town that Jack said was halfway through the circuit, she showed the photos up and down the main street before ending up at a diner for lunch and a pit stop.

"Does the uncanny play wackadoodle with time as well as geography, or is the town retro on purpose?" Beth asked when they were back in the car. "Because it looks like photos I've seen of towns from fifty or sixty years ago."

"I don't know what you mean," Jack said as they drove out of town.

Sure he did, but that was probably another of those things you weren't told until you signed a confidentiality agreement and got your very own decoder ring.

Beth looked out the window at the pasture rolling by and the . . . "Holy . . . ! That's a purple cow!"

"The sunlight on the brown hide probably gives it a purplish hue." Jack's tone was bland, bland, bland.

"Bullshit! That's a purple cow—a whole herd of purple cows—like in the Gelett Burgess poem." Had Burgess written the poem after he'd somehow stumbled across this neighborhood in Wyrd?

"You didn't have any complaints about the burger you ate for lunch."

She turned in her seat to stare at him. "I thought the 'purple burger' was called that because of the purply lettuce they put on it."

Jack's grin was wickedly amused.

Beth studied him. "Is there a neighborhood on Wyrd where pigs can fly?"

"I've never seen a flying pig."

Which didn't really answer her question.

An hour later, while still pondering the existence of purple cows, Beth saw a flash of color in the woodland.

"Jack, slow down. I think I saw something."

Jack glanced in the rearview mirror and hit the brakes. Beth scrambled out of the car and moved toward the man who was running down the road, waving his arms to attract their attention. He had to be one of the people who had gone missing recently—one of the people she was trying to find.

"Beth, wait!" Jack shouted.

She glanced at Jack, then realized he wasn't looking at the man. He was looking at the sky—and the humongous bird that was focused on the running prey.

Beth drew her weapon and shouted, "Get down! Get down!"

Jack opened the back of the vehicle, flipped the lid on one of the coolers, and took out a large object wrapped in brown paper. He pulled out a knife from somewhere and stabbed the paper a few times.

Blood began dripping onto the road.

"Stay near the car," Jack said as he moved to the middle of the road.

Beth moved with him but kept to the side of the road. She stopped a few feet away from the man on the ground, raised her weapon, and aimed at . . .

Standing, the bird would be as tall as she was. That was freaky enough, but . . . It had a woman's face. The beak was there instead of a nose and mouth, but it was still a woman's face on a giant bird's body.

Beth clicked off the safety. *Please go away. I don't want to shoot you. Please go away.*

Jack whistled and made an underhanded throw with both hands, sending the blood-dripping package into the air.

The bird snatched the package out of the air, banked sharply enough that a wingtip would have hit Jack if he hadn't ducked, and flew away.

Beth held her stance a few seconds longer. Then she lowered her weapon and clicked on the safety before her hands began to shake.

"I told you to stay near the car," Jack snapped.

"I'm a cop," Beth snapped back. "My job was to protect the civilian and back up my partner. I took up a position that would allow me to do both."

"You couldn't have shot her."

"Because a nine mil wouldn't have enough firepower?"

"Because she comes from another branch of Arcana, and a conflict between branches would cause no end of problems." Jack glanced at the sky. "We'll discuss this later. Make sure your weapon is secure before you approach him, but let's get him in the car and get out of here. If she has a nest nearby, she'll be back for more meat for her chicks."

Shuddering, Beth secured her weapon and helped Jack haul the man into the back seat. Jack removed a bottle of water from the storage area, handed it to Beth, then said quietly, "I have some sandwiches in another cooler, but we'll wait on that. Don't talk to him. Don't engage and get distracted. We need to stay focused on this road."

Beth opened the cap on the bottle, handed it to the man, then got in the front with Jack.

"Thank you," the man said. "Thank you."

"You're welcome," Beth replied before she stared straight ahead.

Jack said nothing. He just drove with a fierce kind of focus—and glanced in the mirrors often enough for Beth to wonder just how fast those birds could fly.

They found another of the missing men sitting in the middle of the road, petting the gravel and crying.

Beth and Jack hustled him into the vehicle and secured the seat belt.

Before she could reach the front passenger door, Jack closed a hand over her arm. "That's all we can do today. We have to get these two on the last ferry and across the river before the sun goes down."

She almost asked why the men couldn't stay at the hotel in Destiny Park. Then she understood. Whatever else these men had seen that had shaken them so badly, the Arcana didn't want them to see the truth about the ones who lived around Destiny Park.

"Is there some kind of medical personnel who could give them a quick checkup, maybe give them a sedative to help them when they cross the river?" she asked.

Jack nodded. "When we reach Destiny Bay, we'll have cell phone service. You contact the police and tell them to meet the last ferry—and bring an ambulance to take those two to a medical facility that can deal with mental trauma as well as physical injuries. I'll contact Lucas and let him know we're bringing in two of the missing humans."

He gave her arm a comradely squeeze before circling the vehicle and getting in the driver's seat while she got in on the passenger side.

Beth hadn't noticed him removing the key from the ignition when they'd gone out to help the second man, but she noticed now when he inserted the key and started the car. She looked over her shoulder at the men. One was still crying softly. The first man they'd rescued . . . Something wrong with his eyes. She wasn't sure what she was seeing, but he was *off* in a way that made her uneasy about him sitting behind Jack.

"You should buckle your seat belt," she said.

The man didn't answer her, but he obeyed.

Once they were past the gravel road and back on asphalt, Jack put his foot down, and the vehicle raced along the road as if they were in a high-speed pursuit. Maybe they were, except they were chasing the remaining daylight.

When they reached Destiny Bay, Beth and Jack made their phone calls. Neither of the rescued men asked to use a bathroom, and she noticed that Jack didn't suggest it. Since he had more experience dealing with humans who had become . . . untethered . . . by their experience in Wyrd, she figured there was a strong possibility of the men bolting. One of the men, anyway. She had a feeling they were going to have to drag the crier out of the vehicle in order to get him on the ferry.

Jack didn't waste any time. The only thing he said to her as they were leaving Destiny Bay was "Focus on the need to get to Destiny Park quickly. Don't think about anything else."

Words had power here. Intentions mattered. Whatever road Jack was taking now to get them to the park wasn't going to take them through static neighborhoods, and with two men in emotional turmoil of one sort or another, Jack wanted her to stay focused on where they needed to go, while his focus was divided between driving a vehicle at a reckless speed and reaching their destination.

When they pulled into the part of the park that held a variety of vehicles, male Arcana swarmed around the car, opening the doors and pulling the rescued men out of the back seat. Someone opened her door, but before Beth could snarl a warning, she recognized Ethan. He didn't reach for her, just looked relieved by whatever he saw in her face.

Beth stood with Ethan and watched while a man she assumed was a human doctor gave the rescued men a quick checkup before injecting them with a sedative. They were escorted to what looked like an old-time horse-drawn police wagon, complete with bars on the small windows and locks on the door.

She and Jack also rode in a horse-drawn cart, but it was open and practical.

"You and I have to escort them across the river," Jack said. He handed her a slip of paper. "Give that to the police. It's the sedative the doctor used to calm the humans enough to get them to Penwych. The medical people will need that information before they administer anything else."

Beth memorized the name of the drug and the dosage used. When she had a chance, she'd talk to the doctor and find out what the standard procedure was when dealing with rescued individuals.

There was no private place on the ferry to stash the two men and keep them away from the rest of the passengers, but the men had been missing for several weeks and personal hygiene hadn't been a priority, so she didn't have to worry about other people getting too close to her charges, despite curious looks. In fact, several of the passengers opted for outside seats after a few minutes. She didn't blame them. If she didn't have to keep an eye on the men, she would be out there, too, especially after being in a vehicle with them for several hours.

When they reached the Penwych side of the river and the ferry docked, the other passengers hurried out of the cabin. Beth, Jack, and the rescued men were the last ones to disembark, but they weren't alone. A handful of men waited to help her escort her charges to the other end of the pier, where Tom Castelletti and Ian Kuhn waited. She wasn't sure how many men normally worked on the ferry, but she didn't question the need for them as they helped the rescued men reach the end of the pier.

They formed a phalanx around the rescued men, with Beth in the lead, the ferry's crew on either side, and Jack in the rear. No one was going to break loose, run away, or jump into the water—at least not while the Arcana were still somewhat responsible for the fools.

Crewmen were replaced by cops, EMTs, and ambulance personnel. Beth gave the medical personnel the information about the sedative and also emphasized the need for observation due to suspected emotional and mental trauma. She also gave the information to Castelletti and Kuhn. And she obeyed the one don't-mess-with-me order she'd been given by Jack: she didn't step one foot off the pier.

"Detective Fahey," Jack said, coming up behind her. "We have to leave now."

"We need her report," Castelletti said.

Jack gave Castelletti a fierce smile. "She can write it up and send it to you."

"She," Beth growled, "can speak for herself." She looked at the men who had been her colleagues. If she didn't leave now, she'd be stuck on this side of the river, and she really didn't want to stay in Penwych tonight. "We didn't find Yaron Kali. We'll be going back out at first light. It's better if I'm on Wyrd tonight. I'll write up the report, although I've already told you what I can about the men we found during today's search."

Castelletti stared at Jack. Then he looked at her. "Stay in touch."

"I will." She wondered if he was really concerned, or if he was bristling because something about Jack made him nervous.

Back on the ferry, Beth chose an outside seat and watched the crew efficiently cast off.

Jack took the seat beside hers. "We'll be cutting it close."

She glanced at his head. He nodded to acknowledge that the truth about the Arcana would probably be revealed before the ferry reached Wyrd.

"Are you going to join us for the evening meal?" he asked.

"Would it be considered rude if I didn't?"

"That would depend on the reason."

"What I'd really like to do is take a hot shower, get into my jammies, call for a meal from room service, and then read a book before falling asleep. Hopefully in that order."

Jack grinned. "You've certainly earned some quiet time." He didn't speak for a minute. "I'll report to Lucas. You do whatever you need to and get some rest. Tomorrow we'll head out for some of the other neighborhoods, and we'll be staying out for two or three days. We may not find anyone else, Beth, but we'll look."

She nodded. "They'd been missing for several weeks. After that much time, we were lucky to find two of them, weren't we?"

"Yes, we were."

There was still a chance that Detective Kali's husband was alive. There was still a chance that they would find him. Maybe they would find the other two people who were still missing as well.

The ferry ride across the river didn't take that long, but she didn't object when Jack helped her off the ferry and escorted her to the hotel—not when she'd fallen asleep with her head on his shoulder and still felt groggy.

She also didn't object to his insistence that she text him after she got out of the shower to prove she hadn't fallen asleep again and drowned. She wasn't sure if that was Jack's way of dealing with females in general or just a female who wasn't pure Arcana. Either way, he'd had a point. A lot had happened today, and she was exhausted.

It wasn't until she was in bed with one of her cozy fantasy books that she realized that the bird with the woman's face matched Ted Ocampo's description of the bird that had killed Darren Palmer.

55

Beth wasn't surprised when Lucas Frost sat down at her table before she finished breakfast. After all, Ethan Sharpe and Jack Frost had already swung by to take an inventory of what was on her plate.

"Are you checking up on me too?" she asked.

"Should I be?" he asked in return.

"I'm feeling a bit like the new puppy that everyone expects to trip over her own feet and land in her water bowl."

Lucas's laughter was loud enough to draw attention from everyone else in the hotel's dining room.

"Not as bad as that," he finally said, "but your position in terms of your work here hasn't existed until now, so it's not surprising that the men tasked with security around the park are trying to figure you out. Besides, on your current assignment, Jack is responsible for your survival, and that's not something he takes lightly."

"Did that order come from you?"

He didn't answer the question, which made her think that Lucas wasn't the one who had laid that burden on his brother.

"Think of Jack and Ethan as trainers, and you as the trainee,"

Lucas said. "Didn't the police assign you to work with an experienced officer when you first went out to perform your duties?"

She thought about the two jobs she'd had before getting the job in Penwych—the two jobs that hadn't lasted through her probationary period for reasons no one wanted to explain. "Yes, they did." And put that way, Jack's and Ethan's protective attitude toward a rookie made more sense.

"Besides," Lucas added, "you making yourself a target for the harpy to split its attention unnerved Jack, who expected you to follow orders."

"Would Jack have expected Ethan to stay back and let him stand on his own?"

Lucas smiled. "No, he wouldn't. And he's not foolish enough to think females aren't dangerous or capable of protecting themselves. Give him a chance to learn what *you* can do—and forgive him for the moments when he treats you like a puppy." His smile faded. "This choice you're making to find the missing humans. You don't yet appreciate that your survival truly might be at stake. Yesterday was the easy part. Listen to Jack. Believe what he tells you."

They walked out of the dining room together. Beth went up to her room to do the "personal necessaries," as Jack called them. She wondered if that was the typical way Arcana males referred to anything that involved female bodily functions, or if he was still trying to find a way to provide information without giving offense.

She took care of personal necessaries, then checked her soft-sided weekender bag to make sure she had everything she would need if she was going into the unknown for a few days. After a quick debate with herself, she stuffed a roll of toilet paper into her bag, since she didn't know how rough roughing it might be during this search.

Mia Skov escorted Beth to the area where the vehicles were kept before the Arcana woman continued on to the section of the park that she was tending that day. Jack was already there, with a map spread out over the hood of their vehicle.

"Store your gear in the back seat," he said. "Then come and look at this."

The back seat held a couple of coolers and Jack's duffel. Puzzled, Beth set her weekender on the seat next to his duffel, then looked at the cargo space.

"Why are you carrying so many gas cans?" She looked at the map of Wyrd he had spread over the hood. The outline matched what she'd seen at the 13th precinct. The areas that would be Destiny Park, the Teeth, and the land around Destiny Bay were shaded in dark gray. Some areas around the outer ring of the island were shaded in light gray. Probably the static neighborhoods? Everything else was blank. No, not blank. Even as she watched, faint boundary lines moved on the map, redefining the interior neighborhoods.

"Where we end up might not have gas stations, and running low on fuel would be a very bad idea." Jack gave her a long look. "We found two of the missing people yesterday, and frankly, that's two more than I thought we would find."

"There are three more who are missing." Including Yaron Kali.

Jack nodded. "And now you have to choose. You have to focus on one of them if we're going to have any chance of finding that person. The interior of Wyrd . . . Where we're going, the roads can change with intentions. If you try to find all three . . ."

Jack lifted the map and pulled out a sheet of drawing paper. He laid it over the map.

The sketch was of a journey that began with intention and turned into chaos, branching out in so many directions it looked like someone chasing dandelion seeds blown in the wind until it ended with . . .

Beth wasn't sure if the image of their vehicle going over a cliff was meant to be literal or symbolic, but in the sketch, Jack was badly wounded and she wasn't much better off.

"That's what Lysandra saw happening to us?"

"If the focus is scattered, it's highly unlikely that we will return, even if we survive," Jack replied.

Beth pointed to the detailed sketch of what looked like a diner. It was separate from the chaos. "What is that?"

"Our destination. If we can find that place, we should find someone there who needs our help getting home, although not necessarily the person you intended to find."

"You don't recognize the diner?"

Jack shook his head. "I recognize the type of place, but not that specific place."

Five people had come ashore in five different parts of Wyrd. Finding two of them yesterday had beaten the odds and then some. Beth looked at the sketch and thought about what Lucas had said about Jack being responsible for her survival. Someone had laid that burden on the Frost brothers, and she didn't want to think about who might be powerful enough to demand that of Lucas.

Beth rummaged through her weekender and pulled out a missing person flyer from the file she'd made of the missing people. She stuffed the rest of the file under everything else. Then she pulled it out and set it on the hood.

"Could someone take that file to Lucas and ask him to hold on to it until we get back?" she asked. "Having it with me might be a distraction."

Jack opened the file, flipped through the notes about the other people, and nodded. "Yeah. Better to leave this here."

Beth laid the chosen flyer on the map. "We're going after Yaron Kali."

Jack folded the map and the sketch. Placing the flyer on top of the other papers, he put everything in a large manila envelope. "If you're ready, let's go."

"Why are we going to Destiny Bay?" Beth asked when she spotted the water and the boats. "If Yaron Kali was there, couldn't he get transportation to the park or even pay someone to take him across the river?"

"Maybe," Jack replied.

A hesitation in his voice made Beth think there was something else going on. "But . . ."

"I am the trainer," Jack said. "And you are . . . ?"

"The trainee."

"That's correct. So while I see to some business the fishermen want carried back to Lucas, you're going to show the picture of Yaron Kali around the docks and find out if anyone has seen him."

"Yes, sir. Aye, aye, captain."

Jack grinned. "Smart-ass."

It took her less than five minutes to understand that she wasn't there to show Yaron Kali's picture to the groups of men who were working around the docks or the men and women who ran the shops near the water. She was there so that they could get a good look at *her*.

She came in with Jack Frost?

Yes, she did. She was going to be working as a Destiny Park security officer. This was her first assignment. Jack was her trainer.

Not full human, then?

No, she was one-quarter Arcana.

They eyed the gun she carried. One of Ethan Sharpe's weapons?

Yes, he'd selected this one for her to carry.

When they finally looked at the flyer with Yaron Kali's picture, it wasn't quickly dismissed. They looked, they thought, they called to other men and women working in the shops. No one had seen Kali, but the other side of the bay, near the Teeth, was where full humans lived. He might have taken refuge there.

One man returned with a map of Wyrd that ignored the interior and focused on the shoreline, noting docks, small marinas that belonged to the Arcana, and other places to anchor.

Beth pointed to two places that looked like dimples in a skull. Coves? One had a simple *X* and might still be considered part of the bay; the other had a skull and crossbones. "What are those?"

The man pointed to the *X*. "That's where the *Last Breath* anchors—when it does drop anchor. It's a fishing trawler that hauls up more than fish." He hesitated. "A ghost ship."

Beth shivered. "And the other?"

"That's where the *Bonnie Lass* drops anchor when the pirate queen and her first mate come ashore for supplies—or to release any of the crew who have fulfilled the bargain that was made."

"Another ghost ship?"

All the men nodded. The man with the map said, "It's said that the

Bonnie Lass takes her rest at the bottom of Susurration Sound and then rises again to hunt."

"It doesn't sound like a place we would find Yaron Kali."

"If he made a bargain to sail on the *Bonnie Lass*, he won't be leaving until he completes the bargain—or until Captain Sheridan Gray decides to let him go."

"Is there any way to contact the captain and ask?"

The man shook his head. "She's water Arcana from a major branch. You don't want to be messing with her. She talks to the Sorcerer King and the Ferryman and few others."

In other words, if Yaron Kali—or either of the other two missing people—boarded that ship, they were gone for good.

"Tell her about the boat," a woman said.

All the men murmured and finally agreed on the exact spot where a motorboat—not one owned by Arcana—had been spotted near a place where a person would find an interior road. The human saw the two Arcana who were out fishing but didn't raise a friendly hand, despite being anchored on the wrong side of the river, and looked uneasy, almost afraid. When the Arcana were returning a couple of hours later, they saw that boat, with the same human at the wheel, heading for the town directly across the river. They didn't see anyone with him.

The spot where the Arcana had seen the motorboat was almost directly across the river from the town of Jackson, where Yaron Kali lived and worked. It seemed likely that Kali would want to go ashore as quickly as possible—before his colleague had time to change his mind and regret taking him to Wyrd.

Beth wasn't sure what the men meant by an interior road, but she was certain Jack would know—and wouldn't be pleased.

When Jack joined her, the Arcana fishermen showed him the map and the spot where the motorboat had been seen. She was right. He did not look pleased.

At the invitation of the woman who ran one of the shops, Beth made use of the washroom. Then she bought two bottles of juice.

"Are you water, land, or air?" the woman asked.

For a moment, Beth didn't know what she was talking about. Then she understood. "It took special circumstances to see them, but . . ." She touched the sides of her forehead. "Antlers."

"Ah. A forest branch. Most of us around the bay are connected to a water branch, as you might expect."

Lessons. A show of trust to provide information that wouldn't be shared with anyone across the river.

Beth joined Jack, set the bottles of juice in the cup holders between the front seats. "We are going to the place where the boat owned by Kali's colleague was seen?"

"We are," Jack replied. "And there is no telling where we will go from there."

They traveled inland. Beth scanned her side of the road for a flash of color or some debris that might have been left by a careless human. The dirt road was fairly straight, but she wasn't sure that, if they turned around, they would end up back where they started. And if that was true for someone traveling with one of the Arcana . . .

Jack hit the brakes, jolting Beth out of her thoughts.

In front of them, where it hadn't existed a moment ago, was a fork in the road.

He shut off the engine, took a long drink from one of the bottles of juice—and said nothing.

"Jack? What's going on?"

"You lost your focus. You began thinking of many instead of the one you want to find."

"Are you saying I created that road?"

"The road is always there. The fact that it appeared when you lost focus means that, most likely, it's not a direction that will lead to Kali. But it's easy enough for a person to become lost in the neighborhoods if they give in to impulse and follow a road or a path that suddenly appears."

Beth sighed and drank from the other bottle of juice. "Sorry."

"No need to be sorry. That's why you're doing this with me. To learn the dangers."

"Right. You're the trainer; I'm the trainee."

"Rest your brain for a minute. Look at the sky, listen to the birds until you're ready to focus again."

She wanted to get out of the car and stretch her legs, walk a bit, but she didn't dare. Not until she understood how easy it might be to get swallowed up in one of Wyrd's neighborhoods.

After a couple of minutes, she unfolded the missing person flyer and studied the image of Yaron Kali. "All right. I'm ready."

Jack started the car. Beth looked up. The fork in the road faded like the Cheshire cat until there was nothing there.

They stopped at villages, at farmhouses, anywhere a handful of people had built a place to live. No one had seen Yaron Kali, and yet they drove over the one road available to them—as long as she didn't lose focus, didn't lose her intention to find this one man.

The third time they were confronted with so many one-lane roads, riding trails, and game trails that the impression was one of driving into the branches of trees, Jack held to the road while Beth closed her eyes and struggled to stay focused through a pounding headache.

"We'll stop here for the day," Jack said, pulling into the parking lot of what looked like a seedy motel. "The place is cleaner than it looks and has decent water pressure if you want a hot shower. There's also a pizza parlor just down the street, if that's of interest."

"It's the middle of the afternoon," Beth protested.

"You're done, Beth. Staying focused for extended periods of time is exhausting, especially when you're new to doing it. Stay here. I'll get us a room."

It wasn't until he returned with a key and carried his duffel and her weekender inside that she realized he really meant *one* room.

"They didn't have another room free?" She noticed her weekender was on one bed and his duffel was on the other. Still, she hadn't expected to be sharing a room with Jack.

"You need an anchor," he said quietly. "And we both need rest."

"I wouldn't go anywhere."

"You wouldn't mean to go anywhere. That's not the same thing."

"But you know this place. Where are we?"

"Don't ask that question." The tone of voice was a flat warning.

Are we still on the Isle of Wyrd? Right now, seeing the look in Jack's eyes, she didn't dare ask *that* question.

"If it's all right with you, I'm going to take something for this headache and then take a hot shower."

"Go ahead."

Bringing her weekender into the bathroom, Beth took a couple of pills for the headache, then undressed. The bathroom's fixtures were old but clean, and the water pressure was sufficient to help loosen her tight neck and shoulder muscles. By the time she finished her shower and pulled on clean clothes, she thought she might be ready for some food by the time Jack took his shower.

She sat on the side of her bed and watched Jack walk into the bathroom. She heard the shower. She didn't hear anything else until two hours later when Jack woke her up and suggested they get something to eat.

56

Tom Castelletti strode into the team's area of the precinct, swearing under his breath.

Ian Kuhn stared at him. "Did the results from the DNA tests come in already?"

Tom shook his head. "Bonnie Wilson did a runner."

"What?"

"She was supposed to talk to the mayor, the district attorney, and the chief of police this morning to answer questions about this DNA sample that allegedly came from Beth Fahey. Instead, she packed up and left the hotel very early this morning without settling her bill, and, get this—the credit card she'd provided at check-in no longer had enough of a balance to take care of the room and meals because on her way out of town, she withdrew as much cash as she could from that card."

"Is she heading home?"

Tom rubbed his hands over his face. "A cop in her hometown saw something about her on social media and called the precinct early this morning, hoping we could help locate her. Last night there was a storm in that area of the country. Her house was struck by lightning and burned to the ground before the fire department could get the blaze under control."

"Shit."

"That's not all. An anonymous source sent the mayor and the chief of police a list of the casinos where Bonnie Wilson likes to play—and tends to lose. She owes thousands at each of those places—and she plays at places where the debt collectors wear brass knuckles and carry saps . . . and guns."

"Why did they let her keep playing?"

Tom shrugged. "Maybe they were pressuring her now that they realized she couldn't deliver on what she owed."

Kuhn rubbed the back of his neck. "What if she tried to hold off the casinos by telling them she was coming to Penwych to collect money she was owed? With her being on TV and blabbing Fahey's name, do you think those people will come looking to get their money from Fahey if they can't get it from Wilson?"

Swearing, Tom took out his cell phone and called Fahey. The call went to voicemail. "Fahey, it's Castelletti. I need you to check in as soon as you get this message."

"Unless Bonnie Wilson didn't really do a runner, and there is a reason why Fahey can't check in," Kuhn said quietly.

Swearing viciously, Tom called another number—a number he'd hoped he wouldn't need to call while Captain Forrester was away on vacation.

"Frost."

"Mr. Frost, this is Detective Castelletti at the thirteenth precinct. I need to get in touch with Detective Fahey."

"She's searching for the missing people."

"I'm aware of that, but we need to contact her, and she isn't answering her cell phone."

"Most likely, she's currently in a neighborhood where that kind of communication isn't possible. If it's any comfort, Detective Fahey is working with my brother, Jack. He'll look after her."

That wasn't any comfort at all. All the cops had heard rumors about Jack Frost—rumors that made Jack the Ripper sound like a Boy Scout. But rumors were all they had. They couldn't prove anything about anything, and more often than not, there were signs of a violent crime but no body, and without a body, they had nothing.

"If you hear from them, tell Fahey I really need to talk to her."

"I'll tell her." Frost ended the call.

"Should we call the captain?" Kuhn asked.

Tom shook his head. "There's nothing he could do, even if he were here."

"So we wait for something else to happen."

"Yeah. We wait."

57

Colin stood under the shower and thought he would never take hot water for granted again—or being able to use water that wasn't rationed by the bucket.

He'd felt sad to leave Llamalidia, especially since he knew it was unlikely he would ever visit there again. But the cria who had been taking weaving lessons along with him presented him with their work, and the adults had done the finishing so that he had four unique place mats to give to his mother. They weren't coordinated or perfect or anything, but he knew she'd get a kick out of them, just like she would get a kick out of the postcards he'd bought at one of the stores here.

He couldn't tell if the town was retro on purpose, or if the people who lived there felt no need to modernize . . . anything. He could see how a town like this worked for Tia. It provided everything a person needed, but everyone moved at an easy pace.

It was like a pocket of yesterday, he decided as he dressed to go out for dinner and a movie. His mom had packed one dress shirt when she'd sent the second batch of clothes. It was a bit wrinkled now, but he thought it would do well enough with a clean pair of jeans.

Tia's room at the hotel was right across from his. When he was ready, he knocked on her door. She wasn't wearing a dress—he wasn't sure she owned one—but, like him, she'd dressed up a bit for their final night.

"You want burgers and fries again?" Tia asked. "Or we can go for a steak."

"Since we got here in time to have burgers for lunch, let's go for the steak." Colin thought a moment. "Will we have time to eat before the movie?"

"We'll have time. And the movie house has two theaters, so neither of us has to pretend we want to see a romantic comedy if that is one of the choices."

"Action?"

Tia smiled. "You never know what you'll find when you come here. At least, in terms of movies."

They found *Jaws*. Sharing a large tub of popcorn with Tia while the shark terrorized a town, Colin thought it was the best evening he'd had in a long time.

58

Richard turned on the water at a sink in the men's room, washed his hands, and tried to decide what to do now that the check Bonnie Wilson wrote to cover his expenses had bounced. The woman had seemed solid when she'd hired him to keep track of her errant "niece," but when he caught her on the TV, ranting about having proof that the woman he'd been tracking wasn't pure human, he figured it was best to disappear for a couple of days. But disappearing required money, and now he was short of cash.

A toilet flushed. A man stepped out of one of the stalls.

The guy looked familiar. Where had he seen that face before? Maybe in the restaurant? Somewhere else?

The man washed his hands and dried them. He smiled at Richard. "I don't know what you did, but you sure pissed off somebody, and now they want to balance the scales."

Richard felt cold sweat roll down his spine. "I don't know what you're talking about. I don't know you."

"You don't need to know me. I'm just here to do a job. But you do know what I'm talking about. You helped mess up a young woman's life. Now it's time to pay."

Richard spun around and tried to spring for the door, but the garrote was around his neck before he had time to move. He scratched at his neck and tried to grab his attacker, but he couldn't seem to get a grip on the man.

"Wyrd. Arcana," he gasped as the garrote tightened.

"Nah," the man replied. "The Arcana in Wyrd don't use outside contractors, not with who they have in-house. But the bargain I made with another Sorcerer King allows me to take the occasional job—and I do enjoy my work."

The assassin stashed the body in one of the stalls, stowed the garrote, and washed his hands.

Beyond the little he'd been told, he didn't know what the man had done, and he didn't care. The Arcana didn't interfere with humans most of the time, but when someone roused their anger enough to make some adjustments in someone's life, well, fate could be a fickle bitch and send a bolting man right into the path of a predator.

After paying for his meal, the assassin left the restaurant and walked back to his hotel. He'd been given a three-day leave to enjoy the physical world and, hopefully, fulfill this contract. He was careful about not being seen in too many places. It had been a couple of decades since he'd disappeared, but his face was still on wanted posters. Even so, he had enjoyed good food and an evening with a woman who cost enough to give a man company as well as sex. Now he went into the hotel shop that sold toiletries for outrageous prices, as well as books and magazines. He bought a couple of thrillers, a book of crossword puzzles, and a book of sudoku. Taking them up to his room, he packed his things, pleased that the hotel's laundry service had returned his clothes on time.

As the clock on the bedside table passed midnight, he picked up his duffel, checked out, and assured the person at the desk that he'd enjoyed his stay. Then he walked down the street until he reached a dark corner. There, he waited for a particular bus to pick him up again.

59

Beth said nothing when Jack nudged her toast to one side and slid a third of his omelet and two slices of bacon onto her plate.

"You can eat while you're brooding," he said before he turned his attention back to his meal.

"I'm not brooding. I'm thinking."

"You can still eat."

She understood his reasoning. She just wasn't sure her queasy stomach would keep down what she put in it. But she'd thought and thought about what they were doing and why. She thought about how they had driven through some very strange places yesterday—places that made no sense if they were still within the geographical boundaries of Wyrd. And she thought about how she felt like she had jet lag to the nth degree—and how even Jack was showing some weariness this morning.

She ate a bite of the omelet, figuring he would be more willing to talk if she showed some willingness to eat. But she wasn't quite willing to talk about what they needed to talk about, so she said, "What did the fishermen at Destiny Bay want to talk to you about yesterday?"

He refilled his cup of coffee from the pot on the table. "A big game fish has made the Fate River its territory. It's been spotted on and off for the past few months, but the fishermen weren't after a trophy fish; they were casting lines to catch fish for their tables—and to sell any surplus to eateries around the bay. Now that fish has started targeting the fishermen's catch, seeing a fish on a line and biting it in half to avoid getting caught on the hook. They've never seen a fish that looked like this one, so they wanted Lucas to know about it."

Beth ate a slice of bacon, pondering as she chewed. "Are they sure it's a fish?"

"Instead of . . . ?"

"Well, are the men you talked to sure that this fish started out as a wee little fish that avoided being swallowed by other fish until it grew up to be the bully in the river, or was it something else before it acquired fins and gills?"

Jack smiled. "It's a good question. I don't have an answer. But we can ask Lucas when we get back to the park." A beat of silence. "You ready to tell me what you've been brooding about?"

She hadn't been brooding. Not exactly. But she felt the weight of the conclusion she'd come to early this morning when she couldn't sleep.

"People move around," she said after taking a sip of her coffee.

"People do," Jack agreed.

"So we're following the trail of someone who keeps moving through neighborhoods."

Jack inclined his head in agreement.

"But buildings don't move. They don't break loose from their foundations, grow legs, and wander off to the next town to see what it's like there."

"Well, there's that hut that walks around on giant chicken legs, but yes, most buildings stay put."

"That's Baba Yaga's house. That's folklore."

"Sure."

The quick agreement meant the Arcana had a more flexible understanding of things like folklore.

Beth took a steadying breath—and tried not to imagine dumping her coffee on Jack. There was so much she didn't know about Wyrd, it was possible that folklore and myth cozied up to some of the neighborhoods. After all, she'd seen a giant bird with a woman's face, as well as purple cows, so what else lived here that she didn't know about yet?

"The diner in the sketch. The Ladies Three said that was our destination, that we would find someone who needed our help when we found that place." Deep breath in, deep breath out. "I think we should change our intentions. I think we should look for the diner, collect whoever we find there who needs our help, and then go back to Destiny Park. Go home."

Jack studied her. "We might not find Yaron Kali."

"We tried. That has to be enough." She wasn't sure how she would explain that decision to Detective Kali, but every cop knew that sometimes search and rescue changed into an effort to recover a body—and the three people who were still missing could be anywhere.

"All right." He looked pointedly at her plate. "Try to eat a bit more. Even changing our focus to find a particular building, it could still be a long day."

She made the effort because her body needed fuel—and because she didn't want to falter if Jack needed help.

60

"Why are we headed to Fahey's apartment?" Ian Kuhn asked. "She's not back yet, right?"

Tom Castelletti turned on the car's siren when the flashing lights didn't inspire the drivers in front of him to pull the fuck over. "We're going there because Detective Gibson called and requested that we meet her at what she called 'a multiple crime scene.'"

"What does that mean?"

"We'll find out."

Police vehicles of all kinds filled one side of the street. Officers were directing traffic and manning barricades to keep people away from the building.

"This is not good," Kuhn muttered.

When they reached the second floor of the building, Amanda Gibson met them in the hallway, looking grim.

"Do you know where Detective Fahey is?" she asked. "I have a number for her, but she's not picking up."

"She's on assignment across the river," Tom replied. "I was told she might be in an area of Wyrd that doesn't have cell phone service or phones of any kind."

"Is that likely?"

"I wasn't going to argue with Lucas Frost, especially not after he said his brother, Jack, went with Fahey to assist in her inquiries."

"Could she have slipped away from him and come back here?"

Tom barked out a laugh. "Detective, I hope I never find out how much truth there is in the rumors I've heard about Jack Frost. No, she couldn't have slipped past him." He stared at the partially open door. "You want to tell us what's going on?"

"My people are waiting to gather evidence at the primary crime scene. I asked that they not move anything until you had a chance to see it—including the body."

Tom felt a shiver roll down his spine. "All right."

Gibson pushed the door open and walked into the studio apartment.

"Shit," Kuhn said softly.

"Fuck me sideways," Tom said just as softly as he surveyed the damage.

"According to the neighbor across the hall, a woman showed up yesterday evening, pounding on Fahey's door, demanding to be let in," Gibson said. "When no one answered, she began shouting that she needed money, that the spine crackers were looking for her, and she had to give them something. When Fahey still didn't respond, the woman made threats and was verbally abusive. By that time, the neighbor across the hall opened her door just enough to shout that she had called the police. The woman fled before the patrol officers arrived, but they did question the neighbor, and the description of the woman seen through the peephole matched Bonnie Wilson."

"Why trash Fahey's place?" Tom asked.

Gibson gestured to the living area and tiny kitchen. "This vandalism was done by the fathers of the four boys who were killed by Albert Palmer. With Fahey being outed as an 'Arcana spy,' they wanted to cause her some grief. They said they found the lock already broken, so they came in and trashed the place, destroying her personal property. Hearing the noise, the neighbor called the police again, and officers from the twelfth arrived to apprehend the men before they had a chance to flee."

"The men heard the sirens?"

Gibson shook her head. "They had found the primary crime scene and were afraid they would be arrested for murder." A pause. "The body is in the bedroom alcove."

"It smells like an outhouse in here," Kuhn said.

"Two of the men pulled the books off the shelf and urinated on them. Another man made a bowel movement in the kitchen area."

Tom moved toward the bedroom alcove, watching where he stepped. Four men in a small place like this? It didn't look like Fahey had much to destroy, but they ruined everything they could until . . .

He stared at the body, at the mutilated face. No eyes, no ears, and he would bet the medical examiner wouldn't find a tongue. Pinned to the chest with long hat pins were five IOUs marked paid.

"Jesus," Kuhn said, looking over Tom's shoulder. "Someone must have told them where to find her."

Tom nodded. "Someone who knew certain people would respond by taking body parts in lieu of other payment." *Or would those debts be settled once proof was received that Bonnie Wilson would no longer cause trouble?*

A thought occurred to him. "These apartments wouldn't have much soundproofing. He studied the body, then looked at Gibson. "Broken neck?"

She nodded. "The rest was done postmortem."

There was some mercy in that, but he doubted mercy had anything to do with it.

"Do you think the Arcana did this?" Gibson asked.

"Not Lucas Frost or his people," Tom replied. Frost was dangerous, but Tom couldn't see him ordering *this*.

"I need Detective Fahey to come in and make a statement as soon as possible."

"We'll keep trying to contact her." And God help him, he was going to have to call Frost again and tell him about this.

As Tom and Ian stepped out of the apartment, the chain rattled on the door across the hall before it opened. The elderly woman eyed them warily until Tom showed her his ID.

"You work with Beth?" she asked.

"Yes, ma'am," he replied.

"Such a nice young woman." She tried to look between them to see whatever could be seen through the open door. "Those men made a mess of her place, didn't they?"

"Yes, they did."

"It's a good thing her friends came over the other day for the decluttering party."

"Ma'am?"

"A girl about Beth's age and two young men. They all live in small apartments and had rented a storage space together. They came over the other day and took away all the things Beth didn't have room for in her apartment but didn't want to discard. Winter clothes and books and things like that." She paused. "At least, that's what they said, but I wondered if Beth was planning to move soon. I guess she will be now."

Tom's heart pounded. "Do you recall any names?"

"Oh, yes. They were such polite young people. There was Ashley, Ethan, and Jack. They brought over a large pizza. Beth dropped off a couple of slices for me before going back to work." She sighed. "I'll miss her. She was a good neighbor."

Back in the car, Tom closed his eyes for a moment. "The neighbor doesn't know about the body."

"Maybe Bonnie Wilson was the one who broke the lock, intending to hide in Fahey's apartment," Kuhn said. "The spine crackers found her, killed her, and slipped away before the other men showed up."

"And they were quiet. The old lady was already listening for trouble after calling the cops once that night." Tom sighed. "It's Gibson's problem."

"You going to call Captain Forrester?"

"Have to now. And Frost."

"You think Fahey is all right?"

Tom started the car. "Let's hope so."

61

Colin stood outside the building that was a combination bus depot, taxi stand, and the equivalent of a UPS Store where you could drop off packages to be delivered to . . . somewhere else . . . if the somewhere else could still be reached. He had the suitcase his dad had sent when he'd first arrived in Llamalidia, and he had a box of gifts he'd picked up at the trading post, along with the woven place mats and the primer that Tia told him he could keep so that he could continue studying the Llamalidian language.

Tia came out of the building. "There's a bus arriving at eleven o'clock this morning. Its route depends on where the passengers intend to go, but it has a fixed stop at a place where you can transfer to a Destiny Park shuttle bus. We can stow your bags in the depot and go across the street to the diner if you want something to eat."

"That sounds . . ." Colin spotted the man who stepped out of an alley across the street at the same time the man's attention fixed on *him*. As the man hurried across the street, aiming straight for him, Tia took a half step in front of him.

The man hesitated, then seemed to ignore her as he approached Colin. "Hey, buddy. Got any spare change?"

The man carried a day pack over one shoulder, but he looked like he hadn't changed clothes in days, and the body odor was strong enough to knock Colin back a step. But it was the look in the man's eyes that made him wary. Something wrong. Something off. Drugs, maybe? Or had the man been lost in the neighborhoods for so long that he was mentally whacked?

"Change for what?" Tia asked, her stance suddenly reminding Colin that she had been a soldier and had been trained to fight.

The man tried to move closer to Colin. Tia blocked him, forcing him to answer her. "A meal. Maybe a bus ticket?"

"To where?"

He didn't like her asking questions, requiring answers. He turned to Colin. "Where are you headed?"

Tia reached into a pocket, then held out a gold coin. "This will get you a meal at the diner across the street, although they may make you eat it outside."

The man hesitated, then snatched the coin and hurried to the diner.

"You're not getting on a bus with him," Tia said. "Doesn't matter where he says he's going, you don't get on the same bus."

Colin was glad she'd said it. "He's . . ."

"Some people get addicted to wanting to see what's around the next corner. It's not so different from saying "this will be my last drink" and then going on a bender or "this will be my last hit" and then going out the next day desperate to score another hit. He wants to experience the next buzz of the strange, and if the people around him aren't vigilant . . . He won't be able to pull everyone away from their intended destinations, but he can make it harder to reach those stops." She looked at him. "He can make it harder for you to get to Destiny Park because you're young, and he sees you as someone he can manipulate—and I don't think he wants to reach the park where he'd have to deal with someone like the Sorcerer King."

The man came out of the diner. He had a paper bag in one hand. He looked down the street, then hurried across, his attention fixed on Colin again.

"Bus is coming," Tia said quietly.

Colin looked the other way, wondering what excuse he could give for not getting on the bus when he spotted a black SUV making the turn at the intersection. It was dirty, as if it had traveled a lot of miles.

The woman in the passenger seat pointed at the man who was trying to crowd Colin despite Tia's efforts to stay between the boy and the man. When the SUV pulled up close to the building, the woman hopped out and said in a commanding voice, "Yaron Kali!"

The man turned, hesitated, started to back away. But the SUV's driver came around behind him.

"I'm Detective Fahey from the Penwych police. You need to come with us now."

Kali shook his head. "I'm taking the bus to . . . I'm taking the bus."

"No, sir. You're coming with us to Destiny Park. We'll get you home from there."

Before Kali had time to escape, the driver had a handcuff around one of Kali's wrists, had marched him to the vehicle, and forced him into the back seat before attaching the other half of the cuff to some part of the vehicle.

Colin eased around Tia. "Detective Fahey?"

Tia looked surprised. So did the detective, but she had been focused on apprehending the man instead of noticing a teenage boy.

"Colin?" She gave him a big, delighted smile. "Colin Forrester? What . . . ? Have you been here all this time?"

"No. I was . . . someplace else. But my friend"—he indicated Tia—"helped me reach this town. I was waiting for the bus to go to Destiny Park."

"Is that what you want to do? Take the bus? Because we're headed for Destiny Park and can take you with us."

"He'll make it hard for you to get to the park," Tia said, nodding toward the man who seemed to be arguing—or pleading—with the driver.

The driver who was standing outside the vehicle with the door open. In an enclosed space, the body odor would be awesome.

"We'll get him there," Fahey said grimly. She turned to Tia. "I work with Colin's dad, Captain Forrester."

Colin saw Tia relax when he said, "I'll be safe going with Detective Fahey."

"Jack is Arcana," Fahey said. "He'll be able to counter any resistance from our passenger."

Tia sucked in a breath. "Jack . . . Frost?"

Fahey nodded.

Frost. Like Lucas Frost. Who was the Sorcerer King.

"Is there room for my stuff?" Colin gestured to the suitcase and box.

"We'll make it fit." Fahey picked up the suitcase. "Can you get the box?"

"Yeah." He turned toward Tia. "Thanks for everything."

"It was a pleasure to have you around." She looked a little embarrassed. "If you can, send a message and let me know you got home okay."

"I will."

She patted his shoulder and stepped back. Colin picked up the box and went around to the SUV's storage area. As he watched Jack rearrange things to fit in the suitcase and box, Colin wondered why they were carrying so many gas cans.

"They're empty now," Fahey said. "Turns out Jack wasn't kidding when he said we would be traveling in places that didn't have gas stations."

He had a ton of questions he wanted to ask, but only one he really wanted answered since he figured he would be the other person in the back seat. "Could we open the windows?"

"Oh, yeah," Jack said, looking at Kali. Then he looked at Fahey and added, "He's going to be a problem. Keep your weapon secure."

"Come on, Colin," Fahey said as she opened the back door for him. "The sooner we get started, the sooner we'll get home."

"I'd like to talk to you about that," he said quietly.

"When we reach the park," she said just as quietly. "Until then, I need you to help me stay focused on *reaching* the park. Understand?"

He nodded and got in the back seat behind Jack. He kept his head turned enough to keep an eye on Kali because being within reach of the man was a bit like riding in a car with a savage dog and hoping the chain didn't break.

Beth listened to Kali's grumbling and whining until they were several miles out of town. Then she slipped her gun out of the holster, checked that the safety was on, and stowed it in the large purse tucked near her feet. It wouldn't be easy to pull out the gun if there was trouble, but it also wouldn't be in easy reach if Kali made a grab for it. After removing the flyer from her purse, she said, "Stop the car, Jack."

Jack stopped the car and put it in park before looking at her.

Beth released her seat belt and twisted around to face Kali—and hoped she didn't scare the crap out of Colin.

"All right, Mr. Kali. Ever since we left the town, you've been bitching about us interfering with you seeing just one more thing, so we're going to let you out and you can go ahead and see whatever you want to—but first, you're going to give me a couple of answers."

Kali looked sullen. "What answers?"

"What do you want me to tell your wife? Should I tell Detective Kali that we found you and were going to bring you home, but you were selfish enough not to give a damn about what she's been going through because you wanted to see one more thing? Should I tell the administrators at Jackson University that they should hire someone else to fill your position?"

"You have no right to say anything to anyone," Kali snapped. "I've only been gone . . ."

"For weeks." Beth saw the shock in his eyes, but that was quickly replaced by denial. "You've been gone *for weeks*." She thrust the flyer over the seat so that it was right in his face. "You're officially listed as a missing person, and every precinct in the six towns around the Fate River has this flyer posted on a board to remind all the police officers in those towns that the spouse of one of their own is missing."

"I . . ." Kali looked confused.

"The friend who took you across the river in his boat? You *promised* him you would be back in two hours. When the time was long past and he returned to Jackson alone, he went to your house and told your wife what happened. You've been gone for weeks, Mr. Kali. Weeks when your wife waited for the phone call saying you were found alive—or that your body was found. And now you sit there like some five-year-old who had spent an afternoon going on all the rides at the county fair and was whining because the grown-ups said it was time to go home and wouldn't let you go on one more ride."

Kali looked out the window with a yearning that was like a sickness.

"Jack, what are the odds of finding someone again if they've been lost in Wyrd and they walk away from a chance to go home?"

"No odds," Jack replied. "If he walks away now, you should tell his wife to sever all legal bonds with him and consider herself a widow."

Beth hopped out of the SUV and opened the back door. She stared at Kali. "Either you stop whining and come with us to Destiny Park, or I unlock the cuffs and let you go—and I tell your wife you chose to disappear."

"She won't believe you," Kali said. "She loves me."

"I'm a cop. She's a cop. She'll believe me."

Kali hunched in the seat and said nothing.

Beth closed the back door and returned to her seat. She fastened her seat belt and looked at Jack.

Jack grinned. "You're impressive when you're pissed off." He put the car in gear and took off.

If any of the roads had speed limits, she hadn't seen any signs. Not that it would have mattered. She let the world outside the car go by in a blur while she pictured the pavilion and the ornamental lake.

Destiny Park. We're going to Destiny Park.

Several hours into the trip, Beth realized that Jack's speed wasn't just about preventing Yaron Kali from doing anything foolish. Jack wanted to get them back to the park before the sun went down—and Kali saw something the Arcana really didn't want him to see.

62

Lucas, we found Yaron Kali. We need to get him across the river before dark.

Despite the communication reaching him as a faint whisper—which gave him a good idea of how far away Jack was—Lucas heard the strain in his brother's voice. Whatever had happened over the past couple of days had taxed Jack's stamina to its limits. **Can he be trusted if we let him stay overnight?**

No. Jack was gone.

Lucas called Tom Castelletti's cell phone, and looked at the sky as he waited for the man to respond. Even with summer's extra daylight, it was going to be close.

"Castelletti."

"Send your patrol boat," Lucas said. "We found one of your people, and he needs to get across the river *now*."

"Does the person need medical attention?" Castelletti asked.

"I don't know. Assume he will." Lucas ended the call.

Justine and her sisters walked into his office, a question in their eyes.

"They're on their way back," he told the women. "They found Yaron Kali. Jack says the man needs to cross the river tonight."

"We have considered this man's desires and balanced the scales." Justine's voice held a bone-deep cold. "We want you to impose a cost on this man if he ever tries to return."

"What payment will keep the scales balanced?"

She told him. "We snipped off fifteen years from the thread of his life for the trouble he has already caused."

"And the other two people who are still missing?"

The three women looked at one another before Justine said, "They didn't come to the park and seek our help, but they came to Wyrd in secret for a reason. For sanctuary."

"I think when the neighborhoods change places during the autumn equinox, those people will be someplace other than Wyrd," Lysandra said.

"But they will be settled in a place that suits their spirits," Zerah said.

Jack's coming,* Mia Skov said. *He requests assistance.

**Patrol boat is approaching the dock,* Ethan Sharpe said.*

Lucas walked past the Ladies Three. "I'm going to help Jack. Ethan will keep an eye on the patrol boat."

"Beth?" Justine asked.

"I don't know." Jack hadn't mentioned her, but he would have said *something* if she wasn't all right.

Then again, this assignment had tapped out Jack's strength, so he wouldn't make assumptions about Beth.

Lucas strode toward the area where the vehicles were kept. As daylight began to fade, he felt the pull of the stars and the moon. The Arcana couldn't stop the truth of what they were from being revealed. They could only choose who knew that truth. Which meant that getting Yaron Kali on the patrol boat and getting his own people safely out of sight was going to be difficult.

The SUV bulleted up the road and slid to a gravel-spewing stop. Beth hopped out of the passenger seat and stumbled before she righted herself. She looked exhausted, but she didn't look injured, so Lucas focused on the problem that was sitting in the back seat. He opened the back door of the SUV and started to drag the man out before realizing Kali was handcuffed to the vehicle.

No time to let Beth unlock the cuff. Lucas simply grabbed the metal links between the cuffs and yanked, breaking the metal—and possibly a bone in Kali's wrist.

Jack came around to that side of the vehicle. Between them, they hauled a protesting Kali through the park and down the beach to the dock where the patrol boat waited.

"I'll take him," Lucas said, leaving Jack at the end of the dock since Ethan was waiting for him.

Ian Kuhn climbed out of the patrol boat. Good. Someone who was supposed to be familiar with Wyrd and the Arcana.

Lucas swung Kali around so they were face-to-face. "Judgment has been passed for the trouble you've caused. You have forfeited fifteen years of your potential lifespan. Every time you try to set foot on our land again, it will cost you another twenty years. If you're selfish, you'll make your wife a widow within a year. Think about that." He shoved the man toward Kuhn. "Get him out of here."

He and Ethan joined Jack at the end of the dock and waited just long enough to watch the police wrestle Kali into the patrol boat and pull away from the dock. Then the three men hurried up the beach, not stopping until they knew they would be out of sight of the humans on the water.

"Kali isn't the only one we brought back," Jack said. "Beth is taking the other one to the hotel."

"Then I'd better talk to her," Lucas replied. "You should get some rest. You can tell me what happened in the morning."

"She was good, Lucas. She met the challenge and didn't flinch." Jack gave him a tired grin. "And she's pretty impressive when she's pissed off."

High praise coming from Jack Frost.

Lucas headed for the hotel. Whoever Beth Fahey brought back with her was going to have to deal with the truth about the Arcana.

63

Beth smiled at the woman behind the check-in counter. The woman glanced at Colin, then at her.

Yes, Beth thought. *He's human but . . .*

"Whoa," Colin said softly.

Beth turned and stared at Lucas Frost. She'd seen him before in starlight and moonlight, but in the hotel's artificial light, she appreciated that it wasn't just the antlers that made it obvious he wasn't human. There was a subtle difference in his face and the way he moved. And right now . . .

She'd always thought saying someone was swelled with anger was a phrase used only in stories. Lucas hadn't turned into the Hulk, and he wasn't popping the seams of his shirt, but he was *more* than the man she'd seen the other night when he was helping her understand her own heritage. And he was furious.

"Sir." She wasn't certain if he wanted her to use his name in front of the boy. "This is Colin Forrester. He was waiting for the bus that would bring him to Destiny Park, so Jack and I offered him a ride. I was going to get him a hotel room for the night."

"In the private wing," Lucas said.

His voice was deeper, more resonate. More primal. More *powerful.* A sound remembered by the old forests of the world.

"He can have the room next to yours," Lucas added. "You will choose something to eat; the food will be brought to your rooms." He looked at the boy. "You are welcome here, Colin Forrester, as long as you abide by our rules."

"Yes, sir. Thank you," Colin replied.

Lucas focused on Beth. Having spent several hours in a vehicle with Yaron Kali, Beth wanted to fumigate her clothes and take a long shower. It wasn't comfortable having Lucas Frost give her such a thorough, assessing look. Nothing sexual, but definitely not casual.

"Call Tom Castelletti," Lucas said.

"And Captain Forrester?" Beth asked.

Lucas nodded.

"Sir?" Colin waited until Lucas indicated he should continue. "Is it all right if I tell Detective Fahey about the neighborhood where I was staying?"

A beat of silence before Lucas said, "Once she completes her work for your father, Beth will be working for me, so you can tell her anything." Another penetrating look at Beth. "Tonight you need rest. We'll talk in the morning. But understand this, Beth. No matter what Castelletti says or wants, you will not cross the river without my consent—and I do not give my consent."

Lucas walked away.

"Here is your key, Mr. Forrester," the woman said.

Since Colin still held the box of gifts for his folks, Beth took the key, then looked at the suitcase she'd carried into the hotel. Colin's suitcase.

Ashley appeared at her side, carrying two menus from the restaurant. "I'll give you a hand. Jack brought your purse and luggage up from the car and left them outside your room."

Beth sighed, finally appreciating how exhausted she felt. "That's good because my room key is in my purse." Along with the nine mil on loan from Ethan. She'd been so focused on getting Colin up to the hotel and into a room before the boy had to deal with the truth about the Arcana, she hadn't given her own things a thought.

Besides, she didn't think she could have carried her purse and weekender to the hotel along with Colin's suitcase. Not tonight.

"This isn't the usual room service menu," Ashley said, leading them through the hotel corridors. "But tonight you can order anything you want from the hotel's full menu."

When Ashley pressed the spots in the wall mural that unlocked the door to the private wing, Colin whistled softly. "Is this like a secret place in another dimension or something?"

Ashley smiled. "Or something." She opened the door to Colin's room, dropped the menu on the bed, and walked out.

Beth looked at the weekender and purse that had been left to one side of her door, where anyone could have taken them or rifled through the contents. Except this was Wyrd and this was the private wing.

She found her key, opened the door, and used the weekender to keep it propped open.

"Problem?" Ashley asked.

"Just trying to flog my brain into making a mental list of what I need to do tonight," Beth replied.

"There are laundry bags in the closet. Put your clothes in one and leave it outside your room. We'll wash what can be washed and leave the rest to air overnight. The boy's things too."

Colin leaned against his open door. "Really? Awesome. Is there time to take a shower before eating?" Now he looked uneasy. "And there's something else."

Remembering that he wanted to talk to her, Beth said, "The shower comes first for me. Let me know what you want to eat. I'll call down with the order after my shower. I have some calls to make." She looked at Ashley. "Would that cause a problem for the kitchen?" She didn't want to wait a couple of hours for the food, but if she had to, better to order now.

Ashley gave her a strange look. "Anything requested from the private wing receives top priority."

Because the guests in the private wing were people the Arcana didn't want other guests to see.

Ashley left. Beth left her door open until Colin gave her his order.

Then she brought in her things, closed the door—and stripped off the clothes she'd been wearing. She filled the laundry bag with the dirty clothes and opened the door just wide enough to shove the bag into the hallway.

She showered once, sniffed herself, then showered again before she felt clean. Remembering that she had a teenage boy waiting for her to order their meal, she skipped drying her hair and dressed in leggings and a tunic. Casual but acceptable for a meal with friends.

She called the restaurant and placed the order, noting Colin's restraint in not ordering half the menu. Then again, she wasn't sure who was expected to pay for his room and food, so restraint was a good idea.

Having settled herself as best she could, Beth picked up her cell phone, saw all the missed messages and voicemails that had been left over the past couple of days, and called Tom Castelletti.

"Fahey?" Castelletti sounded frazzled. "Are you all right?"

"Tired. It's been a long couple of days. Did you get Yaron Kali across the river okay?"

"He tried to jump overboard halfway across the river. What happened to him?"

"He was obsessed with seeing one more piece of Wyrd and wasn't happy about being cornered into going home."

A pause that felt heavy even over the phone. "Some things have happened while you were away. Detective Gibson wants you to come in tomorrow to answer some questions."

"About what?"

"Four men broke into your apartment and trashed the place."

She sighed. There went her deposit. "Anti-Arcana?"

"Yeah. The fathers of the boys Albert Palmer killed."

"That's better than what they might have done if I'd been home." It made her sharply appreciate that Lucas's offer of a job and a place to live would give her a safety she would no longer have across the river.

"Beth, there's more."

Castelletti calling her by her first name? That couldn't be good. "Just say it."

"Bonnie Wilson was killed in your apartment. Killed and mutilated. Whether it's true or not, indications are that spine crackers working for one of the casinos where she owed a lot of money found where she was hiding and came after her. Finding her body at your place is one of the things Detective Gibson wants to talk about. You should come in first thing tomorrow."

"I can't."

"I can send the patrol boat."

"Doesn't matter. I was given orders not to cross the river."

"Frost gave you *orders*? You're a cop. You don't take orders from him."

"I'm a Penwych police officer for a few more days. After that, he's my boss. I'll be staying here."

Silence. "Are you sure about this?"

"I'm sure. Look. I need to call Captain Forrester and then get something to eat. I'll call you in the morning after I check in with Lucas."

"The captain already knows about the break-in and murder."

"I'm not calling him about that. Colin Forrester is with me."

Castelletti whistled. "You found him?"

"More like he was already on his way to Destiny Park, and we just gave him a lift."

"You taking orders from Frost isn't going to go down easy with the brass."

"I've made my choice. Good night."

Beth ended the call and answered a knock on the door. Not the food.

"Can we talk?" Colin asked.

"You're just in time." Beth stood aside to let him into the room. "I'm about to call your dad."

"Maybe wait?"

"No." Thinking about what was going on in Penwych, even if the boy had no idea what had been happening, she could guess what he wanted to say. "Look, your family is on vacation. If your dad doesn't have to cut it short, they'll be gone for another week. I know you're smart and responsible, but you can't go home and stay on your own. Things are a bit . . . fraught . . . right now. I'll talk to Lucas in the morning and see if he'll agree to letting you stay for a few days."

Colin looked relieved—and eager. "Maybe I can do some chores to help pay for room and board? I helped out at the trading post, so I know how to do some retail now. Or maybe help to maintain the park. There must be a gazillion people working to keep the place tidy."

"Well, we're set for the night, so let's call your dad before I have to recharge my phone." Beth called Captain Forrester's cell phone. It barely rang before he answered.

"Beth? Are you all right?"

"Why is that the first thing everyone has said to me?" It wasn't really a question because, looking at it from the point of view of everyone who had waited for her to make contact, it would have been the first thing she would have wanted to know too.

"Castelletti told me what's going on," Forrester said.

"He just told me too. I've been out of touch for a couple of days, so you probably know more than I do. But that's not the reason I called."

An indrawn breath. A father bracing for news that would change his life. "Colin?"

"He's here with me at the hotel. We got in an hour ago. He'd like to talk to you." Beth handed Colin the phone. She would have left the room to give him some privacy, but the boy latched on to her arm.

"Dad?" A pause. "Yeah, I'm fine. The friend I was staying with said there were signs that I needed to come back to Destiny Park, so that's what I did. Well, I started to when Detective Fahey showed up in that town and offered me a ride. We're waiting for room service." Another pause. "You don't have to come back just for me. Detective—" Colin glanced at her. "Beth thinks I'll be able to hang out here for a few days, like a halfway house between where I was and home."

Beth blinked. Apparently, Captain Forrester did, too, because Colin handed her the phone when someone knocked on the door.

"Food's here," Colin said.

"Destiny Park as a halfway house," Forrester said. "Is that what you think?"

"Colin hasn't had a chance to tell me where he was, so I can't say if his assessment is accurate," Beth replied. "But I did pick up that he was in a neighborhood that had no cell phone service, no internet, and no pizza. The hotel has all three."

"Well." Forrester's laugh sounded relieved. "You're both all right?"

"We spent several hours in a car with a man who hadn't bothered with any kind of hygiene in weeks, but other than that, we're okay."

"Should I set everything on this table?" Colin asked.

"I'd better let you go if you want your share of the food," Forrester said, obviously hearing Colin's question. "The general feeling is I was already out of town when this whole thing sparked, and I should stay out of town with the family. But I'm available if you want to talk."

"Thank you, sir. Good night."

Beth set her cell phone on the bedside table and looked at the dishes filling the small dining table. "I didn't order that much."

"The guy who brought the food said the steaks and scallops are a dinner for two special tonight," Colin replied. "The regular salad comes with that, along with the steak fries. The pizza came with a small antipasto."

"Uh-huh."

"Pizza is good for breakfast, and there is a mini fridge, a microwave, and microwaveable containers for leftovers." Colin beamed at her.

The food was here and Colin was right about pizza for breakfast. Beth took a seat. At least with Colin, she didn't get the "you're not eating enough" look. He was more than willing to take one of the steaks and half the scallops and steak fries. He generously gave her all the salad while he piled a couple of slices of pizza and half the antipasto onto his plate.

"So," Colin said as Beth cut into her filet mignon, "I guess Lucas Frost is Wyrd's Sorcerer King?"

Beth stared at him. How much did the boy know that she should know? "Eat first. Then we'll talk."

"Awesome."

64

Grace Russell sat across from Sheina Kali at a table in the hospital cafeteria and considered what she could—or should—say to this young police officer whose husband was currently sedated and secured to a hospital bed. Comfort or truth?

"You should try to eat something," Grace said gently. "There wasn't much left to choose from at this hour, but it's pretty good for hospital food." She took a spoonful of the chicken noodle soup she'd ordered for herself, hoping Sheina would mimic her.

Sheina picked up her spoon but didn't eat. "He called me a bitch. He's angry because he has to stay here overnight for observation. He's angry that he's secured to the bed like a common criminal. When the doctor asked him about his time in Wyrd, Yaron said he's not saying anything, isn't going to let cowards steal his research. And he blames the boy for the cop focusing on him like he was some pervert and forcing him to come back to Destiny Park—and then letting those men hand him over to the cops who took him across the river before he'd completed this stage of his research."

Grace tried to keep her voice casual. "What boy?"

Sheina shrugged. "He didn't know, didn't ask. Just some boy who knew the cop—some boy who wasn't forced to cross the river."

Charles Forrester was still on vacation. Had anyone on his team called to tell him about the boy? Or would they wait until they could confirm the boy's identity in case it wasn't Forrester's son? Given the current turmoil in Penwych, the boy's presence at Destiny Park might have gotten buried under the necessity of getting Yaron Kali to the trauma unit at the hospital.

"It's standard procedure to secure an agitated patient, especially when they have spent time on Wyrd outside of Destiny Park," Grace said.

"Yaron said one of the men who handed him over to the police told him he was penalized fifteen years for the trouble he caused." Sheina dipped her spoon in her bowl of soup but still didn't eat. "I'm not sure what that means, but Yaron looks older than he did a few weeks ago, and not just because he hasn't showered in days. There's a lot of gray in his hair and lines on his face." She looked at Grace. "He looks middle-aged. Is that possible?"

"It's possible. There was an incident last year of a young man aging seventy years in a matter of hours after shooting three people with a ghost gun." Was that always the case—that you aged the number of years you owed the Arcana rather than having those years deducted from your potential lifespan? Perhaps it depended on what you wanted—or what you had done to earn the Arcana's wrath.

"Maybe after some sleep, your husband will realize he was lucky to be found and brought back across the river," Grace said. "Maybe he'll be satisfied with the research he already has and will write about what he observed."

"He's going to go back. I know he is, and I . . ." Sheina pushed the bowl of soup away, giving up all pretense of eating. "What would you do?"

Grace thought about her father and the last time she saw him, waving to her from a ghost ship. Would Yaron Kali make that kind of effort for his wife? Somehow, she doubted it. "My recommendation? Think about what you want for yourself, not what your husband wants from you. Think about what you need to do to prepare yourself to live without him because it sounds like, one way or another, you're going to be on your own."

Not much comfort in that. Wondering why Sheina had called her for help instead of turning to the cops in the Jackson precinct, Grace also wondered how much Sheina was already on her own.

65

Beth sat at a picnic table near the food stands, enjoying a mug of coffee and a small bowl of summer berries. The food stands weren't open yet, but the hotel buffet had the basics for the staff and for other people who worked at the park.

She wasn't looking forward to talking to Detective Gibson, but she understood why the other detective would want to talk to her. After all, Bonnie Wilson had been killed in her apartment.

Lucas Frost took a seat opposite her and gave her one of those assessing looks. "You look better than you did last night. You slept?"

Beth wasn't sure she *felt* better, but she nodded. "When I almost went face-first into the pizza, Colin steered me toward the bed. I don't remember him clearing up the dishes or putting the remaining food in the mini fridge. I don't remember him going to his room. But I received a text from him just after sunrise telling me that the park's residents can use the hotel's swimming pool before official guest hours and could we go down? So we purchased basic swimwear from the hotel's gift shop and joined Kia Dance for a swim before returning to our rooms to shower and have leftover pizza for breakfast. I'm telling you this so I don't have to explain it to Jack."

"Why would you?" Lucas reached for one of the berries.

"Because Jack is a mother hen."

Lucas's hand stuttered, almost dropping the berry. "I've heard Jack called many things, but never *that*."

"Well, he is. And he's got the hotel staff taking notes for him." She lowered her voice a little. "'Is that *all* you're having for breakfast, Detective Fahey? Just fruit?' When I said I'd already warmed up leftover pizza, which everyone across the river knows has at least three of the essential food groups and is a breakfast staple, they looked horrified."

She admired Lucas's ability to keep a straight face. "And you figure their reaction is due to Jack's interest in your food requirements and not that they're sufficiently horrified on their own?"

"If they want to be horrified, they should watch Colin cruise through the buffet. Teenage boys have a bottomless pit for a stomach."

"But he did leave you some pizza for breakfast."

"He did." Beth ate a berry and braced for what she needed to say. "He'd like to stay here awhile longer. At least until his folks get back from vacation. He's sixteen, and I'm not sure what the labor laws are on Wyrd, but he told me he'd worked at a friend's trading post, so he knows enough about retail to work in the hotel gift shop, or if you think his being in sight might be a problem, he could help the park's groundskeepers, since he'd be one of the gazillion people working, so who would notice him?" She ate another berry. "And his being here for a while might benefit the youngest resident in the Teeth." It was understood that Faulkner's name wouldn't be spoken in any public place, even if there was no one around to overhear her and Lucas. "Colin could be a kind of big brother if a meeting place could be worked out. He's smart enough to understand that some people need to disappear. Maybe he could stay in one of the cabins you rent to guests who want to stay for a few days."

"No. If he stays, he stays at the hotel—because you'll be staying at the hotel until the trouble across the river is settled. You should have time to consider which cottage you want as your home. *Your* home, Beth."

"But he can stay?"

"Until Captain Forrester returns. Then we'll discuss it again." Lucas took another berry. "I think having Colin work with Mia Skov in the park is a better idea. People may notice him when he comes in for meals, but he'll be one of many. I'll consider your suggestion about Colin making contact with the Teeth's new resident."

"Thank you."

"Now to business. Detective Gibson will be arriving around nine o'clock to discuss what happened at your apartment while you were away."

"It's an interview, or an interrogation, not a discussion," Beth corrected.

"It's a discussion." Lucas's smile had the same feral edge she'd seen on Jack's face. "We will listen to what she has to say and consider if there is anything the Arcana here can do to assist her."

"We?"

"Yes, Beth. *We*."

"Colin says you're Wyrd's Sorcerer King. That implies that other places like Wyrd also have Sorcerer Kings." *Did you have anything to do with what happened to Bonnie?*

She didn't think Lucas had heard her thoughts, but he answered as if he had. "The Arcana here have never had an interest in Bonnie Wilson, and we only became aware of you the first time you crossed the river. To the best of my knowledge, she shaped her own fate. But other Arcana were aware of her—and you."

"Do you think one of them killed her?"

Lucas looked toward the river. "All Sorcerer Kings are dangerous, but we're not all equally dangerous. The one who has been aware of you is older and not to be trifled with. Did he kill Bonnie Wilson? Not directly. But when she came to Penwych and caused trouble for you, I think he studied the possibilities of her fate and influenced small things that would cut the thread of her years."

"You can do that?"

"When required. More often, if someone is a threat to us, I banish them and keep them from returning to Wyrd."

"Is that what you did to Yaron Kali?"

"No. I told him what payment would be due if he returned. Whether he returns or not is his choice, and his fate will be determined by that choice." Lucas drew in a breath and let it out slowly. "Enough. You need to find Colin Forrester and inform him that he will be working for Mia as an apprentice groundskeeper, and then you need to get ready for this discussion with the detectives."

Beth drank her cold coffee and watched Lucas walk away. It would be better if Colin was unavailable when the Penwych detectives arrived. They couldn't force the boy to go back with them. Still, it would be sensible to call Captain Forrester and get his official approval.

66

Charles Forrester listened to his cell phone's ringtone and turned to his wife. "Why don't you take the kids down to breakfast? I'll catch up with you as soon as I can."

Aisha gave him an anxious look but nodded and left their room.

He answered the call before it went to voicemail. "Forrester."

"It's Frost. It's early to be calling."

"Apparently, you're the only one who appreciates that since you're the fourth caller this morning. Colin was the first, laying out the whole plan to have a summer job in Destiny Park as one of the groundskeepers."

"A job for the rest of the summer? I see."

Charles stared at the ceiling. "This is news to you? Because Beth

Fahey was my second caller. She thought it was a nifty plan. After the call from Detective Castelletti, I have to agree."

"Oh?"

"The four men who vandalized Beth's apartment are out on bail, and there is no guarantee they won't try something else. Not giving anyone an opportunity to target Colin is sensible."

"But?"

"Castelletti said that Yaron Kali had a psychotic breakdown and is currently in the hospital, secured to a bed and sedated. I've been wondering if Colin wanting to stay . . ." He couldn't think of a polite way of voicing his fear.

"Your son isn't addicted to experiencing the uncanny," Frost said. "He was staying with unusual but gentle beings. I'm guessing he sees time in the park as a way to reacquaint himself with the pace of life on your side of the river."

My side of the river. That says it all, doesn't it? "All right. Summer job, park employee. I guess there are enough adults around to keep an eye on him."

"He won't stray. He has a crush on Beth."

"Oh, God."

Frost laughed. "Jack hasn't given me a full report yet about their search, but Colin thinks Beth is awesome."

Could be worse, Charles thought. *Beth has a good head on her shoulders.*

He ended the call with Frost and went to meet Aisha for breakfast. He'd break the news about Colin's summer job—and then he and Aisha could figure out how soon they could do an overnight trip to Wyrd.

67

Beth tried to shake off the dragging fatigue that made her want to put her head on the table and sleep. She needed to be sharp. She didn't think Detective Gibson would try to trap her into saying something imprudent, but verbal stumbles could create an impression of instability. Not an impression she wanted to project.

Detectives Amanda Gibson, Ian Kuhn, and Tom Castelletti were escorted to the conference table in Lucas Frost's office. Gibson sat between the two men. Beth sat opposite her, with Lucas and Jack flanking her and Ashley Laxton sitting slightly apart from them. Ashley opened a steno pad and held a pen over the paper, ready to make whatever notes were needed.

Or ready to stab someone with the pen.

"Why would Bonnie Wilson go to your apartment and try to see you after making inflammatory allegations against you?" Detective Gibson asked.

"A few days before she showed up in Penwych, Bonnie called me, wanting twenty thousand dollars. She said I would be sorry if I didn't give it her."

"Do you have that kind of money?"

"No, but Bonnie liked to gamble, and I think she made those calls when she was desperate to pay off debts."

"Can you tell me where you were on the night Bonnie Wilson was killed in your apartment?" Detective Gibson asked.

"Not specifically. Jack and I were searching for Yaron Kali. We traveled a lot of miles in a couple of days."

"A lot of miles? You're on an island surrounded by a river. It's not that big."

Beth felt the room do one slow rotation. She rubbed her hands over her face, trying to stay awake. "The island is like Doctor Who's TARDIS. It's bigger on the inside."

Gibson frowned. "Doctor who?"

"Exactly."

Ian Kuhn looked away and struggled not to smile. Apparently, he was the only one who understood the reference.

"One of your neighbors indicated you had moved a lot of your things out of the apartment, almost as if you had anticipated a problem while you were allegedly out of reach."

Jack made a sound that was close to a growl. Castelletti, who was sitting opposite Jack, shifted as if he wanted to push away from the table.

"I anticipated moving because I received another job offer and was going to be relocating. You've seen the size of my studio apartment, Detective. Most of my things had never been unpacked. Some friends helped me move those boxes into storage. The last time I was in my apartment was the morning I reported in to the thirteenth precinct to turn in my firearm to Detective Castelletti. Then I took the ferry to Wyrd and spent three days searching for the people who had gone missing. We found three of them. I didn't know about Bonnie or the vandalism until I returned to the park yesterday evening." Beth yawned. "That's all I can tell you."

Gibson stared at her. "Your apartment has been released. You can come to Penwych and . . ."

"No," Lucas said. "Beth will not be crossing the river. Since the men who vandalized her apartment are on the streets again, a law firm that works with us will look at the apartment and assess the loss of Beth's personal property. They will also discuss releasing Beth from the rest of the lease since she will no longer reside in Penwych. If the landlord is unwilling to break the lease, we will continue to pay the rent, but we'll also make sure the landlord doesn't attempt to lease the apartment to someone else in order to collect double rent. Anything that belongs to Beth that the law firm's team deems salvageable will be packed up and sent here. Everything that was damaged will be photographed and discarded. The landlord can discuss any damage to the furniture with his insurance company since the furnishings belong to him."

Kuhn looked at Beth. "The landlord might try to sue you for property damages."

"That would be unwise," Lucas replied.

An uncomfortable silence filled the room.

"Thanks for your cooperation," Castelletti finally said. "If we have any other questions, we'll be in touch."

After Ashley escorted the Penwych detectives to the ferry, Beth stood up—and braced her hands against the table as the floor seemed to rise and fall. "What the . . . ?"

Lucas eased a hip against the table. "The first day you went out with Jack to find the missing people, making the circuit of static neighborhoods was like driving on a road along the East Coast, going from north to south. Geography changes. People have different customs. But you're in the same time zone. At the end of the day, you're tired. While you were searching for Yaron Kali, you crossed into several of the roaming neighborhoods. That was the equivalent of not only bouncing between time zones but also going back and forth over the international date line several times in the space of two days."

"Is that why we arrived in some neighborhoods several hours *before* we'd left the previous neighborhood?" Beth asked.

"Yes."

"So that's why my body clock feels so screwed up." Which also explained why she crashed so fast between breakfast and the meeting with Gibson.

"What you did was dangerous, Beth. Even pure Arcana normally wouldn't attempt to follow a line of intention that compressed so many places in such a short amount of time."

Beth frowned at Jack. "Then why did you?"

"You needed to do it," Jack said. "You needed to learn while there was someone with you to provide an anchor."

"You're one-quarter Arcana," Lucas said. "That gave you enough protection while you were traveling with Jack. If you'd tried that kind of journey on your own, most likely you would have ended up lost forever or you would be like Yaron Kali—strapped to a bed and heavily sedated."

She ran her hands through her hair—and noticed the tremor in her hands.

"If you hadn't changed the intention to finding the diner instead of the man, I would have called a halt to the search," Jack said. "Or insisted that we stay where we were for a day to rest."

If they had stayed a day to rest, they would have missed Yaron Kali—and Colin. "You gave me a chance to learn in the safest way you could."

"Yes," Lucas said. "If you hadn't experienced it, you might have dismissed the danger as being exaggerated."

Maybe. She'd certainly gone out on this search unaware of the dangers she could face.

"With food, sleep, and mild exercise, you should feel normal in a couple of days," Lucas said. "If you don't, we'll take you to the doctor who lives in the Teeth."

Beth nodded. Then she narrowed her eyes and looked at Jack. "Tell the staff at the hotel that eating pizza for breakfast isn't a mental aberration."

Jack studied her. "Why should I?"

"Because you're a mother hen," Lucas said.

"Well, cluck cluck."

"I'm going to take a nap." Beth pushed away from the table and waited for the room to stop moving. "I can get to the hotel by myself."

She hoped that was true, because if she landed on her face and Jack had to help her reach her room, she would never hear the end of it.

68

Charles Forrester stepped into his team's part of the 13th precinct and stared at Beth Fahey's empty desk. He'd been uneasy about the Arcana's interest in her from the start, but it hadn't occurred to him that *she* was part Arcana. Maybe it should have. However you wanted to label them, humans and the Arcana could mate and produce young. If you met an Arcana on the street, in daylight, most people wouldn't know they weren't talking to another human—and when it came to seduction and sex, seeing the truth revealed by moonlight might not matter in the heat of the moment.

"Captain?"

Charles turned. "Morning, Tom."

"We weren't expecting you back until next week."

"Aisha wanted to get home, so we left the resort a few days early. I came in today to review everything before we cross the river for an overnight trip to visit Colin now that he has a summer job in Destiny Park."

"Colin is going to work across the river?"

"Yes."

"Beth Fahey didn't mention it when Ian and I crossed the river to talk to her about the break-in and Bonnie Wilson's murder."

She must have had her reasons. Since her strained relationship with her colleagues was probably one of those reasons, Charles said, "Did she come in to clear out her desk?"

"Ian packed up what we knew was hers. The box is under the desk. She still has her badge."

"I'll take the box and drop it off to her. And I'll pick up her badge." He'd also check with human resources about sending Beth her last paycheck—after he found out where they should send it.

Castelletti looked uncomfortable. "We didn't do right by her, and I'm sorry if that helped people jump to the wrong conclusions about her."

"The conclusions weren't wrong, Tom. She is part Arcana. Bonnie Wilson's accusation was the spanner in the works, and I think we'll all feel the repercussions for a while."

Ian Kuhn walked into the room, followed by Detectives Grace Russell and Markus Seibert.

"Charles," Grace said with a smile. "I thought you were on vacation."

"Keep thinking that," Charles replied as he shook Markus's hand. "What brings you to Penwych?"

"This morning we were summoned by Alistair Hampton," Seibert said. "He wanted to know why we're not making more of an effort to find his brother, Reginald—and his fiancée, but she's more an afterthought at this point, since he doesn't gain anything financially by making a fuss about her."

"After talking to Hampton this morning, Markus and I agreed that he pressures us in order to go back to the people who continue to control his brother's estate and businesses and tell them he's still making an effort to find Reginald but needs some of his anticipated inheritance in order to continue."

"We also agreed that he really doesn't want anyone to find his brother," Seibert added. "He wants control of the Hampton money. Having Reginald return would interfere with that."

"To appease Alistair and the rest of the Hampton family, we're here making our inquiries in person," Grace said. She paused. "There's some talk going around. To me, it sounds more like a cautionary tale about the importance of parents not bringing children to Destiny Park. The media is trying to rev up the anti-Arcana sentiments again, demanding that the Arcana make the island safe for children."

"Wyrd is not meant for children." At least, not the ones who come from homes that don't endanger the child's physical or mental health. Charles turned to Castelletti. "What happened?"

"There was an incident yesterday." Castelletti looked uncomfortable. "You might be able to get more details from your source."

Grace glanced at the empty desk.

"Yes, Beth," Charles agreed, seeing Grace's look, "but also my son. Colin talked the Arcana into giving him a summer job in the park. He started working there a few days ago."

Grace gave him an uneasy smile. "Then he's close to home."

"Close. What did you hear about the incident?"

"Mother lets her young son run around unsupervised while she's getting her palm read or some such thing," Castelletti said. "The kid is leaning over the ornamental lake's retaining wall, sticking his hand in the water and splashing. A park employee passing by tells the kid not to play in the water because something comes into the lake to breed at this time of year and the hatchlings are hungry. As two more employees approach and tell the kid to stop, the kid gives the employees a 'make me' grin, which you figure is exactly what he does when mommy says *no*, and sticks both arms into the water. Something latches on, the kid panics, and he falls in."

Kuhn took up the story. "The kid is in the water for just a few seconds before the two employees manage to haul him out. But that was enough time for the whatevers to eat one of the kid's arms down to the bone from wrist to elbow. That's the story, anyway. We haven't received the official medical report, which is odd since we should be the ones investigating."

"Jesus." Charles pulled out his cell phone and tapped a number from his contacts list. Three guesses who the employees were who went after the kid. "Colin? Are you all right?"

"Dad! Sure. Why?"

He put his phone on speaker so he wouldn't have to repeat whatever was said. "The lake, Colin?"

"Oh. You heard about that?"

"Yes. I heard."

"I got one bite while I was helping Beth—the darn hatchling just leaped out of the water and latched on to me until I smashed it against the lake's retaining wall. Beth got a couple little bites on her arms. I guess the Arcana don't taste good to the hatchlings when they have another meat option. Lucas and Jack still freaked out that she had me holding her belt while she leaned over the lake's retaining wall and dunked the upper half of her body into the water in order to grab the boy. He was a mess. Lots of little chunks out of his arms and legs, and

I think he lost part of an ear. The Lovecraft patrol boat came and took him to a hospital, since the park only has basic first aid stuff."

"And Beth?"

"Lucas said she's stuck doing office work until she acquires enough sense to match her courage. He was *steamed.*"

Hearing the admiration in Colin's voice—and certain the admiration wasn't aimed at Lucas—Charles sighed. The boy certainly did have a crush on Beth Fahey. "We're taking the ferry this afternoon and spending a night at the hotel. Will you be off work so that we can spend time with you?"

"Everything shuts down before dark, so we can hang for the evening. Is Jazz coming with you?"

"Yes. Why?"

"The Arcana are pissed off about the boy's mom blaming them instead of admitting she wasn't paying attention to her kid, so you're going to have to sign a form before they let you on the ferry. I heard it says that the Arcana aren't responsible if any unsupervised child ends up being mauled or eaten by any carnivores who live in the park. I guess the Arcana have mega-scary lawyers, because when I mentioned that humans tend to sue people when a kid gets run over or mauled or whatever, Lucas smiled and said that wouldn't be a problem after their attorneys explained a few things about fate."

His boy was a bundle of terrifying information. "We'll be over this afternoon."

"Wicked. I have presents. Dad? Could you bring my e-reader?"

"Will I be able to find it in your room?" Charles asked dryly.

"Sure. I think. Mom will know where to look."

"I'll text you after we check in." He ended the call, then looked at all the detectives staring at him.

"I guess being chained to a desk doing grunt work is the equivalent of house arrest," Grace finally said.

"Jack was freaking out." Seibert looked pale. "He meant Jack Frost?"

Charles nodded.

"Did you know your former detective was a holy terror when she was working here?"

"No, and I don't think Lucas Frost knew either when he hired her. I think that aspect of her personality bloomed when she crossed the river." Or after she'd spent a couple of days in Jack Frost's company. Still, he hoped Colin was exaggerating about Jack freaking out.

69

Beth checked the time on the computer and pushed away from the desk. It was time to feed the fishies. The auxiliary computer and desk were tucked into a corner of Lucas's office and looked like they were a planned part of the space. The industrial-sized metal cart that held a large aquarium with a sliding mesh cover had been added yesterday. Lucas and Jack had positioned the cart so that she couldn't ignore the aquarium's inhabitants. They certainly didn't ignore *her.*

She had just wrestled the cover off the bowl of meat that was stored on the lower shelf when Colin appeared in the office archway, glanced around, then stepped into the room.

"I wanted to see how you're doing," he said, eyeing the tank as he walked toward her. "The Arcana are keeping us apart during work hours to avoid another 'conspiracy of foolishness.' "

"Who said that? Lucas or Jack?"

"Actually, it was Ashley, but Mia and Kia agreed. They also agreed that we mean well, but we have a lot to learn before we take another walk around the park."

A variation of her status as the clumsy puppy. "I was given a binder yesterday afternoon of the expected predators that live in Wyrd, including the seasonal ones that use the island as a stopover during a migration or the place where some species come to breed and raise or hatch their young. I have to pass a quiz every morning before I'm allowed outside on my own." She wasn't feeling bitter about that. Not at all. "Hold the bowl while I open the cover on the tank."

"Why do you have hatchlings in a tank, and why are you feeding them?" Colin asked.

"I think this could be called a Frost teaching moment. I have to feed them and observe until I fully appreciate the danger I put myself in."

"You had a reason."

"Oddly enough, that did not impress Lucas, Jack, or anyone else here." Beth slid the mesh to uncover one half of the tank's top. She picked up a large slotted spoon, filled it with small chunks of meat, then held it over the tank. She tipped the spoon, dumping the meat into the tank before the hatchlings began leaping to reach the spoon.

"Whoa," Colin said, watching the feeding frenzy as Beth dumped two more spoonfuls into the tank.

Beth slid the mesh screen to cover that half of the tank, then opened the other side. The hatchlings rushed to the other side, the ones that had already consumed chunks of meat as big as their heads moving slowly enough to give others a chance at a meal. Some of them lifted their heads out of the water, opened mouths filled with sharp teeth, and waited for the meat to fall.

"Wow," Colin said. "When the magic spoon appears, meat falls from the sky."

"Oh, thanks for that image." Finished with the feeding, Beth put the spoon on the lower shelf of the cart while Colin put the cover back on the bowl. "Here's another image for you. Anything that falls from the magic spoon is food, even if it's another hatchling that landed in the spoon and was tipped back into the water."

"Wicked." Then he frowned as he watched a couple of the smaller hatchlings get consumed by the rest. "You put your face in the water when you were reaching for the kid." He thought about that and stared at her. "Your *face*."

"Don't you start. Lucas and Jack are giving me enough grief about that." It was hard to admit you had done something incredibly stupid when everyone else was *telling* you that you had done something incredibly stupid.

"I imagine Captain Forrester will have something to say about it, too, when he arrives this afternoon," Lucas said from the archway.

Beth looked at Colin and mouthed, "Your father?"

He nodded.

She sighed. Then she bristled. If she had to do it again, knowing what she knew now about the hatchlings and how much she had risked, she still would have done it. Or maybe she would have moved faster and hauled the kid off the lake's stone wall and . . . "We need a holding cell."

"A what?" Lucas asked.

"A place to hold misbehaving children."

Silence. Then Lucas, sounding curious, asked, "Does this cell have to be on a foundation?"

"No, but it would be better if it wasn't running around on chicken legs."

"Okay." Lucas walked away.

Colin turned and looked at Beth. "'Okay'? What did he mean by 'okay'? And chicken legs?" He tried to put a hand on her forehead. "Do you have a fever or something?"

"No. My arm hurts where I was bitten, and I'm feeling bitchy because I deserve the desk duty for being complacent about thinking the park was safe—or safer than the rest of Wyrd. And it is, but that doesn't mean it's *safe*. So you be careful, too, and listen to Mia. There are *huge* birds on the island that can strike with such power, it can break an adult human's back, and it can dismember the body in less than a minute to take the meat back to its chicks."

Colin paled. "You know this how?"

"I saw one when Jack and I were out searching for the missing people." She didn't mention—yet—that the harpy bird-woman came from a branch of the Arcana. "The binder I was given has enough information about her kind for me to know a small child who wanders away from a parent is just the right size to haul off before anyone can react to the strike."

"Keep one eye on the sky."

"Words to live by. Literally."

Colin nodded. Then he eyed her. "Chicken legs? Did you really see . . . ?"

It was Colin, and she knew she could share some things with him the same way he had shared things about the Llamalidians with her. "I didn't see a house on chicken legs." She grinned. "But I did see a herd of purple cows."

70

Charles walked toward what looked like an old circus wagon and an exhibit set up on a large metal cart. The sign next to the wagon read:

UNSUPERVISED CHILDREN ARE CAGED HERE. The sign next to the metal cart read: THIS IS WHY. The other sign by the cart had the movable hands of a clock, indicating when the next feeding demonstration would take place.

Since the tank was filled with water and had a mesh screen secured over the top, he assumed the inhabitants were fish of some kind. Not like any fish *he'd* ever seen, but . . .

He turned his head and studied the ornamental lake, thinking about the boy who had been badly injured by something in the lake—and thinking about how the Arcana had chosen to respond to the new accusation that they were negligent about the well-being of people who visited the park. While he and Aisha waited in line to buy passage on the ferry, he'd watched two teenage boys about Colin's age denied passage and watched the person in the booth refuse a mother with a baby in a stroller and a little boy who kept trying to free himself from her hand. When the woman argued that the park should provide some day care for the moms who wanted to get their cards read, one of the ferry's crew stepped onto the dock and just stood there. Then he smiled and asked the woman if the boy knew how to swim.

The question hadn't sufficiently terrified the woman, but the smile had. And that smile had made Charles wonder if he'd finally seen the Ferryman.

Several other people withdrew from the line, dragging their children with them. A couple of parents signed the waiver that required them to take full responsibility for their children while they were visiting Wyrd.

The fare for children was twice that of adults. The Arcana were making a point.

And that wagon and the signs were the second stage of making a point.

"Beth was being snarky when she suggested a holding cell for misbehaving children. She didn't think Lucas would really do it."

Charles looked at the young man wearing a ball cap, sunglasses, and a green T-shirt with "Destiny Park" embroidered on it. *God, he's grown in just these few weeks.*

"Hi, Dad," Colin said.

"Hi, Colin." Charles gave his son a squeeze on the shoulder. "No hugs in public?"

"Yeah. Thanks. I'm trying not to do things that I have to explain as cultural differences—at least for a few more days. Hopefully it won't be much longer before Lucas and Jack decide that the Frost teaching moment has had the desired impact on the new employees and will return the fishies to the lake. Then they won't be giving Beth and me the hairy eyeball all the time. Lucas and Jack, I mean. Not the fishies." Colin finally took a breath. "Where's Mom?"

"Since children can't go unsupervised, she's with Jazz and Davie. They wanted to have their cards read."

Colin eyed the time on the clock by the tank. "You should keep Jazz and Davie away from this side of the lake during feeding time." He turned as if tracking two older teenage boys who were showing interest in the lake. "Dad, I have to go back to work. I need to sweep up the heads before someone picks one up."

Alarmed by those words, Charles followed Colin to the broom, large dustpan, and rolling trash receptacle—and the pile of what looked like moving fish heads. They were about the size of a golf ball and had a flat side covered by a membrane that was transparent enough to show the pulsing organs protected by the bony head.

One of the teens reached for a fish head.

Colin grabbed the broom and blocked the hand. "Don't do that."

The boy straightened. "Yeah? Why not?"

"Because the heads aren't all the way dead yet. If you slip one in your pocket, it will chew through the fabric and then chew its way into your thigh before you can get your jeans unzipped and down. And once it's in your thigh, it will burrow deep in order to hide—and feed. Once it has a safe place, it will keep feeding, and it will grow a stub of its body back—enough for it to go through the next stage of its growth."

"Are you shitting me?"

Colin shook his head. "Wait here." He went back to the tank and removed a bowl and spoon from the lower shelf. When he returned to the mound of heads, he uncovered the bowl, scooped a few chunks of meat onto the spoon, and dropped the meat on top of the mound.

In all the years Charles had been with the police force, in all the things he'd brushed against when dealing with Wyrd, he'd never seen anything as disturbing as a mound of heads surging to consume the meat—or consume each other. A few rolled off the mound and seemed to be trying to reach the feet of the humans watching them.

What are these things? Charles thought.

"Demonstration is over," Jack Frost said, giving Colin a pointed look. "Put the meat away and then sweep up the heads or we'll have visitors in sandals dealing with amputated toes." He focused on the two teenagers. "I think you've seen enough of the park, don't you?"

Something in Jack's voice. Something in his eyes. The teens backed away and headed for the pavilion.

"You've got time to stop at the food stands for a snack before the ferry leaves," Jack called. Then he turned to Charles. "I'll keep an eye on your boy and make sure he keeps his fingers and toes."

"Thanks. I'd like to see Beth if she's available. I brought the personal belongings from her desk at the thirteenth."

"I'm sure she'll appreciate that. She'll also appreciate talking to someone who hasn't pissed her off. This morning she sent Lucas a long e-mail. All it said, over and over, was 'I am not a clumsy puppy.'" Jack grinned. "Lucas will release her from desk duty before she gets discouraged—or mad enough to try to dent his head."

On his way to Lucas's office, Charles passed Colin, who shrugged and said, "Feeding the heads seemed like a good idea."

71

Beth wasn't sure what to say to Captain Forrester except . . . "I intended to go back to the thirteenth to say goodbye after you returned from vacation, but things escalated with Bonnie's murder and Lucas wouldn't let me cross the river."

They were seated on one of the picnic benches near the food stands. Mrs. Forrester, Colin, Jazz, and Davie were at another picnic bench. Beth appreciated being able to talk to Forrester privately.

She slid her badge over to his side of the table. "Thanks for bringing over my personal bits and pieces."

"You're welcome," Forrester replied. "Some things were salvaged from your apartment?"

"Whoever killed Bonnie wasn't interested in destroying my things. They ran her to ground there and took what they wanted—or were paid—to take. The clothes I'd left in the chest of drawers and the closet were washed and are fine. Same with the bathroom supplies.

I'm sorry about Bonnie. I wanted her out of my life, but not that way. Maybe her life would have ended that way regardless, but I keep thinking that it might not have been so brutal if she hadn't come to Penwych and tried to cause trouble for me."

"Her neck was broken, quick and clean," Forrester said. "The rest was done postmortem."

"Still. You know the saying fate can be a fickle bitch? It's taken on a different meaning since I encountered the Arcana."

"I heard your little stunt at the ornamental lake freaked out Jack Frost."

"Okay, I was told there were hatchlings in the lake that were aggressive, but nobody said they were like little piranhas on speed. And I did have Colin holding my belt to keep me from pitching into the lake when I hauled up the boy."

"I'm sure Lucas and Jack found that comforting."

Something in Forrester's tone told her *he* didn't find it comforting.

"If they didn't want me to do what I'm trained to do, they shouldn't have hired a cop to work as park security." Beth hesitated, weighed loyalties. She leaned closer. "There are places like Wyrd all over the world. Convergences of the uncanny. Each of them has a leader called a Sorcerer King. One of those individuals was aware of me for a long time. Maybe knew my mother or grandmother. I'm pretty sure this person was responsible for sending the support money when I lived with Bonnie and also gave me the lump sum when I turned eighteen. Maybe the convergence he rules has a Ladies Three who had read the cards and sketched out the potential lines of my fate, so he watched to see what choices I would make that would shape the path my life would follow. I chose to become a cop, and I chose to become a detective. I ended up in Penwych, working for you, and one day I took the ferry across the river to inquire about a ghost gun that had been used to shoot three people. I met the Arcana in Wyrd. The trouble with the bullyboys and their subsequent deaths may have created ripples in the uncanny, may have shifted something that compelled Lucas to offer me a job and a place to live here. When Bonnie showed up in Penwych to cause trouble for me, I think Lucas received a phone call that put the responsibility for my survival on his and Jack's shoulders. So I get why Jack was upset when I stepped away from the car to back him up when that huge bird was flying in to snatch the man we just found, but what did he expect me to do? He was my partner. I had the nine mil with a full magazine. What did he have? *A roast.* And he got snippy with me?" She took a breath. "I didn't understand it then, but I get it. Whoever made the phone call is the guy Lucas wants to be when he grows up. Or maybe *will* be whether he wants to be or not."

"And you still dove headfirst into a lake full of carnivorous fish," Forrester said quietly.

She sighed.

His answer was a resigned smile. "Will you be all right here, Beth? They've got you living in the hotel."

"That's temporary. There are a couple of available cottages. I get first pick and was encouraged to take my time choosing. I'll do that after the summer rush."

"It's a different life, being here."

She nodded. Then she snorted. "A binder was made up for me that contains, with photos or sketches, all the potentially deadly things that might take up residence in the park. The binder is divided by earth, air, and water. I guess there's nothing that comes here that breathes fire, so we have to make s'mores the old-fashioned way. The binder is further divided by season and has little flags on the pages of the creatures that might be here now. I have to study the flagged pages. There will be quizzes every morning. Colin has to study the flagged pages, too, so that he can identify anything that might want to eat the visitors."

She wasn't sure what else to say to him. They were standing on opposite sides of the river now, but they were still cops, and if a police investigation brought him here, she wanted to help.

"Colin would like to tell you and Mrs. Forrester about his time here and where he was staying, but . . ."

"But a girl Jazz's age might not see the importance of keeping something a secret."

"Yes. So I was thinking Jazz and Davic and I could hang out in the hotel pool while you and Mrs. Forrester have some alone time with Colin."

"Thank you." He seemed to be looking for something else to say. "You'll have a busy summer."

Beth nodded. "Lucas has already said Halloween is the last day the ferry will be running for visitors, and Ashley said the winters are quiet—or have a different kind of visitor."

Forrester swung one leg over the bench, preparing to join his family. "Keep in touch, okay? And not just for police work."

"I will. I'll be all right, sir."

He smiled. "I know you will." As he stood up, he added, "But I'm not so sure about Lucas and Jack."

JULY

72

The fish smacked the lower half of his body against rock once more to be sure the . . . *thing* . . . that had burrowed inside him was dead. It should have been dead when he'd pulped the body against a rock, but he'd felt its head continue to gnaw and burrow, gnaw and burrow.

No way for him to explore Susurration Sound while those things were migrating back to the sea. And no way for *him* to get to the sea. He couldn't seem to adapt to salt water, and the passage called Dead Water didn't have enough fresh water over the salt to keep him safe from ships coming from and going to the Fate River.

So he swam in the river, and he attacked fishing lines whenever he could and avoided nets that might tangle him up. And he remembered he just needed to get through this change of seasons, just needed to get through the summer. After that, he would be who he had been. Reg . . . Reginald Hamp . . . ton. Yes. Reginald Hampton III. Once he was back on land and in control of his life again, he would send the Arcana, his fuck-up brother, and everyone else who was an inconvenience to roast with the devil.

PART FOUR

WHAT GOES AROUND . . .

SEPTEMBER

1

Charles Forrester sat at his desk and looked at the letter placed on top of the rest of his mail. Looked at Beth Fahey's name on the return address. Looked at his two detectives, who seemed overly interested in this piece of mail.

"Don't the Arcana usually call if it's something official?" Tom Castelletti asked.

"They do," Charles replied. "This is personal." He considered how much to explain, then decided he needed to tell his men as much as he could. "This isn't actually a letter to me. It's for Colin. And it's not from Beth. She's the go-between.

"Colin befriended someone while he was staying in Wyrd, and he's been reluctant to say anything about the person or why he communicates by writing letters. He finally told me to talk to Beth." Charles hesitated, weighing his words. "Imagine you made a friend, then discovered that person had needed to disappear in order to stay alive."

"Like witness protection?" Kuhn asked.

"Similar to that," Charles agreed. "You decide not to abandon the friend, but you don't talk about that person to anyone except on a need-to-know basis. This"—Charles held up the letter—"is the only way to keep in touch, and both parties are careful about what is said. But . . ."

"But a slipped detail might be enough if someone was still looking for that person," Castelletti said.

Charles nodded. "Jazz has been inquisitive about Colin's time on the island to the point of being a brat. We're all curious about it, but Aisha and I respect that there are things he *can't* talk about. Jazz kept badgering him for details, promising she wouldn't tell *anyone.* So he told her that someone had said there was a herd of purple cows on the island, but she really couldn't tell anyone else. She promised she wouldn't tell, and then she told her best friend, who also promised not to tell anyone, and within a couple of days the whole school had heard that there were purple cows on the island.

"Colin went ballistic, and Jazz was crying and yelling that it wasn't a big deal because it was just some stupid cows. Then Colin said, 'You made a bargain with me, and you broke it.' "

"Shit," Kuhn said. "That's Arcana talk."

"Yes, it is. Anyway, it escalated to a letter coming for Colin and Jazz getting to the mail first and teasing him by holding up the letter and dancing out of reach until he grabbed her and yanked the letter out of her hand. The next letter that arrived, Jazz took it and not only opened it, she was calling her friend Davie to *read* him the letter when Aisha walked in with some clean laundry. Realizing what was happening, Aisha confiscated the phone and the letter. The next afternoon, Colin put a dead bolt on his bedroom door. He gave Aisha the second key, but his sister is no longer welcome in his room—and he's already talking about going back to Wyrd to work in the park next summer."

"It's just kids spatting," Castelletti said.

"That's part of it. Another part is she's developed a reckless attitude and thinks she can go to Wyrd and have a bigger adventure and then won't share anything with Colin—and he's scared she'll try it and die because he knows more about Wyrd now than I do despite all the years I've interacted with Lucas Frost."

"So the letters come here, and you hand them over to Colin?"

"Yes."

"Carrying secrets can be a heavy weight if there's no one to talk to," Kuhn said.

Charles sighed. "He can talk to Beth. She's carrying the weight of those secrets too."

2

Beth hung the last framed piece of fantasy art, then stepped back to make sure it was level.

Lucas had been right about her waiting until after the summer rush before she moved to her new home. For one thing, Colin had gone with her to see the two available cottages and had strongly lobbied for the one that was more rustic while she considered the one with the remodeled bathroom and kitchen as a better choice. Since there was a "no guests" rule for the cottages in this part of the park—unless your guest lived in another part of Wyrd—Colin's vote didn't matter, but having "the boss" delay her official decision had avoided her butting heads with Colin over something that really wasn't his concern.

Besides, this cottage had newer furniture as well as windows with screens and storms and a screened-in porch where she could sit out at night and not be devoured by insects.

When someone knocked on her front door, she called out, "Come in!" and continued to study the artwork. Then she shrugged. She could rearrange it later if the groupings didn't quite work.

Lucas walked in and looked around. "Are you settling in? Have everything you need?"

Beth nodded. "I still have to go to the Teeth and pick up some groceries so that I have some food on hand." And she needed to bring her list of preferred brands of "female and personal products" to the store there so those items would be stocked from now on.

"Catch the shuttle in the morning and run your errands," Lucas said.

"Okay." She noticed him eyeing the fantasy art. "Do you recognize any relatives?" Lucas was still her boss, and Jack was still her trainer, but she'd discovered over the summer that they would tolerate being teased a little.

"Not any of *my* relatives." Lucas studied the artwork and smiled. "But *you* might find one or two of your ancestors included in those pictures."

When he said things like that, she was never sure if he was teasing or serious. She suspected it was a little of both.

"I'll be heading up to the pavilion around lunchtime," Beth said. "I'm helping Rahele write a note to her friend, a few words at a time."

Nothing was said about why or how a lark could arrange letters into words and make those words into complete sentences. Beth had come to understand how the Arcana balanced those who came to Wyrd and needed to disappear. So she dug through her personal hoard of stationery and note cards and transcribed the words made with letters on wooden blocks, then gave the finished note and a blank envelope to Lucas to address. She didn't *know* where Rahele's friend lived, but she knew where a certain black-haired boy could be found since she had arranged a couple of meetings between the boy and Colin over the summer.

People disappeared—and not everyone wanted to be found.

"Make sure you're somewhere conspicuous when you eat lunch," Lucas said as he opened the door to leave. "Jack worries."

Food wasn't the worry; it was an excuse to keep track of her while she learned her job as park security—and learned which statues in the park weren't really statues. And learned about the place and the people who lived there. Still . . .

Beth waited until she could see Lucas walking down the path back to the pavilion before she grinned and said, "Cluck cluck."

3

Acid walked through another graveyard. He had learned how to feel the boundary that separated one graveyard from the next, but he had no way of telling where he would end up. Blazing sun or frigid cold? Lush jungle or rocky soil that wasn't good for anything except burying the dead?

And what was he? Not alive enough to be living but not truly dead. He occasionally craved food, but he couldn't taste it anymore.

How long had he been walking near railroad tracks that seemed to run through graveyards? A week? A month? A year? Sometimes he found a piece of a newspaper and looked for a date, but that didn't help either because the date could be from a hundred years ago—or it could be in a language that told him he wasn't even close to home.

He wanted to go home.

It wasn't going to happen.

Acid heard the train whistle and looked around. There was a single mausoleum close to the tracks. The rest of the graveyard was almost out of sight. The town must be anticipating the need for more acres filling up with the dead. Which made the mausoleum a distinct landmark.

He removed his wallet and made sure it still held his ID and the slip of newspaper he'd used to write two words. He placed his wallet between the railroad ties and waited. Waited. He couldn't change what was happening to him, this transition from living to dead, but he could decide his fate.

When the train was in sight, when it was too late for the engineer to do *anything* to change the outcome, Acid stepped onto the tracks.

4

Charles Forrester stepped out of his office and joined his men to hear what Officer Leanne Curran had come to report.

"Everything all right in Lovecraft?" he asked.

"Yes, sir. More or less," Curran replied. "Captain Wozniak sends his regards." She fiddled with the strap of her messenger bag. "I have a cousin who investigates railway accidents. He called me last night because he wasn't sure who to contact in Penwych and thought I might know."

"So you came to us?"

Curran withdrew a piece of paper from the messenger bag and laid it on the evidence table. "An incident two days ago. A person stepped onto the tracks in front of a train. No time for the engineer to stop. Since the person stepped onto the tracks and faced the oncoming train, the consensus is it was intentional, and it was suicide."

"But . . . ?"

"The investigators couldn't find a body. There was some evidence on the engine that the train had struck a person—some fragments of flesh and cloth—but there should have been more. When the investigators went back to the spot where the engineer said he saw the person, they found a wallet with ID and a note. That's a printout. They'll send the wallet when they know who to send it to."

Charles looked at the student ID and the two words—"I'm sorry"—that had been printed on a scrap of newspaper from 1953. "This boy has been missing since the spring. It's anyone's guess what he was doing so far from home."

"My cousin sometimes . . ." Curran hesitated. "He said there was a weird vibe at the spot where the boy must have stood right before he stepped onto the tracks. He doesn't mention stuff like that in his reports, but he says sometimes he hears a train whistle when a train shouldn't be on a line. He never sees the train, but he hears the whistle and gets a feeling when it passes through the town where he lives."

The day your cousin sees that train . . . Not something Charles would say to Officer Curran unless her cousin disappeared one day.

"We'll confirm which precinct handles the area of the town where the parents live, and I'll send you the name of the detective who should receive whatever personal effects were found."

"Thank you, sir." Curran started to turn away from the table, then stopped. "I heard Detective Fahey is living across the river now. How's she doing?"

"She's doing all right. Settling into her job as a Destiny Park security officer."

After Castelletti escorted Curran out, Charles looked at the paper. The last bullyboy was finally accounted for, and the parents would have some kind of closure.

And yet . . . Where was the body?

5

"Mommy! Mommy! That man is all bloody and has bones sticking out!"

"There's no one there. That seat is empty."

"But . . . Mommy!"

Acid didn't look at the child. He was seen by some but not by many. And the seat that was his prison and his grave was a cold spot no one dared breach.

He wasn't sure how long it had taken for him to become aware that his attempt to end his existence had failed. That he was a kind of ghost—a haunting—trapped in a passenger car on this train, doomed to ride it until . . .

Bargains made with the Arcana are never broken.

A teenage boy swaggered down the aisle toward the restroom. Chains and leather. Badass attitude. He bared his teeth in a snarling smile as he knocked a book out of an old woman's hands.

Look at me. I'm the big bad here.

Acid turned his head.

The teen, catching movement from a seat that was empty, looked—and froze as the color drained from his face.

"Be care . . . ful," Acid whispered. "Be care . . . ful, or you'll . . . end up . . . like me."

The teen backed away, backed away, scrambled to reach his own seat at the front of the car.

Maybe it would make a difference. Maybe this moment of seeing where he might end up would encourage the teen to make different choices. To change his fate.

A sign appeared near the front of the car, a sign Acid was sure no one else could see.

Years left on your ride: 99

The number changed to 98.

Acid understood. For every person he tried to warn away from the things he had done that had led him to becoming a trapped ghost, the Arcana would deduct one year from the years he'd been condemned to ride the ghost train. He'd thought he'd escaped by leaving the ghost train. He'd escaped nothing.

"I'm sorry."

Would the words ever find their way to his parents? He hoped so.

As the living world rolled by outside the train's windows, Acid wondered if his life would have been different—if *he* would have been different—if he had received a ghostly warning before he'd become one of Dare's Doggs.

6

Standing at the land end of the dock, Lucas Frost watched the ferry take the day's last visitors across the river.

"What happens when the ferry stops running next month?" Beth asked as she joined him.

"The seasonal workers who live across the river will assist in bringing in supplies for the hotel for a couple more weeks," he replied. "But not on the ferry. It will disappear sometime between Halloween and All Soul's Day."

"And it winters where?"

Beth Fahey was tough, and she was inquisitive—and she was becoming more Arcana every day.

"I don't know," Lucas said. "The vessel is part of the Ferryman's domain, and his domain is separate from mine. A couple of days after the spring equinox, the ferry will be at the dock."

"I guess the winter months are quiet."

"Quieter, not quiet. Different kinds of visitors take advantage of the lack of humans."

Beth eyed him. "Does that mean I'm going to get another binder of beings to study, along with morning quizzes?"

Lucas laughed. "Probably. Park security needs to be prepared for the park's visitors." His amusement faded. "It might also be an opportunity for you to take a bus ride and learn how to travel around Wyrd."

"Traveling with Jack?"

"He is your trainer. However, a *short* bus ride of no more than one or two stops could be done with someone else who is pure Arcana. Or even with a group. Katherine Rose goes out on a ride or two during our fallow time in order to refresh her talent—and shop."

"A group outing sounds like fun."

"And you're hoping that if there are more people, Jack won't have you in the crosshairs every moment?"

"That too." She shifted her weight, her body moving away from him, then back. "The other Sorcerer King. Is he still holding you and Jack accountable for my well-being?"

"Not as much as before. It's nothing for you to worry about."

Beth let out a slow breath. "I'll do another circuit around the main trails and call it a day."

"Will you be joining us for the evening meal?"

"I will."

Lucas watched her walk back to the pavilion, then returned his gaze to the river. The ferry would disappear at the end of October, and the ghostly ice cutter, with its skeletal crew, would arrive sometime in November. The Fate River would freeze on both sides over the winter, but the center would remain clear, and the water would be a barrier to anyone who tried to reach the island. A quieter time. After the past few months, he would welcome that quieter time.

7

The fish who sometimes remembered he had not always been a fish swam in the Fate River. He hunted. And he waited, sensing that change would happen soon.

8

Beth studied the contents of her refrigerator. She could be good and have yogurt for breakfast, or she could go to the hotel and have pancakes.

She closed the refrigerator door. It was a pancakes kind of day. Definitely. Besides, the hotel's coffee was better than anything she could make at home.

She went through the routine of checking the cottage, making sure everything was tidy and that the heat was turned down, the stove was turned off—even if she hadn't used the oven or any of the stovetop burners—and the fire she'd lit in the fireplace last night was nothing more than cold ashes. Then she gathered her personal items, wrapped a scarf around her neck, shrugged into her fall coat, and left her cottage.

The air still held some warmth in the middle of the day, but the mornings were autumn crisp with the first hint of winter.

She'd survived her first summer on the Isle of Wyrd, working with Jack, working for Lucas, and becoming part of a community—or straddling the line between two communities. The Arcana were friendly enough with the pure human and mostly human individuals who lived in the cottages and worked on the island year-round, but they weren't going to invite those humans to their private part of the island for dinner.

But Lucas expected *her* to join the Arcana for dinner a couple of nights each week. She wasn't sure why he insisted. It was easy enough for him and Jack—and Ethan—to keep track of her during working hours and see that she wasn't in any distress, so that wasn't the reason. No, Lucas wanted her to feel comfortable around them, wanted her to feel like she *was* one of them—and that was something he didn't do with any of the other cottage residents, even the ones who had been living on Wyrd for years.

Then again, the Frost brothers had been right when they'd said that some of the visitors who came to the pavilion were . . . different, and those visitors somehow knew that they didn't have to hide what they were with her.

She'd dealt with the different. She'd also gone on a couple of bus trips that stopped at static neighborhoods as well as a roaming neighborhood that had disappeared after the autumn equinox. She'd been glad to have Jack riding with her when the bus had stopped there. Not that the residents weren't friendly, but the lure of the uncanny in that place might have led her to a different fate if Jack hadn't been there as an anchor.

It had been another valuable lesson.

As soon as Beth stepped inside the hotel's restaurant, Chase, one of the Arcana who worked in the restaurant during daylight hours, approached her. Since the coffeepot he held was empty, she figured he'd detoured to cross her path on his way to the kitchen.

"It's pancake day," Beth said.

Chase smiled and waited.

"I'm having pancakes for breakfast."

He waited.

"And coffee. And some kind of protein so that Jack won't have a hissy fit."

His smile widened. Then the smile faded. "Katherine Rose has been waiting for you. I'll bring your coffee over as soon as the fresh pot is ready."

Katherine Rose was nibbling on a piece of toast. Since she'd clearly already eaten, Beth figured the toast was a delaying tactic.

After laying her coat on an empty chair, Beth settled in the chair opposite Katherine Rose. "Why is Jack still obsessed with what I eat?"

"You're physically fit, and you're skilled with weapons, so he can't pester you about those things," Katherine Rose replied. "Your food choices are personal but not private, not . . . serious, so he feels he can interact with you about them."

"If he thinks food choices aren't serious, he's never talked to a human woman who has been put on a diet. If he had, he'd know how serious food can be."

"He wouldn't care about a human woman unless she had made a bargain with the Arcana." Katherine Rose sipped her tea as Chase approached their table with a mug and a pot of coffee. He poured, gave the empty spot on the table in front of Beth a pointed look, then left.

Beth added cream and a little sugar to her coffee, then stirred—and stirred some more.

"Is there something I should know?" she asked quietly.

"You should get your food before Jack shows up."

"In a minute. Katherine Rose?"

"I read the cards this morning."

"You read them every morning." And the Ladies Three read the cards, made the sketches, and balanced the scales for Wyrd, for this convergence, to see what might be drawn to this place. It had taken her a while to realize that the Arcana's power could ripple through the strange in the world like a stone dropped into a pond—or it could roll through the world like an earthquake, a tsunami, or a freaking volcano that would erupt, creating or destroying destinies. The Ladies Three were watching for some warning that the Arcana equivalent of an earthquake was going to rock Wyrd along with everything else in the world.

"Katherine Rose? What did you see in the cards?" Beth asked.

"The ferry and the Ferryman will be leaving soon."

"At the end of next month. That's expected, right?"

"Yes. That's expected." Katherine Rose looked pale. "But someone will be returning before then, and death and madness will follow."

9

Hearing the sound he recognized as *boat*, the fish swam deeper.

After the small, savage biters left Susurration Sound and continued on to the ocean, he'd stayed in the sound for the rest of the hot months, occasionally leaving to hunt in the river. But he stayed away from the caves and the long dark passage that led from the sound to . . . somewhere. There were females in those caves—females that were almost human but were something *other* and swam as swiftly as he could. Those females hunted for feasts in the water, so he stayed away from them, understanding that he was prey.

It had been good to stay deep in the sound, but now the lure of *home* was calling to him, pushing him to swim closer to the surface, closer to the shore. Closer to the boats and the lines in the water that teased with food but offered death.

He knew these things, in a way, but what he knew most of all was that a change was coming that compelled him to stay closer to the surface, to a specific part of the shore.

That compelled him to return to an almost forgotten life.

10

Alistair strolled out of the master bedroom suite in one of the wings of the Hampton mansion. It had been almost a year since Reginald disappeared, and during the months when Alistair's lawyers fought with Reginald's lawyers and the boards of directors of the companies where Reginald was the majority shareholder, Alistair had slowly acquired pieces of his brother's personal estate. There were cousins circling to take a bite out of the Hampton fortune, but he was the only one named in Reginald's will since Reginald had ex-wives but no offspring, not even a bastard that had popped out of a side piece.

The will was a strange document since it took into account the possibility of a disappearance. If Reginald disappeared and there was no communication of any kind for six months, Alistair would receive some of the shares in the businesses Reginald controlled. Not enough to give him any power—he was still a minority shareholder—but it provided some additional income from dividends, which he needed. After ten months, Alistair could take up residence in the Hampton mansion—but not make use of the wing that held Reginald's suite of rooms.

He'd gladly moved into the mansion and enjoyed being waited on by a full staff, including a stuffy butler who either didn't know about Reginald's kinkier tastes when it came to sex or, perhaps, was one of the participants. What Reginald had or hadn't done didn't matter. As the new tenant, so to speak, Alistair wanted to be perceived as a solid citizen and good employer. That's why he'd decided to keep his new piece of ass in the penthouse apartment, where his head of security would make sure the bitch didn't leave after Alistair had had some fun. That way no one could ask questions if the bitch sported a black eye or moved like her ribs were bruised.

He could count on Martin Chandler's loyalty—he paid enough for it—but the butler and housekeeper at the mansion weren't under his control yet, and he couldn't be sure there wouldn't be a call to the King's Hill police if a girl had to be punished for disobedience. He'd been too benevolent with Rachel Nightingale, and he'd lost a small fortune because he hadn't broken her down enough to get her to sign over her royalties to him before she vanished. Not a mistake he would make again.

Now, almost a year after Reginald disappeared, the next asset was coming under Alistair's control—the yacht. It was in its slip at the King's Hill marina and ready for him to use.

There wasn't much time left before the yacht would be put in dry dock. He'd invite a few men to come aboard for a fishing party next week. There were rumors of some big game fish that had claimed the Fate River as its territory. They would drink a toast to Reginald and try to hook a trophy fish.

A fitting tribute since Reginald—may the bastard rot in hell—never let him borrow the yacht. He just wished that Reginald could show up for one moment, just long enough to realize that he, Alistair, now controlled the yacht, the house, and would soon control the businesses and be a very wealthy man again.

On the other hand, Reginald had been a truly vicious bastard who had hidden his nature behind learned business techniques and bespoke suits, so it was better if he didn't reappear—unless he managed to die a minute later.

11

The water in this part of the river tasted familiar, and instinct was overwhelming thought. He needed to fling himself onto the shore. Why? He didn't know, so he fought that compulsion. He would die if he beached himself on the shore too soon, and he would die if he was too far from shore when . . . What? Something needed to happen. Something was *going* to happen.

A shape. A sound. Lines thrown into the water, with hooked death at the ends, hidden by tempting bait.

The fish avoided the lines, noticed the one line that was thicker and carried a piece of bait so large the smaller fish were nibbling the edges and not getting anywhere near the hook.

He moved close to the surface because there was something about the shape of the boat—and he heard the voice, the laughter. *Knew* that voice.

He surged upward, broke the surface in a furious leap—and saw *his* yacht filled with humans he wouldn't have bothered to piss on not that long ago. And there, waving the heavy fishing rod and laughing, was his brother, Alistair—the perfect target for his fury.

Shouts of excitement filled the air as the fish returned to the water with a hard slap. He didn't waste time. He never wasted time when he needed to squash a rival. He grabbed the bait at the end of the thick line and headed for the bottom of the river. He couldn't stay out of the water long enough to deal with Alistair, so he would pull Alistair *into* the water and deal with him once and for all.

12

Alistair let out a sound that was part laugh, part scream as the heavy rod was almost ripped from his hands and the line *zizzed* from the reel with a speed that could slice off a finger. He leaned back, fighting to hold the rod, struggling to grab the reel before the monster of a fish could run out all the line.

The other men on the yacht shouted encouragement, but only

Martin Chandler had sense enough to help him steady the rod while he took advantage of moments of slack to wind some of the line back on the reel.

The fish broke the water with an impressive leap and looked right at him with a fury and hatred that seemed . . . unnatural.

Shouts from other men who were taking videos with their phones.

"The hook's set," Chandler said. "That bastard isn't going to shake off the hook, but if he bites through the line . . ."

Alistair wound more of the line—and would have been pulled into the water if Chandler hadn't grabbed him and leaned back.

The line ran out. Alistair reeled some in when the fish got close enough to the boat to create some slack. Out and in. Out and in. He sweated and cursed while Chandler made sure he didn't end up in the river.

"Why isn't it tiring?" one of the men asked. "Shouldn't it be tired by now?"

As if in answer, the line suddenly went slack.

"Bastard bit through—" Chandler began.

The fish leaped into the air close to the side of the yacht, a foot of line dangling from the large hook in its mouth. It arched toward the deck, a monster that must have weighed as much as a man, and fell on Chandler, its teeth ripping the man's arm to the bone before it seemed to gather itself and leap toward Alistair.

Alistair screamed as the fish's jaws closed around his calf. He flailed his hands, looking for something, anything, to defend himself. His hand closed on something metal and heavy. He swung it at the fish's head. Swung it at those eyes that burned with hatred. He swung the metal again and again until the monster's head caved in and the eyes dulled.

Men scrambled. A couple of them tried to staunch the wound in Chandler's arm. A couple of them used what they could find belowdecks to pry open the monster's mouth and free Alistair's leg. A couple more were leaning over the side, puking their guts out.

"Reel in those lines," the captain shouted. "Reel in the lines, and I'll head back to the marina."

A task even frightened men could do.

The captain had sense enough to call for medical assistance, so there was an ambulance waiting at the marina. Chandler was in worse shape, but no one, not even Chandler, argued when Alistair insisted that he be treated first. He was, after all, a Hampton.

Hours later, when he'd been treated and sent home, Alistair listened to the men who had been on the yacht with him, had watched the videos of his battle with the monster fish. He remembered to call the hospital and inquire about Chandler, swallowing his annoyance when he learned his head of security was going to be out of action for several days.

The fish had been hauled to the mansion and was currently in a bathtub full of ice.

"Are you going to have it mounted?" one man asked. "It would be a helluva thing to put over the fireplace."

"But the head is damaged," another man said.

"Mount it so that side is against the wall."

"It's got a big dimple on the other side, like something bit off a chunk."

Alistair thought about the hatred in the fish's eyes and couldn't imagine wanting to see those eyes every time he walked into a room.

"I'm not going to mount it." He waited until they were all looking at him. "I'm going to have a feast, and you're all invited. Tomorrow it will be one year since my brother's disappearance, and we'll serve that fish as the main course in his honor."

13

"Forrester."

"Captain? This is Officer Laci Tower. I work with Captain Russell."

Charles braced a forearm on his desk. A cop from King's Hill wouldn't be calling him unless there was a problem that involved Wyrd. And why wasn't Grace Russell the person making the call? "What can I do for you, Officer Tower?"

"Captain Russell asked me to inform you that Yaron Kali, Detective Kali's husband, died yesterday. A massive heart attack. He was in a stolen boat and almost within reach of Wyrd's shore when he collapsed."

"He tried to get back to Wyrd on the sly."

"It looks that way. It was his second attempt since his initial disappearance in the spring."

Charles rubbed his forehead. Experiencing the uncanny could become an addiction as compelling and dangerous as any other kind—or that brush with the strange could leave a person fearful of leaving their house in case the strange touched them again. "How old was he?"

"Thirty-five if you go by his birth date."

"How old according to the coroner?"

A hesitation. "Late eighties."

"You'd like me to find out what bargain Kali made with the Arcana, or what penalties were placed on him if he tried to reach Wyrd again?"

"Yes."

"I'll make inquiries and get back to you."

"Thank you."

Charles ended the call. He got up, got a glass of water, and informed his team.

"Wyrd?" Ian Kuhn asked.

"Sounds that way," Charles replied.

"Is one of us going to have to go over there?" Tom Castelletti asked.

Charles shook his head. "I'll make a phone call."

An awkward silence.

He returned to his office and placed the call. "Beth? It's Charles Forrester."

"Wow, that was fast," Beth said. "I just saw the e-mail from Colin asking about a summer job in the park."

"Pardon me?"

"Oh. Ah."

"It sounds like Colin and I have something to discuss when I get home."

"Now that I've pulled my foot out of my mouth, what can I do for you, Captain?"

"Yaron Kali."

"I know. I helped arrange for a couple of men from Destiny Bay to return the boat and Kali's body to the Jackson marina. How is Detective Kali?"

"I'm guessing that, in some ways, she had prepared herself for her husband disappearing again for good. Him going this way?" Easier in some ways to have a body and a funeral—and closure. But there was still an unanswered question. "What bargain did Kali make, or break, with the Arcana that aged a man in his midthirties to his late eighties? That's what Detective Kali would like to know."

He waited. Then Beth said, "I'll ask and call you back."

Charles sat back. Cops who dealt with Wyrd tended to burn out—or became too tangled in the uncanny. He'd dealt with Lucas Frost for years and watched his team change every few years while he'd stayed grounded enough to see some of the truths about the Arcana and still be able to cross the river. Still be able to sleep at night.

Wasn't that his worry about Colin? That the boy would become entangled and not be satisfied with a world that wasn't spiced by the strange? Except the world, *all* the world, *was* spiced by the strange. So maybe this exposure was better.

Maybe. He'd talk to Lucas Frost before he made a decision. Could he make the decision? The boy was almost seventeen now.

His phone rang, saving him from thinking about that discussion. "Forrester."

"Captain," Beth said. "If a person enters Wyrd without going through Destiny Park, the penalties depend on, for want of another description, what kind of disturbance they cause in the Force, if you . . ."

"I got the reference," Charles said.

"Okay. The other two men we found had come ashore, blundered around in a static neighborhood, and were found on the main road that runs around the whole outside of the island. Their presence didn't cause much of a ripple in those neighborhoods, so the penalty for them was five years deducted from their potential number of years to live."

"They forfeited five years of their lives for making a foolish decision."

"Yes. Plus, they'll probably spend several years in therapy to get past whatever they saw. Yaron Kali, unfortunately, had a forceful enough personality that his presence, and his wandering from place to place within Wyrd, created disturbances that twitched other people's lines of fate in those neighborhoods. Not badly, but enough that the penalty for *his* blundering around Wyrd was fifteen years. When he was being escorted to the dock, Lucas set the terms: Kali would forfeit twenty years of his life every time he set foot on Wyrd's shore. He didn't actually set foot on the island, but he was close enough for the penalty to kick in, and it sounds like this was his second time?"

"Yes. Why didn't Lucas just ban him?"

"Kali had to make his own decision, make his own choice. Lucas gave him a chance. Banning him would have kept Kali away from Wyrd, but he wouldn't have chosen to step away and live with his wife and do his work. He could have spent his life looking for another convergence of the uncanny." A hesitation. "Captain, if Colin had gotten on a bus with Yaron Kali, it's unlikely he would have reached Destiny Park. You could have lost your son because of a man's need to see more and more of the uncanny in a way that was breaking his sanity. And he still tried to go back. Twice."

Charles waited, almost feeling her balancing loyalties.

"Maybe Lucas's decision to give Yaron a choice wasn't so much about Yaron's fate as it was about Detective Kali's," Beth added quietly.

"I don't think I should share that information."

"No. You shouldn't."

"Thank you, Beth." A pause. "How are you doing?"

"I'm doing fine, Captain. I'm doing just fine. This place . . . It feels like home."

Charles ended the call. He would get out for a bit. Take a walk down to the river. And he would think about choices and fate before he called Officer Tower to relay some of the information he'd learned about Yaron Kali.

14

Lucas scanned the area between the food stands and the communication center and rental cabins. He reached for his cell phone to call his security officer when he spotted Beth and Katherine Rose.

"Beth!" he called. "With me."

Beth hesitated a moment, said something to Katherine Rose, then headed toward him.

"Problem?" he asked.

"What goes around comes around," she replied.

"Meaning?"

"I don't know. Neither does Katherine Rose. But she's disturbed by what she saw in the cards today."

Lucas headed for the dock. "The Ferryman wants to see both of us."

"Why does he want to see me?"

He had wondered that himself, so he said nothing.

They stood on the dock and watched the ferry's crew secure the vessel and close up the cabin for the night. The crew nodded to Lucas and Beth in passing.

Were these Arcana anxious to get away from the water—and the Ferryman—for some reason, or had they been told to make themselves scarce while things were said?

The Ferryman stepped onto the dock and looked at the river before he turned and walked toward Lucas. The Sorcerer King's domain ended at the shore where the Ferryman's domain began. Meeting at the dock put them on equal footing.

Interesting that the Ferryman wanted equal footing for this meeting, but Lucas thought he understood why when the other Arcana looked at Beth.

"The police boats should keep an eye on the river for a few hours tonight," the Ferryman said. "Instinct should be enough to bring *what is* close enough to shore to survive the transformation back to *what was*, but he might need help getting to shore."

"Transformation?" Lucas asked.

"A coin for a ride across the river is a simple bargain," the Ferryman replied. "But it is not a bargain I will allow to be broken."

"This happened a year ago?"

The Ferryman nodded.

Beth didn't look at the men. She frowned at the dock. "So there is a . . ."

"Fish."

"Fish out there who is about to turn back into a man sometime this evening?"

"Yes."

"So he might pop up to the surface anywhere in the river and flail around while he tries to remember what to do with his reacquired arms and legs?"

"Yes."

"This man has been a fish for a year? What would have happened if another fish ate him?"

The Ferryman shrugged. "Meat is meat. As long as the coin that holds the transformation remains in the flesh, *what is* will remain *what is* until the payment for breaking the bargain is complete. If the flesh dies before the payment is complete and the coin is removed, *what is* will still change back to *what was*."

Lucas looked at Beth. "You should make the calls to your police contacts to get the patrol boats out as soon as possible."

"How much time before the transformation?" she asked.

"Soon," the Ferryman replied.

Beth hurried back up the beach to the communications cabin.

Lucas watched her for a moment, then turned back to the other Arcana. "You gave her this task to delay her from understanding the truth. Do you suspect? Or do you know?"

The Ferryman smiled. "Does it matter?"

15

Alistair watched the faces of his guests as the main course, brought out on a specially made wooden serving platter, was placed on the table. He'd invited the men who had been with him on the yacht and had filled the other chairs at the table with some of King's Hill's politicians, a couple of actors who had recently starred in a successful play, and some society women who might have been fucking some of the men at the table.

He'd refused to allow his chef to cook the fish with its head and tail still on the body, so those parts had been reconstructed using aspic. He'd wanted the rest of the fish to be presented in one piece, but it hadn't been physically possible to cook the fucking thing without cutting it up. Now he had to admit that his chef had been clever about dividing the fish into the number of pieces needed to feed his guests, but it was all arranged on the board to *look* like the fish was still the monstrous adversary he'd fought.

His servants plated the pieces of fish and offered the various dishes of vegetables before retreating to one side of the dining room. The men who had been with him had already shown everyone else the videos they'd taken of his battle—and the fish's attack on Martin Chandler and himself before he subdued it.

He was no longer the younger brother who never quite measured up. Now he had the wealth and the power backed by the Hampton name. Now . . .

The mayor of King's Hill put down his utensils and reached for his wine. "What kind of fish did you say this was? It tastes . . . odd."

"It might be the way the chef prepared it," Alistair replied. He stabbed at his piece and ate a mouthful. "Tastes fine to me."

His guests ate small amounts of the fish, but it was obvious none of them liked it. Damn that chef. He should have brought in someone who specialized in preparing seafood instead of letting a nobody cook create such an important meal.

"What is that?" One of the actors shoved her chair back from the table and stared at her plate.

Her companion poked at her piece of fish with his fork. "It's . . . God! It's the broken skull of a small fish. Look at those teeth."

The woman clapped a hand over her mouth and stumbled away from the table. A servant waved her to the door and hurried her out of the room.

"Pretty funny her getting squeamish like that," one of Alistair's friends said. "I heard she'd swallow anything—or anyone."

Some of the men laughed. The rest looked insulted or angry.

Alistair stabbed at his piece of fish and hit something hard. Not caring how it looked, he used his fork and fingers to dig through the flesh until he found what had been hidden. He held up a silver coin. "What the fuck?"

Exclamations. Sounds of disgust—and fear—as everyone shoved away from the table.

He looked around the table. Looked at the meat on his plate. It was cooked, but it no longer looked like fish.

In another part of the mansion, someone started screaming.

16

Charles Forrester sat across from Grace Russell, Markus Seibert, and Laci Tower. He'd come to Russell's precinct in King's Hill because she was the one scrambling to investigate a bizarre dinner party where Alistair Hampton had served his brother, Reginald Hampton III, as the main course.

"Videos taken by Alistair's friends show him catching a game fish that doesn't look like anything the local fish and game people recognize," Russell said. "But he hooked it and fought it until it bit through the line, leaped into the boat, and attacked Martin Chandler and Alistair. I don't think those videos were faked."

"The videos weren't faked," Charles said. "Alistair Hampton caught an unknown species of game fish. I considered the possibility that, as a twisted joke, Alistair had arranged for the fish to transform into a shape resembling his brother while his guests were eating, and then letting them think they'd eaten human flesh. However, the Arcana said they have never made a bargain with Alistair Hampton."

"But they might have made one with Reginald Hampton?" Seibert asked.

"'He made a bargain with us, and he broke it.' That's what I was told. I was also told that if Reginald had eluded fishermen for one more day, what he owed the Arcana would have been paid in full, and he would have transformed back into a man. That's why we were alerted the other evening that there might be a man in the water and the patrol boats should be on the lookout."

"So it's just bad luck?" Russell said. "Alistair Hampton goes out fishing with friends; hooks the game fish everyone has been trying to catch; kills it in what looks like self-defense, since the fish *did* attack Hampton's head of security; and then serves the damn thing for dinner on the anniversary of his brother's disappearance."

"Some might call it fate," Charles replied. "What goes around comes around."

"We found a young woman in Hampton's penthouse apartment," Seibert said. "She'd been beaten and locked in a bedroom. En suite bathroom provided water, but she had no food and no medical attention. Turns out that was typical of Alistair's treatment of her. Chandler was bringing her food, but he's been out of it on painkillers while his arm heals, and no one else had been instructed to go in and look after her."

"Between finding her and that dinner party, I doubt Alistair will recover from the scandal," Russell said. "Especially with the rumors going around that he somehow realized the fish was Reginald and he beat its head in to stop his brother from returning and retaking control of the family's wealth. Do you think that's possible?"

Charles looked into her tired eyes. "Unless he admits it, we'll never know."

"Well, according to the butler at the Hampton mansion, Alistair is currently under a doctor's care for a nervous breakdown and is recovering at an unknown location. Since Albert Palmer's shooting four boys while they were wild dogs may be a precedent, depending on how the courts work things out, Alistair may be facing criminal charges for his brother's death. He'll certainly be facing charges for the woman's assault and imprisonment."

Their meeting concluded, Charles said nothing while Russell escorted him out of her precinct. As he opened the outer door, she said, "Do you think the Arcana knew what was going to happen?"

He considered what to say. "They make bargains with us, Grace. They don't care about our morality, only their own. They didn't make a bargain with Alistair Hampton, but they were aware of him because they had helped a woman escape from his abuse."

"Rachel Nightingale. His fiancée. She went missing almost a year ago."

Charles hesitated.

Russell nodded. "Between you and me."

"Yaron Kali knew the penalty he would pay if he returned to Wyrd, but he was given a choice—not for his sake but for Detective Kali's. Perhaps the Arcana's decision to do nothing to stop what happened with Alistair and Reginald Hampton was their way of protecting someone else."

17

Lucas Frost placed a sheet of paper with six addresses on his desk, then laid a key ring with six keys on top of it. He wasn't sure whose idea it was to put plastic caps on the keys to color-coordinate them with stickers next to the addresses—or where or when the caps and stickers were purchased. It was simple and practical, but he had the feeling that it was also meant to annoy *because* it was simple and practical.

"There are six residences currently available in the Teeth. I want you to look them over and choose the one you think will be the best fit for the newest resident."

Beth Fahey eyed the keys and the addresses, then looked him in the eyes. "Is there a reason you want me out of the park today?"

"No." It was interesting that that was her first assumption. "You have lived across the river. You would know what a human woman would need to settle in comfortably."

"Shouldn't she choose her own home?"

He'd had a few months to observe how Beth balanced loyalties. She might be a bit reckless with her own life while performing her duties, but never with someone else's. "She'll be going through her return transformation next week. Some people make the transition easily and only need a couple of days to readjust to the human form. Others need longer to recover. In this case, having a home where she can put away her belongings while making the mental and emotional adjustments would be helpful."

"What can you tell me about her?" Beth asked. "Is there anything specific she would need?"

"She is a writer, so she will need a place to work within her home. She also has a publisher and agent who will be allowed to visit Wyrd and stay at the hotel or in one of the guest cabins."

"No outsiders visit the Teeth. I remember." Beth stared at the paper and the keys. "I read a variety of books. Would I have heard of her?"

"Not yet. Her name is Rahele Larke."

She looked at him, then at the paper. "Ah."

"You should pack an overnight bag, in case you miss the last shuttle coming back to the park."

"Not necessary."

No, it wouldn't be. He could see she understood. Her body might be mostly human, but her heart—and her understanding of the uncanny—were Arcana.

He held out an envelope. "While you're there, you could deliver this."

Beth looked at the name, looked at the address, and then looked at the list. She took the envelope—and smiled.

18

For form's sake, Beth visited the two potential residences that were on the bay side of the Teeth. There wasn't much to distinguish the houses in that part of Wyrd. Most were one story with a loft or attic for storage. Some had one bedroom; others had two. All of them faced the street and had tiny front lawns. What made them different was that the backyards weren't divided, making the interior of a whole block of houses a community space. Sure, there was some privacy and personal space, but the whole contained paths that connected the houses; had a community vegetable garden that everyone planted, tended, and harvested; had fruit growing from trees and bushes; had some kind of water feature. It would be important for your immediate neighbors to get along, for personalities to mesh. She kept that in mind as she stepped off the horse-drawn double-decker bus that could fit a dozen people if they didn't mind being friendly.

She looked at what was considered the central business district in the Teeth. There were businesses at either end where supplies could be brought in by water; but here was the library, the post office, a general store and small grocery store, a pharmacy that shared a building with the doctor's and dentist's offices. There was even a small theater where concerts and plays were put on, and where movies were shown. Every shop humans really needed could be found in the Teeth on a small scale. But there were other considerations for a person who would want to catch Destiny Park's shuttle in order to use the park's internet, who would want to stay in contact with a few people beyond Wyrd.

Beth looked at the house in the block near the theater. A good place with two bedrooms and plenty of natural light. The kitchen seemed to be the dominant room, and she imagined someone who had a passion for cooking or baking would enjoy living there. It was a possibility.

The last house. Beth opened the front door, then went directly to the back door and opened it, making sure the screen door was off the latch. Wondering if a particular resident would be curious enough to investigate, she wandered through the house. A modest kitchen with fairly new appliances, including a microwave. The main bedroom and bathroom were a comfortable size.

She tested the water to make sure it ran clear, since there was no telling how long it had been since someone had lived here. All the rooms had a layer of dust and needed a good cleaning. She'd ask Lucas about how that could be done.

She stepped into the second bedroom. Hearing the squeak of the screen door, she smiled as she walked to the center of the room and waited, listening to cautious footsteps getting closer and closer.

"A writer is going to be moving in soon," she said. "This would be a great room for her office. It has plenty of built-in bookcases, a desk for her laptop, and another desk by a window where she could take care of paperwork." She looked over her shoulder. "What do you think?"

"You're the police." His dark eyes looked too old for his age and held a wariness that bruised her heart. The skin on his arms that wasn't covered by the sweatshirt's pushed-up sleeves carried the scars of his previous life.

"I worked for the police when I lived across the river. Now I work for Lucas Frost as security in Destiny Park and here in the Teeth." She tipped her head to indicate the room. "What do you think? A good house for a writer? I understand Betsy Richens and Rya Hedden have houses in this block."

"They do."

Beth nodded. "I think this will be a good place, the right place." Reaching into her jacket pocket, she held out an envelope and smiled when he recognized Lucas's handwriting. "Special delivery."

19

Rachel twittered her objections to being wrapped up and carried in a closed basket. Lucas had explained a couple of times that it was for her own safety, that humans sometimes panicked when it was time to return to their original form.

She wouldn't panic. *She* would be sensible.

She would have flown away and hidden if she'd been awake enough to understand what Lucas was doing when he took her from her cage and wrapped her in a soft cloth.

"Not far now," Lucas said.

They moved quietly, the Arcana. Rachel heard the wheels of a cart, heard the pony's steady hoofbeats. But she didn't hear the Arcana as they followed the paths to the moon gate. She wasn't sure how many of them had come with her and Lucas.

She didn't want to go back across the river. Ashley had told her Alistair Hampton was no longer a threat, but people who worked for him might come after her. The Hamptons were wealthy. Even if she left the towns around the Fate River, they could find her easily enough. A new name wouldn't protect her if she started writing again.

But Beth Fahey had told her the Arcana had selected a house for her here on the island, and she would be safe. Beth said Rachel's personal things, including her books, had been brought to the house so it would be easy for her to move in once she got back on her feet. Literally.

Of course, she'd *had* feet. It was getting used to having hands again and not being able to fly that would take some adjustment.

Lucas set the basket on the ground, opened it, and gathered Rachel in his hands.

"You were Rachel Nightingale," Lucas said. "You are now Rahele Larke. This is what you looked like when you were human."

Beth held up a book. Rachel cocked her head and looked at the human on the back cover. She couldn't remember if that face was considered pretty or plain, couldn't remember how her body had felt before she'd become a starved survivor of Alistair's cruel affection. She looked and tried to remember who she had been before she'd known Alistair Hampton.

Beth handed off the book and went around the side of the moon gate. Kia Dance went around the other side, carrying a long robe.

"Are you ready?" Lucas asked.

Ready to be transformed, or ready to meet whatever fate had in store for her?

She twittered softly.

"The gate is held for transformation," Ashley Laxton said.

Lucas unwrapped the cloth around Rachel's body but kept his hands around her. "You'll be tempted to fly through the gate, but you need to walk. The change is immediate, and you don't want to twist an ankle by landing wrong on the other side of the gate." He paused. "Words have power, Rahele Larke. Intentions matter, especially when you walk through a moon gate. Know who you want to be."

She needed to be human again. She understood that. The lark needed to become a valued memory, and a woman needed to pick up the pieces of her life.

Lucas raised his hands, freeing her.

She walked to the moon gate, through the moon gate . . . and would have fallen if Beth and Kia hadn't grabbed her arms and eased her to the ground.

"You did great," Beth whispered as she and Kia bundled Rachel into the robe, tucking it around her before Lucas joined them and went down on one knee.

"It might take your brain a day or two to tick all the boxes, as humans say, so your vision might be . . . odd. And your voice. Ashley, Beth, or Kia will be with you at all times while you adjust to your human form. They'll help you in whatever way you need. Do you understand?"

She couldn't seem to talk or twitter, so she nodded.

Lucas picked her up and carried her to the small cart and the pony. He settled her in the back of the cart with Beth and Kia before leading the way back through the park to the Arcana's private land.

Rachel closed her eyes. Trying to sort out her vision was giving her a vicious headache, like wearing glasses that were too strong to be useful. She kept her eyes closed when Lucas picked her up again and carried her up some stairs.

Inside now. The air felt different, smelled different.

A door opened. Movement. Beth and Kia talking quietly. Lucas setting her down on cloth. Sheets? A bed?

Rachel opened her eyes. Visuals were less confusing. Not good yet, but less confusing.

Lucas had left, but Ashley arrived bringing food and water. With help, Rachel sipped the water and the broth. With help, she became reacquainted with her fingers and hands, with ankles and knees. They helped her into the bathroom, helped her take a sponge bath, helped her put on pajamas.

Ashley went out, then returned a short while later carrying a laptop. She turned it on and opened the word-processing program. "You probably don't have the coordination yet to write things down, so I brought you this. You can peck out a message using one finger instead of a beak." She grinned at Rachel.

"Is there anything you would like to eat?" Beth asked.

"Within reason," Kia added. "Your innards have some adjusting to do too."

Rachel had an answer to *that*. With one finger, she typed, "No worms."

The women laughed.

OCTOBER

20

While Jack patrolled the park, Lucas kept an eye on the pavilion and reviewed the résumés of the seasonal workers. Some had already indicated their interest in returning next spring to work in the food stands or in the hotel. He needed to decide on the other possible employees, giving those with experience in the park priority—including Colin Forrester.

Justine and her sisters had considered the possible fates of every potential employee, had advised him not to offer jobs to a few of them, even if they had been suitable this year. After all, even Wyrd wasn't immune to changes. But they had suggested that he offer Colin Forrester a job again next summer. He would discuss that suggestion in more detail, but for now he tucked Colin's letter into the employee file.

His phone rang just as he was about to close up his office and help Jack round up the last visitors who needed to be herded to the ferry.

"Frost."

"Is she safe?"

Lucas drew in a slow breath. He'd been expecting this call for weeks, had been surprised that it hadn't come. "Beth Fahey is as safe as a woman with courage can be."

The silence on the line pricked the territorial side of his nature. "She is settled here, has made friends here, is building a life here. She is Arcana, and she is the only one who has the right to determine her fate."

He wondered if Beth realized the subtle changes over the past few months. She probably thought the grace with which she now moved with the world was due to the various exercise classes she participated in at the hotel. That might be part of it, but more was due to embracing a heritage that had been dormant for most of her life and had awakened when she had touched the strange. She moved like the Arcana now, and humans would sense the difference, even if they didn't understand the difference.

"You helped her when she was young," Lucas said. "Helping her then gave her the chance to make her own choices now. I have no right to interfere with her fate. Neither do you." When he didn't pick up any ripple of anger, he added, "If you wish, I can call you from time to time and let you know how she's doing."

"That would be welcome."

Lucas waited a moment after the call ended. Then he put down the receiver. He had wondered if the other Sorcerer King would insist on Beth resettling in the convergence he ruled. The Kings rarely challenged each other. That let too much of the strange into the world. But Lucas Frost, Sorcerer King of the Isle of Wyrd, would have defended Beth's right to choose her own fate.

He felt relieved that his father had agreed.

21

Rahele Larke was grateful for all the help Ashley Laxton and Kia Dance had given her over the past couple of weeks while she relearned how to use a human body, but she was glad Beth Fahey was the one escorting her to her new home.

"I'm nervous."

Beth gave her an understanding smile. "Stands to reason. The new can be stressful as well as exciting, and living in the Teeth . . . Well, think of it as living in a town populated entirely by people who are in witness protection."

"Which is why guests aren't allowed."

"And why only the businesses have telephones, although there is a phone box every couple of blocks."

"No cell phones or internet."

"Nope. But there are the essentials."

"Bookstore?"

Beth grinned. "Yes. And a small library within sight of your house. If you can't find what you're looking for, you can always take the shuttle up to the hotel and treat yourself to a massage and a fancy lunch, then sit in the lounge and load up your e-reader."

"I appreciate all of you buying me a new e-reader and setting up an account in my name, along with all the other documentation that has been provided." Rahele hesitated. "I'm a little confused about the books I found in it."

"Oh, we all chose a favorite book, and Ashley downloaded the selections."

"That explains why some of the choices are a bit . . ."

"Terrifying?"

"I was going to say 'unusual.'"

"Everything in Wyrd feels unusual at first, and then it doesn't."

The shuttle pulled up at the closest stop. Beth picked up Rahele's suitcase and said, "I've got this. Are you steady enough?"

"Yes." She'd worked hard to walk again, use her arms and hands again. But sometimes her perception of where the ground was in relation to her feet was still a little bit off, so being cautious was wise.

Not much of a yard, Rahele thought as Beth opened the front door and then stood aside to let her go in first.

"The street side of the houses don't have much variety," Beth said. "It's the backyards that are special. I'll put your suitcase in your bedroom and help you unpack in a minute. Go back to the kitchen and see for yourself."

Rahele opened the back door and looked out. Then she stepped out. There was a patio and some furniture. There were a couple of large pots filled with earth but empty of plants. Beyond that . . .

She stepped carefully as she moved from patio to gravel path. She couldn't see all of it. The path curved, providing an open kind of privacy. She heard water, but wasn't ready to do much exploring yet.

As she returned to the patio, Beth walked out of the house, looked over Rahele's shoulder, and smiled at someone.

"Rahele?"

Rahele turned, her heart in her throat at the thought of confronting a stranger. But the black-haired, dark-eyed boy stopped at the edge of the patio, as if understanding her need not to have her space invaded, and gave her a hesitant smile.

She didn't recognize the boy, but the eyes . . . "Faulkner?"

The hesitant smile turned into a confident grin. He held out the bowl he carried. "I picked some apples for you."

ACKNOWLEDGMENTS

My thanks to Blair Boone, Debra Dixon, and Jennifer Crow for being this book's first readers and for providing encouragement and feedback in the story's roughest stage; to Doranna Durgin for maintaining the website; to Ashley Laxton for running the Anne Bishop Fan Group and Spoiler Fan Group pages on Facebook; to Anne Sowards and Jennifer Jackson for the feedback that helps me write a better story; to all the publicity and marketing folks at PRH who help get the book into readers' hands; and to Pat Feidner for always being supportive and encouraging.

A special thanks to the following people, who offered their names for characters: Edwena Benjamin Bang, Leanne Kathrine Curran, Kia Dance, Tia Downing, Amanda Gibson, Rya Reynolds-Hedden, Sheina Kali, Ian Kuhn, James Lamb (permission from Rachel Lamb), Ashley Laxton, Jenn PT Lee (Wing Kei Lee), Alan Naylor, Emma Ocampo, Betsy Richens, Markus Seibert, Mia Skov, Jeni Rose Slown, and Laci Tower.